THE URGING

Barbara turned, with her back pressed against the glass door. The lights went on again all at once—with a brighter, more fierce glow than ever before. She spoke softly, fighting to keep back a scream, "Please . . . let me go."

Slowly the dense air stirred around her, fluttering her skirt against her legs, holding it there. She felt as if she were suspended in fluid—buoyed up by the spice-laden air . . . as the pressure moved in on her, touching her, caressing her. It glided over her thighs and stroked her breasts. Teasing. Tantalizing. Urging her to respond.

Then she was responding . . . as she never had before in her life . . . to the most irresistible power ever to make a woman its own. . . .

ⓈSIGNET BOOKS (0451)

HAUNTING PASSION

- [ ] **DARK WINDOW by Linda Crockett Gray.** When Barbara Ashcroff's wonderful husband, T.J., suddenly died, Barbara found that desire had not died in her. But the two new men in her life had a rival for her passion and possession. For desire had not died in T.J. either. (169824—$4.99)

- [ ] **GODBODY by Theodore Sturgeon.** Was he seducer or savior? Good or evil? When he came to this small town, meek, mild men discovered the raw power of lust. Sensually starved women learned the ecstacy of fulfillment. Icy hearts melted. Should he be worshipped or destroyed? Find the extraordinary answer in this mind-exploding novel by the Nebula and Hugo award-winning author Stephen King calls "one of the greatest!" (163044—$3.95)

- [ ] **THE GIRL IN A SWING by Richard Adams.** "Astonishing... sublime eroticism and gruesome nightmare... an absolutely terrifying ghost story, as gripping and psychologically penetrating as anything in James or Poe. Richard Adams has written with marvelous tact and narrative power, a strange, beautiful, haunting book."—*The New York Times Book Review* (163060—$5.95)

- [ ] **THE MIRACLE by Irving Wallace.** Natale Rinaldi, a ravishingly beautiful, tragically blind Italian actress, becomes lost in a maze of dark lust and mysterious love... as people from around the world are drawn together at one extraordinary moment in time and caught up in a miracle whose true nature you will never predict.... (158962—$4.95)

- [ ] **PEARL by Tabitha King.** After arriving in Nodd's Ridge, Maine, to claim her inheritance, Pearl Dickenson becomes involved with two men whose rivalry explodes into violence, and threatens the fabric of everyday life in the small community. "Powerful... truly masterful."—*Washington Post Book World* (162625—$4.95)

Prices slightly higher in Canada

Buy them at your local bookstore or use this convenient coupon for ordering.

NEW AMERICAN LIBRARY
P.O. Box 999, Bergenfield, New Jersey 07621

Please send me the books I have checked above. I am enclosing $_____ (please add $1.00 to this order to cover postage and handling). Send check or money order—no cash or C.O.D.'s. Prices and numbers are subject to change without notice.

Name_____

Address_____

City _____ State _____ Zip Code _____

Allow 4-6 weeks for delivery.
This offer is subject to withdrawal without notice.

DARK WINDOW

Linda Crockett Gray

A SIGNET BOOK

SIGNET
Published by the Penguin Group
Penguin Books USA Inc., 375 Hudson Street,
New York, New York 10014, U.S.A.
Penguin Books Ltd, 27 Wrights Lane,
London W8 5TZ, England
Penguin Books Australia Ltd, Ringwood,
Victoria, Australia
Penguin Books Canada Ltd, 2801 John Street,
Markham, Ontario, Canada L3R 1B4
Penguin Books (N.Z.) Ltd, 182-190 Wairau Road,
Auckland 10, New Zealand

Penguin Books Ltd, Registered Offices:
Harmondsworth, Middlesex, England

First published by Signet, an imprint of New American Library,
a division of Penguin Books USA Inc.

First Printing, April, 1991
10 9 8 7 6 5 4 3 2 1

Copyright © Linda Crockett Gray
All rights reserved

 REGISTERED TRADEMARK—MARCA REGISTRADA

Printed in the United States of America

Without limiting the rights under copyright reserved above, no part of this publication may be reproduced, stored in or introduced into a retrieval system, or transmitted, in any form, or by any means (electronic, mechanical, photocopying, recording, or otherwise), without the prior written permission of both the copyright owner and the above publisher of this book.

PUBLISHER'S NOTE
This is a work of fiction. Names, characters, places, and incidents either are the product of the author's imagination or are used fictitiously, and any resemblance to actual persons, living or dead, events, or locales is entirely coincidental.

BOOKS ARE AVAILABLE AT QUANTITY DISCOUNTS WHEN USED TO PROMOTE PRODUCTS OR SERVICES. FOR INFORMATION PLEASE WRITE TO PREMIUM MARKETING DIVISION, PENGUIN BOOKS USA INC., 375 HUDSON STREET, NEW YORK, NEW YORK 10014.

CHAPTER 1

> I dwell in Possibility—
> A fairer house than Prose—
> More numerous of Windows—
> Superior—for doors.
> *Emily Dickinson*

EVEN BEFORE SHE caught the slight movement in the shadowy darkness of the room, Barbara knew T.J. was there. When he found her engrossed in one project or another, he often stood back and waited, watching silently, until some uncanny sense gradually nagged at her and she would look up and notice him. It was his idea of being amusing. He'd give her one of his disarming smiles that she usually found impossible not to return, apologize halfheartedly for interrupting, then promptly launch into whatever it was he wanted. In this case, he wanted her.

"Let's go to bed, babe," he said softly as he placed a wineglass on her desktop. Sherry. One drink before retiring. It had become a familiar signal that Barbara immediately recognized. T.J. wanted her to unwind, then he wanted her to come to bed to make love.

"Just a second." She was reluctant to call it quits for the night. The kids were in their rooms, asleep. The house was finally quiet. T.J. had held a late conference with a client over the final blueprints for a remodeling project. Outside, the full moon had turned the uppermost branches of the surrounding trees to alabaster. Swatches of light streamed through the beveled glass bay window of her study and across the pale carpet. In her rare solitude, Barbara had been grappling with a play by Pirandello, reading the dialogue silently and trying to conjure up the characters. Six of them. Suspended in an unfinished play, seeking their author—and completion. Within the circle of light from her desk lamp, her cap of copper-colored hair remained motionless while she bent over the thick textbook, scanning a few more lines.

When a character is born, he instantly acquires his own independence, even from his own author.

Studiously she made a streak of yellow highlighter over the passage and read on.

"Barbara . . . it's late."

Without looking up, she stalled him. "Just a little longer. I want to do well in this class, and there is so much outside reading. It's not easy to keep up with these college kids," she sighed as she flipped to the next page. "I was just getting used to making the assignments, now I'm doing them."

T.J. crossed his arms and leaned against the wall. Tall, blond, and beautifully proportioned, he radiated restless energy even standing still. "In the overall scheme of things, I doubt if this particular English Lit. assignment will have any cosmic significance," T.J. teased, lowering his hands to his hips. "You said yourself, the course is only a bureaucratic requirement. They check off a yes or a no to update your certificate. The specific grade you make won't matter. A respectable B would be sufficient," he observed with gentle humor. "Give yourself a break, and come to bed. It's almost midnight."

From the shadowy perimeter beyond the range of the light on the desk, T.J. stepped closer and began to rub her shoulders. The scent of his cologne, sweet bay and faintly almond, drifted around her. Dhatri. Named after some obscure Hindu god of creation. T.J. had worn nothing else for years. Besides bringing her sherry, his freshly applied Dhatri was another sure sign that he was feeling amorous.

"According to the Almanac, the moon is in Sagittarius," he announced with mock seriousness. One of his college professors had started him reading the *Farmer's Almanac* years before in a landscape architecture class in North Carolina. T.J. enjoyed quoting the little yellow-covered book with its weather forecasts, planting tables, and occasional outrageous tidbits of folk wisdom. Some of the information was helpful. Some was merely humorous. But T.J. frequently used the snippets of almanac wisdom to amuse her and the kids or occasionally to get across a point.

"The Almanac says that when the moon is in Sagittarius, the time is right for romance and optimism, planting onions, and pulling teeth," he informed her. "I wouldn't want you to let a propitious moment like this pass without taking advantage of it."

Barbara let her head droop and drew in a deep breath. She exhaled slowly as the pressure of his thumbs between her shoulder blades glided back and forth over the tense muscles there. He took her yellow marker and placed it between the pages of the textbook and closed it. Then he kissed her fingers and went back to his massage. Lolling her head slightly with the motion of his hands, Barbara reached out and picked up the glass of sherry.

"Okay. I surrender." She managed a weak smile. "But don't kid yourself. I know you're trying to get me all loose and liquored up so you can have your will of me. Sagittarius or not, no teeth pulling," she warned him.

"Planting onions is out too?" T.J. answered with a hint of laughter in his voice. "Never mind. I'll settle for the romance. Nothing like a little body friction to level out the old brain waves and make you really relax." Still standing behind her, he moved his hands over her shoulders, sliding them down the front of her shirt, over her breasts. The gentle massaging motion became distinctly erotic. "I've been waiting all day to have you to myself."

"Whoa there, Bozo." Barbara stopped him. "Before you get carried away, how about a little of that action farther down," she pleaded, glancing back at him hopefully. The trek from the remote student parking area, across the College of Charleston campus to class, to the library, then back to the car had left her feet aching by the end of the day. "How about it?" She swiveled around in her chair and thrust one leg into the air. "Foot rub?"

"One erogenous zone is as good as the next," he said, shrugging. He caught the foot in one hand and began to knead the sole with his thumbs.

Barbara took a slow sip of the sherry and sighed again. "That feels so good."

"I don't know why you put yourself through all this."

T.J. studied her face solemnly. "I hate it when you hurt." His long, strong fingers worked away while he spoke. "You know you don't have to teach again this year."

She'd heard that comment more times than she cared to count. The previous year, after both kids were settled in elementary school, she'd started substituting in the secondary English classes in the area. It was supposed to be an occasional thing. But in the spring, one tenth-grade English teacher at Charleston High had taken ill, and Barbara had filled in for a few weeks. She'd loved it. When the teacher opted not to return, she'd agreed to finish out the school year for him. For the upcoming fall, she'd been offered a full-time slot, a vacancy left by another teacher who was relocating. She'd promptly accepted; T.J. had been grumbling periodically since.

"I know I don't have to work," she covered old territory again. They certainly didn't need the money. "But it keeps me in touch with what's going on with kids these days. Consider it training for when Eliot and Miranda pubesce. Besides, it keeps my intellectual juices flowing."

T.J. studied her a moment, then he smiled. "I love it when you talk dirty."

Barbara ignored him. "Even this," she said, nudging the textbook for the Modern Drama class that she'd put aside for the night. "Reading this stuff is fun in a weird kind of way. It's stimulating."

"You used to find me stimulating." T.J. pretended to pout. But he shifted to her left foot and resumed the massage.

"I still find you stimulating. Without a doubt." She took another sip of sherry. With her eyes closed, she let the sweet liquid linger on her tongue. It seemed to move through her body, smoothing out all the little rough spots along the way. The intermingled aroma of the drink and the Dhatri drifted on the air. "Rub my feet and I'll follow you anywhere." Blissfully she sighed again.

"That good, huh?"

Barbara nodded.

"The things we learn too late," T.J. muttered. "If I'd known when I was younger that a shot of sherry and a foot rub would get results with the ladies, I'd never have made it through school."

Barbara cracked one eye and looked at him dubiously. His sandy-colored hair, razor-cut and combed back, gleamed in the lamplight. His generous mouth and not-quite-aquiline nose were imperfect enough to add character and softness to his otherwise handsome face.

He knew he had her attention. "In my youthful naiveté, I thought blowing in a girl's ear or breathing down the neck of her blouse would turn her on. I'd go for a tit any chance I got, but it never occurred to me to grab a foot." His smooth tanned skin, like sculpted caramel in the glow of the fluorescent light, showed traces of laugh lines. Half-hidden by the shadowy lashes, his blue-green eyes narrowed speculatively at his audience of one. Barbara caught the glint of amusement they held.

Nice routine but she wasn't buying it. "You did all right with the ladies, regardless of technique," she countered. "Besides, foot rubs and sherry may not work with everyone. I may have a distinctly personal fetish."

"That's fine by me." T.J. abandoned the foot ministrations abruptly. "Let's get naked. We'll work on some distinctly personal fetishes of mine."

"Whatever happened to the romance you mentioned? What happened to the sweet talk? Just 'Let's get naked?' " Barbara arched her eyebrows and rolled her eyes melodramatically. "I thought you had a bit more imagination, more finesse." She shook her head as she reached under the desk for her shoes.

"You want imagination. You want finesse?" T.J. leaned forward, whispering in a conspiratorial tone. "How about tonight we try something adventurous. Maybe even ethnic? With costumes?" He paused a few seconds. "I got it. We'll play Zorro and the senorita." He took her hand and gently pulled her to her feet as he stood. "You can wear black pantyhose. That's all. You get the mask and whip. I get the rose in my teeth and castinets." He pulled her closer, poised with clasped hands in tango position. "An' we spe'k nothin' but Spanish."

"We don't know any Spanish," Barbara reminded him. "We can hardly order food in a Mexican restaurant."

"Who's not being imaginative? Pretend we know Spanish," he declared emphatically. "Use a lot of body language." He puckered his lips. "Senorita kiss'a me mucho."

"That sounds more like Italian. Bad Italian, I might add." Barbara laughed, glancing around the room before she reached back and switched off the light. "Did you set the Sonitrol?"

"We're all turned on for the night," T.J. assured her with an evil glint in his eye. "Including the Sonitrol."

"You're outrageous."

"Whenever possible."

Arm in arm, they strolled past the glass-enclosed atrium that sat at the hub of the unique four-winged house. "You take Eliot to the bathroom," said Barbara. "I'll get Miranda. They spent the afternoon out in the hammock drinking iced tea."

T.J. nodded understandingly. Iced tea, especially in quantity, had a way of running right through the kids.

Moments later, bathroom duties completed, they met again in the hallway and proceeded on to their bedroom.

"I love looking at you in the moonlight," T.J. said as they undressed against a backdrop of moonlight flooding the grounds outside. He'd pushed the sliders partway open so the soft summer breeze swept in from the river.

"I just hope no one is out there enjoying the view," Barbara joked. She was standing cross-armed, looking out at the softly illuminated grass and the Ashley River beyond. Its shifting surface caught the light like a trail of sequins gleaming silver and jet. "I often wonder if some fisherman or duck hunter could be out there in the marsh, huddled in his boat, watching with binoculars." Barbara's focus shifted as she saw T.J.'s reflection in the glass slider. He eased up behind her and wrapped his arms around her, enveloping her reflection in his so there was only one form visible.

"If there's anyone out there, he's about to get a real good show," T.J. promised, moving close against her. Wordlessly he took her hand and led her to bed. He kissed her lips, lightly at first, then her neck. He let her slide into the middle of the bed while he followed, his kisses gradually moving downward. Outside, the marsh grass gently swayed in the night breeze, making silken sounds.

"Before I forget," T.J. murmured a bit unevenly, forcing himself to break away, "I'd better set the clock. Don't move." He lunged across the bed and grabbed the alarm. With Barbara's summer school schedule, they had both started getting up earlier, by quarter to six, so they could spend some time together and collect their thoughts before Eliot and Miranda awoke. During that amiable quiet time after awakening, T.J. would make coffee and bring in the paper and read while she showered. Then he'd shower and dress while she got her school papers in order and planned her itinerary. If neither hit a snag, they'd have breakfast together. This routine all depended on the alarm going off on time.

"I've been thinking," he began as he rejoined her on the bed. "We've had a damned unspectacular summer this year. I want to do something really special for next year. Maybe for June, for our anniversary." He was trying to sound nonchalant, but there was a hint of something else in his tone.

"What have you got in mind?" She gazed up at his shadowed face, sliding her arms around his neck to draw him nearer. From the satisfied gleam in his eye she guessed he'd already settled on a plan.

"I was thinking that we should all go to the islands. Bahamas. To Eleuthera. Sprawl out on the beach. Snorkle until our fingers look like raisins. We could stay at the Wellesley."

Barbara looked at him suspiciously. "Every time we've been there, you and I have either made a baby or been about to deliver one. You're not trying to tell me something? You do remember the simple but effective surgical procedure that transpired in Tom Palmer's office?"

"No more babies." He grinned down at her. "I just think it would be great to take the kids there and see where things got started, so to speak." He sounded as if he'd played this through already, imagining them all there together. "I'd like to see the pavilion and the hotel again. Maybe do some sailing. Take a look at whatever changes have been made since we were there last. You know, the relentless encroachment of civilization bit," he added, sounding slightly rehearsed. "A little business and a lot of pleasure?" His shoulders shone like chiseled marble in the moonlight.

Barbara glided her fingertips over the curve of his neck and back, remembering. "I've thought about going back there with the kids." Almost ten years earlier, when they had gone to Eleuthera for a delayed honeymoon, T.J. had managed to get in on the beginning of a massive resort development that was taking over one end of the island. His contribution had been creating the design for restoring and modernizing a hilltop observation pavilion. From that vantage point, hotel guests could watch the spectacular sunsets and oversee the activity in the marina below. The original structure, a gingerbread Victorian-style gazebo from a private estate, had deteriorated irreparably from years of exposure to the sun and wind. T.J.'s restoration, complete with inset glass skylights for stargazing and paddle-style overhead fans for comfort, retained the charm of the original, but added state-of-the-art digital telescopes and maps to make the facility informative as well as picturesque.

"You're sure all you want to do is play tourist?" Barbara questioned him. "You have the proportions correct? More pleasure than business? No abandoning us while you go off and get involved in a new project? We are talking family vacation here." T.J. had a tendency to get sidetracked by work. Near the end of her pregnancy with Miranda, they had gone to Eleuthera to check on the progress of the pavilion. T.J. had left her at the beach, bobbing like a cork with her snorkle, "for about an hour," while he went off to a conference. He hadn't shown up again until sunset and found her waddling along the beach alone in her tent bathing suit with the arrow on the tummy, looking for shells.

He had, however, brought a peace offering, a picnic dinner of champagne and caviar and beautiful iced melon balls. They feasted and argued over names for their child-to-be. T.J.'s names, both Terrence and Jamison, were dismissed as too pretentious for the kid they envisioned. They had already named Eliot after Barbara's favorite poet, T. S., and if this second child were a another boy, they decided on John. For a girl, the debate got livelier.

"How about an S? Susan or Stephanie?" T.J. offered.

"I don't think so."

"Maybe something with an A, like Amy or Amanda," T.J. suggested. "Amy Ashcroft." He practiced the name out loud.

"Too cutesy," Barbara argued. "She needs something special, something with character, something that fits a kid but will have a certain elegance when she's a woman." She stared at the last traces of the sun as it disappeared behind the crimson water. For a long time she was silent. "Miranda. From *The Tempest*. Miranda Ashcroft." As soon as she said it aloud, they both knew it was perfect.

Now as they lay embracing, Barbara smiled at the prospect of taking the children to the islands. She could show her daughter the exact place where she had stopped being "the baby" and became Miranda. She could let Eliot and Miranda snorkel and find all kinds of icky things in the water. Both kids could enjoy T.J.'s hilltop pavilion.

"They'd love it. I'd love it."

"Good," T.J. replied, brushing her lips lightly with his, then returning to linger a moment. "It's settled. And just because we decided no more kids doesn't mean we have to stop going through the motions, here, there, anywhere . . . I love those motions." He breathed the words against her cheek. The scent of Dhatri was everywhere, like incense, fired by his body heat. T.J. groaned softly and pulled Barbara closer, cupping his hands under her buttocks so she could feel every inch of skin on skin.

"Wriggle up a bit so we have a little more room to undulate." Barbara said the last word slowly, then laughed softly. She'd once read an article about "love-talk." She'd been startled by the statistics listing the percentage of couples who used slang words when they made love. "What the heck would they say that for?" she'd muttered. "They all sound so blunt and so gross. Like graffiti. We could come up with something more erotic than these," she told T.J., pointing at the series of quoted phrases.

"Reads like stuff I used to hide under my mattress," he acknowledged. "We could do better."

They went on for weeks, leafing through the dictionary and thesaurus and books on sex, laughing themselves silly at the substitutes. Then she hit *undulate* in a totally different context and it became the hands-down winner. The word itself reverberated with the humor that permeated their lives. But with peculiar eloquence, it described the motion of hands and bodies in the near-silence of their lovemaking. So *undulate*, murmured teasingly or in earnest, brought smiles, sighs, and passion in the night.

"I will always undulate with you, anywhere . . . always . . ." He rolled above her, looking deep into her eyes, stroking the copper curls that framed her face.

"Is that a promise?"

"It's a promise. You better believe it."

In the morning, T.J. was dead. Lying there tranquilly against his pillow, lips half parted, he remained motionless when the alarm went off. Barbara finally crawled across him to silence it.

"Hey, Bozo. This is your job," she complained sleepily. "Quit playing possum." Only when she put the clock back in place and reeled back to stare bleary-eyed at him did she realize that the body beneath her hand was unnaturally cool and still. Instantly she retracted the hand. Then she touched him again.

"Oh, my God." She struggled into an upright position and stared at his serene face, trying to comprehend. "Oh, no. Not you. No . . . T.J. . . ." Slowly she reached up and placed her hand against his cheek. It was all so remarkably peaceful.

"No." She shook her head from side to side as slow tears welled up and spilled over, trailing down her cheeks. "Poor baby." She let her fingertips caress his cheek and settle lightly on his lips.

In the early-morning stillness of the house they built together, on the bed where they had so often loved each other into ecstacy and exhaustion, Barbara Ashcroft wept alone. There would be no shrieks of anguish, no lamenting for others to witness. That wasn't her way at all. Her innate reserve would not permit so public a display. But for the moment, while she still had him all to herself, she didn't hold back the tears.

"Tom, this is Barbara." Her voice was even and controlled as she spoke.

"What's wrong?" Tom Palmer knew a call to a physician's home at six-fifteen in the morning wasn't likely to be a social one.

"T.J. is dead." Barbara swallowed, then managed to get the words out distinctly.

"What?"

"He's here, at home, in bed. He died during the night."

There was a momentary silence, then a quick expulsion of breath that sounded as if Palmer had been hoping somehow it wasn't true. "Geez, Barb." It was almost a groan. Besides being their family doctor and neighbor, Palmer was T.J.'s friend. "I'll be right over." He was off the line before she could even respond. Mechanically she placed the telephone back in its cradle and walked over to the bedroom window.

Outside, the sun was just beginning to filter through the upper branches of Wordsworth, the tallest and oldest of the four massive oaks that surrounded their home. T.J. had bought the lot the first year they had come to Charleston. He was working on several designs for houses farther inland along the same strip closer to the country club, but spotted the location on the point in a flyover when the development was just begun.

He fell in love with the four impressive oaks towering over the tangle of palmetto bushes, evergreens, and Virginia creeper, with the marsh grass and the river spreading out behind them. Then, it was only a jumble of vegetation at the end of a narrow dirt road in an undeveloped section of Harborview. On one side the Wappoo

Creek headed off to the country club. The other looked across the Ashley River toward the southern tip of the Charleston peninsula and had been proposed as a bird sanctuary. But the proposal hadn't passed the legislature, so the area became a new development. A road was cut in. The lots went on sale. And when they did, T.J. bought.

First, because the area was boggy, they had brought in truckload after truckload of fill. Then T.J. spent two years coming up with the right floorplan. "They were here first," T.J. said of the oaks and the shrubs. "We'll just ease in here among them and try not to antagonize Mother Nature in the process." He set the cross-shaped house up on a raised base in case of flooding, then built up the surrounding land, without disturbing the oaks at all. They stood intact, like aged sentinels, between each wing.

So the four oaks became members of their extended family. Wordsworth, stately and broad, with moss-bedecked limbs, provided a tranquil presence on the north between the family room and the bedroom wing facing the creekside. Poe, secluded near the back of the house to the east, shoulders hunched against the river winds, loomed between the bedroom and the study-workroom. On the south, Keats, more slender and younger than the others, overlooked the study and the kitchen-dining areas. At the front of the double lot stood Byron, T.J.'s favorite, with its trunk coiled in ivy and its low, dramatic, outstretched branches hung with rope swings. Byron was situated between the kitchen and den and shaded the gravel drive curving up to the entrance.

T.J. had also seen to it that the surrounding area around was landscaped. He wanted to accentuate the natural and secluded setting on the slight promontory at the end of the access road. So he brought in Luster Johns, an elderly fellow from the nursery who knew the climate well. Luster helped set up draining channels and raised buffers, natural seawalls camouflaged by native plants that needed little care. For color in season, the natural green was augmented by masses of oleander bushes, azaleas, camelias, and jasmine.

Because every view was unobstructed, T.J. designed the outer walls primarily of glass, with floor-to-ceiling windows, stationary panels, or sliding doors all around. He used grayish-bronze reflective glass that mirrored the foliage, so from the outside, the house, with its cedar uprights, blended into the setting. But in exchange for the beauty and serenity the surrounding plants provided, T.J. planned that the clear glass panels would eventually hold stained and leaded designs.

"When the lights are on, we'll give nature something back, something to enjoy," he insisted.

They hired a quiet-mannered local glass artisan, Craig Kerfberg, to design and make the first windows. But gradually Barbara became so caught up in the process of cutting and leading the creations, she moved from onlooker, to assistant, to craftsman. She helped with the eight wildflower panels in the kitchen, creating the most cheerful corner of the house. For the bathroom, Barbara had done a panel of deep purple irises, rich and elegant and exotic. "For Wordsworth," she declared with genuine concern for that particular viewer outside.

For Miranda's room, she and Kerfberg had done a huge rainbow, with pansies instead of a pot of gold at its end. Eliot got hot air balloons, four multicolored ones, against a brilliant blue sky. On rainy days or during the dull winter months, or when a moonless night engulfed the yard in darkness, the house had its own bright colors to share.

But there were windows still to be done. T.J.'s master plan also included a number of other indoor and outdoor projects. Walkways. Decking. A gazebo. A dock for when the kids were old enough for boating and jetskiing. "We never got to finish." Barbara stood looking out at Wordsworth. "T.J. . . ." She breathed his name in the still of the room. "What will I do? We had so much we didn't get to." She drew in a steadying breath and wiped away the remaining tears. Tom Palmer would be arriving to make it all final and real.

"I guess this is goodbye." Barbara crossed once more to the bed and put her hand on T.J.'s chest. Deep inside, a voice she could not acknowledge kept screaming *No* over and over until it became a single incoherent wail underlying everything else. Solemnly she bent forward and kissed his forehead. Then she stood, took another deep breath, straightened her shoulders, and headed for the front. From now on, T.J.'s body would be in someone else's care. Other people would hear and mourn. He no longer was hers.

Tom Palmer examined T.J. for only a few moments before speculating that the probable cause of death seemed to have been an aneurysm in the brain. "Quick, no pain," he told her. Then he called the medical examiner's office and began the legal formalities that were required.

"You want anything?" Palmer asked, eyeing Barbara cautiously as he led her down the hallway toward the atrium. "I could give you a tranquilizer," he offered. Barbara stopped and pressed her forehead against the cool glass that enclosed the inner garden. She stared at the pots of geraniums and begonias inside.

"I don't want any drugs. I've got to keep my head clear and help the kids to get through this. I'll manage on my own resources," she insisted. Then she moved on toward the kitchen, almost robotlike as she filled the coffee maker, got out mugs, then plopped a can of frozen orange juice into the sink to defrost. Palmer followed her.

"I guess I'd better call my professor and tell him I won't be in class today," she spoke at last. "I'm supposed to have a test this week." Her voice trailed off as she reached for the telephone. She stopped, remembering what T.J. had said the night before. *In the overall scheme of things, I doubt if this assignment will have any cosmic significance.* At the moment, it seemed ludicrous that she could even think about a class or a test while T.J. was in the other room dead. *In the overall scheme of things* . . . His words kept drifting back.

"Barbara?" Tom Palmer's voice prodded her into the present. "Barbara, as your physician and friend, I'm telling you to sit down here a minute." He spoke gently, but he had a firm grip on her arm. "Let's just talk a bit and discuss what must be done. First of all, I think you should have someone here with you. I'm doing the calling," he said evenly. "Do you want me to start with Karen and have her come over?"

"Karen. Yes, Karen," Barbara replied dully. Karen Belcazzio was her best friend. She would want to be here. "And Louis," Barbara added. Karen's husband, Louis, would need to be on hand. He would have to take care of whatever loose ends there would be at the architectural firm.

Barbara sat watching the coffee drip into the pot while Tom Palmer dialed the Belcazzios' number. When he told Louis the grim news, Barbara sat motionless a few seconds before she made herself get up. Resolutely she crossed the room and took the telephone.

"You shouldn't have to do this. This is my job," she said quietly, her whispery voice a bit more hushed than usual. "They should hear it from me." She spoke to Louis for almost a minute before Karen got on the other line. Then the litany began again, "T.J. died peacefully in his sleep last night. We think it was an aneurysm." That was the message she would be repeating all day to everyone who must be told.

When she finished speaking to the Belcazzios, she patted Tom on the shoulder sympathetically. He turned and hugged her without saying a word. He was hurting too.

"Coffee," she offered. Palmer nodded. Silence once more filled the room.

Moments later Barbara looked out under the wildflower panels and saw the beige van from the medical examiner's office gliding up the curving gravel driveway. "Could you hold them off for a little while? I've got to tell the kids."

Palmer opened his mouth to protest, but Barbara raised one finger to silence him. "I have to be the one to tell them," she insisted. "I want them to see him as he is, quietly and peacefully lying in his own bed. It's not so bad, really." She breathed in to check a new onrush of tears. "It's better that they see how it is, so they won't imagine something far worse." Her voice cracked before she finished the statement, but she stopped and steadied herself and didn't cry.

Palmer shrugged and surrendered. He stood watching her as she walked out of the room, her stance erect and brave. When the low van pulled to a halt beneath Byron, Palmer stepped out to greet its occupants.

Eliot and Miranda listened, bleary-eyed and silent, as Barbara told them that their daddy had gone to sleep last night and had something go wrong in his body. "He died," she told them solemnly. "But I don't think he hurt at all." Then they hugged and wept together in Miranda's big bed until Eliot asked if he could see his father, just as Barbara said he could.

Together they went into the bedroom where T.J. still lay undisturbed. Eliot never spoke at all. For a long time, he stood at the foot of the bed and looked. Then he touched and nodded. He sighed. And wept.

Miranda rested her head on T.J's chest and patted him. Then she patted his hand, his cheek, his shoulder. She smoothed his covers as if he were the child and she the parent gently tucking him in and checking that all was as it should be.

"Bye, Daddy," she said over and over. "Bye, Daddy." It was a slow and sorrowful ritual, but Barbara felt this was far more important to the children than any of the more formal ceremonies that would follow. She'd had her private farewell. They were having theirs.

"The men are going to come in. Daddy's spirit has gone from here. He's gone somewhere special. But there are things that have to happen now. Dr. Palmer and the men have to take care of the body. They'll have to take it away to do it," she said softly. "We'll see it again later. You two come with me." She waited for the children to respond. Miranda gave T.J. one final pat. Then she came and took her mother's hand. Eliot took one more look, then nodded. He wiped the palms of his hands against each cheek. Stiffly, he backed away. He reached Barbara's side and slid his arm around her waist. At nine, he already came up to her chest. Like his dad, he would be tall one day. She put her arm securely around his narrow shoulders. "Let's go," she said, turning and leading the children from the room.

Tom Palmer and the gray-suited men were still standing in the driveway when Barbara brought the kids into the kitchen.

"I'll tell Dr. Palmer and the others that they can come in now." She made certain the children knew they would no longer have the house to themselves. "You two sit here and sip some juice," she told them before she left. Tom had told her the medical examiner would have to do some routine work, but Barbara didn't care what went on down the hall. All those labors were inconsequential. What mattered was that T.J. didn't live there any more. Without warning or spectacle, T.J. had left them all.

"Rob?" Barbara's soft voice trembled more from weariness than from emotion. This was the twelfth call she'd made since morning. Her shoulders ached and her arms felt weighted as she held the phone. "This is Bobbie."

"What's wrong?" Rob Johnstone picked up on her distress immediately, even long distance. Usually their conversations were upbeat, rapid exchanges. "Have you read . . ." or "Have you seen . ." They had kept in touch this way through the ten years of "the marriage," as he and Barbara called it. There had been brief visits in person and long silences between, but between Rob and Barbara, some invisible thread remained unbroken. They were friends. Whenever they spoke again, the time lapsed and the space between diminished into insignificance. Particularly now, something compelled her to contact Rob again, some need for continuity.

"T.J. died quietly in his sleep last night."

"Oh, Bobbie." His voice was barely audible. "What a damn shame."

"I know." She leaned one hip against the kitchen counter and nodded.

"You want me to come up? Are you all right for now?"

"You don't have to come," she assured him. "There really isn't anything anyone can do. Some of the family will be arriving. Things will be pretty grim here for the next few days." She hesitated a second. "I'll be okay."

Rob didn't say anything right away. "I know you'll be okay," he acknowledged. "But I'd like to come up anyway. If not now, then as soon as you feel like having me there. I have a play in production. I'm getting everything blocked out and walked though." He was obviously trying to adjust his schedule. "I guess the Belcazzios will help you out."

"They've already been here," Barbara told him. "My folks are on the way up. T.J.'s parents and his brother are arriving tonight."

"How are the kids? Dumb question under the circumstances," he muttered apologetically.

"The kids are doing all right. It was very calm. An aneurysm."

Again there was a brief silence. "Look, how about giving you a couple of weeks to let things settle there. Then I can assign a student director and arrange to come up for a few days. Nothing hectic. I just want to see you and the kids. To touch base. It's been a while."

"Sure." Rob knew her well enough to understand she'd function well under pressure. But it would be the aftermath, when all the activity subsided and the company had departed, that would be most difficult for her. His visit would give her something beyond this first hurdle to think about.

"Good. I'll get things organized on my end," he said. "Meanwhile, if you need anything, or just want to talk, call me, night or day. I'll check in with you next Sunday for sure." His voice, solid and reassuring, soothed her. "I sure am sorry about this, Bobbie."

Barbara didn't reply. She simply nodded against the telephone receiver.

"I'll be seeing you," he said quietly. "Count on it. Okay?"

"Okay."

Then he paused and hung up.

Barbara stared down at the list of phone numbers with checks beside them, indicating that they had been called already. She'd retreated to the study to make the calls, searching out some place quiet and away from the other activities in the house, a place where the kids wouldn't have to hear the details over and over. Now a small hand rested on her arm, gently commanding her attention.

"Come and have some tea, Momma. Karen and I made some tea." Miranda's deep bluish-green eyes were puffy from crying. Her long reddish blonde hair was pulled back and neatly tied with a ribbon. She was wearing her apron with the quilted duck on the bib front. T.J. had called Miranda's latest phase the "little mother syndrome." Barbara assured him that it was something all seven-year-olds went through. For now, it was one way Miranda could manage this catastrophe.

"Thank you. Tea is a lovely idea." Barbara hugged the little girl. "I think we could all use a cup of tea."

"I think so, too," Miranda replied in her maternal voice. "Maybe after, you should rest."

Barbara felt a small smile tilt the edges of her lips. It was a strangely uncomfortable sensation for that day. "Thank goodness for you." She contemplated the calm, earnest expression on Miranda's face. "Maybe I will take a nap," Barbara conceded. "Maybe we both should. I'd feel better if you rested with me."

"Maybe." Miranda refused to commit herself. Without another word, she tugged Barbara's hand and led her toward the kitchen.

Karen Belcazzio had set out tea and sourdough biscuits. She was diligently making a shopping list after scrutinizing the contents of the refrigerator. Her sleek black hair, pulled back in a chignon, contrasted more than usual with her skin. Pale bluish semicircles beneath her eyes showed the strain she shared with her friend.

"You look tired," Barbara pulled Karen away from her listmaking and hugged her.

"Neither one of us would make the cover of *Lear's*," Karen kidded her. "I think we'd both better eat something nourishing before we drop. This is going to be one heck of a long day. It's really rough going, my friend." Her bottom lip quivered as she spoke.

The two of them had managed to hold up pretty well as long as they were busy. But every once in a while, talking face to face, they would catch the stark emptiness in each other's eyes. Then all the hurt would rise dangerously close to the surface and conversation became very difficult for them.

"Let's sit down." Barbara waved them both toward the food. It was still early in the day, and neither one of them had eaten anything. "I forgot I was running on empty," she noted. Miranda was already at the breakfast nook in the raised corner area adjoining the kitchen. She was pouring tea, carefully, not spilling a drop. "How about Eliot?" Barbara glanced around.

"He said he'd like to be alone," Karen lowered her voice. "I took his tea and biscuits into the atrium." Her dark eyes shifted toward the glassed-in garden down the hallway. Barbara stepped over and looked toward the center of the house. Eliot was barely visible amid the potted plants, sitting inside the glass room with his back against the panes, staring up through the skylight at the solar panels that rimmed the north end of the sloping roof.

"So, I guess we leave him alone," Barbara concluded. She watched him a moment longer before turning away to give her full attention to Miranda and Karen at the table.

"You want some jam?" Karen passed the jar to the now-silent Miranda, who was engrossed in spreading butter on her steaming biscuit.

"Please," Miranda replied without looking up.

The two women raised their cups for their first sip. Then they sighed, lowering them simultaneously. There was a hesitant exchange of half smiles as they reached out and linked hands.

"This is really awful," Barbara said softly.

"It stinks," Karen squeezed her friend's hand. "It really stinks."

"I heard about Mr. A. at band practice." Kent Nelson said, shifting his feet and looking more gangly than usual. At sixteen, he already stood six feet four inches and managed to resemble an embarrassed ostrich whenever he was not in full motion. On the football field with the marching band, he looked like a weathervane, swinging his French horn from side to side and goose-stepping to the rhythm. But on the basketball court, his movements became liquid. There, all the awkwardness was gone; he was transformed into a gazelle, loping, leaping, totally at ease. Now he was having a difficult time standing still. He towered over Barbara Ashcroft, flapping his arms uncertainly.

"I sure am sorry, Mrs. A.," his voice was gentle. "I thought I'd better come over and help around the house, maybe with the yard. You'll be having visitors, I guess. It was busy at our house when Grandad died."

Barbara shifted her eyes from the tall, lanky young man to the long expanse of land behind him. Kent had spent most of the past year working with Barbara and the kids and the aged nurseryman, Luster Johns, landscaping the place. They'd started around the perimeter facing the water, where a bulldozer had made ridges called "berms" to act as natural seawalls in case of heavy storms. They covered the ridges with variegated shrubs, sprigged in plants, and laid sod to help conceal the underground watering system that now wound like a labyrinth out to the grassed-in portions.

T.J. was there to supervise, off and on, until summer came—hot, clear, and dry, perfect for the building trade. Then he was so busy that he hadn't even taken a vacation, much less found time for the lawn work. So it had been Luster Johns, a rail-straight figure who still lived on the backriver, who took over as crew chief, pointing his wrinkled ebony hand and narrowing his eyes as he gave directions. Kent and Barbara sweated and supplied the heavy labor while Eliot and Miranda followed Mr. Johns, listening to his tales and assisting where they could.

Luster Johns taught them the names of native plants and showed them where to plant them around the berms where the water system didn't reach. He used drought-tolerant varieties that could survive on rainfall alone and required no special care. They also restored the wild look that the trucks of landfill and the construction process had obliterated.

"Turnin' it back to nature" was what the soft-spoken

Mr. Johns called his brand of low-maintenance landscaping—the same thing that the conservation books now were promoting and calling xeriscape. Luster just called it "nature sense." He'd lived on the South Carolina coast near Charleston all his life. His grandfather, who remembered and passed down tales of the slave days and had taught Luster the Gullah language, had lived on the same plot of land in his time. Luster knew about floods and tides and storm surges. He'd seen drought and downpours, icestorms and hurricanes, and he knew what survived. He also knew that using freshwater irrigation was gradually going to be a problem in the coastal areas, where lowering the water table made the incursion of salt water a real danger.

"Too many folks using too much water," Luster summed up the problem succinctly. Rather than plant showy, water-loving plants that depleted the freshwater resources, Luster advised T.J. to go natural. It was impractical to try to transform the three-acre plot around the house into a grassy flatland punctuated by cultivated gardens. "Let Nature do the most work free," Luster counseled. "Low-care, low-cost." When the landscaping was completed, Kent took as much pride in the result as the Ashcrofts and Luster Johns. But even with the low-maintenance factor, the portions nearer the house needed some care before the influx of visitors.

Barbara stepped outside and walked with Kent into the shady area under Byron. It was the first she'd been out of the house all day. "Even Luster would admit this looks a little too natural," she conceded, contemplating the drive and entryway in particular. "It needs cutting."

"The band director said it would be all right if I missed practice for the rest of the week," Kent added. "I figured you might need me. I just want to do something, anything to help."

"I know the feeling," Barbara assured him. "I keep thinking we should all be doing something. But no one seems to know what that something should be."

"You want me to go ahead now and cut the grass?" He still had not managed to let his eyes meet hers for more than a fleeting second.

"Please," Barbara patted his arm. "You know where everything is."

"I'll take care of it." He suddenly sounded more assured.

"I really appreciate your coming over like this." Barbara patted him again. "We're all a little at loose ends."

"I just had to do something, Mrs. A." His wide brown eyes dipped down to meet hers. Then, like a puppy eager to please, he managed a slight smile.

"I'll try to get Eliot out here to give you a hand," Barbara added. "He's been cooped up in the house all day. I think he could use some constructive activity."

"Sure." Kent bobbed his head up and down, just like Luster Johns often did. "Send him on." He strolled off around the kitchen wing toward the garage on the southern corner of the house, where the riding mower and all the lawn equipment were stored.

Barbara stayed in the shade a moment, watching a heron wading in the marsh grass along the river. Someone on a jet ski was bobbing, barely visible, on the fringe, making some adjustment or another. Farther out, some kids in a flat-bottomed boat were drifting by, trailing fishing lines. Everything seemed strangely normal. In a little over four hours, her folks would be arriving by airplane. Then T.J.'s would arrive. The cycle of grief and consolation would begin again. But for now, it was a bright, breezy summer day, a day for children to be outside. She turned back toward the house.

"Kent is here to spruce up the yard." Barbara rested her hand on Eliot's shoulder as she spoke. He had left the atrium and had sequestered himself in the den, apparently absorbed in watching an old videotaped movie.

"Don't you think a little fresh air would do you some good?" She knelt down beside the silent, sandy-haired boy.

"Is Mr. Johns here?"

"No. Just Kent. I haven't called Mr. Johns yet. I guess I'll have to do that." She rubbed his shoulder, trying to make some physical contact to ease his remoteness.

Eliot poked at his glasses and kept staring at the television screen. "You know how you said Dad's spirit was gone?"

"I remember."

"Remember when my lizard died? Bartholemew?"

"I remember Bartholemew."

"Well, Mr. Johns said when something dies, it just steps a little bit away. He says its spirit stays near for awhile. For a couple of days. It kinda' watches over us till we're okay. Then it gets to go off with the other spirits. He says we shouldn't feel sad, just cause we can't see 'em like we used to." The young boy struggled to connect the old nurseryman's folk philosophy with his own feelings. "When I think about Dad, I hope he's still around." His small voice wavered. "I'm trying not to be sad." He hesitated and took a few slow breaths. "But I'm not too good at it." He nudged his glasses again, sliding them further up his nose.

Barbara stared at the thoughtful face of her son, still turned toward the television screen. This was the first real conversation they had shared all day. He was handling the sorrow with as much courage as any nine-year-old could muster.

"Sometimes we'll feel the sadness more than others. Like today. It's too soon for any of us to be okay." Barbara leaned forward and kissed the top of his head. "I'm sure Mr. Johns would agree. We'll just have to take this one day at a time. I still think it might help to go outside, just for a change. The yard could use some work."

"Maybe Kent will let me drive the mower." Eliot shifted thoughts and clicked off the set, adjusting his glasses again. "I think I'll feel better out there." He swung around and managed a small smile for his mother.

"I'm glad," she said, giving him a long hug.

"We'll be all right," Eliot insisted, patting her back. "Daddy will still be with us. Just like Bartholemew." He jutted out his chin confidently. And suddenly there was T.J., years younger and more innocent, shining in the face of their son.

"Thank you, Mr. Johns," Barbara breathed as Eliot bounded outside. She picked up the remote control and placed it on the shelf above the television. "I sure hope T.J. and Bartholemew are with all of us," she murmured as she turned down the hallway toward the kitchen. "We need all the help we can get."

"Listen, Barbara." Ernie Engler's bald head glistened in the light from the fluorescent tubes overhead. "It is perfectly reasonable for you to stay out for awhile. You might need to think things over and reestablish your priorities." He peered over his eyeglasses, which made him look far older than the fortyish years that he was. He knew she didn't need the income.

"I want to teach," Barbara replied calmly. "I need something normal, some regular routine in my life. Teaching will give me some outside structure," she stressed. "Besides, I like it."

When Ernie Engler asked her to come in ahead of schedule for a preschool conference, Barbara had guessed this was what her principal wanted to discuss. Like everyone else, he wanted to see for himself how she was bearing up after the shock of T.J.'s death.

"Anyone else would have to be bribed to take the remedial classes," Ernie grinned at her nervously. "You're the first really good teacher who ever asked for them."

"T.J. used to give me that same bewildered look," Barbara responded. "He never did understand what the kick is in dealing with . . . well, he called them throwbacks," she admitted. T.J. had taken her return to teaching about as seriously as other husbands took their spouses' interest in gourmet cooking or needlework. He looked on it as a time-consuming hobby, one with the added penalty of Barbara's grading papers at home.

"He could spend a year restoring an old building that wasn't functional or attractive when he started, turn it into a doctor's office or a business complex, then gloat over the results," Barbara continued. "I get kids who don't read or write particularly well, and teach them how to do both things better. I think that's worth gloating about too." She tilted her shoulders in a slight shrug. "I could see the similarity. My results are just less public."

"Hey, you don't need to convince me." Ernie rocked

back in his chair. He was suddenly far more relaxed with her than he had expected to be. "You're good. The kids put out for you. In a manner of speaking," he added hastily, immediately wishing he hadn't phrased it quite that way. There was something about Barbara Ashcroft that encouraged a certain reticence in the people who knew her. Even the "throwbacks" took a protective attitude toward the slim, copper-haired woman with the whispery voice who seemed incredibly vulnerable next to some of them. They generally cleaned up their language and avoided any extreme that might offend her.

"They do work hard," Barbara rephrased his comment, getting him off the hook.

"So you're really sure about this?" Engler was more relieved than he showed. Replacing a Remedial English teacher less than two weeks before school resumed was a nightmare he'd been dreading.

"I'm sure about this year," she said honestly. "One year at a time is all I can handle right now," she said solemnly. With T.J. gone and the old rhythms of her life gone too, she needed time to readjust and examine her options.

"Teachers report back—" Engler began.

"Next Tuesday," Barbara supplied the information. "I'll be here bright and early," she promised.

"Now you remember this." Engler reached forward and placed his hand on her wrist. "If at any time things get too rough, if anyone gives you any trouble, if you need a few days leave to take some time for yourself," his anxious face furrowed in concern, "you buzz me and I'll do whatever it takes, even take over your class." He stopped on that one, realizing what he might be letting himself in for. Then he nodded. "Even that. I mean it. No questions asked."

"I may take you up on some of that," Barbara replied.

"Cathy and I really want you to know how much we regret what happened." He removed his hand from her wrist. "It was a shock for the whole community."

"Tell Cathy that I appreciate your concern." Barbara had said a variation of that phrase innumerable times lately. "Thanks, Ernie, for being so considerate."

Engler cleared his throat and picked up his pencil, not knowing what else to say.

"See you next week." Barbara stood and picked up her purse and a new workbook that some publisher had sent for her to examine. "Thanks again for taking the extra time with me." She summoned a tight smile and left.

Instead of turning toward the front of the long, two-story high school, Barbara went in the opposite direction, up the stairs into the room she'd been assigned for the upcoming year, the one that would be totally hers. Inside, the bare walls and empty chalkboards were bleak and spiritless. The pale green walls accentuated the bland, institutional look.

"What we need is a little life in this place," Barbara said, then paused as she caught the irony of her own words. T.J.'s death had changed everything, even the ease with which simple clichés fell into place. Throughout the final weeks of her summer-school course, the ironies had surfaced again and again in her class discussions of the plays they studied. Themes of death, suicide, alienation, and the inability to feel any emotion were woven through the modern plays they were assigned. Like Pirandello's six characters, Barbara felt abandoned, abridged, incomplete, cut off before the ending was clear. Diligently, Barbara buried herself in the literature each night, earning the A's that she wanted but steeling herself against the echoes of her own grief in all the selections she read. And all the while, the distant voice within cried out its constant *No*.

"This is my room, my kids." She stiffened and cast a critical eye over the bare classroom before she left. "Plants. We definitely need plants. And some pictures." She could feel the momentum picking up. "Thank goodness for the throwbacks."

Downstairs, rows of desks were lined up in the gymnasium, newly varnished after the old scars and graffiti had been sanded off over the summer. The signboard that would post the dates of football games and dances now only read "Orientation of Freshmen. August 27th." But the promise was there. New students would be coming, and many of the old students would be returning, most of them taller and more mature than they had been just a few months before. They'd be poking their heads in the door to give Mrs. A. a rundown of their vacation or summer job or current romance. "Take it as it comes," Barbara said out loud, smiling as she headed for her car.

"Somethin' the matter? That ol' rheumatiz grieving you?" Mattie Johns looked at her father warily. Luster had been sitting on the porch since he'd come home from the nursery that afternoon, smoking his pipe and staring out over marsh grass along the sidecreek.

"I'm jus' listenin'," Luster said in his soft raspy voice that seemed to come from a long way off. He never broke the rhythm he'd set with the cane-backed rocker, and he never took his eyes from the shimmery surface of the water as it turned to amber in the setting sun.

"You want some dinner? I can bring a plate out here."

"In a while. In a while," he answered gently, clearly wanting to be left alone. The breeze slipping through the branches of the moss-hung live oaks almost swallowed up the sound of his voice. Mattie sighed and turned back into the kitchen.

"What's the matter with Grampa?" Willie Dodd asked her, looking out the window at the top of Luster's head, moving forward and back as he rocked away outside. Willie Dodd had been up in his room doing homework ever since he'd come home from his college classes that day. Being summoned to dinner without having Luster at the head of the table to give the blessing made him uneasy.

"The spirit is reaching out to him," she said simply. "Didn't you say Sonny Pierce brought in some wood today?"

"Big pieces. Three of them. Maybe four feet tall. He put 'em out by Grampa's workbench."

"Then I guess that's what's happening." She turned over the pieces of chicken sizzling in the pan. "He must feel the spirit reaching out. Time to do some more pieces. Just leave him be." She put each portion on the folded paper towels she'd spread out on the blue cornflower platter. "We'll just go ahead without him tonight." She patted Willie Dodd's shoulder. "You know how it is when he gets like this."

"I know." Willie Dodd smiled and nodded, relieved now that Luster's behavior made sense. It was often this way before Grampa started working on one of his sculptures. He'd get quiet for a couple of days while he waited for inspiration. Luster Johns called it "listenin'." He said the spirit would come close and talk to him and tell him what to do. He never called it "God" or "Nature" or anything that other folks made stiff and proper with capital letters. It was just "the spirit," the same one that he spoke to every morning and every night. The same one that first told him ten years earlier, when he was almost seventy and his wife of fifty years had passed on, to take an old oak root and find the face in it. With a chain saw and some chisels, Luster had worked for days until he saw her. That first face had been beautiful. Serene and full-lipped. He'd rubbed it smooth with sandpaper, then buffed it with ashes to burnish the wood just so. Then he polished two dark pebbles and set them in for eyes. And he had his Inez there again, carved in oak, eternal, patiently waiting with him for the time that he would join her on the other side.

Inez was still out back in the garden beyond the workbench with the others: the bulldog, the squirrel, the pelican, and the children—Nathaniel and Lizabeth—like they were years before they died. Luster kept the ones that were family and the ones that belonged there. But from time to time, when they needed the money, like for Willie Dodd's college, he let the others go, and the spirit didn't seem to mind at all.

The museum in downtown Charleston had one Luster Johns original in its sculpture garden. The curator bought the doe-eyed Indian girl right out of the nursery when he'd come down for mulch one fall. Luster's boss, Everett Pierce, had put the girl, a slender figure only three feet tall, on display after Sonny Pierce drove Luster home one day and spotted her on the porch where he'd been putting the finish on her. After that, Sonny would come and get whatever he had done, and Everett would show off all the pieces right in with the plants and flowers. Then a writer for the newspaper took an interest and did a nice piece in the feature section. From then on, Luster's pieces never sat on display for long.

There were always buyers, often art buffs who had seen the article or the museum's Indian maid and wished to add "a Johns" to their own collection. A restaurant bought an old fellow with a corncob pipe for its entryway. Everett Pierce bought and donated the one that looked like Christ to the Catholic school, even though he wasn't Catholic. Pierce kept one, an old woman with a watering can, for the nursery. And he made sure that any good-sized stumps, or driftwood, or lengths of fallen cypress or cedar were saved and stored in the warehouse until Luster knew it was time to carve again.

Apparently now it was time.

"Can't rush Grampa," Mattie ladled out the corn and string beans onto her son's plate.

"I'm just glad he isn't feeling poorly," Willie Dodd replied.

"You know what he says," she reminded him. "When the time comes, it comes. I don't think Grampa's time is here yet."

"Praise the Lord," Willie murmured.

"I think Grampa's out there doin' somethin' just like that," Mattie noted with a patient smile.

Before Luster came in that night, the sun had long set and the soft cover of darkness had closed in around the house where he had been born seventy-nine years before. "I don't know what's to come of this one." Luster stood in the clearing out behind his workbench, looking over the pieces of wood Sonny had brought that afternoon. "Never did no angel before," he told Inez. "Why you suppose we're goin' to need an angel?"

He reached out one long-fingered wrinkled hand and ran it over the rough surface of each of the three pieces of wood. He liked the cypress the best. It had a solid feel. Insect repellent. Two short limbs butted out near the top. They sort of looked like wings. Then he stood erect, his head crooked slightly to one side. For a while he didn't move at all. "Maybe more angels. Lots of angels. Now why would we need lots of angels?"

He stared at the wood again.

"Well, if they in there, I'll find 'em, that's for sure." He gave the second piece, the cedar, another close look. "Ev'ry back is fitted to the burden," Luster muttered philosophically. "Get a good rest, fust and fo'most. Night, Inez. Night, ev'rybody." Half smiling, he looked up at the night sky, dotted with stars. "Night ev'rybody," he said again, and slowly headed inside toward the lamplight.

CHAPTER 2

> How lonesome the Wind must feel Nights—
> When people have put out the Lights
> And everything that has an Inn
> Closes the shutter and goes in—
> *Emily Dickinson*

LOUIS BELCAZZIO shrugged and flapped his hands over the typed agenda, the stacked folders, and the various sets of paper-clipped pages spread out over the table surface in front of him. "Okay you guys. Let's go. Hey, I'm calling the meeting to order." He aimed the comments at Barbara and Mark Ward, who were huddled at the opposite end of the long conference table, scrutinizing some sketches Mark had brought. "Come on, you two. Sit. Let's act like a company," he proposed, feeling increasingly foolish seated there at the far end alone, like an oriental potentate.

"Sorry, Louis," Mark apologized, picking up the crisp, blue-lined sheets of drafting paper. He started rerolling them into a neat tight tube as he walked the length of the room and took his customary seat to Louis's left. Louis waved Barbara toward the right-hand chair, the one that had been T.J.'s. With the three of them in place, the August partners' meeting of Ashcroft and Belcazzio, Architects could commence.

"Are you sure you're up to this?" Louis narrowed his bright button eyes at Barbara. His brows merged into a single line.

"I'm all right," she responded quickly, giving him a tight smile. "Really." In the five weeks since T.J.'s death, Louis had seen that same all-purpose smile countless times as he watched Barbara carry on. Still, he couldn't dispel the uneasiness he felt whenever that smile materialized. It didn't dissolve the desolation deep in her eyes. On the surface, everything she did seemed unnervingly normal, typically contained. With quiet dignity, she had weathered the funeral and the aftermath remarkably well, including finishing her graduate classes at the College of Charleston. She'd taken the children to movies and shopped for back-to-school clothes as usual. This week, she'd arranged for a sitter and started her pre-opening departmental sessions at the high school.

Everything seemed to have fallen into place with an efficiency more typical of T.J. Ashcroft than Barbara. T.J. had taken care of her and the kids with a thoroughness that even Louis had not expected. Jack Clayton, T.J.'s attorney, had overseen all the family's legal affairs, handling and filing all the insurance and Social Security forms. There had been a number of them, all requiring the same grim documentation.

T.J. had left directions for the funeral—simple, precise, and modest. With meticulous care, he'd had term policies that covered the house, the office building housing the business, even both cars; now the insurance paid off them all. The considerable sum from his full life policy would be diverted by Clayton into a variety of investments and bank certificates. Barbara would never have to worry about money. "Financially, you are set for life," Clayton had assured her while Louis and Karen Belcazzio sat with her one evening during that first bleak week. All it took was a few signatures. Clayton had completed the transactions without further involving her.

The only concern that Barbara had to deal with directly was the operation of the architectural firm. Curiously, T.J. had involved her more after his death than he had ever before. He'd stipulated that for a full year she serve in his place in the partners' meetings. He also put a lock on selling any of his fifty-one percent of the business he had started when he first came to Charleston over a decade before. Six years into that decade, to accommodate an expanding clientele, Louis Belcazzio was taken in as a partner. Ashcroft, Architect became Ashcroft and Belcazzio and prospered.

Now they had twenty-six-year-old staff architect Mark Ward, two draftsmen, a fine reputation, a list of long-standing clients, and ongoing consulting agreements with two engineers and five local developers. There were also three office workers who handled their secretarial work and bookkeeping. However, for the firm to maintain T.J.'s standards, there was a void to be filled. The company needed an experienced architect with a flair for restoration and period work, one who could handle contemporary design as well. Filling that post had made this afternoon's meeting necessary.

"Maybe we should review some of the pending business first," Louis said, looking over his half-glasses a bit apologetically at his two associates. He wasn't used to running the show. He and T.J. usually shared the responsibility in their own relaxed style. Louis was finding the entire procedure more difficult than he'd expected. "T.J. had a few things in the works. We have to decide whether we'll follow through with them or back out." He passed copies of two project proposals to each of them. Louis smoothed his close-trimmed, gray-streaked beard and gave the others a moment to scan the material.

"Don't these depend on whether you have someone to take them over and make sure they're executed correctly?" Barbara got right to the point. Louis had already told her that he and Mark Ward couldn't absorb any more of T.J.'s workload. "You and T.J. always said that plans were only lines. Making the vision come off the page requires a caretaker." Her hazel eyes met his steadily. "Who's going to be their caretaker now?"

Louis's mouth felt dry. "I guess that moves us on to the second item on the agenda," he said stiffly. For the time being, he put T.J.'s two proposals aside. "We have put out some feelers for a new associate," he noted. "Let me go over the material I've got so far."

Louis slid a few manila folders over and opened the top one. "Jeff McMillan. Savannah. Thirty-seven. BA. Divorced. He and T.J. were not in the same class but they were at UNC at Chapel Hill together. They've both worked in restoration." Louis tugged at his tie, uncomfortable at the uncustomary formality of the suit he'd worn for Barbara's benefit. Usually these meetings were conducted in shirtsleeves over orange juice, coffee, and corned beef. He passed copies of the architect's resumé to each of them. "McMillan could most likely pick up on these projects where T.J. left off. He's good. He's available. He would accept a year trial before either of us makes a decision about partnership. And he's close enough to commute back and forth to Savannah for any leftover business while he eases out of the firm he's with there."

"Shouldn't we invite him up here to look around and meet everyone?" Barbara barely got the words out when Louis shifted his eyes and gave Mark a distressed look. Behind his wire-rimmed glasses, Mark's face was rigid. He glanced at the papers he still held clasped in his hands.

"Oh," she licked her lips. "You already have."

"We asked him to drive up a couple of weeks ago," Louis said gently. "I didn't want to bring it up to you until we'd done some groundwork. I figured I'd find out for sure if he was interested and if he seemed to fit in, then I'd bring it up here."

Mark Ward had turned ashen. He watched with soft blue eyes, cautiously awaiting Barbara's reaction.

"So, tell me how it went with Mr. McMillan." Barbara's all-purpose smile was in place.

Louis could feel the sweat trickling down inside his shirt. "It went very well." He leaned forward and propped his elbows on the conference table. His bush of thick dark hair, streaked, not as extensively as the beard, with highlights of gray, quivered as he nodded enthusiastically. "It went real good, in fact. He's sharp. He's been with a big high-profile firm, but he likes the relaxed pace of our outfit. He knows his stuff." He was watching Barbara's intent expression as he enumerated the positives. "Word is that he's a bit of a workaholic. Socializes well. Like I said, he's divorced. No kids. He's got no real ties to Savannah." He shrugged slightly. "We like him," he concluded.

Barbara hesitated then shifted her attention to the remaining manila folders in front of Louis. "What about the other ones?" she questioned him cautiously.

"A couple looked promising. Bridges. And Weller." Louis nodded, lifting the next two folders from the stack. "We had them come in, too." Louis pressed on. Mark

Ward still sat motionless, studying Barbara across the tabletop.

"Bridges wants to run the world, and the business, his way." Louis assessed the next candidate on the list. "He's a grandstander. Goes after big projects. No real appreciation for detail. Not what you'd call subtle."

Mark Ward smiled and nodded silently in agreement.

"The other guy, Weller, wants too much money right off and too big a slice of the pie," Louis continued. "He wants to buy half of T.J.'s shares now and have an option to buy the rest in a year. T.J. wanted you to hold onto everything for a year. If you do decide to sell any of it, I want to buy enough to keep the controlling interest. T.J. set a certain style and established standards that we're known for, and I don't want that changed. I don't think he would either."

Barbara drew in her lips thoughtfully. "So that brings us back to this Mr. McMillan. What do you think?" She turned her attention to Mark Ward. His eyebrows shot up in surprise.

"Uh . . ." He swallowed and moistened his lips with the tip of his tongue.

Barbara suddenly had the feeling that at these partners' meetings, at least the ones before this, Ward had been given very little opportunity to offer his ideas. He was not a partner, but T.J. and Louis had him sit in regularly on the sessions so he wouldn't miss any important decisions. Now she could imagine how those meetings went. T.J. had an unmistakable dynamism, a momentum that often overwhelmed anyone around him. He could be awesome—if not impossible—when it came to having his way. But he was also brilliant, and Mark Ward had idolized him. So that only left Louis as the voice of conservatism.

"We have to make a decision," Barbara said for her own benefit as well as for Mark's. "We just have to make sure it's the right one," she added reassuringly. "So, Mark, I assume you met these men?"

"Yes." Mark cleared his throat. "Yes, I did."

"Well, what do you think?" she pressed.

Mark paused, looked from her to Louis and back, then

let out a slow breath. Besides the prospect of anyone taking T.J.'s place in the firm or altering "the style" that Louis mentioned, T.J.'s death alone had been difficult for Ward to deal with. He shrugged almost apologetically. "I agree with Louis. I think McMillan is our best bet." Gradually, his color was returning to normal. "He brought some slides. He's done some nice work. Offices. Townhouses. He's good on preservation. He's a stickler for quality. He's done some nice interiors." Mark made each comment thoughtfully, as if he were recalling specific projects as he framed his remarks. "And he's done some contemporary offices that are very clean, real elegant."

"You think he would fit in here?" Barbara studied Mark's lean chiseled face and the solemn eyes behind the steel-framed glasses. As an associate architect, Mark would have to work as closely with the newcomer as he had with T.J.

"He seems to be pretty easygoing on the outside. Kind of intense about his work. Sort of like the rest of us," Mark added, almost managing to smile this time. "I could work with him. I think he'd be an asset to the business." He made the last part sound objective and quite professional.

"You don't think we should keep the position open for awhile and continue looking?" Barbara had known there would be a search for a new associate, but she hadn't expected the void left by T.J. to be filled so soon. The haste seemed vaguely like a sacrilege.

"I think he's the best suited for us all around," Mark concluded sincerely, becoming increasingly expansive under the attention Barbara was giving to his opinion. "I doubt if we'd find anyone better. Not in the position to transfer in so readily."

Now Barbara leaned back in her chair as her eyes darkened with the glimmer of some indefinable emotion. "Louis?" She waited to hear from her friend.

"I agree with Mark. I didn't expect to click so fast, but I think McMillan's our man. This is a quirky situation. Experienced restorationists don't just shift locations often. We're lucky he's only down the road in Savannah and that the timing suits him." Louis turned the focus back on Barbara. "How about you? Do you want to meet McMillan before we reach a final decision?" He studied her, trying to read behind her mask of reserve.

"I don't think I really need to check him out. I trust your instincts." Barbara shook her head slightly. "You're the experts when it comes to evaluating his credentials. You have to work with him." She looked from one man to the other. "If you're satisfied, then offer him the position."

"Done," Louis proclaimed, clearly relieved. "I'll draft the offer in writing. I guess that solves the first issue on the agenda as well." He picked up the two proposals they had initially discussed. "If McMillan accepts, he can start in with these. We'll have him look them over, decide whether he wants to take them on, and go from there. Agreed?" He looked at the others for confirmation. "Now if you don't mind my getting out of this damn jacket," he groaned good-naturedly, "I'd like to finish the other business in comfort."

"Please do," Barbara urged him. She was used to a more casual version of Louis. Seeing him in jacket and tie had added a sense of distance between them that made her somewhat defensive.

"Now, I need to engage in some blatant nepotism," Louis proceeded, stroking his beard like a mischievous genie in shirtsleeves. "I'd like to contract my wife for the Aames project. And Mark needs her for the medical offices he's doing." All three of them knew Karen Belcazzio regularly did the architectural renderings they needed. Her results were excellent; there was no real need for discussion. "Agreed?"

Everyone nodded.

The remaining items were familiar, routine considerations. In order to appear more organized for Barbara's benefit, Louis had weeded through most of the financial details and simply enumerated them and suggested that the bills listed be paid as usual.

"That's it. So let's go home," Louis concluded the meeting. He shoved all his paperwork into a neat pile.

"That's it?" Barbara asked.

"That's it," Louis assured her, knowing full well that some of their board meetings were more rambling and often considerably more heated. But for an introductory round, this version would do. "That's it," he repeated, trying not to sound too anxious to be out of there. He was having trouble keeping memories of some of the past meetings when T.J. sat next to him, laughing and arguing, from coming crashing in on him. "Let's go to my place and unwind," he suggested, standing and pulling out Barbara's chair. "I'll fix you a drink and you can pick up the kids. How about it, Mark?" he asked the younger man. "You have time for a detour?" Louis glanced at his watch as he and Mark Ward followed Barbara down the hallway toward the rear exit of Ashcroft and Belcazzio.

"I've got a meeting. Committee for the River Run." Mark had been a cross-country medalist in college and had started training for the Charleston Run the past few months. "They're blocking out the routing and revising some rules. They need the input of runners. Sorry." He hesitated, then glanced at his own watch and offered a distracted half-grin. "Got to go."

"No problem. See you Monday." Louis waved as they parted just outside the door. Mark got in his car and drove off. Louis walked with Barbara toward her vehicle.

Under the sweeping branches of an oak tree at the end of the paved area, she halted, looking at the metal signs marking the spaces reserved for Ashcroft and Belcazzio. She'd parked in the one with T.J.'s name. "Louis, what about the name of the company?"

"What about it?"

"I mean, now that T.J.'s gone . . ."

"The name stays." Louis guessed precisely what was bothering her. "It was Ashcroft when I got here, it will stay Ashcroft as long as I have a say."

"What about this McMillan, or even Mark?" Barbara inclined her head toward the office building they had just left. "Shouldn't they be added eventually?"

"If there were any suggestion of a change—which there is not—it would be a darn poor move to ever consider dropping Ashcroft. Because of T.J., we're known as a restoration firm. He left his signature on this firm just as he did on every building he worked on. This company is T.J.'s baby, always will be. Besides, he was too precise a taskmaster, too efficient at brainwashing Mark and me, and too ornery to cross, to ever let us take his name off anything." Louis grinned as he took Barbara's keys from her hand and opened the door for her. "He set the standards. He'll always get top billing. We'll worry about any add-ons later."

"I guess I just needed to hear that out loud. Sometimes it seems like there isn't anything left." She pressed her lips together in a thin line, holding back whatever other thoughts were struggling inside her.

Louis put his arm around her shoulder. "I began to feel that way back in the conference room. We used to have some hellish arguments in there," he reminisced. "Most of them Mark avoided and I lost. T.J. had the knack of seeing things that we would have missed. And he hung in there like a pit bull until we got the point. He was tenacious, that's for sure." His eyes glistened with emotion. "Usually he was right. Once in a while, he wasn't. Then we'd yell a lot. He'd see my point. He'd surrender and laugh his ass off. He loved a good fight." He lowered his voice, trying to smooth the occasional break. "No matter what we do, we'll always hear T.J. somewhere in our heads, or feel him peering over our shoulders, making us look at things from another perspective. And he'll be cackling that outrageous laugh of his when we come up with that one missing element that makes it all work. He was quite a character."

Louis's thick-lipped smile wavered and faded completely. He stiffened his stocky body and sniffed, struggling to keep his composure. He thrust out his lower lip and stared off toward the street, in an attempt to appear pensive. But Barbara recognized the symptoms and reached out and hugged the portly little man. She was familiar with the tightness that made it difficult to speak and the rush of tears that came surging from nowhere when a sudden memory surfaced. She'd experienced the devastating haste with which waves of grief and reminiscence swept aside the mundane, suspending everything else in the real world while the sense of loss held her breathless.

"He was quite a character," she said softly.

For a moment they just held and patted each other.

"But he was one S.O.B. when he wanted to be," Louis muttered, assuming the gruff, bearlike demeanor with which he could conceal his sorrow. "I'd hate to piss him off, even now," he tried to joke. "If we misspelled his name on the stationery, we'd probably hear from him."

They looked at each other and exchanged small sad smiles.

"Let's go home and have that drink now," Barbara spoke first. "We'd better bail out Karen. My babysitter had an appointment, so she's had my kids most of the afternoon. She's probably as much in need of a drink as we are."

"You take the lead. I'll follow." Louis proceeded over two spaces, peeled off the tan covering that he called his "birdshit shield," stuffed it into the trunk, and got into his car. When Barbara pulled out into the thickening late-afternoon traffic, maneuvering her silver Mazda westward toward the Ashley River Bridge, Louis kept right behind her in his low sportscar, a candy-apple red Mercedes convertible Karen had bought him three months before as his fiftieth birthday present. T.J. and Barbara had hidden it in their garage for a full week before the morning of the unveiling.

She narrowed her eyes against the glare of the sun as she concentrated on getting into the right-hand lane. Halfway across the massive bridge, with the Charleston peninsula behind her, she finally let the tense smile fade from her lips. For a while, alone in her car, she could drop the act. Everyone said she was handling the situation well. She was so serene, so competent, more resilient than anyone had expected her to be. It wasn't too difficult with strangers. But it was hardest with a few close friends. They suspected. And they were watching her.

"But not here," Barbara thought. She felt her lower lip begin to quiver as she glimpsed her exit ahead. Once she picked up the kids at Karen's, she'd drive deeper into the wooded subdivision, heading home to the house she and T.J. had built out on the point. No one monitored her there. Each return trip was like going into a deep dive. The requisite errands, the pace, and the strident voices of that outside world were left behind. She could immerse herself in the slow time of the house on Harborview.

She liked to ease back into it gently, following the winding road without haste, so the final turn up the long driveway toward Byron could sweep clean the clutter of that day. Secure in her own realm and T.J.'s, she could reclaim part of what they'd shared. In small flashes and for fleeting moments, she would have him again in the things he created and the children he had loved.

"Hi, kids. Hi, Karen," Barbara called out. She was on stage again as she stepped out of her car and waved to the trio in the yard. Louis swerved past her in the driveway and swung into his garage. Even there, he pulled out the car cover and tucked his baby in. Miranda and Eliot came loping across the grass. "You two ready to go home?" Barbara asked. The kids had abandoned Karen and the half-inflated football they'd been scrambling over. "Hey, you're losing something." She grinned at Miranda, whose tiny flowered bikini top was dangling precariously just above her navel.

Miranda's pink-tipped nose turned up indifferently at the comment. "It doesn't matter. There's no one here 'cept Eliot." At seven, she was too much of a tomboy to make concessions to modesty.

"Well, let me hitch it up anyhow, so you won't lose it," Barbara suggested. Miranda arched her eyebrows and assumed a pained expression, but she condescended to hoist the garment into place and turn her back so her mother could retie the slender neck cords. Barbara pushed Miranda's tidy long braid, obviously Karen's handiwork, to one side.

By now Eliot had strolled over to join them at the edge of the Belcazzios' driveway. His cheeks were ruddy from a day in Karen's pool, but behind his narrow-framed glasses, his hazel eyes were dark and reserved.

"How did your meeting go?" He watched closely as Barbara finished with Miranda's suit and looked up at him.

"Pretty good," Barbara replied. She gave a gentle toss to Miranda's braid, as the youngster leaned against her.

Eliot waited for more details. He figured there were going to be some changes at his father's company. He wanted a full report.

"We're taking on a new architect. A fellow from Savannah. He'll probably be working on some of your dad's projects. Karen is going to do some drawings. Mark is getting ready for the fall cross-country run. I guess that's about it. Ashcroft and Belcazzio is going strong." She reached out and smoothed the shoulder of his shirt. "It still is Ashcroft and Belcazzio," she added. His somber face turned suddenly boyish again.

"Good. So let's go home." He started around to the passenger side of the car.

"Whoa. How about a few thank-you's?" she insisted, halting him.

"There have been a lot of those already," Karen assured her, coming across to join them. She'd unfastened her hair, long and dark but braided like Miranda's, and deftly untwisted it, catching a few loose strands and pulling it back into an elegant knot, listening to Barbara's summary. Now she tapped the toes of her shoes on the driveway, shaking off the loose dirt. "They thanked me after the juice and hot dogs, after the pizza, after the peach cobbler and . . ."

"It sounds like you've been running a delicatessen," Barbara said, laughing.

"We had a great time. I thanked Karen for letting us swim," Eliot added with a slightly patronizing tone.

"Karen let us finger-paint," Miranda announced, clasping her mother's hand. "We painted all over her tablecloth."

"You did what?" Barbara's eyes widened.

"It's all right. It was an art project. We did it on purpose. It's for some special occasion, as soon as I think one up," Karen explained hastily. "I was tired of the dreary old tablecloths I had, so I enlisted your talented children to decorate one for me. We spread it out on the back porch, got a few pots of paint, and went to work."

"It was pretty messy," Eliot said, trying to sound unenthused. He was usually the tidy one, much like T.J. had been. "But it turned out all right. We dipped flowers and leaves in the paint and pressed them down. Even the veins showed."

"We stuck them all over. And we finger-painted the stems and some ladybugs." Miranda beamed up at her mother. "It was great."

"I can imagine." Barbara chuckled, knowing how wholeheartedly Miranda would have thrown herself into the action. It was the kind of up-to-the-elbows activity she loved.

"I had to hose them down when we finished," Karen added, anticipating the next question. "We can't show you the finished product until it dries. When it's ready, we'll unveil their work." Karen gave a sidelong look from the proud faces of the children to the limp football they'd left behind on the lawn. "Say . . . you two pick up the ball and put it in the garage for next time." Her tone had become more serious. "And go out the back and check that there aren't any wet towels left around."

"We already took care of the towels," Miranda reminded her.

"It wouldn't hurt to take another look, just to be sure we didn't miss anything," Karen flicked her fingers, shooing them off. "Scoot."

Eliot hung back, smiling mischievously. "You're just trying to get rid of us for awhile, aren't you? You grown-ups want to talk. Like you always do," he added.

"I would like a few words with your mother." Karen reached out and tweaked his nose gently. "Without big ears, if you don't mind."

"I thought so." Eliot cackled, sounding just like his father. "Come on, Miranda," he said patiently. "Let's go find something to do." The two of them strolled off side by side.

"You aren't in a rush, are you? Come on in for a drink," Karen suggested, turning her attention back to Barbara. "Lemonade?"

"Back at the office Louis offered me something a little stronger." Barbara draped her arm through Karen's.

"Ahh, then that's why he disappeared so fast. I'd bet he's whipping up a pitcher of daiquiris. Nice timing." The two of them strode toward the house.

Barbara gave her friend a cautious, sidelong look. "You've got me wondering. What are the few words you wanted to tell me? Something about the kids?"

"Oh, no," Karen countered quickly. "Everything is fine with them. They were a real pleasure to have around." She slid off her soiled sneakers and left them by the front door.

"If you don't mind, I think I'll ditch these, too." Barbara slipped off her high heels and left them in the mirrored and marble foyer. In stockinged feet, they proceeded into the interior, a vast elegant ivory and crystal room that T.J. had once called Sugar-Plum Fairyland. In single file, they crossed to the far end of the formal living area that ran the full depth of the Belcazzios' house. A wall of glass opened onto a spectacular view of the back few holes of the country club and Wappoo Creek farther out. The only sound beyond their voices was the chomp and growl of the blender from the kitchen.

"Come on, what is it you want to talk to me about?" Barbara prodded.

Past the terraced pool area outside, the yard swooped down to the manicured thirteenth fairway. Eliot and Miranda were already out back, lying on their stomachs, floating leaf-boats across the churning waters of the jacuzzi that Louis had apparently turned on. Karen led her friend to the cluster of wicker chairs facing the outside so they could sit and enjoy the view.

"It's about the new architect who's joining the firm."

"You already know who he is?" Barbara glanced at Karen fleetingly then locked back onto the kids.

"Outside, you mentioned Savannah. The only one from Savannah was McMillan. I figured you'd go with him. He seemed pretty sharp."

"You met him?" Barbara's eyebrows arched a fraction; the quick look faltered before zeroing back on the children.

"Louis and I had him over for dinner when he was up here."

"Of course."

Karen raked her toes into the thick carpeting. "Anyway, from what I understand, once McMillan has officially accepted the offer, things will have to move pretty quickly."

"In what respect?" Barbara kept the same polite expression that made Karen's toes dig deeper. The sound of the blender had ceased.

"As soon as we can arrange it, Louis thinks we should have a cocktail reception to welcome him. We need to introduce him to our friends and our clients. We were thinking we'd have the reception here." Under previous circumstances, business parties had alternated between Barbara's and T.J.'s and the Belcazzios'. Generally the ones at the Ashcrofts were relaxed affairs. While guests mingled on the shaded lawn and enjoyed the food and the river view, T.J. would often give informal tours, showing off the house he'd designed.

"I think having it here would make sense," Barbara spoke after a heavy silence.

Karen breathed an audible sigh of relief. "I'm glad you think so. We really don't want to put you through anything stressful," she spoke in a gentle, concerned voice. "But there is something else."

Barbara's noncommittal look held no clues to what she was thinking.

"We would like you officially cohosting with us. We'd like our names and yours on the invitations," Karen proposed. "It won't be for a couple of weeks. Probably the weekend after Labor Day. Everyone will want to see you." She studied the still, unreadable expression on Barbara's face. "Entertaining here at our house, with a semibusiness group, might be good for you. It may help you to ease back into the social scene. Not that you've missed much lately."

"So, do you think you might be up to a little socializing?" Louis's voice came from slightly behind Barbara.

The pale carpet had muffled any sound of his approach. He stepped between them, bending slightly to offer each of them a tall, frosted glass from the tray he carried.

Barbara stirred the iced mixture with a slender straw. "Sure. I can handle it."

Karen leaned forward. "I know it must seem like you're getting hit with a lot of changes in one day."

Barbara took a long sip of the daiquiri and sighed approval. "No. It's fine. The party makes sense," she assured them, propping her feet, like Karen had done, on the seat of an empty chair. She remembered sitting in this exact way before. She was sure that other time she had looked relaxed.

"You don't feel like we're rushing you too much?" Louis asked as he settled down next to Karen.

"The timing is all right." Barbara traced the top edge of her glass with a fingertip. "Summer's over. Things shift gears in the fall. I can understand the importance of getting things moving ahead. A party to introduce this McMillan is good, businesswise."

"And you're not too uncomfortable about the idea of hostessing?" Karen stirred her own drink.

"I feel uncomfortable now," Barbara answered honestly. "Not because of the party. It's tough getting used to planning anything without T.J." She took another long sip of the daiquiri to loosen the knot in her shoulders that had begun steadily inching its way upwards.

"We don't want to rush you."

"Quit worrying. Over Labor Day, I'll get my courage up." She looked from one pair of somber, assessing eyes to the next. "Really." She reached across and patted Karen's arm. "Really. I'll be fine. I know I should be there, otherwise a lot of folks we've known for years will be the ones who will be uncomfortable. We'll all do fine." Barbara smiled again, scrupulously pushing the right buttons and saying the right things, hoping to ease the wariness in the Belcazzios' twin stares.

"If you're sure."

"I'm sure. Besides, I may have reinforcements. There's an outside chance that Rob will finally make it up at the same time. He's been juggling his schedule, and he mentioned Labor Day weekend or the next one as possibilities."

"It might help all around to have another old friend on the sidelines." Louis tilted his head to one side and smiled tentatively. "Should we call and tell him we could use the company?"

"I'll call him," Barbara promised. "How about setting an exact date for this coming-out party?" She regarded her companions with amusement.

The tiny worry lines at the corners of Karen's eyes softened. "We'll make it the tenth. Saturday evening. That will give us the rest of the weekend to clean up and recuperate."

"Okay. The tenth." Barbara leaned back against the cushioned headrest, watching the children, now absorbed in enticing a bushy-tailed squirrel off the fairway. T.J. used to call squirrels "tree rats," which only made the children find them more fascinating. Barbara was the one who kept a sack of raw peanuts, unshelled, in the garage so Eliot and Miranda had a constant supply to feed the beasts. But she'd often seen T.J. scatter a few extra handfulls at the base of Byron when the autumn chill set in, thinking no one was looking.

"Another drink?" Louis offered.

"Please," Barbara answered without moving. The back of her neck felt rock hard from tension. Her temples pulsed with a dull, angry rhythm. She'd pulled it off again. She convinced them that she had it all under control. There was no need for anyone to know otherwise. She was getting better and better at doing her public self convincingly. Her private self still needed work. And time.

Inside, she'd been functioning on auto-pilot since T.J.'s death. At first the numbness was strangely comforting. But the safety of that muffled sense of remoteness was seductive. Lately, even with school about to resume and the requisite activities at home and work piling up, the numbness hadn't eased like the books on grieving said it would. The acute sense of separation, the feeling of being hopelessly out of sync with her friends and the rest of the world had begun to feel dangerously comfortable.

The possibility that she would pull back too far emotionally began to worry her. Somehow, she had to hang onto life, to reconnect. The party and Rob's visit would help.

"Cheers." Louis handed her a refilled glass and raised his own in salute.

"Cheers." Like a puppet, Barbara raised her glass.

It was almost dark when she loaded the kids in the car and headed for home. Louis stood in the driveway with his arm around Karen's shoulders as he watched them drive off. "Well. What do you think?"

Karen shook her head slightly. "I'm not sure."

"She seems to think she can handle it."

"She seems to think she can handle everything," Karen replied. "It's really scary, Lou."

"How so? She's doing darn well as far as I can tell."

"That's just it. She's handling everything too well." Karen turned to meet him eye to eye. "The friend I knew had this very pleasant off-kilter way about her. She'd occasionally run a whole cycle on the washing machine and forget to add the soap. Or she'd fix dinner and not remember to put the spaghetti in the boiling water. Just a little dipsy." Karen's pale and beautiful face, like one in a pre-Raphaelite painting, had a wistful, sad look. "Now she gets the kids places on time, she keeps the house tidy and the lawnwork done. She makes lists."

"So do you," he reminded her.

"But that's me. I've always been that way. For her, it's all too neat and organized and civilized." Her voice cracked. "I miss the old Barbara. This one is trying to be Miss Perfect, going about her business without missing a detail, just like T.J. did. But for him, that kind of disciplined thinking was natural. He was always stepping in, spotting whatever wasn't taken care of, and fixing it." Karen's dark liquid eyes glistened with tears. "When Barbara does it, it's creepy. I don't like it. Even Rob said he was getting some strange readings when they talked. He's worried about her. So am I."

"Maybe this is just the way she needs to operate for a while," Louis tried to console her. "Maybe taking care of details keeps her mind occupied so she can make it through each day."

"I don't know what she's thinking. She won't open up to me any more. Rob says she's a little evasive on the phone at times. That's why he keeps calling us. He was ready to come up the last week of summer school, but she told him she had to study for exams. Then she told him the next Monday that the weather had been great and he should have come after all. He just wants to keep posted as to what's going on."

"Maybe she's just keeping everyone at a distance for a while because the hurt is just too much."

"That's fine, up to a point," Karen conceded. "Then she puts on one of those damn smiles and cuts us off completely. She's like a mama bear. She comes out to do what's necessary, collects her young, goes back into that house, and she absolutely hibernates. Miranda told me she even started baking bread." Karen made the activity sound vaguely deranged.

"We'll do what we can to draw Mama Bear out of her den and let her know that she still belongs out here. Today at the meeting she did just fine. The party will be another good start. Getting Rob up here may help. Sooner or later, she'll come around without so much coaxing."

Karen directed one last apprehensive look down the roadway. "I sure hope you're right. I want the old Barbara, my Barbara, back again. I know you miss T.J. So do I," she said softly. "But I miss Barbara more."

It was after ten when Barbara stepped out of the hot bath and let the water drain. Wrapped in her tee-shirt nightie and a flannel robe that had been T.J.'s, she went in to check on the kids. Usually she'd left each of their bathroom lights switched on and their doors pushed partway open so the glow into each bedroom illuminated the route from bed to commode. Miranda awoke in the night and would find her way to the bathroom and back to bed. But even though Eliot was older, he was the deeper sleeper. If he drank a lot in the evening, and if no one made him take a late stop, and if he were really exhausted, he'd occasionally wet the bed. One time it happened on a spring night when he and T.J. had gone to a baseball game, overdid the colas and hot dogs, and come in late, gloating about "the guys' night out." Afterwards, Eliot had been so embarrassed over the bedwetting, he'd moped about the house for a week.

Tom Palmer had said Eliot would outgrow it when he got closer to puberty. His hormones would kick in and his sleeping patterns would change. But until then, just to be safe, on most nights Eliot had to be roused and led like a rag doll to the toilet. With a little encouragement, he would stand docilely before the commode, do his business, and be led back to bed without noticeably waking from a sound sleep.

He'd made it dry through the first two nights right after T.J.'s death. There were relatives visiting, no one was monitoring the kids' soda consumption, and Barbara was too tired to remember to make the late round. But he wet the bed once, the night after the funeral. Barbara heard him rummaging in the linen closet at three in the morning, crying to himself, as he tried to locate clean sheets. That one wet bed had brought a lot into focus for her. There was no backup, no one to catch what she missed. Either she did whatever was needed, or it didn't get done. So she started Karen's system of making lists. The one that included "set Sonitrol" and ended "bathroom run" was taped to the light on her study desk. No matter how tired she was, she'd remember the bereft expression on Eliot's face grappling with his peed sheets, and she'd trudge over to his room, whisper his name, lead him to the bathroom and back, and tuck him in.

Now back in the study, she returned to the old lesson plans left by the teacher who had taught the remedial classes before her. Ernie Engler, the principal, had gathered up a box of similar material for her from other teachers at the district curriculum center. "The bottom line is individualizing. Getting each kid to do the best he can do with what he's got." Engler had summed up their approach, telling her nothing she hadn't already figured out herself. "But the tricky part is simply getting them to quit fooling around and get to work."

"I'd better quit fooling around myself," Barbara said as she slid pages from one stack to another, trying to pick out the successful units and restructure them to suit her own ideas. School would begin the middle of the next week. She'd have the new group for three days, then they'd all be off for Labor Day weekend. First impressions, hers and theirs, were crucial. Diligently she scribbled notes in the regular square spaces that indicated each session of that first week, until the lines blurred and the notations looked hazy, and the longed-for weariness finally overtook her.

She'd been making a practice of staying up alone in the study, reading or working on class material, determined not to roam the house, feeling the emptiness. She couldn't go into her bedroom at all after dark until she was too tired to lie awake and think. Sometimes, as Tom Palmer had suggested, she'd take a hot bath and drink a glass of sherry, to help her relax and drop off. He'd given her some sleeping tablets, but she hadn't used them yet, simply because she didn't want to get into a routine that might lead to some kind of dependency.

Wearily, with elbows propped on the desktop, Barbara pressed her palms against her eyes, easing their slight burning until she yawned and broke the silence of the room. Yawning a second time, she raked her fingers through her hair. Then she pushed it all into place again, arching her back and stretching as she drew in another deep breath. Tom had said deep breathing would help relieve the stress, so she closed her eyes, straightened her position, and inhaled slowly, easily. Suddenly, she sniffed again, and again, more sharply, recognizing the scent. Dhatri. It was the unmistakable heady, aromatic blend of bay and almond that T.J. had worn. Barbara snapped her head from one side to the other, scanning the area anxiously. She sniffed again.

"T.J.?" she whispered as the phantom scent filled her with an old longing. "Oh T.J." She cupped her hands around her eyes and stared out into the dim room, beyond the pale circumference of the desk lamp, half expecting to see him standing there, reminding her that it was late and it was time for them to go to bed.

There was no one, nothing, in the shadows. She inhaled slowly again. The familiar fragrance made her flesh tingle. She rubbed one hand over her forearm, erasing the goose bumps. When she glanced about this time, her eye caught the pale gold glimmer, just beyond the harsher edge of the circle of light that encompassed her papers. Her sherry. She reached out tentatively, then closed her fingers around the slender, half-filled glass that was sitting there. In bewilderment, she stared at the glass, trying to recall when she must have gotten up and brought it. Before the bath? After tucking in the kids? When she'd checked the Sonitrol? Sherry didn't need a place on the list stuck to the lamp. She usually just worked it in. But this time, she couldn't remember when.

A gentle cool current of air crept in from nowhere, wound around, enveloping her, bringing closer the savory Dhatri, even stronger than before. She tugged the lapels of the robe against her neck, shivering with the inexplicable chill.

"I don't like this." Barbara's anxious eyes once more scanned the darkened room. All the windows were closed for the night, no air conditioning was on. There was no reason to feel a draft. But what had her off center was that she couldn't remember filling the glass.

Sometimes, on other nights, she would take her sherry over near the windows, sit there for awhile in the loveseat by the worktable, waiting for the liquor to glide through her limbs and quiet the lonely whisper within. But tonight she couldn't remember going anywhere near the liquor cabinet across the hall.

The room was so silent that the only sound beyond the hollow ringing she heard was the pump and rush of her own pulse. She peered harder into the shadowed corners, straining to see and hear something in this cushioned atmosphere. "Late-night heebie-jeebies." She fought off the nervousness.

Hastily she swallowed the sherry in two nervous gulps. "I don't like this one bit." She put down the empty glass, clicked off the study light, and hurried out into the hallway. Without looking back or stopping to check one last time on the children, she went straight into her bedroom.

She pitched her robe onto the end of the bed, scrambling past it and sliding hurriedly between the sheets. She knew she must look foolish, skittering about like a startled kitten, but panic was welling up inside.

"I'm all right. It's late. I'm a little stressed out," she reasoned. Her whole body felt clammy. She had done this as a child, crossing her room in the dark, crawling into bed and covering her head. She'd lie there absolutely rigid until the ghosts and monsters of her fantasies had been banished from corners and under beds or supplanted by other, more benign dreams. Later there were bullies and practical jokers in the real world who thought that scaring girls was fun. But she'd outgrown all that. At least she thought she had. She was too big now to pull the covers up over her head and cringe in the warm space beneath them. She simply drew them to her chin and lay there, feeling childish, staring outside at Wordsworth, reluctant to turn and look toward the hallway in case some spectre had followed her and lurked on the threshold, needing only her fear to invite him in.

"This is really stupid," she muttered between clenched teeth. She lay there, assuring herself that whatever she'd experienced in the study that night—the scent, the chill, the sense of some other presence in the room with her—was nothing more than the combined effect of exhaustion, memory, and perhaps some wishful thinking. T.J. had died July seventeenth, five weeks before. It was possible that unconsciously she'd picked up on the date on a calendar or felt the similarities between this night and the one when T.J. died. The moonlight, the solitude, the weariness, and the loneliness had her playing mind games. She was sure that was all it was.

Outside, in the still August night, Wordsworth curved his leafy branches across the full, bright moon of Indian summer. Over the past year, Barbara and T.J. had spent countless peaceful hours lying there in the dark, gazing out at the ancient tree, watching the easy motion of the leaves. But now, her nights alone with Wordsworth were the saddest times of all. On many levels she'd accepted the empty place in bed next to her and the absence of laughter and lovemaking in the pale light of stars and moon. She missed being held and hugged and kissed. On some level she was so numb she felt as if she had shrunk and was almost lost inside her body. Still, she struggled with the greater dread of knowing that after the night of sleep would come a morning. Another day would begin with her, alone.

In the morning, Wordsworth would be there, rugged and old and twisted from the river winds, his boughs well-nested by chirping birds and squabbling squirrels. But there would be no T.J. to roll over and poke down the snooze button on the alarm or mutter faint curses at the morning serenade outside. That once-delicious time between the first alarm and the delayed one would no longer be spent gently nudging each other awake. Instead, Barbara used those moments purposefully reassembling the composed version of herself she showed the children and the rest of the world.

"If you're out there somewhere, goodnight, Bozo," she whispered aloud. They were a silly few words to say. She knew that. But she'd been saying goodnight to T.J. for years. And perhaps to keep from letting him slip into a void more final than she could bear, she had continued to murmur them each night since his death.

"Goodnight, Bozo," she would breathe softly as she lay there remembering, lamenting. "I miss you." Just saying goodnight, like a final prayer before she let go of the day, somehow diminished the boundaries between what was real and what was not. If she could sleep and dream like she sometimes did, T.J. would be there, waiting for her on the other side of consciousness.

Closing her eyes, Barbara waited in the silence for the tension to leave her as it always had before. But tonight was different. Tonight the boundaries had blurred before the words were said, while she was still awake. "Please help me, T.J.," she said, as an invocation, a summons for solace from the ambiguities of the night. "Help me not to be crazy. Help me not to be afraid." She closed her eyes and squeezed the edge of the covers until her hands ached.

Resolutely, she rolled over, compelling herself to face

the bedroom door. "Please let there be no one there." Abruptly she opened her eyes.

There was no creature lurking in the opening between her room and the hallway.

As her eyes adjusted, Barbara peered at the shifting shadows beyond the doorway. The hall was darker than it should have been. She realized that must have contributed to the uneasiness that made her flight from the study into her room more eerie. Either the children's bathroom doors had been inadvertently closed, or their lights were off.

"I'm really not up to any more of this," Barbara groaned, closing her eyes again, trying to dredge up more composure from her depleted reservoir. If the children did get up in the remaining hours, they would be fumbling in the dark, trying to find their way. But she knew if she went out there now in the pitch black and accidentally stepped on one misplaced toy, one dropped sock or clammy tennis shoe, or felt any movement of air, she'd lose control and let out with a scream that would most likely bring the youngsters shrieking from their beds. "Come on. I just want a little time off duty," she complained. Leaving on the appropriate lights had always been T.J.'s job. She tossed over onto her side, trying to ignore the problem and not feel guilty.

It didn't work.

"All right, damn it. I'll get it," she muttered. She finally cracked open one eye and looked again. Now the whitish glow from one bathroom or the other again illuminated the hallway. "Thank goodness." She leaned up on one elbow, listening for the sound of a flush.

" 'Night Miranda," she called softly, waiting for the mumbled response that would mark her seven-year-old's progress.

No one replied.

"Miranda?" she tried again. "Eliot?"

Not a sound.

But the faint sweet scent of bay laurel now was there with her again. And the cool air in the room made the skin on her arms prickle. "This isn't funny." This time, childish or not, the covers went all the way up and over her head.

Luster Johns sat up and looked at the even stripes of pale bright moonlight pouring in across his bed through the blinds. Sitting upright, he tilted his head to one side and then to the other, listening. Outside, not a leaf stirred. He peeled back the top cover, a faded, circular-patterned quilt that Inez had made the Christmas before she died. He wrapped it, warm side in, around his angular shoulders, eased to the side of the bed, and poked his knobby feet into his slippers.

He headed straight out past the workbench, round toward the clearing in the moonlight. "You okay, folks?" he rasped softly. "You okay, Inez?" He rested his fingertips on her shoulder and peered down at the carved figure a moment, then he stooped and kissed her cheek before moving on. "Nathaniel?" He patted the one of the young black boy, his middle son. "And how 'bout you?" He paused in front of the winged young female carved from cypress, the first of the angels he'd finished. "You sho' look mighty purty out here 'neath the new moon. Dun' myse'f proud with you." He stood, drawing the quilt more snugly around his shoulders, gazing up into the clear night sky. "Sho' hope yo' is pleased up there."

Mattie watched her father from the porch for a long time before she followed him out. Every so often, he would look up at the moon, then he'd stop to address the next one of his sculptures and rest his hand on it. Then he'd move around the circle a little more, turn and look up again. She waited until he'd visited each one of them before she walked right out in the center to join him. She looked up at the bright starry sky before she spoke.

"Somethin' troublin' you, Ol' Paw?" she said softly.

Luster nodded. "The haunts is out. I guess it's just the full moon opened the door a bit mo' wide than usual," he said quietly, scanning with pinched, raisin eyes the sky just above the treetops. "I could feel them comin' closer tonight. I could feel them all the way inside. I jus' figured I'd better come out to keep these folks from being all spooked."

Mattie kept looking at the stars contentedly. She didn't want it to sound like she was rushing him. "So, you got them all calmed down?"

"Bes' I could. It ain't done, though. I just don' like the feeling that's afoot." He paused, looking upward and listening again. Beyond the clearing, the trees stood with upper branches bathed in light, motionless in the still damp air. "Haunts can get real persnickity. These ones are real close. Too close. And they feel stubborn-like."

"What you mean by stubborn-like?"

"Kind of grudgin'. Ornery. Like they's just lurkin' around, lookin' for trouble." He narrowed his eyes, looking over his circle of wood carvings like a daddy jaybird taking count of his fledglings.

"I didn't think haunts stayed 'round for long."

"They ain't s'posed to stay on for more than a few days. But if they take a mind to, fo' one reason or 'nother, maybe just to keep an eye out fo' the ones they love, they can hang about longer. Trouble is, if they stay 'round too long, haunts forget what they's stayin' for. They forget what livin' folks is really all about. Then they meddle. They just get up to no good, just up to mischi'f. I don't want no haunt makin' mischi'f around here. Get on with you. Go." Luster shook his hands in the air, pointing his crossed fingers, for luck, in each direction. He paused. Then he pursed his lips and whistled low as if he were calling a pet home.

Mattie knew her father's wind whistle. She'd heard him use it time and again when the still air was heavy and oppressive. He'd call the wind to stir things up and clear away the dead air. Now he was calling it to sweep away the haunts that he'd warned off with his hex sign.

"Come on, wind," Luster said with gentleness. He whistled again. The treetops remained motionless.

"I'd feel better if you'd come on, Ol' Paw," she said good-humoredly. "It's time to put yourself back into bed where you belong." Mattie reached out and rested her hand on Luster's quilt-covered shoulder.

Luster nodded. "Probably right. Probably need to rest.

Spirit knows I've been dillydallying. Maybe that's what this is all about. Maybe it just called me out here to worry me a bit." He tilted his head toward the remaining two stumps, still uncut, waiting by the workbench. "Tomorrow I'd better start in on that cedar piece and look for the angel. Then I'll get on to the next one." He shook his head slightly and stroked the side of his chin with his fingers. "Spirit said angels. I only did this one. Guess I needed a little nudgin'." He slipped his arm under Mattie's and headed back to the house. "Night, Inez. Night, all. Tomorrow, I'll get on with it."

CHAPTER 3

> The poetry of earth is never dead:
> When all the birds are faint with the hot sun,
> And hide in cooling trees, a voice will run
> From hedge to hedge about the new-mown mead:
> *John Keats*

THROUGH THE CLEAR panes beneath the stained-glass wildflowers in the kitchen windows, Barbara Ashcroft looked out at the threesome standing beyond Keats. They were lined up on the southeast lawn like judges in a reviewing stand, staring toward the rear of the house where the marsh grass and the gray river beyond spread out toward the tip of the Charleston peninsula. They seemed to be zeroed in on something. Barbara listened a moment, expecting to hear the low purr of a passing boat or the buzz of jetskis. But there was only silence.

Eliot had his arms crossed over his chest, a carbon copy of his father except for the eyeglasses. He seemed smaller than usual next to Rob Johnstone, whose six foot five inch long-legged form was clad in khaki slacks and faded madras shirt. Miranda held Rob's hand, swinging it back and forth, occasionally shifting her gaze from the river, way up to his face, then back to the river as they talked. From the kitchen, Barbara could see their mouths moving but she couldn't hear voices. The slight river breeze from the north swept the sounds the other way.

She watched them a moment longer, then turned back to the cans of orange juice on the counter. Labor Day weekend had come and gone, dragging with it a hot, humid blanket of listless air. Then there had been a few cooler mornings, offering some relief after an unseasonably hot summer. Now Rob was here for the party to welcome McMillan to the firm, and the sultry mantle of Indian summer had descended again.

Even with the breeze, standing outside for a few minutes was insufferable. Regardless, the children had apparently insisted on showing him around the grounds before breakfast. Barbara slid the orange concentrate from the can into the blender and added yogurt, a banana, and a handful of ice cubes, intent on concocting something cool for her explorers when they came back in. Fruit smoothies would do nicely.

Glancing up again, she saw all three of them drop abruptly to a crouch. In a half-circle, poking aside bits of dull green grass, they began inspecting the ground, turning leaves over and probing the soil with their fingers. Eliot's sandy hair clung in wet strands to his forehead. His glasses kept slipping down the bridge of his nose. Barbara put out three extra hand towels by the sink, made a note to have the optometrist adjust Eliot's frames, then put four apple dumplings in the microwave. She gave the fruit smoothie another pulse, put on the coffeemaker, and waited a little longer. They were all still poking about in the grass.

"Hey, how about a time-out for breakfast?" She cranked open one window and called for them all to come in. "Anyone hungry?" Without protest, all three slightly wilted individuals started for the house.

"We were talking poetry," Miranda announced as she led the perspiring procession into the kitchen. Rob tugged at the front of his damp shirt and silently signaled that he was going down the hall to make a quick change. Barbara took a shaker and doused the hot apple dumplings with cinnamon sugar. Miranda looked over at the platter and immediately headed for the sink to wash up.

"Rob told us part of a poem about a grasshopper and a cricket. By Keats," Eliot announced with eyebrows arched as he jerked his thumb in the direction of the tree outside. "It was one we hadn't heard before." Any poem by one of their tree-poets surrounding the house generally impressed the youngsters. From time to time Barbara had made it a point to read them a few lines by one namesake or the other. Usually Wordsworth, Byron, and Keats were too long-winded or a bit too esoteric, so she had to be selective. The melancholy and mysterious works of Poe were the only ones that could hold their attention for long, and she had definitely not felt up to reading anything of his lately. But Keats sounded promising.

"Did you like the poem?"

"I guess so," Eliot shrugged. "Mr. Johns always says crickets are good luck. Keats sort of said the same thing. He said their chirping is like the sound of the earth talking. It always is whispering something somewhere. Rob says Keats means their chirping lets us know that something is always alive and doing things, even if we don't see it. I guess it's a pretty neat idea," Eliot concluded, shrugging again. He joined Miranda at sinkside.

"We tried to find a cricket to bring inside." Miranda stuck out her lips in a disgruntled pout as she wiped her wet hands on a towel, then passed it to her brother. "Rob said Mr. Johns is right about them being lucky. The Chinese have special little cages to carry them in because it's really lucky to have one in the house. We could hear one outside, but we couldn't find it."

"Rob said we might look again tonight," Eliot added. "When the sun drops and it starts to cool off, we'll hear lots of them." He kept looking toward the table at the tall glasses with the pale fruit smoothie. Barbara had dropped a couple of stemmed cherries and a sprig of mint leaves on the top for an added festive touch. "I bet you guys are going to talk a lot now, aren't you?" Eliot eyed her with a calculating expression.

"Probably."

"Can I take my stuff into the den so I can watch TV?"

"Me too?" Miranda followed her brother to the table. Her face was flushed from the heat outside. "Is the fire still going?" Her blue-green eyes danced with enthusiasm.

Since this September morning was almost as hot and humid as much of August had been, Barbara had been surprised to see a small neat fire in the fireplace in the den that morning when she peeked in to see if Rob was awake. The large fireplace, framed by brass-rimmed glass doors, opened into both sides of the combined den and guestroom. When they had guests, one side could be closed off from the other by maneuvering sliding panels into place. The sofa opened into a queen-sized bed. But when only the family was home, everyone could gather in that wing. The sitting area with the TV and stereo, T.J.'s pool table, and Barbara's sewing corner all opened onto each other. Even though they all could be involved in different activities, the room itself created a sense of easy camaraderie that invited conversation. But that had been before T.J.'s death. Barbara had spent most of her time working in the opposite wing of the house, in the study, since then. The kids camped out in the den to play music, do homework, or watch TV.

"Sure, you to can eat in the den. The fire is still going," Barbara assured her daughter. "But it has to stay small," she cautioned her. "Otherwise the air conditioner will go crazy. Don't try to talk Rob into adding more logs," she added, knowing how much Miranda loved to see a roaring blaze.

It had been Miranda, with Eliot trailing behind, who had slipped into the den at six-thirty that morning while Barbara was still asleep in her room, oblivious to the fact that her houseguest was being roused by two small intruders.

"Maybe you two could come back about lunchtime," Rob had groaned at the two inquisitive faces staring down at him. When they didn't budge, he propped himself on one elbow and stared back at them. "I guess you must be the welcoming committee. Nice to see you two again." He smoothed back his hair and greeted the duo.

"Good morning, sir," Eliot responded politely. It had been well over a year since he had seen Rob Johnstone, and then it was just an afternoon visit while he was passing through Charleston. However, Eliot heard Rob's name and bits of phone conversations so often, it felt like he was a special family friend. Eliot just wasn't quite sure whether a handshake or a hug was in order. So he held back, slightly behind Miranda, curious but cautious.

"Momma said you'd be getting in late last night," Miranda began, with her customary torrent of chatter. "We were asleep, so we didn't get to see you. Boy, I didn't remember that you were so long." She pointed to the end of the fold-out bed where his feet jutted off into space.

"Well, one of the hazards of being tall," Rob said solemnly, "is that when you lay down, you are long."

"I'll say," Miranda replied thoughtfully.

Eliot cut his eyes toward Rob. The tall man was amusing. Eliot vaguely remembered that about him now. He'd say funny things, quiet things, and when you got the point, you'd smile.

"Wait till you see the tablecloth we made. It's at Karen's house." Suddenly Miranda piled onto the sofa bed, starting right in with how much they had to show him. Eliot waited a bit, then leaped after her.

By the time Barbara had awakened, dressed, and prowled through the house in search of company, she discovered both children and Rob were already up and gone. When she saw the fire in the fireplace, she knew it had to have been Miranda's idea.

"Come back if you want seconds." Barbara handed each of the kids a lap tray. "Just don't spill anything. And don't sit too close to the TV. Try to give Rob a little privacy," she called after them as they filed off into the hallway. Rob was already coming toward them.

"Don't worry, I get plenty of privacy at home," he told them, stepping aside to let the twosome move past with their trays. "Privacy is one of the fringe benefits of living alone." Eliot glanced back over his shoulder, his mouth tilted up at one corner in a lopsided smile, amused again, then he proceeded on after Miranda.

"Well, good morning. Looks like they got you started early." Barbara shrugged apologetically. "Have some breakfast."

"I had forgotten there was still a six-thirty A.M. on weekends," Rob replied with a low chuckle as he followed her to the corner nook. "Not that I mind," he quickly assured her. "The children are charming, even at that hour. It was nice out there until the sun really broke through." He nodded toward the expansive grounds. "I got the grand tour. We visited a few cranes in the marsh, a lizard's grave, a couple of rabbit holes, and an owl's nest. I've heard all about Luster Johns and saving water and where the sprinklers are hidden. We looked at the solar panels on the roof, ate peaches, buried the pits, and searched for crickets. It was fun. It gave us a chance to get used to each other again." His warm brown eyes shifted toward the hallway. "They sure have grown."

"Kids have a way of doing that."

"I guess they do." Rob looked at her in earnest. "You all look good. They talked about T.J. a bit. They sure seem to be doing all right." He slid onto the bench in the nook and clasped his glass of juice and yogurt. "How about you?" Barbara had taken the seat across from him and was reaching out to pour their coffee. "How are you?"

The sudden shift in the tone of the conversation made her hand hesitate in midair. They hadn't had much time to talk other than superficially the night before. She'd gone to pick him up at the airport at eleven, then his flight was delayed until almost midnight. By the time they got to her house and set him up in the den, they were both too tired and too wise to start in on a long discussion. Now the kids were gone, the amenities over. In the uncompromising light of day, Rob studied her face. It was time for grownup talk.

"Actually, I'm doing pretty well. I've been busy." She spoke with more ease than she felt. "Between keeping up with Eliot and Miranda here and the kids in my classes at school, I don't have much time to sit around and feel sorry for myself. Needless to say, I've got Louis and Karen hovering on the sidelines, keeping an eye on me." She smiled, but she couldn't keep the slight edge of irritation from her voice. "Frankly, I get the feeling everyone is watching and waiting for me to do something dramatic. That probably sounds a little paranoid."

"It doesn't sound paranoid." Rob leaned back and draped one arm comfortably along the cushioned back of the bench seat. "I imagine that Louis and Karen and a number of other folks are watching, just to make sure you're doing all right. I can see where that might get a bit trying for you, though," he admitted. Since T.J.'s death, he'd been careful to limit his calls to once a week to keep from giving her the feeling that he was being too inquisitive. But he discreetly made a second and sometimes a third weekly call to the Belcazzios just to hear about her progress from their vantage point.

"The trouble with all of this is there isn't anything dramatic to do. Besides, it would be out of character for me. Showmanship was T.J.'s department." She shrugged slightly. "I'm simply hanging in there, finding out that the adjusting phase is a little bumpy. It takes more time than I realized." She glanced out toward the hallway as if she were making certain that neither of the children were making a return trip. "I haven't been acting morbid or anything," she added with gentle humor, stirring a scoop of creamer into her coffee then watching as the powder disappeared under the surface. "I've been keeping up with all the things I'm supposed to do, but I'm still pretty numb. And I've been sticking around home a lot. Maybe that's what worries Karen and Louis."

"You mean staying in?"

"They must think I'm avoiding them. I used to hike over and drop in after dinner. Now I stay home. I'm just taking things one day at a time, regrouping, and working at getting back my equilibrium."

"Eliot said you've been spending time reading."

Barbara gave him a curious look, surprised that Eliot had even noticed, much less mentioned it to Rob. "I had a lot to do for the courses I was taking."

"I don't think he was talking about textbooks."

Barbara's expression momentarily darkened, then the polite smile appeared. "He must have noticed I got some books from the library. Self-help things."

"About death and grieving?"

"About that. About changes." Barbara hedged slightly. She looked up at Rob's soft brown eyes, gentle and sympathetic, but unconvinced. "Okay, I got out some books about grief," she conceded. "You know me, always the good student. If there's a question, I look the answer up in a book."

"So what's the question?"

For a moment her eyes locked on to his. Then she arched her eyebrows thoughtfully. "I suppose 'Why him?' or maybe 'Why me?' I guess that's what everyone asks. Needless to say, there were no easy answers." She tossed her head back, running her fingers through the tangle of copper curls. "So I'm trying to move on to 'What's next?' "

"That sounds a bit more positive."

Barbara glanced out the window beneath the row of wildflowers. "I guess it does," she said softly. "On the good days, I'm sure everything is slowly falling into place just like it should. Then there are the not-so-good days." Her voice, naturally whispery, became even softer.

"What about those days?" Rob pressed her to go on.

She cupped her hands around the coffee mug. "They slip up on me. Every once in a while, I'll get really caught up in something—reading or cooking or grading papers or whatever. I actually forget what's happened. For a moment, I think he's still here." This time she avoided meeting Rob's eyes at all. "There have been a couple of times, late at night when I'm working in the study, I actually look up and expect to see him standing there or sitting at the worktable by the window." She glanced toward the hallway a bit cautiously. "It's spooky how the mind plays tricks on us. In the books, they say it's a spinoff of the denial phase," she noted with a half-smile. "Obviously it's happened to other people, and they've made it through. We're going to be okay too."

"It sounds like you're doing all the right things."

"I've always done the right things." She cut him a wistful, slightly amused look. "I've been a good little girl. That's why I had such a nice, uncomplicated, orderly life. Except for this." She fluttered a hand toward the center of the house, and for the first time, her voice wavered. She paused for a moment to take a sip of her coffee.

"No, even this went like a well-rehearsed play," she amended her comment. "T.J.'s death and the days after it were so peaceful and civilized and proper. Maybe that's what's so unnerving about it. It all went so smoothly, so quickly. One day he was here, the next day he wasn't. There was no time to say goodbye. No time to help. I just woke up and he was gone." She stopped and licked her lips, trying to ease the sudden dryness. "He'd already made all the right arrangements. It was easy for me to do the right things. I just had to make a few calls and show up for the ceremony."

Rob watched her intently. Her hazel eyes, greenish, flecked with gold, were wide and preoccupied. He waited and said nothing.

"When T.J. died, it didn't feel real. I saw what was going on and it all registered somewhere. But it didn't click. I kept wondering, where's the rest of it. Is this how it ends? Not anything like T.S. Eliot said. Not with a bang. Not a whimper. Just silence." Barbara leaned forward, studying the mug in her hands, trying to explain her ambivalent feelings. "Intellectually, I know it's real. T.J. is dead and I am dealing with that. But in here . . ." she spoke slowly, resting one open hand on her chest over her heart, "it's just not settled. I have the strangest feeling that something about it isn't over. Like something else is supposed to happen before the actual ending occurs." She broke off in frustration, staring unfocused off into space. "Something says there has to be more. There has to be a real ending." She shook her head in distress, trying to articulate the peculiar sense of expectation that had lingered since his death.

"You feel like you're still waiting for the other shoe to drop?"

"Something like that," she acknowledged. "Like the process is incomplete. It's nothing I can put my finger on." She glanced up at him with a slightly guarded expression. "I don't want you to say anything to Karen and Louis. Whatever this is, it's probably just another phase. I just haven't found the right word for it yet. I certainly won't let it overwhelm me. It's just a little disconcerting at times." She began attentively cutting into the warm dumpling.

"I can relate to some of what you say," Rob sympathized, vaguely beginning to understand now why she had delayed his visit and why the Belcazzios felt that she was not as serene as she acted. "I know when my dad died a few years ago, it all seemed very anticlimactic. He was seventy-one. Seemed perfectly fit. He was playing golf one day, had a faint spell, went in for a checkup, and they put him right into heart surgery. He didn't wake up." He shook his head slightly. "It didn't seem right. He'd been such a feisty old fellow. He did everything with such style and energy. Like with T.J. My dad and I never said our goodbyes either. It took a while before the finality really registered. A long while."

Barbara was listening and nodding and poking at the last few pieces of dumpling with her fork, but she didn't look up.

"It eventually does register," he assured her in a gentle voice.

"I guess it will," she answered. They sat eating in silence, comforted by the sweet scent of cinnamon and apple and the rich coffee aroma. Barely audible in the distance, the bouncy background music and staccato voices from the children's cartoon show added a counterpoint to the tranquility in the sunlit kitchen.

"This is really a beautiful place," Rob spoke at last. "T.J. did a great job with the design. When I was here last year, you were just moving in. It was a little hard to grasp the overall effect. There were boxes everywhere, construction litter outside, and none of the grounds were landscaped."

"And it was raining," Barbara recalled.

"Right. Now it looks like everything has been here forever. The way the house rises like an island surrounded by greenery, and the flow from inside to outside is spectacular. Not showy spectacular," he stressed, "but thoughtful spectacular. The ridges for flood control make great sense. This Luster Johns fellow that the children mentioned did amazing things with the planting."

"Luster is a very thoughtful, very deliberate man," Barbara acknowledged. "Near the end of the construction, he would come out here and walk around the area, planning it out in his head. Sometimes he'd sit out there under one of the trees on a little folding stool, smoking his pipe. He'd look around, then he'd pick up and move to the next tree." She gazed out past the glass wildflowers toward Keats. "One day it poured, and Luster came inside. He moved from window to window with his stool, studying each view. Eventually he and T.J. got together and looked out the windows, then they put on raincoats and walked the area together."

"The results are impressive." Rob's eyes followed Barbara's to the sloping yard, the buffers covered with plants, the large oaks, and the more dense undergrowth beyond. Set on a point at the end of a cul-de-sac, the house seemed part of a separate world, civilized but unspoiled.

"There are still some things that aren't finished completely." Barbara's voice carried a note of resignation. "We were going to put in a walkway and a dock, and lots of decking and a gazebo with a hot tub out by the bedroom. We already have the solar pipes and an auxiliary tank over my room." Her focus shifted abruptly back to the kitchen windows set aglow by the midmorning sun. She reached out and rubbed her fingertips over the dull leading between the petals. "There are some windows we never got to."

"The ones I've seen so far are beautiful." Rob tried to ease their conversation in another direction. "You've done an incredible job. Miranda showed me her rainbow this morning, then naturally Eliot trooped me into his room to see his balloons." He glanced up at the row of pink and light-orange flowers surrounding that corner of the kitchen. "And these wildflowers are lovely, even if I'm not a morning person. I see now what T.J. meant about the windows being designed so you don't need draperies."

Barbara bit her lower lip lightly and glanced away. "I'm not so sure anymore," she ventured. "When T.J. was here, we used to kid about people being able to look in, about putting on a show for them. It was just a joke. The reflective glass stops that and you can only see out. But lately, the plate windows that aren't finished bother me. The show-biz joke hasn't been so amusing, especially at night after the children are asleep and I'm the only one around. Sometimes I feel like I'm in a fishbowl and there's a cat on the loose. I've been worried about prowlers or peeping Toms."

"This is a pretty remote area," Rob acknowledged. "It wouldn't hurt to take a few extra precautions."

"Oh, we've got good security," Barbara insisted. She shook her head, realizing he hadn't quite understood her point. "I can lock the doors and windows and turn the Sonitrol on. I know we're safe. But I still can't really relax. If I'm in a room with a clear plate window, I keep getting a weird feeling like there might be someone around, watching." She took a deep breath and adjusted her smile. "I get enough of that on-stage feeling outside the house. I don't need it here too."

"If that's the feeling you're getting, there might be something to it," Rob glanced out over the contoured terrain. "I'm sure there were articles in the paper about T.J.'s death. They could make someone curious enough to snoop. I've always figured it was smart to listen to your instincts."

He was sorry the instant he said it. But the way the house was set off from the others farther inland in the development and screened from the street by the thick undergrowth did more than assure the privacy T.J. had wanted. Now, listening to her, after having explored the grounds and pathways with the children, Rob realized the landscaping could give an intruder cover, at least up to the large oaks. "Maybe you should have the police drive by for a couple of weeks. They could swing through the driveway to check things out," he suggested, trying to ease the anxious look his remark had produced. "It might make you feel better knowing they'll be keeping an eye out for anything peculiar. An occasional patrol car sure would discourage anyone who doesn't belong here from wandering around."

"The police have plenty to do without coming all the way out here. I'd feel foolish asking them to make a special trip just because I'm nervous." Barbara licked her lips. "It's probably just a passing thing. When I'm tired and a little down, my imagination gets a bit overactive. Everything will settle back to normal soon enough," she insisted, tossing her head in a deliberately casual manner. "Besides, if anyone does come snooping, he'll probably get chased off by one the indigenous spooks," she said flippantly, diligently trying to make light of the situation. "Luster Johns says that there are all kinds of spirits about."

"Spooks? Spirits?" Rob deadpanned.

"Right, spooks. The locals call them haunts. Sort of like guardian angels. After Eliot's lizard Bartholemew died, Luster told Eliot that his spirit would linger a while as a haunt, checking on the ones he left behind. Then it moves on. It made Eliot feel a lot better about Bartholemew. It made him feel better after T.J. died, too."

"You're not suggesting that any of you believe that stuff . . ." Rob was feeling increasingly uncomfortable with the direction Barbara's conversation, however playful, was leading. "And you're not suggesting that T.J. might still be around."

"Of course not. I'm kidding. It's just an old folktale." Barbara smiled and fluttered a hand, but there was an indefinable shift deep in her eyes that Rob found disturbing. Just as Karen and Louis Belcazzio had cautioned him, Rob felt she was trying too hard. "But I have to admit," she added in a teasing tone, "if he were still around, I certainly wouldn't worry about anyone stepping foot on our place. He'd run them off in a heartbeat."

"I think you'll have to settle for guardian angels in uniforms and patrol cars."

Again Rob saw that sudden shadowy look.

"No patrol car. No fuss." Barbara poured them both more coffee. "This whole fishbowl business can be solved relatively simply," she proceeded, clearly shifting mental gears. "I've been thinking about getting drapes for the windows I haven't done in the bedroom and the study. When I'm grading papers late at night or when I'm in my room, I'd feel better with something nontransparent between me and the great outdoors. You're good with colors and fabric. How about going shopping with me today?" She looked at him expectantly. "If they can't see in, they won't have any reason to skulk around out there."

Rob hesitated, measuring her for a moment. "Do you still remember the time I skulked around the back of the sorority house?"

"And scared the wits out of me," Barbara remembered, instantly nodding, her eyes narrowing with the recollection. She kept smiling, but the eyes stared off into space, registering a trace of some dark emotion. "I didn't think either of us would ever get over that one. I don't know which of us was more upset."

Years before, when they were in college and Barbara was "Bobbie," Rob had helped her decorate a float for the USC homecoming parade on Halloween weekend. The crew of volunteers had labored through dinner and into the night to complete the structure, and every so often, someone was sent into the sorority house for coffee, or tissue paper, or staples, or nails, or whatever was needed. On one of her trips, as a joke, Rob pulled a piece of tarpaulin over his head and hid in the bushes, waiting in ambush. When she returned, he jumped out in the dark, dragging his foot and lurching at her like Frankenstein's monster.

She caught one glimpse of the shrouded, six-foot-five figure coming for her, dropped the bag of doughnuts she was carrying and started running, wide-eyed and speechless, toward the lighted area where the others were still at work.

The rest of the float crew looked up and laughed at the spectacle. From their vantage point, Rob, with his paint-stained tarpaulin flapping with each long-legged stride, looked more like a ragamuffin Icabod Crane than a demon in pursuit. But Barbara desperately dove into their midst, clinging to her roommate, refusing to turn face-to-face with the monster who was stalking her. Only afterwards, when she heard Rob's distinctive voice apologizing profusely, the terror eased and she began to calm down.

"Don't ever do anything like that again." She was barely able to breathe the words. "Not ever." It was not a reprimand; it was a plea.

"No more practical jokes," Rob promised, dumbfounded by her reaction. "It was a stupid thing to do anyhow." He could feel her trembling as he held her close, soothing her. That was the only time he'd ever seen her lose control. It was more chilling because she never uttered a syllable. She just fled. He'd never forgotten the expression of sheer panic on her face. This morning, he thought he'd caught a glimmer of something milder but faintly similar as he listened to her talk of haunts and spooks and watched her across the kitchen table, sixteen years later.

"I know I overreacted," she'd told him later that night as they'd sat on the front steps of the sorority house. "It wasn't your fault. I had a bad fright when I was little."

"What kind of fright?" He kept his arm around her as they huddled there together in the aftermath.

"Some big kids in our neighborhood, guys about thirteen. Real gross characters. They used to pick on my girlfriends and me every once in a while. When I was about eight, they got us really big time. It was almost dark and Jenny Lassiter and I were cutting down an alley on the way from her house to mine. The boys came by on their bikes. Instead of their usual yell-and-split routine, this time they stopped and grabbed Jenny and me. They shoved us in one of those huge metal garbage dumpsters with the lid that slams." She licked her lips then as she told him what had happened.

"The dumpster smelled horrible. It was pitch-black inside. Jenny and I were frantic, crying and trying to shove the lid up so we could get out. But we weren't tall enough. Then something in there with us moved. Something big and dark and shapeless stood and pushed the lid open. When there was enough light, we could see him. It was a bum. He was hairy and dirty and he started yelling at us to get the hell out of his place. We were shrieking and scrambling to get away from him, knees and elbows flying. He grabbed us. Me first. I thought he was going to kill me. But he was only boosting me up. He just wanted to get rid of us. He pitched me out the opening."

Rob stared at her, mesmerized, as the details of her childhood tale turned his prank into something increasingly grotesque and fearsome.

"I can't tell you what it felt like to have his hands on me." Even in the retelling years later, Barbara clutched her arms across her chest protectively. "He dropped

Jenny out after me. We ran home, crying until we threw up. My Mom called the police. When they got there and looked in the dumpster, of course the man was gone. I think the boys got chewed out later for being bullies. That was about all the police could do. But Jenny and I were sick for days. My Mom trashed the clothes I'd been wearing. I showered until I scrubbed myself red. I scrubbed for weeks. But I couldn't wash away the pictures in my head."

"I am so sorry," Rob repeated dismally.

Barbara reached out and patted his arm, more composed after she'd talked about it. "You weren't the only boogey man chasing me tonight," she comforted him. "You had no way of knowing that I'd fall apart like I did. Neither did I," she added softly. "It was a long time ago. I thought I had all that under control."

But now as they sat in the kitchen, surrounded by the aroma of apple dumplings and cinnamon and coffee, Rob wondered how close to the surface that memory had come once more. How close it was now. How futile an occasional patrol car in the driveway would seem. At night, alone, surrounded by glass, he could understand how she could feel dangerously near the dark abyss where moving shadows and shapes could menace her. Whether T.J. designed the house for draperies or not, if they would help hold back the spectres until she felt secure again, Rob would see that she got them.

"Let's go take a look at the windows you want done." He downed the last of his coffee and slid out of the snug nook. "We should be able to take care of this in no time."

"I was hoping you'd say that." She slid out after him. "Let me get a measuring tape and a notepad." They were already out on the counter, side by side, near the telephone.

Minutes later, she stood next to him as they surveyed the study from the center of the cathedral-ceilinged room. "I was thinking of something fairly heavy, with a strong pattern," she suggested. The warm apricot-colored carpet and soft-cushioned chairs and loveseat a few shades darker gave the room a warm, tranquil look. Tall built-in bookshelves lined the inner walls. A large desk and a comfortable reading area was set off to one side. On the opposite side of the room was a drafting table and a tall, padded stool. Nearby was a computer setup with two screens and a printer. The end of the room that jutted out between Poe on the northeast and Keats to the southeast was almost entirely glass, creating the illusion that the side walls simply ended and that section merged with the outside.

A magnificent beveled and leaded bay window, which T.J. had rescued from the demolition of an old hurricane-damaged hotel, dominated the end of the room, facing the southeast, where a bend in the river scooped back around toward the house. A broad, scarred solid oak door was set across trestles in the bay.

"I guess you can tell this room is a place for works in progress as well as being one itself. That's my worktable for the stained glass, but it's just temporary," Barbara explained. "I was planning on moving everything out to the garage once I finished the big projects." Storage shelves and upright slots underneath the table housed her materials—sheets of glass, patterns, and tools. A motorized grinder sat unplugged on one end. Goggles and heavy scissors hung on hooks. The area was flooded in sunlight. On either end of the protruding bay, reflective panels of thermal glass with upright cypress support beams served as walls. Reflective sliders on Poe's side offered access to the yard and the marsh beyond. Then on Keats's side, in addition to a single slider, there was a floor-length panel of ordinary plate glass. Like the rough worktable, the plain glass seemed temporary and inconsistent with the overall design.

"I can see why you might want to have drapes to close off the bay window after dark. That's quite an expanse." Rob tilted his head toward the marshside. "But what about this?" He turned toward the protected grassy stretch where Keats stood. "I gather this is for one of your stained-glass projects. What do you have in mind for here?" He pointed to the long panel.

"That was supposed to be something outdoorsy and interesting. The winter view on that side is essentially in monotone." She stood with her hands on her hips looking at the space. "T.J. made a sketch that looked like driftwood on a beach. He'd even picked out some really beautiful glass. That caramel piece for one, and the oak-grained pieces." She pointed to a few sheets standing on end in one upright bin beneath the table. "With all that's happened lately, I don't know when I'll get around to working on it." She contemplated the array of tools and lead caming strips that lay unused at the back of the work surface. "Maybe one day," she said, shrugging.

"This will be a spectacular location for one of your leaded pieces," Rob said, standing back and eyeing the rectangular area. "Honestly, because of all this sunlight, I'd pass on the driftwood idea and go for something more colorful. With this cathedral ceiling, you might try a really ornate pattern, for a rich and opulent feel. Pick up the rosy apricot in the room and add some gold and green for contrast."

"Believe me, rosy apricot and opulent were not in T.J.'s master plan," she assured him. "He was after a restrained, contemporary look for this room. It was sort of a think-tank, a place for him to work without the kids underfoot.'"

"But that was his idea. The room is yours now. Do what makes you comfortable."

"The driftwood is okay. I'll get around to it in time." Barbara sidestepped his comment. She moved toward the hallway and glanced at her watch a bit impatiently. "Right now, it needs a quick fix." She paused while he stood there, still contemplating the blank space. For the first time, Barbara really looked at the window space as if it were hers. "Maybe we can find rich and opulent draperies with apricot and gold and green."

Rob turned and grinned at her. In the light, she noticed the touches of gray in his hair were more prominent than they had been the year before. She hadn't given much thought to aging and the changes that would bring to any of them. "Rob. It's getting late. Next item on the agenda." She avoided looking at T.J.'s work area. "Come on down to the bedroom."

"The bedroom? Best offer I've had in weeks."

"Only weeks?" Barbara glanced back over her shoulder as he headed out the door. "I'd have thought you were in greater demand."

"As a matter of fact, I am." Rob chuckled good-naturedly and crossed the room to follow her. "If you really want details . . ."

"Please, spare me." Barbara crossed her arms and waited for him by the atrium. "I'd prefer to maintain my illusions."

"Illusions? About me? After all these years?" he kidded her. "I thought we'd known each other too long to have any illusions left."

"I've kept a few carefully guarded and blissfully intact," she declared. "I don't want to find out anything now that will send me back to edit my memories. I like them as they are."

"We've had some good ones," Rob agreed. "PG-rated, but very nice." Barbara knew what the PG rating implied. They had once been sweethearts when they were undergraduates at USC, both too cautious and too practical to automatically think that being in love meant sleeping with one another. It seemed the timing or the logistics were always off. Barbara was at USC on scholarship, a junior, and only nineteen when they met. Rob was five years older and had taken some courses during his hitch in the Navy. But by the time he transferred in to USC, the curriculum requirements put him two semesters behind her.

So they had sometimes been friends, sometimes romantic lovers who walked hand in hand across the campus on rainy days. Both English majors, they would sit through avant-garde plays and old movies, whispering in the dark. And afterwards, sometimes they would dissect and discuss and often argue. Other times, they kissed on porches and beneath trees and at dances until their lips were tender and Barbara's cheeks were red with stubble burn. Weekends they would go to dimly lit hangouts where the beer was cold and the music loud, and they would dance, and perspire, and hold each other.

But there were always interruptions. That first summer, Barbara's stepfather retired and moved with her mother to Florida. She went along to help them refurbish the house they bought. Rob stayed in school straight through. By the time she returned in the fall for her senior year, he'd changed his major to theater and was caught up in stagecraft and performing. He'd also decided to apply to New York University for graduate school.

She graduated the following May, barely twenty and anxious to teach in secondary school. She and her roommate both took jobs in Charleston, a little over a hundred miles to the southeast. Rob had one semester to complete before going on to NYU. "Do you think we're doomed to be ships that pass in the night?" she had kidded him during one of their hectic weekend commutes, perhaps testing his response.

"I don't know. If it's meant to be, we'll head the same way sooner or later," he said with the same easygoing, philosophical manner that made being with him so comfortable from the beginning. It also made him frustratingly elusive. Rob said he loved her but he had not offered to change his direction nor did he ask her to change hers. It wasn't his nature or hers to press for more.

Over the years, they'd kept in touch and visited from time to time, but along the way, there were other lovers and other friends for both of them. Rob finished his Master's at NYU and took a teaching job in performing arts at a progressive junior college in Florida. Barbara had taught in Charleston for three years and was about to go back to graduate school herself. Then she strolled into a cafe courtyard at the height of Charleston's Spoleto Festival and caught the end of a lecture on historic preservation.

The lecturer was a middle-aged local architect named Belcazzio. The fuzzy-haired speaker used beautiful drawings of Charleston landmarks to illustrate methods of adapting their design for functional modern offices and hotels. The younger blonde man who stared at her legs while he listened, then stood and offered her his seat when she started to leave, was a visitor from North Carolina, T.J. Ashcroft. When the lecture ended, T.J. bought her a coke, looked into her eyes, and talked for eight hours straight. He spoke poetically of restoring proud old homes and buildings into living, beloved structures and of building striking new homes in harmony with their setting. He was charming, ambitious, very bright, and he captivated her with his energy and intensity.

"Look. We belong together," he'd told her that first evening, pausing to look at their reflection in a shop window as they strolled along through the historic district, listening to the street musicians play. He was right. Golden and slim, they looked wonderful side by side. There had been no question that night that people in love sleep together.

Only a month later, T.J. moved into an old house in Charleston, began renovating the downstairs into an office, and married Barbara Hendricks. Almost a year after that, when the Spoleto festival was approaching, Barbara wrote Rob as she had sporadically over the years. "You'll have to come and see us," she had insisted. "I want you to meet T.J."

Eliot was six months old when that first meeting finally took place. Rob was driving to New York to visit friends for Christmas. He accepted her invitation to stop over on the way and have dinner with "the Ashcrofts."

Not surprisingly, T.J. and Rob had liked each other. They shared a similar wide range of interests, a perversity of wit, and a liking for history that gave them a good deal to talk about. But Barbara suspected that beneath it all, the good-natured relationship between the two men was possible because they weren't rivals. There was no subtle contest over territorial rights or priority. Rob had never tried to claim her. And T.J. knew she had never slept with Rob. The first relationship had been romantic and idealized, the second far more passionate and permanent. So there was a distinctive easiness between them. She settled back and watched the intent expressions on two different faces—T.J.'s handsome, fair, animated and relaxed; and Rob's, more angular, tanned from the Florida sunshine, and furrowed from laughter. Then, everyone knew the rules. It had been remarkably uncomplicated. At least it had seemed to be.

Now, as Rob walked with her along the corridor to the bedroom she and T.J. had shared, kidding about the women in his life, Barbara felt inexplicably uncomfortable. Her bedroom was her personal retreat; it was where she and T.J. had made love. Suddenly she felt as if she were exposing an intimate part of her life, a part that Rob had never really known.

"Let me warn you—I couldn't sleep the other night so I did a real quick coverup in my room. Effective but very primitive," she apologized as they stopped at the door. At the farthest end of the room, the wide expanse of glass panels and sliders that extended out under the trees was partially covered by peach-colored sheets supported by ducting tape and tacks.

"Reminds me of some of the sets I've used. But if it works, it works." Rob followed her inside.

"I guess you noticed, I have this thing about apricot," Barbara said lightly as they moved farther into the master bedroom. The pastel-striped chairs and the minutely flowered wallpaper were a more delicate echo of the colors in the study. "T.J. said it has all sorts of scientific significance. Something about the diffusion of light and psychology. I simply like the feeling it gives a room."

"Now this room looks like you," Rob said instantly. "This is soft," he observed, smiling at the delicate framed seashells on the walls and the rows of odd-shaped perfume containers on the dressing table. "The rest of the house has a sharper edge. I remember you like this." He spoke his thoughts aloud, with a tenderness that took her by surprise.

Suddenly Barbara felt her cheeks turn hot.

Rob turned and caught the uncertain expression on her face. "I'm sorry," he immediately apologized, realizing he'd overstepped some unspoken boundaries. "I didn't mean to get personal, but this is such a lovely, gentle room." By now Barbara's face had turned a deep rose. "Before I put my other foot in my mouth, let's just get on with the business about the drapes. These have definitely got to go," he gestured toward the uneven but functional sheeting.

"You mean now?"

"If we're going to get the measurements right."

"Right." Barbara nodded, then grabbed the first sheet and tugged at it, relieved to have something physical to do, something neutral, until she could get herself back in control. Somehow between her and her friend, the parameters had changed. And being in the bedroom together made it clear. Neither of them was insulated by the old standards. The proprieties of innocence or "the marriage" no longer applied. She and Rob were meeting this time on unfamiliar terms. Whatever illusions they may have held about each other, whatever polite distance they may have maintained in the past, all that was changing. The ground rules would need reinventing.

While Rob measured the space to be covered, Barbara held back, dutifully jotting down the figures he called out for length and width. But for a while they avoided meeting each other's eyes, reluctant to try again until the old facades were in place and at least some of the old barriers secured.

"Welcome, you two. Welcome." Karen Belcazzio gave Barbara and Rob each a quick hug, then led them inside. It was six-thirty. Guests were due at seven. The casual gathering of forty had escalated to a guest list closer to a hundred and was considerably more formal than they'd originally planned. "You look great, both of you," Karen declared, hurrying them along. "Barbara, honey, just put your things in my room. Then take a look at the goodies from Fancy's in the kitchen. The caterer did a really elegant job." She glanced over her shoulder and hesitated, making certain that Barbara was heading off in the opposite direction. "And you come with me." Karen grasped Rob's hand and started leading him through the house toward the bar. All around the crystal and ivory room, ashtrays and coasters dotted the flat surfaces in anticipation of the influx of guests.

Ahead, the sitting area along the rear windows facing the golf course had been stripped of the wicker furniture to accommodate a bar and a candlelit buffet table. To the northeast, over Wappoo Creek, the low clouds beyond were striped pinkish orange from the setting sun.

Louis stood talking with the young bartender, watching the fellow slice lemons with rapid and ruthless precision. With an elfin grin, he took a toothpick, speared a couple of the olives set out in silver bowls on the service bar, then popped them into his mouth. "Glad you got here." Louis shook Rob's hand and took a quick look past him toward the doorway. "How do you think she's doing?" he asked bluntly, still munching on the olives.

"Pretty well," Rob replied a bit cautiously. He knew the Belcazzios would want to get his perspective, but he hadn't expected an immediate inquisition.

"You get the feeling she's putting on a good front for all of us?" Louis asked, narrowing his bright button eyes and trying, unsuccessfully this time, to impale a cocktail onion.

"Bobbie is the kind of person who would try to make the best of anything," Rob replied diplomatically. "I think she may be working overtime on this one, though." His words prompted a knowing nod from both Belcazzios.

"I used to think she let T.J. run the show too much. He was the one who made all the big plans; she just smiled and went along." Louis's voice was hushed. "He was a dynamo. At work and at home. We both figured she would be lost without him." He gave Karen a weak nod. "Like we said on the phone, we're a little surprised at how well she seems to be doing. She took charge without missing a beat. Maybe we just underestimated her." Now it was Rob who lifted his brows thoughtfully and nodded.

"Now what about this drapery business?" Karen pressed Rob for details. She'd called the Ashcroft household earlier in the day and got Kent Nelson. He'd come to cut the grass and keep an eye on the children while Rob and Barbara shopped. "She didn't seem concerned about those windows until lately. Suddenly they have to be done. What do you make of it?" The threesome were huddled near the bar, conferring quietly, able to talk for the first time since Rob had arrived the night before.

"She says the house seems a bit too wide open now with only her and the children there. I think she's gradually adjusting to living differently. Maybe a few drapes will ease some of the strangeness."

Karen tilted her head to one side attentively like an elegant feline, suddenly alert but not necessarily ready to pounce. "You feel there is something strange there?" She studied him closely.

"I don't. She does."

Karen shook her head slightly. "I've been over there a number of times in the past weeks. Mostly on trumped-up excuses about planning for tonight. I didn't notice anything peculiar, other than her being a bit remote. What does she mean by strange?"

"She didn't use the word strange. She just talked about feeling a little overexposed. She feels she needs a buffer between her and the world."

"I don't like it," Karen whispered. "She never needed a buffer before. I think there's more to this than simply covering up some windows. I don't know if she's intent on shutting the world out or herself in. But either way, the draperies become walls. They do more than buffer, they cut things off from other things. They isolate. T.J. wouldn't have liked it one bit."

Towering over both the Belcazzios, Rob gave Karen a slightly patronizing smile. "T.J. doesn't have to like it," he replied with an uncharacteristic edge to his voice. "The draperies we ordered today are for Bobbie. For her peace of mind. It will take a week or so to finish them. After they get installed, she may not like the effect. They may end up being a temporary measure," he offered, softening his response. "But she's a bit uptight now. That's understandable." His expression warmed suddenly as he glanced toward the kitchen. Two other pairs of eyes followed his. Barbara was just inside the doorway, speaking with the catering staff, but she was gradually working her way toward them.

"I guess we'd better start loosening her up," Louis suggested, handing Rob two glasses of pale peach Zinfandel. "Give her one of these." Then the doorbell chimed, and Barbara looked over at Karen and the two men uncertainly.

"Guests are arriving." With a slight wave, Karen took

charge. On cue, one of the temporary help stepped forward to respond to the bell. "Keep an eye on her," Karen told both men. "Make sure one of us is always with her. I don't want her to feel like she's alone here."

"A hundred guests and she's going to feel alone," Louis muttered.

Karen shot him a warning look. "You know what I mean . . ." Not at all amused, she lifted her chin, looking down her aristocratic nose at Louis, who stood a good two inches shorter than she.

"We'll take care of it," Rob answered for both of them.

"But do it inconspicuously."

"A chubby guy with a beard and a monolith with a suntan and you ask us not to be conspicuous?" Louis nudged Rob's arm and chuckled.

"Louis . . ."

"We'll manage," Rob promised, avoiding antagonizing Karen any further.

"I think we could use some music." Karen tapped Louis on the shirtfront. "Make yourself useful, chubby guy with the beard. Then meet me up front." With an accommodating grin, Louis moved off toward the CD. "And you," she turned to Rob, "you can simply make yourself at home."

Once a steady flow of guests began arriving, Rob stood back by the windows overlooking the fairway awhile, people watching from a distance. With the soft background music as a constant, the flow of guests gradually took on the look of an orderly, genteel dance. Louis and Karen and Barbara and the new associate, McMillan, formed a crescent, receiving inside the foyer, shaking hands with the newcomers, making introductions, and directing the guests toward the open bar. The clockwise flow moved from the bar to the candlelit buffet set along the windows, then back into the center of the room. Black-vested serving staff with trays of hors d'oeuvres and glasses of champagne wove their way amid those standing talking, offering more and taking away empties. As the sky outside darkened, the dancers circled and paused and changed partners with unhurried, civilized grace.

Pensively, Rob watched a minidrama repeating itself at the entrance. Louis's beaming smile and bobbing head made him look like a fuzzy-haired Santa in a dark business suit. McMillan had worn a tux and had an air of self-command and authority that indicated he was totally at ease in his new surroundings. Karen—regal and graceful in her ivory gown, welcoming all—reminded him of an image from a poem, Our Lady of the Snows. Dressed in a full-sleeved silk shirt and softly draped slacks, both a deep shade of emerald green, Barbara seemed to be the least intense of the three. Her copper hair shifted softly with each movement as she smiled and exchanged pleasantries with the guests as they arrived. Occasionally she'd glance his way with a glint of good-humored tolerance in her expression.

He could tell by the way hugs and kisses were exchanged that there were comments and condolences about T.J. being offered. Barbara kept her smile intact and seemed to handle her part reasonably well. Detached for the moment, Rob could understand what she meant about feeling that people were watching her. They were. After the guests moved on a bit, or as they stood in groups, drinking and eating and talking, there would be curious, deliberate glances in her direction. Occasionally as the evening progressed and he spent longer segments of time with her, they would inspect him, with tentative, appraising expressions. Whenever he caught them in the act, he would return their speculative scrutiny with a noncommittal look. Then they would usually smile politely and go back to their conversations.

"Paranoid" was what Barbara had called the feeling of being watched. In public, she felt everyone was waiting for her to do something dramatic. At home, it translated into the fishbowl effect. Now Rob was feeling the same subtle tension himself. Even at this gathering of clients and friends where the new man, Jeff McMillan, was the honored guest, Barbara was constantly under observation. She wasn't imagining that part. He could sympa-

DARK WINDOW 91

thize with her longing to be offstage and off duty at least in her own house.

Rob waited until the stream of arrivals dwindled to the occasional latecomers, before he moved in on his next mission. Throughout the house, the hum of conversation and bursts of soft laughter added a gentle accompaniment to the candlelight and music. "Everything seems under control now." He touched Barbara's arm lightly, drawing her aside. "How about sitting down for awhile and getting some food in you. I'm sure these folks can do without you. Take a break. Get off your feet," he insisted, turning his back and screening her from the guests.

"I guess I could use rescuing," Barbara replied quietly, without significantly altering her pleasant public expression. "Thanks." Only her eyes registered relief. "Let's duck out onto the patio and take a breather."

"You go first. I'll load up a couple of plates and bring them out." Across the room, Rob caught a glimpse of the McMillan fellow, looking over at them with obvious interest. "On second thought, let's both get out of here for a few minutes. I'll come back for the food." He stared at McMillan until the fellow nodded genially then looked away. At least for the moment, he would buffer her from the intrusion a bit.

Definitely more than a bit decadent. Barbara smiled to herself, recalling the comment Rob had made about the ornate pattern of her new bedroom draperies when they'd picked out the fabric almost two weeks earlier. The sample had been labeled "Oriental Delight," and they'd both spotted it instantly. The background was a pale apricot, like her carpeting, but across it paraded arrogant, wide-tailed birds, mythic creatures, woven in shades of peach, salmon, and deep orange. They were interlaced with garlands of pale ivory peonies and white chrysanthemums and foliage of green and gold.

"Does that mean you like them?" One worker stopped.

"Yes. They are absolutely beautiful." She voiced her approval to both men from Warren's Interiors, who had come to install the hardware and hang her purchases.

"Well, what do you two think?" She turned to the smaller onlookers. Miranda was sprawled across the bed on her stomach; Eliot had propped himself cross-legged with his back against the headboard.

"They're better than the ones in the study," Miranda offered grudgingly. She considered her mother's disappointed expression and sighed. "The birds are really pretty," she added politely.

"They're called phoenixes. In China the phoenix is the symbol for the sun." Barbara tried to stir up a little enthusiasm. "According to the legend, when the day is ending, the phoenix builds a nest of sweet-smelling wood, bursts into flame, and turns to ash."

Miranda was fiddling with a loose thread on the bedspread, but Eliot sat forward, listening attentively.

"After the ashes cool, or after night passes," Barbara pressed on, "a new phoenix arises from the ashes, and a new day begins." She waved her hand in an arc, marking the course through the heavens. "It soars through the sky, bringing light." There was a momentary silence as the two workmen finishing up took a long deliberate look at the birds on the drapes.

Eliot adjusted his glasses and moved closer, inspecting the fabulous creatures. "I like the story better than I like the draperies," he concluded, then he turned and loped out of the room.

"Me too," Miranda slid off the bed, following him.

"So much for my attempt at cultural enrichment," Barbara muttered. She turned her attention to the two workmen, who were now packing up drills and screwdrivers and ladders, getting ready to vacate. "Thank you, gentlemen. Nice work." She tested the pulls a few times before the men left the room. She loved the sense of control she had when she pulled the cord, opening and closing the draperies at will. "I'm going to enjoy these," she said quietly. It had taken two weeks to get the draperies made and delivered. None of the ready-made ones she and Rob had looked at that weekend had suited her. She'd been tired, confused, and was almost ready to give up on draperies altogether until they tried Warren's. Now the study looked snug and homey with the striped rust and melon pattern, and her bedroom had been transformed into a Turkish harem, only more subtle. She was glad she'd followed through.

"Hi Mrs. A. I came up to stock up your firewood supply." Kent Nelson reached the front steps just as the two workmen climbed into their truck. "Mr. Johns told me to move it inside while it's still dry. You'll be needing it next month."

"If not sooner," Barbara agreed, remembering the fire Rob and the kids had made a couple of weeks before when the outside temperature was pushing ninety.

"You need anything else done while I'm here?" Kent asked hopefully as he followed her into the house.

"You can tell me what you think of the new draperies. Come on and take a look." Barbara led him toward the study first. "I have to warn you, neither of the kids is particularly enthused about them," she informed him as they halted just outside the doorway. "So if you don't like them, fudge a bit. Humor me."

For the first few seconds, he simply stood there while she pulled the cord, silently taking in the change.

"Well. Say something."

"I guess they're all right." Kent looked embarrassed as he passed judgment. "My mom has curtains on all our windows. I kinda liked the windows here better with nothing." He sounded apologetic.

"Boy, when you humor me, you certainly underplay it," Barbara kidded him. "You were supposed to say they look great, or nice, or charming."

"Okay. They're nice," Kent agreed, grinning sheepishly.

"Chivalrous, but unconvincing," Barbara sighed. "Go get the firewood. I'll put in some muffins for you and the children."

"Hey. Is Kent here?" Eliot had heard the voices and intercepted them in the hall.

"Come and help me get some wood." Kent put his arm on Eliot's shoulder as the two of them strode off together.

Eliot glanced over his shoulder at his mother then back

at Kent. "You didn't like the dumb things either, did you?"

Kent gave Barbara another apologetic look, but he didn't answer.

"Did you see the ones in Mom's room?"

Kent shook his head.

"They have these phoenix birds, from China." The front door closed behind them, shutting off the sound of Eliot's voice. Kent had become a regular fixture lately, stopping by after school to rake the yard, or mulch around the plants, or carry out garbage, or pitch a few balls to help Eliot with his baseball swing or give Miranda a hand with her latest hobby, bug catching. Since Rob's poetic discourse on grasshoppers and crickets, Miranda had been probing nooks and crannies in pursuit of the small critters. The few she'd managed to catch hadn't made a sound. But Kent was willing to go along on her bug safaris, and he'd carry her home on his shoulders when they returned from the marsh, soggy but elated with their various finds. However, it was the practical, less spectacular minutes he spent with Eliot that made Barbara the most grateful. Like the two of them carrying firewood.

Just as she poured herself a cup of coffee and checked that the oven was preheated, she heard the front door close. Two sets of footsteps went up the hall. Then there was a second trip. Kent strode out toward the woodpile at the end of the yard with Eliot at his heels. Both of them carried another armload of firewood back into the house. Only one set of footsteps returned.

"Eliot showed me the drapes in your room, Mrs. A." Kent reported to the kitchen for the promised muffins. "I like the birds. And the story about the phoenix was neat."

"At least Eliot gets a kick out of that part." Barbara leaned against the counter, sipping her coffee. "I guess he mentioned that he disapproves of the ones in the study. He says they're boring. They both do." She landed the cup and started filling the muffin tins.

"Eliot was griping a bit," Kent admitted. "I haven't heard from Miranda." He stood shifting feet, watching her scooping the batch of batter into the indentations in the tray. "The drapes are a lot different from what they're used to. I guess the kids remember Mr. A. telling everyone that the windows wouldn't need anything." It sounded like an accusation. He glanced at her uneasily, then shifted his eyes away as if weighing whether to say more or edit whatever else Eliot might have told him. "They'll get used to the drapes in a while," Kent concluded. He crossed his arms, trying to appear philosophical. "You know how kids are."

Barbara gave him a sidelong look, sensing something disquieting in his guarded delivery. He was having a hard time being the children's confidant and hers as well.

"I know Eliot and Miranda are probably hurting more than they show," she said gently. "I don't want to make things more difficult for them. I suppose I could have done a little more groundwork explaining the draperies to them. I make mistakes. I need your help." She rested her hand on Kent's crossed arms. "We all do. If I get off track or push too far or miss a point, tell me. I need all the input I can get."

"You can count on me, Mrs. A." Kent managed a shy, tentative smile, but there was still a trace of uncertainty in his manner.

Barbara made her voice sound relaxed and confident. "I'm sure you're right about this all working out in time. For now, however, try rounding up the little dears and bringing them in here for some seminutritional peacemaking," she suggested, determined to ease the tension of the moment. "Blueberry muffins might get that disgruntled look off Eliot's face, at least for a while, and they'll look wonderful on Miranda."

By nine o'clock that night, both children were sleeping. Barbara poured herself a glass of sherry. She drank the first one quickly, then filled a second before she retreated to the study to check a stack of student assignments.

I guess they remember Mr. A. telling everyone the windows wouldn't need anything. Kent's halting explanation kept echoing, tugging at her between the sentences on the students' pages, like an indictment for some unspoken offense. Had she violated some crucial principle? Had she been disrespectful? Had her additions detracted so blatantly from T.J.'s master plan? She kept recalling Eliot's scowl. The shift in Miranda's eyes. And Kent's. In a child's mind, it could all come down to a question of loyalty, perhaps. She had broken faith by not keeping things the way T.J. had left them.

By ten-thirty, Barbara put away her papers, poured herself another glass of sherry and stared at the melon-striped drapes covering the beveled bay window and the vacant plate glass next to the sliders. "They really aren't that bad," she murmured, wishing someone would agree with her. "I like them," she said, weaving slightly as she withdrew into her room. How many glasses of sherry was this, she wondered. The third, or fourth? She'd been medicating herself occasionally at night with an extra glass or two. Whatever the number, she felt more relaxed than she had in weeks. She changed into pajamas, finished the last sip, set the alarm, and slid between the sheets. "Goodnight, Bozo," she whispered as she had each night before. "I'm sorry if you didn't plan it this way. I didn't either." She sighed and closed her eyes. Protected by peonies and phoenixes she fell asleep rapidly and slept without dreams.

"Eliot!" Barbara shrieked from the study, "Get in here right this minute." Her voice echoed through the house.

Miranda reached the study first, her blue eyes wide and eager to take in whatever disaster had provoked the angry summons. Eliot followed, his sandy hair slicked down, still wet from his morning shower, and his eyes wide and bewildered behind his glasses.

"Eliot. Did you do this?" Barbara waved one hand towards the rectangular space at the end of the room. The drape that had hung over the single glass panel was neatly folded and placed on the floor beneath it. The wider ones that had covered the bay were also down. The curtain rods and every screw that had supported them were arranged neatly beside the draperies on the rug.

"Did you do this?" Barbara repeated icily.

"No, ma'm," Eliot replied promptly.

"I know you don't like them," Barbara kept at him, "but this is unacceptable."

"I didn't do it. I really didn't, Mother," Eliot insisted, blinking in confusion. The "mother" part slowed Barbara down. Eliot only used that word with that tone when Barbara was mistaken. She stood very still and rubbed her temples with her fingertips, trying to ease the headache that had been little more than a dull, stuffy feeling when she awoke. Now it was pulsing.

"All right." She turned more calmly to address Miranda. "Do you know anything about this?"

"I'm too short," Miranda observed. "So's Eliot." Her heart-shaped face tilted up toward the top of the glass where the screws had left small holes in the wall. "We couldn't reach."

"So it seems," Barbara looked from one child to the other. They both stared at the windows with a dull expression of disbelief. "We have to get to school now. But if either of you should happen to recall anything that may have caused this," she deliberately left them an opportunity to save face, "I would appreciate your mentioning it to me within the next twenty-four hours. Nothing has been damaged. I'm not going to lynch anyone." She watched their eyes shift from the window to the draperies and accoutrements on the floor. "Now let's finish getting ready."

"Yes, Mother," they both said at once. But they didn't move. They seemed too interested in waiting to see what she was going to do next.

"Go and load up your schoolbags," Barbara dismissed them. "Now." They hurried out into the corridor. She rubbed the back of her neck, quietly cursing for overdoing the sherry the night before.

"Too short," Barbara muttered to herself as she turned her attention to the folded draperies. "But we do have ladders and footstools." She bent down to pick up the first panel. Suddenly she felt the cool current of air. The scent of Dhatri, strong and unmistakable, engulfed her. She braced one hand upon the floor to steady herself as the aroma closed in like the heavy, moist atmosphere before a storm. Dhatri filled her nose, coating her throat with each breath, almost overpowering her. The room tilted and rolled and began to recede. She dropped to her knees, clutching her throat, panting and gagging, struggling for air.

Abruptly, it was over. The first breath came. Then the pressure subsided and shifted into a gentle, circular pattern, dissipating the heavy concentration of the scent. Desperate for another breath of the fresh air, Barbara gulped it in, then struggled to her feet, the panel still in her hand, feeling as if she had suddenly surfaced after being forcefully submerged. Her skin was moist with sweat. Her hands were shaking. The next breath, then next, came pure and clear. She breathed in again. And again, slowly, feeling some control returning with each inhalation.

"Anxiety attack." She had read about them in one of the books she'd checked out from the library. They were periods of panic that often happen after a death in the family. The heart raced, the muscles tensed, breathing was labored. Sometimes one came on because of feelings of guilt or remorse or anger. Or being hung over. She rubbed her hand over her face and throat, embarrassed by the last possibility. Whether she liked admitting it or not, she'd drunk more than enough to relax last night. It was no accident that she hadn't even counted the refills. She'd been feeling guilty about the draperies, so she'd numbed herself quite thoroughly.

But perhaps she wasn't numb enough.

Another kind of chill inched its way up her spine. "Was I the one who did this?" She locked onto the bare spaces where the rods had been. She knew the human mind played tricks, and all manner of possibilities were in there somewhere. She had watched the installation from begining to end. She knew exactly how it was done. And she knew T.J. would want them down. Her mouth was dry and cottony, then it tasted like she needed to throw up.

Cautiously, Barbara lifted the panel to her nose. Only the faintest trace of the bay-almond aroma lingered in the dense, tweed weave. But it was T.J.'s scent. "Why is this happening to me?" she moaned. Arms limp, she stared out the window at the tall, arching boughs of Keats, searching for some reality beyond this room.

"This is crazy. T.J., what's going on?" She broke off abruptly realizing that she'd turned toward the loveseat and was talking as if he were there. He often had been. She and T.J. had worked out the final details of the house in that bay alcove. She sat on the stool at the workbench, cutting or grinding the pieces of stained glass for one of the now finished windows. He sprawled on the loveseat at the end of the worktable, sketching and thinking out loud. He said this northeast glass window was "her" window, hers and Keats's, since that was more her tree than any of the others. And he designed the airy, driftwood pattern to complete the room without obstructing her view. But he hadn't planned any draperies.

"It hurts so much to see the things we never finished," she said softly. Her eyes brimmed with tears. "I have unfinished places in here, too." She clutched the panel against her chest. "Please. Don't let me be crazy. Just let me hang on a little longer. Until I'm strong enough."

"Mother?" Miranda poked her head into the room. "Mom?" She inched into the room. "I thought I heard you talking."

Barbara turned to see the somber face of the little girl. "I guess I was muttering," she answered quickly, trying to blink back the tears and make light of her one-sided conversation.

"I was afraid Mr. Johns had come early."

"He's not coming until after school. You'll get to see him," Barbara assured her.

"Good. I want to show him some of my bugs."

"I'm ready, Mother," Eliot announced formally from the corridor.

"Okay." Her lips formed the stiff response. "Go get your jackets and get in the car. I'll be right there." She placed the drapery panel across the flat worktable. Rapidly she made certain that the glass sliders were locked. They still were. She collected her school papers from the desk and walked briskly toward the entry, pausing only to reset the Sonitrol. She had checked it first of all when she'd discovered the dismantled draperies. It had been on all night. No intruder could have done this while they slept. Nor was there any open window, no cracked door that could have caused the sudden swirl of scented air nor the second flow that cleansed the aroma of Dhatri from the room.

"I'm not going to fall apart," Barbara uttered at last in the still house, before she turned and pulled closed the door. "I'm not letting anyone down." She stalked out the side walkway towards the car where Eliot and Miranda were waiting.

"I thought your Momma had some store men comin' to put up those curtains." Luster Johns kept his raspy voice low that afternoon. He walked with Miranda around the house like he did every few weeks when he came, just to make sure all the plants and trees were doing well and that all the little outside chores he'd left for Kent were done. Only this time, Luster's routine varied from the usual one.

With Miranda zigzagging alongside, he kept taking little side trips right up to the house, putting his dark hand on the wood support beams on the outside walls, then pausing. He'd done the same thing with each of the trees. He'd laid his hands on them, standing straight and looking off into nowhere in particular. Inside the study, Barbara and Kent Nelson were busy with the stepladder and a utility stool set up on either side of the window, balancing a curtain rod between them. Eliot was at floor level between them, passing up tools and screws and looking utterly miserable.

"Two workers did put them up. Yesterday. Only someone took them down again. So Momma and Kent are putting them back." Miranda barely looked up. She was watching the ground by their feet, scouting for creepy crawling anythings.

Luster stopped, set open his folding stool, and sat down a moment. "You mean that someone took all the curtain rods and the curtains down?" he asked, rubbing his knees. The weather had started to change almost overnight. All the aches and pains that came with fall and old age were worse the last night, and he'd been restless again. He'd gone out and talked with Inez for almost an hour, sitting there in the light of the full moon, surrounded by his carvings. Luster knew full moons made peculiar things happen, but last night he'd felt the closeness of the spirits like he hadn't felt in years. Now it sounded mighty peculiar that Barbara Ashcroft's new curtains were down.

"Only the ones in the study."

"I see," Luster replied, waiting for Miranda to say more.

"She actually thought Eliot did it," she added, scrunching up her face with childlike disdain. "He's too short. Besides, Eliot never does anything wrong. He wouldn't dare mess with Momma's new drapes."

Luster leaned forward, bending over to help Miranda scour the area for more bugs. "Anything else messed with inside?" Luster asked quietly, trying not to sound too interested. "Or outside?"

"Nope. But boy, was Mom mad when she found all that stuff on the floor. I heard her muttering out loud."

"I guess I'd mutter too."

"She's been doing a lot of that lately," Miranda told him. "She says things sort of to herself. Sometimes I think she's talking to my dad."

"I do some of that with my Inez. Hard to learn to hold it in when you got something to say." Luster's dark currant eyes lingered on the pretty child, with the reddish-blonde hair like her mother and the cool blue-green eyes of her father. Then he looked a long time at the house. He had liked T.J. Ashcroft. He had liked the way T.J. talked about living in harmony with nature, then built a house that did just that. He loved the house and four old oaks and the sprawling grounds crisscrossed by possum trails. He loved the children most of all. And he had a special soft place in his heart for the gentle woman who watched over them so caringly and seemed content to please. But something was not right here.

He had thought of it when he was passing time, talking with Inez the night before. He had counted off the days back to the one when he'd heard that T.J. Ashcroft had died. And it came up on a full moon. Counting again, he recalled he'd felt the same unrest on the full moons since, one in August, now this one in September. Somehow it all fit in with the spirit telling him to carve those angels.

He'd thought about bringing his down-the-lane neighbor, Sister Gertrude Kelly, the conjur woman, with him when he came this time. But all he had to do was deliver some new plants to replace the summer plants in the atrium and make sure that young Kent had done his part with the mulch and the firewood. Having an unfamiliar woman make the rounds with him might put everyone off. He wanted to see them just like normal and take a look around, in case he was way off track.

However, he had stopped to talk with Sister Gertrude before he came. And they talked a long time about the ill feeling that had crept upon them with the past full moon. Something deep in the eyes of the copper-haired woman when she greeted him that day said she'd felt it too. Without words, those eyes spoke of things uneasy afoot. And when he laid on hands and listened to the house and the trees, he could feel something there. Something lingering. Something hanging 'round. Not necessarily something bad, but something there.

"You want to help me bring the new plants in?" Luster prodded Miranda from her close inspection of a few ants on one of Keats's exposed roots. "Might have something for you tucked away." That brought the cap of blondish curls bouncing up and caused her eyes to gleam with interest.

"Let's go," Miranda tugged his lean wrinkled hand and almost yanked the campstool out from under him. "Show me what you brought."

"I said might have." Luster strolled without haste toward the nursery truck. Miranda kept bouncing ahead, clutching his stool, then waiting impatiently for him to catch up.

"Does it have feet?" Miranda looked up at him hopefully. "Lots of feet?"

"Not sayin'."

"Does it wiggle?"

"Nope."

"Swim?"

"Wait and see." He reached the open-backed pickup, placed the campstool in the rear compartment, then opened the passenger door and lifted a glass box the size of a small fish tank from the front seat. "I thought you could use a new friend." Luster produced a delicate terrarium with a lid of carved wood strips. He made her turn around slowly, three times for luck, then he placed it in her hands. Inside was a layer of dark soil, some green leafy plants, and a large magnificent cricket, the color of indigo.

"It's so beautiful . . ." She oohed and aahhed over the creature. "I've never seen any like this one."

"It's kinda' special. I got it from a friend out my way."

"Does it sing?"

" 'Sposed to."

"What does it eat?"

"Little bits of fruit, crumbs, lettuce. Once in a while, jus' a smidge of sugar. They like sugar."

"Does it have a name?"

"None that I know. You pick one. Jus' remember that it's a he. Only he's can do the singing."

"I think I'll call him Henry."

"Henry is a good name. Whatch'a say, Henry?" He stooped over and clicked his tongue like Sister Gertrude told him. The cricket flexed its wings. "He's listening. He's jus' not ready. You jus' get him settled somewhere and click like I did. He'll get those old wings rubbing together and he'll fiddle you a song."

"I'll take him to my room right now. Wait till Eliot sees him."

Luster watched her carry the cricket cage into the house, then he took out the hand truck and loaded it with pots of yellow chrysanthemums for the atrium. T.J. had blocked out the rotation of the plants he wanted and filed a copy with Everett Pierce at the nursery. First of fall meant chrysanthemums, yellow and gold ones. Mid October, he'd change them for rust and orange. In November, everything would be replaced by narcissus. Poinsettias at Christmas. And a live cedar tree, bagged and ready to pot outside after the holidays. Nothing would die or be wasted. The faded plants would be cut back, set outside, mulched to protect them, then allowed to rest and grow the next year in the yard. "They're just slumming for a while," T.J. had kidded about the atrium plants. "Once they got tired of being around people, we'll put them outside where they belong." Luster liked the plan from the start.

"Bringing some sunshine inside," Luster called out as he steered the handtruck down the corridor toward the glass atrium. "Anyone want to help?"

"I will." Eliot bounded out of the study, clearly relieved to have something to do other than pass screws up to his mother and Kent.

"Let's give these sad old geraniums a vacation." Luster directed the switchover. "They've been cooped up too long. Make some room." He wriggled a long finger, showing Eliot what to slide out of the way first.

After one more trip to the truck and back, Luster completed the transformation in the center of the house. He declared the geraniums too "leggy" to be planted as is and decided to take them back to Pierce's Nursery for some propagating. But the tiered granite steps of the atrium were lined with cheerful clusters of chrysanthemums, and the entire area took on a lighter, livelier look.

"What are those?" Eliot watched while Luster placed little bundles of fabric tied with twine under the foliage of several of the plants.

"Just some stuff to help them grow," Luster answered quietly, slipping the packets out of sight. Sister Gertrude had given him the seven small conjur bags "jus' in case," so if he got there and felt there might be spirits about, he could do something right away. She called it "puttin' down the juju," putting them on notice, so the spirits would know they weren't welcome. Luster set four of them in the atrium, but he held back three just as he'd been told.

"Go wash up first, then ask your Momma to come and take a look," Luster directed his helper. "Scoot." He waved Eliot off toward the kitchen. He hesitated a moment, then hurried off in the opposite direction. He wedged a small bag under the bedframe in Barbara's room, one under the mattress of Eliot's bed. Then he crossed the hall and tapped gently on Miranda's door. "I'll be goin' soon and I just wanted to see how you and Henry were doin'."

"He hasn't made a noise yet," Miranda came to tell him, pouting noticeably.

"Then I guess it's time to try a little sugar," Luster suggested, with a knowing wink. "Just a few grains."

"I'll try." Miranda arched her brows, then pranced past him. It only took a few seconds for Luster to slip the last conjur bag between the mattress and box springs of her bed.

"This is beautiful," Barbara declared, when they all convened by the large glass cubicle filled with yellow and white mums. Kent stood next to her, carrying the stepstool and the few tools they'd been using. "Now how do I keep them this fresh?" She seemed a bit more relaxed now that she and Kent had the draperies back in place.

"Just mist them a bit in the mornings," Luster told her. "Don't let them get too wet."

"Do I mist Henry too?" Miranda came bounding back from depositing the sprinkle of sugar in the cage, obviously hoping someone would press her for details.

Eliot did. "All right. Who's Henry?"

The high broken chirp of the cricket answered for her. Miranda gave Luster Johns a smug look. "It worked." A second trill, longer and more enthusiastic than the first, sent a cheerful sound throughout the house.

"Henry might take a little getting used to," Barbara stared uncertainly down the hallway. The cricket let out another long trill. Kent and Eliot were already following Miranda, intent on meeting her roommate.

"You just let old Henry chase the gloom away," Luster said in his raspy, gentle voice. "He'll bring you good luck. He'll be watchin' out for you and the children." His calm, wise eyes held Barbara's a moment until she looked away.

Awkwardly, she cleared her throat. "Well, then I guess I'd better go and meet him." She tried to sound agreeable.

Luster glanced at his watch. "I have to get the truck back before Mr. Pierce closes up shop. You just rest easy tonight," he stated earnestly before he set off toward the door. "You got a cricket in the house now. Everything's going to be just fine."

Once he pulled onto the bridge toward the Charleston peninsula, Luster checked his watch again. Sister Gertrude told him to come to see her after he'd done what she had said. "Somethin's there," he would tell the conjur woman. In the atrium he had felt it most of all, even after he'd moved in the new plants and hauled the old ones outside. The granite floor that served as a heat sink for the solar setup on the roof was cool. Unnaturally cool. So he put the conjur bags like she'd directed, north, south, east, and west. And he'd hidden the others where they would guard the family against bad dreams. But he'd have to tell Sister Gertrude about the heat being drained from the floor and about the curtains and the rods being taken down. And how it took two full-grown people to put them back.

"Come on Henry, do your stuff," Luster said hopefully as he drove along. Sister Gertrude had told him that sometimes it only took a little nudge to get meddlesome spirits on their way. "They forgets where they s'posed to be," she said. The conjur bags and the cricket might be enough. He'd just have to wait and see. Thinking of the lonely widow talking to herself touched a tender place inside. There was a slender line of difference between talking like he talked to Inez and holding onto someone who needs to cross over. Haunts had a way of taking advantage, overstaying their welcome, and turning things sour.

Luster tried to whistle, but the tight knot in his chest made the few bursts he managed to let out sound flat and unmelodic. He needed to get home safe. All he wanted was to sit out on his porch in his rocker, smoke his pipe, feel the ancient river breeze, and to let Sister Gertrude's jujus do their work.

CHAPTER 4

> Perhaps they do not go so far
> As we who stay, suppose—
> Perhaps come closer, for the lapse
> Of their corporeal clothes—
> *Emily Dickinson*

BARBARA NEVER EVEN made it into the study with the book of poems Rob sent her. When it came in the mail and she saw his return address, she opened it at once. It wasn't particularly imposing, just a sturdy paperbound engagement calendar, The Book of Days, each week set off with an illustration and a quote by Emily Dickinson. But she flipped it open to October and read the small verse there about hope, "the thing with feathers that perches in the soul and sings a tune without the words and never stops—at all—" It reminded her of Keats and his cricket and about Miranda's Henry. She was hooked. She ended up leafing through every page, slowly, pensively, in her breakfast nook, letting her coffee get cold in the process.

"Any good stuff in the mail?" Eliot asked the same question T.J. usually had when he came in after work, only Eliot pushed aside the unopened letters on the counter. He poured two glasses of lemonade instead of flipping through the stack like T.J. would have done. "I thought I saw you bring a package."

"This is it. A book from Rob."

"Is it about tree houses?" Eliot plopped a couple of ice cubes in each glass, raising the level of liquid even with the rim. He'd been outside with his best friend Billie Hobach, rummaging in the garage for rope and lumber, intent on constructing something as yet unspecified.

"No. These are poems."

"Oh." His hopeful expression vanished. "When I talked to Rob last Sunday, he said he'd once seen a book on tree houses and he'd look around for it at the bookstore. I thought maybe that was it."

"I guess he's still looking. Is that what you and Billie are working on out there? A tree house?"

"We're just in the planning stage," he responded seriously. Barbara had to look away to keep from reacting. There was so much T.J. in her son. Gestures, phrases, even the interest in building were part of T.J.'s intangible legacy. The simplest exchange could trigger an immediate response that could knock her off kilter for hours. Hearing about his project "in the planning stage" brought back memories of T.J. and had her ricocheting between a smile and tears.

"You guys be careful out there."

"Sure. See ya', Mom," Eliot said, sounding more like himself. He grabbed the two drinks, sipped a half an inch off both of them, and elbowed his way out the garage door to where Billie was waiting.

"See ya'," she replied, trying to sound as happy-go-lucky as he did. It was an act she had to work at even harder since the drapery incident. Every morning since she and Kent had put the rods back up, she'd awakened early and made the rounds, checking to see if they'd been touched again. They hadn't. Every night, after she'd graded papers, she avoided the sherry, fearing that she might inadvertently drink too much, feel too guilty or too lonely, and get up and do something she couldn't remember. For two weeks everything had been blissfully calm. Even that made her uncomfortable.

"Mr. Johns is here." Miranda streaked past and bounded out the front entry. Barbara put her book aside for the moment and followed. She could usually hear the nursery pickup truck coming down the driveway. But this time, there was no sound until she saw it coming around the far side of the house; then she realized why Miranda had spotted it first and had come racing from her bedroom. Luster had used the old construction route that cut around off the main road and came in from the southeast through the woodsy area behind the house. As the pickup bobbled across the lawn and eased to a stop, Barbara could see the two good-sized tree stumps in the back. She guessed he'd been picking up supplies for a couple of projects of his that were also "in the planning stage."

"How's Henry doing?" Luster asked, sliding out one long leg then the next and climbing down to greet Miranda.

"He's been singing every day. He's been great. I don't even have to give him sugar any more. You want to come and see him?" She grabbed his hand and started leading him toward the house.

"Wait, wait. Easy now, little lady. I got som'thin' for you and your brother and your Mama." He patted her shoulder, then turned toward the back of the truck, popped down the tailgate, and pulled back a pile of canvas. "Found you folks a beauty. A real beauty." He rolled a huge pumpkin onto the gate.

"It's a giant one." Miranda was bouncing up and down, dancing around him as he hoisted it up against his chest.

"Jus' was finishing some deliveries and thought I'd stop in a bit." Luster bobbed his head and smiled when he spotted Barbara in the doorway. "Found a pumpkin. Time for jack-o'-lanterns."

"This will make a wonderful one." Barbara stepped back, holding open the door to let him in. Mentally she crossed off "pumpkin" from her marketing list.

"Eliot!" Miranda let out a piercing yell, aiming in the general direction of the garage. "Eliot! Billie! Come here. See what Mr. Johns brought. Hurry."

"Open the door, and then call them," Barbara pleaded, wincing at the noise. The serenity of her Saturday afternoon was rapidly evaporating. Still bouncing, Miranda raced to summon the boys.

"Hey, this is great," Eliot said. He and Billie Hobach came strolling in, trying not to look too eager. "Wow, we could really do a lot with this guy. How about it? Big old snaggletoothed grin." Eliot made an arch with his finger on the pumpkin where the mouth would go. "Let's do it." He nudged his buddy.

Luster had put the pumpkin on the counter, then backed off, grinning as the children closed in on it, thumping the sides and rubbing their hands over the smooth surface and the stubby rough stem on top. "You jus' be careful usin' any knife," he cautioned them. "Don't want no one short of fingers for Halloween."

"No. Wait. Let's do it tonight when Kent comes," Miranda insisted, clearly not wanting to let the boys take over. "He's good at making things. He can help us. We'll have it all done when Mom comes home."

"How about it?" Eliot turned to his mother. "Can we work on this with Kent while you're at the Belcazzios' tonight? Billie could spend the night and help out?"

"We can make it real spooky and everything," Miranda added, scrunching up her face and wriggling her fingers enthusiastically.

"Please," Eliot pleaded. He glanced at his buddy, then back at Barbara.

Carving the pumpkin was something the family had usually done together at the kitchen table each year. T.J. had generally sketched out an appropriately maniacal face with marker. Then he and Barbara would take turns cutting out the features and the kids would scoop out the inside, or "the guts," as Miranda joyfully called the pulp and seeds. While they carved, they'd have apple juice and doughnuts and make it a party.

"All right," Barbara agreed. She hadn't really been looking forward to having to run the show alone. "I'll give Kent a call and warn him, but he'll be in charge. You guys will have to do as he says. And remember what Mr. Johns said about being very careful. No fooling around, and no cuts."

"No problem," Eliot agreed. Satisfied, he and Billie went back outside. Miranda grabbed Luster's hand again and started leading him away to see her cricket. "Henry stays in my room." Suddenly, everyone was gone. The kitchen was quiet again and Barbara was left standing there by herself.

"I guess it's just you and me, kid," she joked, giving the pumpkin a perfunctory pat in an attempt to curb some vague disappointment. Somehow most of the potentially traumatic occasions she'd been bracing herself for weren't turning out to be so monumental as she feared, at least not for the children. Even this departure from pre-Halloween "tradition" had slipped through easily.

"You, me, and Emily," she amended her comment, glancing over at the open book. She freshened her coffee and went back to her reading. She already had her plans for the evening. Karen and Louis were having her over for dinner with a few friends—nothing special, just a quiet evening of good conversation and good food. Karen had come over earlier in the week to see the new drapes and had finally spoken out about Barbara's reclusiveness. Since the McMillan party, she had retreated again.

"You're overdoing it with the mother bear routine," Karen had declared, starting out a bit shaky in the study, but gaining in momentum over coffee in the kitchen nook. "You're going to turn into a hermit if you don't force yourself to have some kind of social life. I don't want you to go weird on us."

The choice of wording struck a disturbingly sensitive chord. Barbara simply shrugged, wondering if the kids mentioned the incident of the draperies coming down.

"You need some time out with adults." Karen insisted that Barbara would forget how grown folks had fun if she didn't get out more, "sans children." The reception for McMillan had been a start. An informal dinner gathering would be the next step. "The guys will probably end up in front of the TV with some football game, but the rest of us can put up our feet and visit. Just girl talk." Barbara was looking forward to just that, a casual evening with friends, with a few lingering misgivings for being self-indulgent.

"Now that everything is settled . . ." Barbara tucked her feet up under her, flipped to the next page of the book, read a few lines and grew suddenly somber. She contemplated the passage that seemed strangely apt.

I can wade in Grief
Whole pools of it
I'm used to that
But the least push of Joy
Breaks up my feet
And I tip—drunken—

Let no Pebble smile
Twas the New Liquor
That was all . . .

"You and Karen must be in cahoots," Barbara mused, recognizing herself in Emily's words. Grieving had become comfortable and familiar and safe.

As Karen had said in the gentlest possible way, she'd been overdoing the responsible single parent bit. "Your eyes don't sparkle and you don't even smile the same way," Karen told her that afternoon when she was finally able to articulate her feelings. "You're not really open to anything except working and running the house. Like you're embarrassed to slack off or be happy about anything. That's not like you." In an instant a wistfulness softened her worried expression. "We used to giggle. I miss that." Karen said it lovingly. She didn't back down even when Barbara's eyes and her own filled with tears. "You're going to feel the hurt forever, but you just can't stop enjoying people and having fun. It's been almost three months. T.J. wouldn't have wanted you to become a drudge."

Grim faced, they sat staring at each other across a sudden heavy silence.

"You're probably right," Barbara finally conceded. She couldn't admit that allowing herself to laugh, letting house chores go, even shopping by herself without dragging the kids along was trickier now. Slacking off let in the loneliness. All the additional baggage she was carrying was strangely comforting. It gave her structure and made each day less risky than proceeding undirected or unscheduled.

"The children get plenty of time with you. But enough is enough. You don't want to make them all clingy. Give them some breathing space, too," Karen suggested. "Lighten up."

"All right. I'll try to lighten up," Barbara had promised. Now she patted the pages of the book reassuringly as she had patted Karen's arm that day. "No more wading in grief," she had agreed. "I'll be better company.

And I'll try not to get too uptight if I happen to enjoy myself."

While Miranda crouched in front of the terrarium, making little clicking sounds to get Henry to perform for him, Luster slipped a couple of dark juniper berries under the dresser. Her back was turned so he checked on the small fabric juju bag in her bed. It was still there, tucked in between the mattress and box springs. He figured the ones in Barbara and Eliot's rooms were equally intact. The big blue cricket preened awhile, then flexed his wings and fiddled out a string of chirps.

"Told you," Miranda beamed, without taking her eyes from the cricket. "Good job, Henry," she said softly, nose-to-nose with him except for the glass separating them.

Luster eased around the other way, reached into his pocket, and rolled a couple more dark blue berries into Miranda's open closet door. They disappeared amid the jumble of tennis shoes and toys. "Got yourself a songbird, all right," he chuckled, coming closer to peer over her shoulder. "Plenty of good luck comin' with that one." He watched a little while longer. "Everythin' been runnin' smooth around here?" he asked her, lowering his raspy voice to little more than a whisper.

Miranda turned and grinned at him. "Everything's been fine."

"Smooth as smoke?" He'd felt nothing peculiar when he put his hands on the glass walls or on the timbers of the house. In the study, the draperies were open, but hanging there just as they had been the last few times he'd come by. He just wanted to be sure he hadn't missed anything.

"Smooth as smoke," she answered, nodding.

"Tha's real good to know." He stood a moment longer. "Must get these ol' bones moving and get on my way." He rested his hand on her head. "Got to spread a little plant food before I leave."

"Can I help?"

"You can come along to keep me company. I could use someone who don't mind gettin' a little dirty to scoop ash and refill my cans from time to time." He gave her a speculative look.

"I'll get my shoes." Miranda rummaged in the closet for her favorite sneakers. The first one was on top, but she had to dig a little for its mate. Fleetingly she glanced at one berry exposed by her search, flicked it with the back of her hand, and sent it skittering somewhere deeper into the clutter. Luster smiled.

"So long, Henry. Enjoyed the show." Luster started on ahead while Miranda finished stuffing her feet into her shoes. It only took him a moment to move along the corridor and roll a few juniper berries into the far corners of Barbara's room and Eliot's, "markin' " the place so the magic would know where to come.

The glass-enclosed garden in the center of the house was still aglow with the pots of bright yellow and brilliant white mums he'd put there two weeks before. He stopped in and plucked off the faded chrysanthemum blooms, then felt each of the four jujus hidden under the foliage. The packets were precisely where he'd left them. This time, the floor was warm. Everything seemed peaceful.

"I'm ready," Miranda called as she caught up with him.

Luster stopped at the kitchen entry to tell Barbara about his next trip before they went outside. "I'll be back with a little squirt of fertilizer for the flowers down the hall next week. Don't want them getting droopy before the new mums are ready." He'd been careful to make each visit seem as natural as he could, so the family would get used to having him coming about more frequently than usual. He didn't stay for long, just enough to do some small task, to visit with the children, and take a look around. Sister Gertrude Kelly had told him to keep checking regular. Even if it felt like whatever was lurking about had taken the hint and left, she'd cautioned Luster that haunts were tricksters. They'd play possum for a while then come back up to no good, meaner than before.

It was time already for another full moon. Sister Gertrude had told him the jujus she already gave him would last a month. She said he'd only need to replace them just a few days before Halloween, when all manner of spirits would come to pull their pranks. But even with Sister Gertrude's assurances that it would be two more weeks until their power would weaken, Luster wasn't taking any chances. He figured a little extra insurance couldn't hurt, so he'd brought a few charms of his own to help strengthen the magic.

For all his years on the backrivers, while he waded through the marshy areas along the banks after sweetgrass for the fine woven baskets Inez made in her time and her mother before her, other "swampers" were out there harvesting certain roots and plants for the local conjur-doctors. From them, he'd learned to use the native plants to heal and to protect. The juniper was what he needed now, ancient plants of tranquility, of refuge, of sanctuary. The juniper berries were ones he'd collected himself, one of the many things of nature that he'd been taught had special powers. He'd also brought a string of garlic to hang in the house to keep the spirits away.

For the outside, Luster had brought ashes. He'd used the juniper leaves and branches and made a fire out by the woodshed the past three evenings at dusk. When the fire was hot and snapped and sizzled and the rich scent hung like incense in the night, he scooped handfulls of berries onto the bonfire. After the flames died down, he gathered the ashes and crushed them to powder, then poured them into two old dented watering cans and a plastic sack. With the ash, he would ring the house, so everyone inside that circle would be safe. Scattered about inside, like amulets, unseen but potent, the dark juniper berries would draw the power of the ring into each part of the house, making each room a refuge that the spirits could not enter.

"Mr. Johns, there aren't any plants there," Miranda commented when Luster trickled a thin line of ash across a barren area, careful not to skip a space and leave an opening in the dark ring he was pouring.

"No matter," he replied, bent and intent on his work. "When the rain comes, it will all wash into the ground and something will start to grow. Nothin' is wasted in nature. It all comes back and helps somehow."

"But I don't think anything's going to grow on the sidewalk," Miranda persisted. She'd made four trips to refill the ash supply in the watering can, and she had dark powder up to her elbows and smudges on her face. She was slightly bewildered by the strip he'd poured across the front walkway.

"We'll just have to wait and see," Luster kidded her, diligently continuing on with his line of ash. "It may wash off to one side or the other and help the grass to grow."

"The grass already grows. Kent has to cut it every week."

"Tonight he won't be cuttin' no grass," Luster countered, eager to get his companion onto a different subject. "He'll be helpin' you cut pumpkin and you'll be havin' a big time. When I come here next, I expect to see a real nice jack-o'-lantern all lighted up inside, grinnin' out the window at me."

"Yeah. We'll fix him up real good. Maybe with a hat. And with ears," Miranda was staring off toward the house. "Last year we put him out on the front porch on a little table. My dad used big old walnuts for his eyes." She crooked her fingers to show the size. "A squirrel took them. So we used ping-pong balls instead. Dad painted the dark spots on them. They were funny." Her voice suddenly sounded strained and hushed.

Luster turned to look at her. She had her lips pressed together. Her eyes brimmed with tears. She stood still, looking at the house, her slim shoulders sagging. "I wish my dad were here." Luster followed her line of vision past Keats toward the loveseat just inside the study window where T.J. often sat. The rust and melon draperies were pulled open now to let in the light.

"Always is hard, rememberin'. Brings some happy, some sad. Jus' know in your heart that your daddy is somewhere else now, bein' at peace with all of nature," Luster comforted the youngster. Her eyes had raccoon rings where she'd swiped away at the tears with her sooty hands.

"I wish he were here."

"I know, sugah'," Luster said quietly, wondering how many times Miranda and Eliot and even Barbara had made the same wish, silently or aloud. To the one well-versed in backwater lore, it sounded uncomfortably like an invitation. "How 'bout fetching me a refill in the other ash can?" Luster tilted his head toward the second old watering can, set out by the back of the truck. Diverted again, Miranda bounded off to get it.

"Don' you come round here, haunts. Go where you belong," Luster whispered three times, throwing a pinch of ash over his left shoulder with each recitation. He hastily spit on the ground. Then he saw Miranda returning with the second can and went back to pouring his circle. "Time soon to put out nuts for the squirrels and carrots for the rabbits." Luster started in on a new tack. "I was thinkin' instead of just scattering 'em, we should set up a little place outside, special like, so they know where to look and so you can watch 'em. Jus' wondering where that should be."

Miranda puckered her lips up, scanning the area. "Maybe around the back so they won't have to cross the driveway," she suggested. "Somewhere safe."

Luster nodded, still swinging the watering can as he moved along, patiently extending the juniper ash line. "Everyone needs somewhere safe," he answered, echoing her words.

By the time he'd come full circle under Wordsworth where he'd begun, Miranda had located just the right spot for the animal feeders. "I'll get a couple of short stumps, cut smooth on top, and we'll put them out here back against the bushes," he promised.

Using the hose, they washed up together in the side yard, one holding while the other scrubbed. "You better do somethin' about that face," he cautioned her. "You look like the tar baby." He handed her his handkerchief, dipped in water. At first the effect only worsened, but by the second rinsing, Miranda looked far more presentable.

She helped him wash out the watering cans. Then they checked the water in his radiator. "Got to take care of your 'quipment. Specially whatever gets you from here to there." He gave the hood and windshield a quick spray while she loaded the two empty watering cans back into the truck.

"What are you making with the stumps you already have?" Miranda asked. Luster slid into the front seat of the pickup, ready to leave.

"Angels."

"Aren't they too short?"

Luster glanced over his shoulder at the two pieces in the back. "How tall are angels 'sposed to be?"

"Big." She stretched her hand up over her head, signifying the size she'd imagined.

"I don't know," Luster drawled. "Seems to me that big is something we worry about in this world. I think angels don' have to fret over stuff like that. They jus' have to be good, and good don' come in certain sizes." His bright currant eyes narrowed as he took a long look at the tree trunks. "I can see the angels when I look real hard."

Miranda contemplated the two pieces of rough wood. "So some of them can be little like me?"

"Jus' like you."

Miranda simply stood back, smiling slowly and looking at the bark-covered trunks.

"Maybe your Momma will bring you out to see them when I finish," he offered. "I got some other things of mine to show off, too."

"I'd like that," Miranda answered without shifting her attention from the sturdy stumps.

Luster waited a few seconds before he turned on the ignition. Seeing her standing there, with that rapt expression on her face, he wanted to prolong the moment as long as he could. The sound of jetskis out beyond the marshgrass did it for him.

"I hate it when they come in close like that. They chase away all the birds," Miranda said, craning her neck to see who was passing by. "And they stink. Smells like gasoline."

"See you in a couple of days," Luster called out. As the pickup rolled off, Miranda lingered, waving, watching until the would-be angels in the back disappeared behind the hedges that lined the drive.

Somberly she looked down at her blackened shoes and the dark rings around her ankles. Her sneakers were what got her from here to there, and they were in sorry shape. She turned back to where the garden hose lay coiled on the lawn. Dragging the hose with her, she stood on the front walk, took off the shoes, and sprayed them and herself clean. Then she washed down the sidewalk so the area was spotless.

"Frankie would have laughed his buns off if he'd heard about this one," Ginny Parma declared. She dropped her armload of textbooks on the table of the teachers' lounge and collapsed into the nearest chair facing Barbara Ashcroft.

"I wondered what happened to you." Barbara checked the time. "The period is almost over."

"I was having an adventure," Ginny answered, sliding her ample posterior more comfortably into the chair. Younger than Barbara by six years, dark-haired and decidedly Rubenesque, Ginny taught in the language department just down the hall from Barbara's English classroom. After two months sharing a planning period each day, they had become in-school friends. "Frankie was always telling me to get an extra set of keys made and buy one of those little magnetic boxes for the car. But no . . ." Ginny heaved a breath and tugged at the front of her blouse, flapping it to cool herself down. "Naturally, I never got around to having backup keys made. So when I stopped at the doughnut shop for coffee this morning, I locked one set in the car with my purse, which of course had the second key in it. I had to borrow money and take a taxi to school."

"Again?" Bobby Joe Hawkins, the shop teacher, asked loud enough for everyone to hear. Barbara could see him grinning behind his newspaper.

Ginny Parma rolled her eyes and laughed out loud. "Now, you hush. I don't keep track of your little idiosyncrasies, so you just don't keep count of mine." She and Bobby Joe had been badgering each other since the school year began. Both were single, both good-humored, both a bit overweight—they reminded her of Tweedledum and Tweedledee.

"Wasn't it last week that you locked yourself out of the house?" Bobby Joe asked, not so innocently.

Ginny stabbed a blood-red fingernail in his direction. "I said hush. You're just like Frankie. Only he'd be crowing, 'I told you so' every three seconds."

"I could do that." Bobby Joe dropped the paper and looked at her obligingly.

"No. Please. I hear enough from him already. Permanent tape loop." Ginny tapped her finger against her temple.

Barbara glanced at her watch again and took a last swallow of coffee just as the bell to end that period rang. All the teachers gathered their materials and headed off to their classrooms.

"You talk about your brother a lot," Barbara noted, sticking with Ginny as they navigated their way through the crowded hallway.

"Frankie and I were real close," Ginny answered, nodding. "Growing up we fought constantly, but we were close. Italian families are like that. Lots of screaming and lots of nagging. But a lot of good things, too. My brother was a real character." She took a sidestep to avoid two students linked in an embrace. "If I didn't talk about him, I'd feel like I was letting him down. No—more like I was cutting him off. I won't do that to Frankie. I didn't kill him, that darn motorcycle did. It took away a lot from me. But I'm not giving up everything."

She stopped and fumbled with the knob on her classroom door, blinked her long dark lashes, and gave Barbara a thoughtful look. Outspoken and consistently bubbly, Ginny had a brashness that irritated some people. But that energy was part of the appeal that kept her Latin and Spanish classes packed. "Does it bother you, me talking about him?"

"No. I like the way you talk about your brother," Barbara said simply.

"Like he's still around?" Ginny grinned. "That's the only way that makes sense to me." She walked in and dropped her books on her desk then came back to talk a little longer. "Frankie and I used to share an awful lot. We still do. It's just that he's not here anymore." She pointed to the open space between them. "He's here." She touched her temple like she had earlier in the teachers' lounge.

"I feel that way about T.J."

"Mine gets worse," Ginny said, leaning closer, lowering her voice conspiratorially. The first few students filed into her room. "When our folks moved to Florida and told us we could have the house and save rent instead of waiting for them to die and sell it, we both gave up our apartments and moved back in. After three years as housemates, I just got used to havin' him around." She glanced over to make sure none of the students were hanging around within listening distance. "It's been almost a year now since he died, and I still talk to him. At home. In the car. Basically when no one else is around."

Barbara licked her lips, finding all this reassuringly familiar.

"Sometimes I'll walk through the house and think I'm going to see him there, sitting at the dining room table, or sprawled out on the sofa," Ginny went on. "Or I get frustrated and I'll say right out 'Frankie, I had a lousy day' or 'Have you seen the TV guide?' Once in a while I think I hear him in the next room. Or I'll be puttering in the garage and get the strangest feeling that he's right there. He was always working on that darn motorcycle." Her expression softened and became more serious. "Sounds crazy. But that's what I feel."

Barbara bit her lower lip, framing her words cautiously. "I miss having T.J. there to say things to. Especially things about the house or friends or news that the kids aren't the least bit interested in. Sometimes I talk to him anyway." She made the confession hastily. "I even tell him goodnight."

"Well, I've asked Frankie to answer the phone," Ginny admitted, shrugging. " 'Specially when I'm in the tub or similarly indisposed. Unfortunately, he never does," she drawled. "So, maybe this means you and I are a bit wacked out. But we're basically harmless," she joked, patting Barbara on the arm.

"I was afraid I was the only one . . ." Barbara began.

". . . Who's nuts?" Ginny guessed what Barbara was going to say. "Who's to say what's crazy and what's normal? Frankie dying at twenty-seven wasn't normal. T.J. was what, mid-thirties?"

"Thirty-six."

"Now that's crazy. How is anyone supposed to handle that kind of crazy?" She didn't even pause for an answer. "I read all kinds of things when Frankie died, trying not to be bitter and to come to terms with what they called 'losing a family member.' Only Frankie wasn't lost. I was at the cemetery. I know precisely where he is," she said bluntly, staring out over the river of jean-clad students moving along the hall. "I had a real tense time with all the philosophical mumbo-jumbo I kept running into. I finally gave up trying to cope and simply started talking to Frankie. I felt better from then on. I figure I'll make up my own way of handling this. And I'll keep doing it until they lock me up."

"Request a double room. I guess they'll have to lock me up, too." Barbara eased toward her classroom. The congestion in the hall had thinned, a clear indication that the tardy bell was about to ring. "Talk to you later."

"Just remember that you aren't the Lone Ranger when it comes to weirdness. There's a lot of us having a rough time dealing with this kind of thing. We all get a little unhinged. But don't give up anything you don't have to. We're all taught to be such wimps. Accept. Accept." She took a few quick steps to the right of her. "That's bullshit." Her pretty dark eyes flashed with indignation. "What's gone is gone, but you should fight to hold on to what's not gone. Take the good times and the good feelings with you. Even if that means talking to air. Just hang in there," Ginny whispered before retracing her steps to her own classroom.

"Thanks." Barbara ducked into her doorway just as the bell rang. Two stragglers, the romantic duo she and Ginny had passed further down the hall, squeaked in right behind her, then ambled toward their desks. "Okay, let's get settled." She summoned the students to order, feeling better than she had in weeks.

DARK WINDOW

* * *

When it came to Halloween, Louis and Karen Belcazzios' home was becoming a favorite stop for the children in the neighborhood. Barbara's house, set off alone at the end of the cul-de-sac, was too remote and too isolated for the little ones to trek to, so she and Karen had decided to combine efforts and make their joint base of operations the Belcazzios', closer to civilization.

"You're sure you want to have a big production this year?" Barbara had asked Karen point blank. The previous year the two had transformed the Belcazzios' front porch and foyer into Count Dracula's palace and dressed as vampires. This year Karen and Miranda had decided to be witches.

"This is my kind of fun. I get to dress up funny, enjoy the kids, feed them all sorts of disgustingly wonderful treats, then send them all home. The next day the cleaning lady comes and resurrects the place," Karen said delightedly. "Of course, I want to do it." So they hung yards of netting and transformed the foyer into a spider-webbed witches' den, complete with a smoky cauldron. But the white carpets were off limits.

Like the previous year, Louis had a few friends in to eat and watch football while the women supervised the action at the front door. This year, clad in black leotard and tights, pointed ears, and whiskers, Barbara was the witches' cat, officially in charge of keeping the serving dishes filled. Karen, in a layered black gown and a pointed hat, with her dark hair teased and wispy around her shoulders, managed the traffic flow. Miranda, the junior witch, helped them pack grab bags. Rather than just hand out treats at the door, she was to invite the children to come inside, let them show off their costumes, use the guest powder room if necessary, then help themselves to the goodies. "Sort of an all-purpose pit stop," Karen had proclaimed.

"Your art project turned out nicely," Barbara whispered her praise to Miranda while they waited for the first arrivals. Beneath the punchbowl and trays of foods was the festive tablecloth that sported fingerpainted and carefully pressed imprints of bugs and autumn leaves.

Miranda and Eliot had squeezed in some ghosts the past week, specifically for Halloween night. "These are really clever." Barbara traced a familiar white handprint, which two dark fingerprint eyes had transformed into a ragged-tailed ghost.

Miranda beamed, then abruptly turned her attention to the group of costumed figures crossing the yard. "If they don't get it all messed up, we can save it for next year." She cautiously placed a few extra napkins under the edges of the doughnut tray to catch any falling sugar.

"Come in, children, welcome, welcome." Karen's deliberately crackling voice was appropriately witchy but not particularly scary. Stationed by the old cauldron that the children would have to reach into for their bags of goodies, she made a grand sweeping gesture to guide them inside. "Welcome to all you ghosties and ghoulies and long-legged beasties and things that go bump in the night."

"Oooh, say that again," Miranda insisted, delighted with the phrase.

"Ghosties and ghoulies and long-legged beasties and things that go bump in the night," Karen repeated, this time reaching out to tickle Miranda when she reached the "bump." Two incoming visitors stopped, obviously willing to be tickled by the witch lady, too.

Karen obliged, until Miranda was repeating the lines perfectly, adding an enthusiastic "Oh, yeah" at the end. "I've got to try this on Dr. Palmer," Miranda insisted as she flounced off towards the den to show off to the group watching football in there.

"I think we could have done without the incantation," Barbara said lightly once Miranda was well on her way. "I have a feeling I'll be hearing it for weeks." It was already echoing in her head.

"It's just a silly old thing." Karen watched the bobbing step of Miranda. Undoubtedly she was keeping cadence to the words she was repeating on the way. "Besides, I think it's an old prayer, not an incantation . . ." Karen turned and winked at Barbara. "It goes on with 'Good Lord deliver us', or something like that. We children," she confided with great melodrama, "thrive on the bizarre."

"I can't dispute that." Barbara picked up a few napkins and scooped up some crumbs. "I think I'd better check in on the bizarre goings-on in the den, just in case Miranda is upstaging the game."

"Don't forget to eat. Sandwich makings are in the kitchen," Karen reminded her. "You'd better help yourself while there's plenty. Louis and Tom are infamous for devastating a good roast, and I think McMillan is running them a good second . . . or third." She turned her attention to the sound of more youngsters crossing the yard. "Send Miranda back quickly," Karen called after her. "More kids."

Barbara steered Miranda back to her front-door duties, then paused in the kitchen, taking Karen's advice to go ahead and eat. At least she could put a sandwich together and take a few bites between callers.

"Time out. I'm here for a refill." Jeff McMillan plopped his plate down next to hers. "You want me to slice some off for you?" He grasped the carving knife and aimed for the rarest part.

"A little more done for me."

"Sure enough," McMillan responded, slicing off the outer portion for her. "Just say when." He continued carving thin, even layers and stacking them on her plate. Whenever she had been invited over for dinner or for a drink, Jeff McMillan was there, often with a few other friends. Tonight the gathering was rounded out by the down-the-street neighbor Andy Reeves, whose wife was out of town, and Tom and Sibyl Palmer, whose children were out with Eliot making the rounds. But Barbara wasn't comfortable with the way the tall blond architect had made himself at home in Karen's kitchen any more than she was with the way he'd made his place at Ashcroft and Belcazzio, Architects.

She'd only stopped in at the firm briefly in the past week to sign some papers. But she glanced in the doorway of T.J.'s office long enough to notice that the furniture had been rearranged, the room repainted, and McMillan's nameplate hung on the door. Louis told her that two of T.J.'s projects, a strip of specialty shops and the restoration of a Charleston single house, were now McMillan's—a few weeks behind schedule, but apparently in competent hands. She tried to sound pleased.

"Is it the cat suit or my company that's inhibiting our conversation?" McMillan asked now, looking at Barbara from whiskers to toes. She'd been standing by watching him carve, saying nothing.

"I'm sorry. I guess I'm a little preoccupied. I have to keep an ear out for the kids coming and going."

"Like I've got mine tuned to the ball game," he observed, nodding. "I guess we're both preoccupied. I was hoping sooner or later we'd get to know each other a little better." He looked at her again, more intent than before. "I know now is not a good time for either of us. But Louis said he'd picked you up to eliminate having all the cars lined up out front." He kept his voice low as he slid the last slice of roast beef on her open bun. "When this event tonight is over, maybe you should let me drive you and the kids back to your house. I keep getting the feeling that unless you and I work out some kind of friendship voluntarily, we're going to spend the rest of our days having Louis and Karen inviting us to functions and wondering if we'll even speak."

"We've been speaking," Barbara insisted.

"I think they may have something a bit more friendly in mind. Surely you've noticed some subtle pressure to get us on better terms."

"I can't say I have. I don't think Karen and Louis are worried about me getting on better terms with anyone." Barbara felt her coloring deepen, realizing she may have been naive about the Belcazzios' strategy.

"I'm not saying they want us to be bosom buddies," McMillan sighed philosophically. "Adults who do things together socially don't have to be madly in love. They just have to be reasonably comfortable with each other. We're obviously not. But we could be. I'm divorced. You're widowed. I assume at some point you'll have functions to attend and you'll consider going with an escort. I think Karen and Louis see some advantages for both of us. They're simply trying to get us into circulation. No one likes a vacuum."

"I'm just not ready to circulate," Barbara protested. She took a soft drink out of the refrigerator and started filling her glass with ice.

"Fine. I'm not interested in getting into anything that demands too much of my attention either." He followed her, nodding agreeably as he helped himself to a soda. "I'm not inferring you aren't attractive and all that," he added quickly. "But I'm well aware of your circumstances and you need to understand mine. I could use some social contacts, but I'm concentrating on establishing myself here professionally. I want to fit into the community, that's all." He took a swallow straight from the can.

"I thought you'd been doing that very well." Somehow the sting of seeing his nameplate on T.J.'s door seeped into her comment.

"Ah, do I detect a bit of waspishness beneath that charming facade?" McMillan gave her a sidelong glance, arching his brows, clearly amused.

"It's no facade. I am charming. Usually," Barbara added, shrugging apologetically.

"So I've been told." He studied the face behind the cat whiskers, feature by feature. "Louis and Karen speak of you in the most glowing of terms." There was a definite hint of laughter in his voice. "And that brings us back to our current dilemma, developing some kind of a workable friendship. You aren't ready to circulate and I'm not interested in anything complicated. So how do we get Karen and Louis to relax and end their helpful efforts on our behalf?"

"I haven't the faintest," Barbara answered honestly.

"I have a suggestion. We at least make an attempt to appear to be on better terms," McMillan proposed. "Tonight I'll take you home. You invite me in for a drink. We talk. Just enough to convince them we are adult enough to be sociable. Nothing more. We say pleasant but impersonal things about our chat. They'll feel better. The tension will be off. And we can go about our business."

"I hope they're not going to keep doing this kind of thing," Barbara muttered, feeling embarrassed.

"Of course they will," McMillan said shaking his head. "Married friends want everyone all paired up. They like couples, or at least sets of two. Personally, I think it's some kind of a conspiracy." He leaned against the counter, smiling with a slightly cynical twist. "I know you already have one male friend, the fellow who was at the reception last month. But I understand he lives out of state."

"I really don't see what Rob has to do with this."

"That's just my point. He's not here enough to be helpful. I am. If we keep everyone content, just by being friendly to each other, we'll both fit in easier. Functions do come up where it is appropriate to have an escort," McMillan noted, fixing her steadily with his intense brown eyes. "We could come in handy for each other. What you'd be doing, what we'd both be doing, is buying some time and some freedom. You don't seem like the type who's meant to stay at home alone. Having me to call would get you out occasionally, without the usual pressure. Eventually you may meet someone who does interest you, but until then . . ." He shrugged accommodatingly, "it might be nice to have a pal."

"A pal?" Barbara found McMillan's choice of the term somewhat amusing.

"Why not? We all need a pal once in a while."

"A pal who doesn't mind being a mere convenience?" Barbara pressed.

"Right. I could use a night out once in a while with someone bright and easy to look at. So could you. If you bail me out when I get in a bind or if they start playing matchmaker for me, I'll do the same for you. No strings. Just pals. Deal?" He held out his hand.

Barbara hesitated, then returned the handshake. "Pals. Deal."

"So what do you say, pal?" McMillan helped himself to one of the backup doughnuts still in the box. "You want a ride home, Mrs. Ashcroft?"

"If we're going to be pals, call me Barbara. What should I call you?"

"Just McMillan. My parents named me Jeoffrey. If you want me to answer, don't try that one."

"I'd be delighted, McMillan," Barbara agreed. "Perhaps you could stay for a drink," she added cheerfully.

"A drink? What a friendly gesture. See you after the fourth quarter," he added, with a quick glance toward the Belcazzios' den. Sandwich in one hand, doughnut in the other, he strolled off.

Barbara stood staring at her plate. *You don't seem like the type who's meant to stay at home alone.* McMillan's words echoed in her ears as she munched her sandwich alone at the counter. She knew he was right. It had been three months since T.J. died, and life did go on. There were functions she and T.J. had attended that she would not feel at ease going to alone. And she didn't want a date. "Couples." She could imagine Karen setting up more casual dinners and bringing in other available men. And it all would be done with the kindest intentions. Her friends would want her to be happy again. To them, that meant married or at least paired up occasionally.

"Spare me," Barbara muttered out loud, summoned by the sound of more Halloween callers knocking on the door.

"Trick or treat!" The high-pitched voices sliced through to where she stood. Barbara shook her head, remembering. Last year she'd stood in the exact same place and heard the same sounds. T.J. was in the den watching football with Louis, and they all ordered pizza and drank a lot of beer. Tom and Sibyl Palmer were there, just like now, and Andy and his wife Terri, who was pregnant at the time. Couples. Just like McMillan said. And when it was over, they'd gone home and made love. Barbara licked her lips, feeling a little ill. "T.J. . . ."

"Ghosties and ghoulies and long legged beasties," Miranda was chanting as she led the latest round of trick-or-treaters past the end of the kitchen toward the drinks and doughnuts.

"Things that go bump in the night," Barbara completed the phrase involuntarily. That previous year, when the party ended, she and T.J. had gone home and put the kids to bed. Then they sat on the loveseat and watched the moon. And they talked about the windows. Actually, T.J. did the talking. The sudden recollection brought another part of that night into focus. Over pizza earlier that particular evening, she told Karen and Sibyl Palmer that she was thinking about going back to teaching. T.J. overheard and kept teasing her, saying there weren't enough hours in the day to keep up with two kids and the house, much less add an outside job. "We've got projects to last us until we're at least ninety," he told the others. "I'll just keep reminding you so you won't get sidetracked."

That night, sitting on the loveseat, he'd begun by making the point again that he'd prefer her being a full-time wife and mother. There had been an edge to his voice that made her start to bristle. "We don't need the money. You can use your talents here or with some volunteer work with the festival, not at some school with a bunch of throwbacks," he'd stressed, as if the subject were closed.

But it wasn't. She hadn't argued then. It was late. They were both tired. T.J. had been disgruntled because his team lost the football game. The harvest moon outside was beautiful. *In the cosmic scheme of things* . . . She mentally shifted priorities. She sat there quietly, drawing in tranquility from the night. Then T.J. started to get romantic, and they realized they weren't too tired after all.

It wasn't until months later that she quietly went ahead, checked into the program, and signed up for the classes she needed to update her certificate. T.J. was slightly stiff-faced when she told him about it, and he gave her the same reasons for wanting her at home, but he didn't turn it into a confrontation. "Okay. Give it a shot. Just make sure we come first," he said, half-smiling, half-pouting, like Miranda often did. He was trying to sound playful. Barbara discreetly overlooked the remoteness in his eyes.

"Trick or treat!" Suddenly time shifted once more. Now Barbara recognized the voices of Eliot and the Palmer children returning from their door-to-door wanderings. The evening would soon be ending. The game would be over. Tom and Sibyl would take their kids home. Barbara was vaguely relieved that McMillan would drive her and her children up the road to their house. And when the kids were in bed, at least for a while, she could show him around and she wouldn't be wandering through the house alone. She'd have a pal. When he left, she could do what Ginny Parma said. She could hold on to the good memories. She could sit on the loveseat, look out the window, and tell T.J. that in the cosmic scheme of things, the window hadn't really mattered at all.

"Ghosties and ghoulies and long-legged beasties," Miranda chanted rhythmically, sending a slow chill up Barbara's spine.

"And things that go bump in the night," Barbara completed it again. The image of the neatly folded draperies and the dismantled rods surfaced. T.J. had said they had enough projects to keep them busy at home until they were ninety. *I'll just keep reminding you so you won't get sidetracked.* Barbara tried shrugging off the ominous connection. "I did it," she muttered to herself. "I felt guilty and I drank too much and I did it." She hurried to the sink and ran some water over a paper towel. Pressing it to her throat, she stared out the window, trying to ease the queasiness she felt. *In the cosmic scheme of things* . . . She inhaled and blew out a breath several times in succession. She couldn't think of a convincing closure. "Just a slight anxiety attack," she told herself. "Relax. We're going to be all right." It sounded hollow, even to her.

In the morning, Barbara lay in bed without moving several seconds, trying to figure out what had roused her so early on a Sunday. She listened for the chirp of the cricket. Sometimes Henry's salute to the dawn would nudge at her. But the house was silent. Even Henry wasn't awake yet.

It took her a moment more to figure out what was off kilter. Light. The room was too light. She rolled over and saw the early morning sun making the outer leaves on Wordsworth sparkle like sequins against the deeper green. Someone had pulled the phoenix draperies wide open. Slowly she propped herself up on one elbow, to see if anything else was out of place. She sniffed the air.

It was the aroma of the coffee that made the knot in her chest slack off. Somehow that vital sign signaled a major breakthrough. T.J. used to wake early on Sundays, make coffee, then spend some time reading the paper or working at his drafting board until the homey scent lured Barbara down to join him. Then one by one, the family would wander into the study. They'd sprawl on the sunlit carpet or lounge on the loveseat while sections of the paper made the rounds from one pair of hands to the next.

Since T.J. died, the Sunday gatherings had been shifted to the kitchen. The outings T.J. initiated for brunch, then a quiet drive to a park or beach or historic attraction near Charleston, had been suspended. It was Eliot who'd mentioned that they should take another boat ride soon. He and Miranda loved the tour boats to Fort Sumter, especially in the fall when the harbor was grim and gray. Next to that, they liked the park farther up the Ashley River at Charles Towne Landing, with its bike trails and its museum, and Fort Moultrie, where Edgar Allan Poe, their favorite poet, had served. Barbara realized they hadn't been off the premises on a Sunday for almost three months.

"Miranda," Barbara guessed, smiling to herself as she strolled barefoot toward the kitchen. They'd brought some leftover Halloween doughnuts home from Karen's the previous night, and Miranda had decided they would have them for breakfast. Before she went to bed Barbara filled the machine and put coffee in the filter so all she had to do when she awoke was turn on the switch. It smelled like Miranda had already been up and started the lazy Sunday for her.

"Morning." Barbara's soft greeting floated through the kitchen, hanging without destination in the silence of the unoccupied room. The coffee was brewed. No doughnuts were out. "Miranda? Eliot?" Puzzled, Barbara backtracked around the atrium and down the hall. She stopped first at Eliot's doorway and smiled when she glimpsed the rumpled sandy hair protruding from the cocoonlike roll of blankets. She hesitated, listening to his steady breathing, then crossed the corridor to Miranda's room. All her covers were scattered on the floor beside the chest of drawers where they usually were each morning. With lips half parted, and limbs outstretched in peppermint-striped footie pajamas, Miranda, like her brother, was still very much asleep.

"Trick or treat," Barbara sighed, starting back toward the kitchen, still drawn by the delicious smell of the coffee. Surely Miranda had been up and opened the draperies, she told herself. She'd turned on the coffeemaker, decided she was still tired from Halloween, and had gone back to bed.

She let them sleep. It had been a long night for all of them. When they returned from the Belcazzios', Barbara had taken off her cat costume, changed to slacks and a shirt, and started McMillan on a quick tour of the house, both of them carrying a glass of brandy. Then the children's nocturnal parade began. There had already been a trip each for a drink of water. Then one for a pinch of celery for Henry.

"Momma." The sleepy voice of Miranda interrupted their discussion of the passive solar system in the atrium.

"What is it, baby?" Barbara and McMillan were standing in the glass room, in the midst of the newer arrivals, the rust and deep gold chrysanthemums and the jack-o'-lantern that Luster had brought. The warm floor was radiating its heat out into the house. Barbara excused herself and headed down the hallway.

"The toilet won't stop flowing," Miranda announced, standing just inside her bathroom door. "I wiggled the handle but it keeps on swooshing."

"Let me see if I can fix it." Barbara poked her head out into the hall. "A bit of a problem here. Just make yourself at home."

McMillan nodded, content to explore farther on his own.

Barbara tried jiggling the handle, then took the lid off the tank and tugged at the chain inside. Minutes later, she returned, flustered and slightly embarrassed. "I can't get it to stop," she shrugged. "The water just keeps on draining. T.J. put some special valves in and I don't know how they work. Something must be out of adjustment."

"Plumbing fixtures—one of my minor fields," McMillan said, smiling. "Let me take a look at it. I'm not licensed, but I am good with my hands."

Barbara led the way. The toilet still had a steady ripple of water cascading down into its interior. "I'm sorry this happened, but I am glad you are here," she said, taking his glass, then stepping back to watch over his shoulder.

McMillan removed the tank lid and rolled up his shirtsleeve. After several minutes of fumbling with the apparatus inside the tank, he surrendered. "Beats me," he shrugged. "Seems like something is wrong with the way the seal fits around the opening. I can't get it to seat right. Probably needs to be replaced. I could turn the water off."

"Do that. I'll call a plumber in the morning. Or maybe we can do without it till Monday." She watched him turn the valve at the back of the commode. The water trickled a moment, then stopped.

"Try it tomorrow and see if it works. If not, just shut it off again," he suggested. "Sometimes these things just get testy." He stood looking at the commode a few seconds, then shrugged and started rolling his sleeves back down.

"Come on. I'll show you the study."

"Mom." A second voice came from the opposite side of the hallway.

"Yes, Eliot," Barbara answered softly.

"I have a tummyache."

"I'll be there in a minute," she called back. "He's probably eaten too much. I'd better get him something to settle his stomach."

"Mom. My tummy hurts, too," Miranda piped in.

"I have a sinking feeling that this might just go on and on," McMillan sighed. "Look, pal, you've got your hands full, and it's late. I think I'd better just take off." He glanced at the study, then back down the hallway toward the bedrooms. "We can finish the guided tour some other time. Besides, it might be a good idea to put Louis and Karen at ease. I'll drive by and beep my horn on the way past and leave them wondering if it was merely a goodnight honk or a sign of progress."

"I doubt if they're concerned. They're probably in bed already." Barbara laughed softly as she escorted him to the door.

"Don't kid yourself. They're most likely watching the clock, wondering what we're doing. At least this way, they'll figure I didn't get pushy and take advantage of you."

"They wouldn't have let you drive us home if they even suspected you'd do anything like that," Barbara answered candidly.

McMillan paused and looked at her closely. "You're right. They do watch out for you. They're very protective, in a nice way, of course. I'm beginning to see why. You have a special gentleness about you," he noted, keeping his dark eyes locked onto hers. "That's very rare these days. Most women have a harder edge, or else they pretend they do in order to keep from being walked on. You have a softness that makes you seem very vulnerable."

"You make me sound like Mary Milquetoast," Barbara protested. *Like a wimp*. Ginny Parma's phrase came looping back to her.

"I meant it as a compliment. You're also a lot more gutsy and more complicated than I suspected. But you do emanate a certain sweetness. I find that very appealing."

"Don't start to find it too appealing, pal." Barbara's polite smile became slightly rigid as she tried to lighten the conversation. "Remember you're not interested and neither am I."

McMillan studied her with an indulgent look for a long moment. "I'm flexible. I can always amend my position. I don't waste my time on frivolous causes. You are definitely not in the frivolous category."

"I don't particularly like the direction this conversation is going. I thought we had a no-strings, no-pressure deal."

"We do. But I made that deal with a lady in a cat suit.

Watching you here on your own turf with your kids had an effect that I didn't expect. I'm not usually privy to this much domesticity," he said, with a careful balance of humor and sincerity. "Regardless, I don't want to foul up our agreement. Pals. I'll be your convenient buddy until you say otherwise. I'm back on track."

"I'm relieved to hear that."

"However, pal," he leaned down and brushed a parting kiss that was borderline brotherly on her cheek, "whether you admit it or not, Barbara, you were never meant to be a loner. You do the mother thing magnificently, but after a while, you're going to get tired of being the one doing all the hugging and fetching. Miranda and Eliot are simply not enough. When you realize that, you and I may need to do some renegotiating."

"You're waffling again. You really have to go." Barbara opened the door. "I have to check on Eliot's bellyache."

"And Miranda's. Good luck with the plumbing. 'Night, pal." He ducked out into the night.

Barbara had stirred up an Alka-Seltzer for Eliot and one for Miranda, set the Sonitrol, and switched off the lights before McMillan's car cleared the far end of the driveway. After she turned into the bedroom wing, she could hear the distant beep of a car horn. She peeked into Eliot's bedroom to deliver the drink, but he was once more rolled up in his blankets, sound asleep. With a relieved sigh, she stepped back into the hallway and drank the Alka-Seltzer herself. " 'Night pal," she murmured.

Miranda was awake enough to drink the second glassful. While she did, just to test the toilet system, Barbara turned back on the water supply to Miranda's commode. The water swooshed, but then the trickle ceased. "Trick or treat," Barbara said happily, heading on into her own room.

With only the light from the moon, she crossed to the sliders and stood looking out at Wordsworth and the pale marsh grass farther off, remembering other nights. "Goodnight, Bozo," she said aloud, then pulled closed the phoenix drapes.

... *Never meant to be a loner.* McMillan's comment was unsettlingly similar to what T.J. had said to her time and again in many ways. *You're the part of me I never imagined was missing until I found you. We belong together,* he'd said from the very first time they'd made love. *I'll take care of you.* He'd promised he'd never leave her.

T.J. knew she wasn't a loner. He knew that as much as she needed to be loved by someone, she also needed to feel secure enough to give her love. So he surrounded her with his confidence, his dreams, his energy, his love, his passion, and even this house, and he made her feel safe. *You do the wife, lover, friend, and mother part, I'll do the rest,* he'd promised. T.J. had provided the tangible things, but without him, some invisible emotional shield was gone. She was doing what McMillan called "the mother thing" magnificently. She was a gifted teacher. But bit by bit, she could feel part of her was dying, almost like she was shutting down circuits, closing off those other feelings that the children and work did not involve. *Miranda and Eliot are simply not enough,* McMillan had said. *You're going to get tired of being the one doing all the hugging.*

Barbara slid into her bed, which seemed larger and emptier than it had lately. "T.J., I'm so sorry we can't make love ever again. I feel . . . neutered." She grasped for the right word, whispering to the pillow next to hers. "I got used to being hugged and hugging back. I liked feeling sexy." She felt her chin begin to tremble. "I don't like being like this."

A soft sound from somewhere down the hallway suddenly jolted her back to a maternal alert. "No . . ." She guessed it was Miranda on the way to the bathroom. "Don't flush," she called. She flung back the covers, hoping to intercept the sleepy youngster before she touched the temperamental commode and started it swooshing again. Her foot caught on the drooping bedspread and slowed her progress. Muttering, she hurried on toward the dimly lit room, cautious to turn on the hall light so she wouldn't seem to leap out of nowhere and frighten the child.

"Miranda," she said softly, so the youngster would know she was coming. The flushing sound halted her. "Not again," she groaned, giving Miranda a few seconds before she stepped in. "Miranda?" she repeated, deliberately.

"Hi, Momma," the child replied, droopy-eyed but smiling angelically.

Barbara took her by the hand and walked with her to the bed. "We had fun tonight with all the kids."

"We sure did," Miranda responded, with a dreamy voice, as she wriggled back under her still-warm covers.

The commode was still swooshing, but Barbara didn't rush. The warm smell of the child brought back memories of holding her as a tiny baby, all powdered and sweet and totally dependent. Miranda didn't need her in that way now. She was growing up, growing away. "Yes, we had lots of fun," Barbara agreed, kissing her forehead as she tucked the youngster in. Thoughtfully, Barbara stood looking down at her, pondering McMillan's comment. *Not enough . . .*

She started for the bathroom, ready to deal with the cantankerous toilet. But when she stepped in and reached for the turnoff valve, the noise and the flow abruptly stopped. There was not even a trickle of water. The room was eerily silent and unusually cool. The entire house seemed strangely still, as if everything were muffled. Except for Henry. He waited until she had quickly retreated from the lighted bathroom and was almost to her bed. Then he chirped, a long, clear, triumphant trill.

Henry began chirping again the next morning as Barbara filled her coffee mug, zapped a cold muffin in the microwave to revive it, then looked out the window toward the driveway, searching for the Sunday newspaper. Frowning, she leaned forward, unable to see it anywhere near the sidewalk where it usually landed. Unperturbed, she located several unread sections of the newspaper from the day before, tucked them under her arm, and carried them with the coffee and muffin to the study. On the way, she turned off the Sonitrol so she wouldn't set off the alarm inadvertently when the newsboy finally made his delivery. Until then, she would start the day on the loveseat, waiting for the others to come and join her, just like they used to when T.J. was there.

Unlike the draperies in her bedroom, the ones here were still drawn, giving the study a dull and somber look, not at all like the cozy sunlit atmosphere she'd hoped for when she bought them. Even the air felt chillier than in the other rooms. Undaunted, she crossed the carpet soundlessly, put her muffin on the table with the newspaper, and switched on the light by her end of the loveseat. The thick Sunday newspaper she'd been looking for, removed from its plastic bag, lay scattered next to the lamp base on the tabletop, as if it had been leafed through, section by section, then casually set aside.

She stood without moving for several seconds. Her mug of coffee, still clutched in her hand, sent pale circles of steam into the cool air. The scenario she found herself in was familiar—the quiet, calm study, the coffee, the newspaper. But those other times, T.J. had done it all. He'd have browsed the headlines and comics then have left the paper out for her. Sometimes he'd be sitting quietly watching her enter the room, then she'd look toward his drafting table and they'd both smile. T.J. would wait there for her to bring him his good-morning kiss. Almost mechanically, she turned and glanced across the room.

"I don't like this, T.J., I don't understand what is going on." She began to sink slowly onto one end of the loveseat, holding her coffee mug in both hands to keep it steady. "I don't know what's happening here," she whispered. She stopped abruptly, staring at the single panel she and Kent had rehung weeks before. Leaning forward on the seat, she peered beyond the bright space of her lamplight at the drapery. Something about it didn't look right.

"Oh, my God," she groaned. Dully, she put aside the coffee mug, then stepped toward the panel, reaching out hesitantly to inspect the eerie effect. The entire length of the panel had been slashed into straight, even strips. Both the loose-weave inner drape and the solid lining closer to the glass hung like rolls of gauze bandages, edge to edge, touching but no longer connected. The straight cuts were surgically neat and precise, with no uneven edges, no frayed threads, just long slashes from the curtain rod through the hem. As she lifted one slender strip upward, cupping it in her hand almost in an attempt to comfort the damaged fabric, the faint fragrance of bay and almond rose with the cloth. Dhatri. She stood immobilized, staring at the fabric, breathing in the scent.

"I didn't do this. I couldn't have." She stared bleakly at the cloth. "I didn't do this," she repeated, touching the dangling pieces of fabric with her fingertips. "I couldn't." Slowly, she backed away and sat on the loveseat, the color drained from her face, searching for a plausible explanation. "I couldn't." She had had only one brandy with McMillan. But she remembered the Sonitrol had still been activated, so no outsider could have come in. It had to be an inside job. Slowly the tears welled in her eyes. Fragments of the children's chant kept echoing through her mind. "Ghosties and ghoulies . . ."

"T.J. Help me. I'm frightened, T.J." She rocked back and forth, hugging herself. Those other ominous, rhythmic words kept coming. *Things that go bump in the night.* Part of her was again that terrified child in the dumpster with something undefined moving near her in the dark. Only now it was broad daylight.

"T.J. Please." She breathed in shallow, quick gasps. "You know I don't handle weird things well at all. If you're here, please make this stop. I don't want to be . . . haunted." She found it difficult to say the word out loud. She'd often read it. Charleston had a long tradition of hauntings—moving objects, phantom images, hazy presences from the past. Until now they had just been charming tales, stories that appeared in children's books or collections on local color. Even Luster's backriver folktales were often about haunts. She'd even heard him talk of restless souls, separated lovers, or tormented voyagers with some mission of their own that kept them lingering among the living. But they were only stories to entertain the children. She hadn't given them a serious thought, until now.

"Why me?" Barbara shuddered. "T.J., why?" She shook her head from side to side, realizing how crazy it all seemed. Not only had she accepted the presence of some type of spirit in her home, but she'd assumed there was some rationale, some reason for its existence and its actions. She'd called this presence by her husband's name.

In the gray brittle silence of the room there hung a peculiar sense of expectation, as if something were waiting for her to act. There was no sound, no movement but her own.

"What is it you want me to do?"

No response, only stillness and the scent of Dhatri.

She finally stood, looking at the draperies. "Okay. Have it your way." She went out to the garage, located the toolbox, and carried it and the stepstool over to the window. "Is this what you want me to do?" She climbed up with the philips-head screwdriver in one hand. "Is this what it's all about?"

Methodically, she removed each hook and let the draperies drop to the floor. Then she undid each screw and dismantled the curtain rods. When she finished, the exposed glass let the golden warming light of morning into the room, illuminating everything, even T.J.'s drafting table.

Outside, Keats stood silhouetted in the morning sunlight. His outstretched branches cast weblike patterns across the grass. Barbara watched them intently, attempting to decipher some message of reassurance in their dance.

Carefully she folded the ruined draperies, stacked the rods on top, then carried the entire armful out into the garage. "Sorry, Bozo." Her robe reeked of the Dhatri. Every breath was sickeningly saturated. Trembling, she peeled off the robe and gown, wadded them together and stuffed them into a huge trash bag with the draperies, then tied it all closed. Naked and shivering and sobbing softly, she left them there, closed the door, and hurried down the hall to her bathroom.

"I'm sorry," she repeated, standing under the steady warm flow of water in the shower. "I'm so sorry." Like a ritual of atonement and purification, she scrubbed herself ferociously, rubbing until her skin hurt. Then she shampooed her hair, trying to eliminate the insidious smell.

If she were haunted, or crazy, or both, no one must know. Nothing must disrupt the lives of her children. They'd lost enough as it was. Whether the things that were happening made sense or not, she'd hang on for the kids' sake as well as her own. No scenes. No one must suspect. Everything must be normal and calm.

Dried off and dressed, this time in slacks and a sweater, she finally went back down to the hall. Ginny Parma said to hold onto what was hers. But as she stood in the study doorway, the increased lightness and warmth of the room did not lift her spirits. She could still smell traces of the Dhatri. Purposefully, she stalked out into the garage and returned with two aerosol cans of Raid. For a while at least she had to get the smell out. "Time to bomb the house anyway. Let's make a clean sweep of it." She spread the old newspapers, fanlike, on the carpet.

"Hey, sleepyheads, get up. Get dressed." She went into each bedroom to rouse the youngsters.

"Dressed? Are we going somewhere neat today?" Eliot's sleepy voice greeted her. He blinked, reached for his eyeglasses, then grinned up at her hopefully. "Can we go exploring?" Eliot persisted. "Like to Folly Beach, or over to Patriot's Point. Somewhere?" he pleaded.

"We'll see, as soon as Miranda gets up," Barbara called, heading across the hall to get her daughter moving. Henry greeted her with a long, elaborate series of chirps.

"We're going to have to take Henry with us, or at least move him outside," Barbara explained the short-term evacuation she had planned. "We certainly can't fumigate the house and leave him inside."

"Okay." Miranda bounced out of bed and made a quick dash for the bathroom. "Mom, can I flush?" she called out from behind the half-closed door.

"Sure," Barbara answered, keeping her voice steady and cheerful. She knew which knob to turn now if anything went wrong. *We'll get through this. We'll be all right*, she kept repeating inwardly as she made the bed.

Miranda came back and rummaged in her closet for something to wear. "Yuck." She shook a small black beadlike object from one shoe. Barbara picked it up as it rolled toward her. Tiny and wrinkled, the berry looked like several others she'd vacuumed up in the past week. "You're going to have to empty your pockets at the door or simply stop bringing all your science projects inside," Barbara told her. "I've found these things all over the house."

"I didn't bring them in. I like bugs, not old seeds. Here's another one." She picked the juniper berry off the closet floor and handed it over.

"Maybe they get caught in your clothes. Or in your shoes. Just try to be more careful," Barbara urged her.

"They're just old berries."

"Regardless."

"Okay. I'll be careful," Miranda said obstinately. "But I don't see what the big deal is."

Barbara paused, deliberating whether or not to launch into a lecture on "the proper way to talk to your mother." In the cosmic scheme of things, a few berries probably didn't matter at all. "Let's just go," she said instead. The lecture could wait.

"The kids and I are going to Sarasota for Thanksgiving." Barbara tried to make her announcement nonchalantly at the sandwich shop after the theater. Louis and Karen Belcazzio exchanged mystified looks. This was the second public outing Louis and Karen had instigated with her and McMillan. The first had been a group excursion to a football game the first weekend of November. Now this evening he had escorted her to the Center for the Arts for a charity benefit, a performance by the College of Charleston theater department. Farther down the table, Tom Palmer and Mark Ward were listening intently to Sibyl Palmer's explanation of the somewhat bewildering play they had all attended.

Besides the Belcazzios, only McMillan heard and registered any reaction to Barbara's statement. He lifted an eyebrow and looked at her more directly. "I thought your folks were coming here."

"Is there something wrong with your stepfather again?" Karen Belcazzio sounded concerned.

"Pete's in fine shape," Barbara assured her. "They're both fine. We've just been talking and they thought it might be a good idea for us to spend the holiday away from here. The weather in Florida is beautiful. They've offered to take the kids to Disney and MGM Studios. Eliot and Miranda are both excited." She avoided looking up from her plate. "They figure maybe I could use a break."

"They're right." Karen shrugged. "Some Florida sunshine and someone else doing the cooking may be just what you need. I swear you look thinner every time I see you."

Barbara's free hand moved toward her throat. Self-consciously she tugged at her strand of silver beads. Karen immediately leaned forward. "You look fine," Karen apologized, resting her hand on Barbara's arm. "Just a bit thinner than usual. I can't help it, I worry about you."

"I've been putting in some late hours," Barbara admitted. She didn't say how little she had been eating or how uneasy her nights had been. She'd deliberately been overloading herself to combat the cycles of guilt and depression and doubt. Since the destruction of the drapes, there had been no other dramatic occurrences, nothing to confirm or explain what had happened Halloween night. But she still felt a distinctly unsettling sensation whenever she was in a room alone, particularly late at night when the children were asleep. Every night she had drawn the phoenix drapes, half anticipating, half dreading they would be shredded like the others in the morning. They hadn't been harmed. But the uncertainty kept her on edge. And there was no one she dared to tell. Not even Ginny.

"I think a few days away from here—from the house— will make it easier," Barbara said softly. "I'm not sure I'm up to the turkey and thankfulness agenda here just yet."

"I can understand that part of it. But there are other

possibilities." Karen rolled her eyes toward McMillan. "We could do Thanksgiving at our house."

"I love you for thinking of me, but I think you'd have trouble convincing the kids to pass up Disney and MGM for football games in Louis's den."

"I see your point," Karen answered, nodding.

"If you're going to Florida, bring me back some cigars," Louis interrupted, rubbing his beard. "Some of those fat Cuban ones." He grinned. "I love 'em."

"Do it and you'll be sorry," Karen objected. "Remember the last time Barbara visited her folks, she brought back that humidor of Tampa cigars for you." She was wagging an elegant finger beneath his nose. "You were ecstatic. But every room in the house reeked of cigar smoke for months. You stick to your pipe," Karen admonished him. "I can live with that."

"So bring me some oranges," Louis chuckled. "I'll smoke 'em for breakfast."

"When are you leaving?" McMillan asked.

"Next Wednesday night." Barbara avoided making eye contact. "We're flying."

"Do you want me to drop you and the kids off at the airport?" he offered. "No sense you having to struggle with luggage and a parking place."

Barbara forced a smile, wishing she'd handled her announcement differently and had already asked Karen to see them off instead. Trying to duck McMillan's offer now would only make an awkward issue out of something she wanted to keep uncomplicated. Besides, Barbara noticed, Karen was smiling again, obviously pleased at the way she and McMillan seemed to be getting along. "Sure, I'd appreciate your help." She hoped it sounded sincere.

"Good." McMillan stared at her a few more seconds than she found comfortable. Calmly he turned his attention back to the other conversation. He'd inherited T.J.'s project for renovating the exterior of an old Charleston home and converting the interior into an open-space theater. Mark Ward was working closely with him. Behind his circular-lensed glasses, the younger architect's Arctic blue eyes were bright with enthusiasm.

"If they had done the play we just saw in a structure like T.J. designed—with stairwells and landings and performing stations on various levels—then all of us would have felt drawn into the play." Ward's slender hands revolved to emphasize his words. Barbara found his gestures and intensity remarkably familiar, only it was not T.J. but Rob Johnstone whose attitudes she recognized. "This kind of theater promotes a vital interaction," Mark declared. She'd heard Rob say the same words.

"I still don't like the ending," Louis muttered. "Somehow burying a kid in the backyard isn't my idea of good entertainment."

Mark Ward ignored the comment and turned once more to earnest conversation with the others at his end of the table.

"Whatever happened to musical comedies?" Louis went on, unperturbed. "A big clutch at the end and it's happily ever after." He took another bite of his salami on rye. "I like the kind of play you go home and get naked after."

"Louis, really." Exasperated, Karen gave her husband a poke on the arm to silence him. Barbara felt an involuntary smile creep across her lips. T.J. would have agreed completely with Louis's irreverent attitude. Any event was a success if the evening ended with them in bed, undulating. Their word evoked memories that made her smile soften. When she glanced up again, Jeff McMillan was looking straight at her, with a softness in his expression disturbingly similar to one she remembered seeing before on T.J. *Come on to bed,* he would say. More shaken than she cared to admit, Barbara focused on the conversation farther down, trying to seem as if she were actually interested in the issues being discussed.

"I hope you have a pleasant visit with your folks and get some rest," McMillan said as he shoved Barbara's suitcase behind the counter and handed her the plane tickets with the luggage tags attached. "Personally, I think it might make a nice division between what's past and what's coming next. Deep down, I think you're running away," he said gently. "One last flight before you succumb to my charm."

"I really don't think I'm doing anything, except taking a breather," Barbara replied wearily. All through the day, she'd been barely hanging on, fighting the hysteria that had been building since morning.

At dawn, she'd awakened again, suddenly tugged awake by no sound or movement she could remember. The phoenix drapes were open wide. In the morning light, she could see the contents of her suitcase, packed the night before, strewn about her room. Even the lingerie and bathing suits were out of their separate plastic bags, as if there had been a silent explosion in the night. And the cold was back, close and heavy, and the Dhatri was everywhere. For a while she'd been too stunned to move.

Then she leapt from the bed and raced to Miranda's room. The contents of children's suitcase, open on Miranda's dresser, had not been moved at all. Frantically, she packed again, before the children awoke and wandered in to find her room in chaos. She didn't say a word. She just put everything in order. She even took out the suitcases and locked them in the hall closet, ready to go. She was getting all of them out of there—putting some physical distance between them and this presence in her home. Perhaps away from Charleston, she could sleep without dreams, wake without fear, and regain her composure, so somehow she could maintain her sanity.

Already Eliot and Miranda had eased to the front of the line, ready to board the plane. As they disappeared into the loading tunnel, Barbara glanced after them apprehensively. "I'm just very tired."

McMillan gave her a sympathetic pat on the shoulder. "Superwoman is wearing down," he said good-naturedly. "Mother of the Year finds out she's merely human." His tone was more amused than critical.

"Something like that," Barbara acknowledged, shrugging. "Time to go."

"Hold it." McMillan caught her arm. "Before you slip out of here, I just want to give you something to think about. In regard to an earlier conversation we had about us being pals. I was watching you the other night after the play. I know there's a lot going on in your head, and some of it has to do with me. I just want you to know, our situation is flexible. And I can be very discreet. Pals can be lovers," he said without any equivocation. "And no one has to know."

Disconcerted, Barbara crossed her arms and glanced toward the loading ramp. "I really don't think this is the time—"

"Time is relative," he interrupted her. "Look, I know you're worried. But you're interested, and you have the right to do something about it. You're ready to step back into the real world, pal." He placed a hand on either shoulder and pulled her closer. "When you come back rested and sun bronzed, I'm going to be waiting for you. The first chance I get, I'm going to scoop you up into my arms and carry you off to my place. Then we'll have dinner and good wine." His lips were close to hers. "There'll be no running toilets, no kids, no chaperones. You can stop being a mother and give yourself a chance to be a woman again." His warm breath caressed her neck as he deliberately bypassed her mouth and placed a gentle kiss below her ear. "Have a safe flight. And think about me."

Barbara opened her mouth to protest, but she was totally disarmed by his frankness.

"We'll pick this up where we left off," McMillan beamed down at her. "Right now you'd better get on board. Your children are probably reporting you lost," he added and stepped back a few paces. "It isn't like you to be late."

"You can be such a smartass," Barbara responded, using one of T.J.'s favorite terms.

"Ah, the wench has spirit," McMillan teased her. "Beneath that serene exterior lurks the . . ."

Barbara didn't wait to hear the rest of it. With copper curls bouncing and her chin somewhat more elevated than usual, she turned into the loading tunnel toward the plane.

Moments later, she stared out at the landing field as the rumble of the engines intensified. Smoothly the plane moved onto the runway. The blue beacons outlining the dark surface were already lighted, although the sun had not yet quite set. It was that peculiar in-between time, where day and night were indistinct from each other and all the boundaries blurred.

Eliot and Miranda each claimed a window seat and sat with noses pressed against the glass. For them, this was a welcome adventure. For her, leaning limply against the tall reclining seat, it was a desperate attempt to regroup, to reassure herself that she would be all right.

Haunted. The word had surfaced in her consciousness a hundred times a day. *Haunted.* She had run out of explanations and excuses for the things that happened. She was tired and afraid and confused. "I want to go home," she sighed inwardly. "I just want to go home." Instead, she was leaving the only home she felt was hers. She was worn out from trying to be in control, when all the while, she knew she wasn't. She wanted to feel someone's arms enfold her and close out the world. Even with T.J. gone, she wanted that feeling again. And she felt guilty for wanting it.

"Hang on. Hang on." She fought back the tears. Wearily she let the acceleration of the plane press her back against the headrest. "I'm no loner," she lamented silently, closing her eyes and feeling as if somehow she had failed.

The words of Louis Belcazzio came back to her. *A big clutch at the end and it's happily ever after.* That's how it was supposed to be. A little sugar-coated, to be sure, Barbara admitted. But it at least had a comprehensible pattern. You knew when you got to the end.

Let me get to the end of this. Barbara breathed a silent prayer. *Just let me get through this.* Far to the west, the thick clouds were outlined in gold from the setting sun. Gradually the plane rose above them. She contemplated the faces of her children, silhouetted against the oval windows. For the first time in months, she felt like someone else was finally in charge, at least for the next hour. For a while, she was free. Little by little, the sky darkened. The steady roar of the jet engines eased away her cares and slowly stole away her consciousness.

* * *

Luster kept his back turned to the marsh to block the wind while he pulled the hand truck and a couple of short lengths of one-by-sixes out of the back of the truck. He'd wedged them between the gallon pots of ferns and the four larger pots of gardenias that he'd brought. He'd wrapped the gardenia branches in plastic sheeting to keep the buds from getting bruised in transit.

Luster hadn't planned on working at all for the nursery over Thanksgiving weekend, but Everett Pierce had said Mrs. A. had called before she left and requested something aromatic, something different, to replace the mums in the atrium. The gardenia bushes, full of creamy velvet-petaled flowers, would perfume the air and add a certain serenity before it was time to bring in the Christmas cedar and pots of poinsettias.

Everett Pierce had also said the young fellow, Kent, would be there to help with the lifting. Luster figured that delivering the plants himself would give him the opportunity to take a good look around the Ashcroft household inside and out. Despite the fact that both Eliot and Miranda had seemed to be in high spirits the weekend before the trip, Mrs. A. looked tense and tired and kept to herself the last few times when he dropped by. That wasn't like her, and it had him worried.

Kent met him in the front yard with the key that Mrs. A. had left with him, went inside first, and hurriedly pressed the buttons to disengage the Sonitrol security system. Luster stayed out on the stoop with the hand truck until Kent came back to get him.

"You go ahead and load up the old plants first," Luster directed, giving Kent the hand truck. "Jus' put them all out in front of the palmettos on the far side of the drive. I'll stake out the space, then I'll just be checking 'round the yard." He strolled outside again.

The trail of juniper ash had been totally absorbed into the grass and the part that crossed the walkway was washed or worn away, but he'd brought a fresh supply to replenish it. He made a brisk circuit of the premises, the trickle of ash from his watering can darkening the grass with each step. He paused only occasionally to rest his hand on the building and each of the large oaks. Each time, he felt a slight chill run up through his arm, like a hushed whisper, a warning that all was not as tranquil as he'd hoped. Once he completed the ash circle, he went back inside, checking room to room for his other precautionary measures. The string of garlic he'd given Mrs. A. before Halloween still hung in the kitchen. But none of the juniper berries he'd sprinkled about were evident anywhere.

"How's it comin'?" He paused at the atrium long enough to help Kent maneuver the second load of pots up over the door frame.

"No problem so far," Kent replied.

"Keep 'em rollin'. We'll sink 'em in and mulch 'em later. I'll come out and help you lift down the gardenias when you get this place emptied." Luster stood back and watched the young man wheel away the cartload of faded mums. He waited until he heard the outside door close before he moved down toward the bedrooms to check on the second set of juju bags he'd hidden there before Halloween.

The one under Eliot's mattress was intact. So was the one in Miranda's room. But he found no trace of the charmed pouch he'd poked between the mattress and the frame in Barbara's room. On hands and knees, he crouched low and groped under the bed, his leathery fingers spread wide. He swept back and forth in case the juju had worked loose and fallen onto the carpet. He was stretched partway under when he felt the peculiar movement of the covers against his arm and shoulder as a cool current of air glided by. Hurriedly, he scrambled to his feet and stepped out into the hall, guessing that the sudden shift in air meant Kent was returning and had opened the front door. But the young fellow was nowhere in sight, and there was no sound to suggest he was nearby.

Luster walked on toward the atrium, eyes narrowed, head cocked to the side. Then he stepped into the glass enclosure, planning to poke his fingers into several of the remaining corner pots to determine whether Sister Gertrude Kelly's little bags were there. He picked up one pot, turning it, trying to locate the bag. He shook loose some of the dark potting soil, making certain the juju bag hadn't been pushed below the surface during a watering. It wasn't there. He crossed diagonally to the next pot. No bag, nowhere. He tried the third, then the last corner pot. All gone. But as he stood alone in the glass-walled room, still holding one pot, Luster felt the chilled stream moving around him again, heavier and thicker than before. Within the cubicle, the leaves and flowers on the remaining plants all quivered, only for a few seconds. Luster puckered up his lips, trying to believe he'd just been imagining. The leaves shuddered again, then everything grew still. Slowly, the hairs on the back of his neck began to stand on end.

"I guess I'd better sweep this out before we move the new plants in," Kent said when he came back for the third and final load and looked at the water spots and soil spilled on the granite floor. "I'll get the broom from the garage."

"You go ahead here. I'll get the broom." Luster passed him the pot of flowers he was still holding, then left the rest for Kent to load. "I need to count the bags of mulch anyways, so's we're sure to have enough to winterize these mums." He strode off, head erect, pace even, pretending he'd noticed nothing at all.

The four bags of mulch he'd brought in the previous weekend were stacked near the outer door of the garage, just as he left them, one on top of the other in two stacks. Beyond them, where Mrs. A. usually set out things destined for the trash, was a bulging green garbage bag and two of the long boxes labeled curtain rods. Luster bumped one with his foot, wondering if he should go ahead and pitch it for her so she wouldn't have to do it when she got back. The discarded box felt heavy. He bent over and gave it a shake. Curious, he opened one end and saw the rod inside. The other similar box held a second rod. He nudged the bag. It felt soft. He hoisted it onto the bags of mulch so he could see better, then undid the twister.

The smell that arose was sweet and vaguely familiar, but Luster placed the melon-striped fabric immediately.

He'd seen it hanging in the study. But not lately, he realized, remembering the window was unobstructed the last few times he made his walk around. Reaching into the bag, Luster grabbed a fistful of the material and pulled it up into the light. The fabric spread out over his hand in wide strips, like a cluster of oversized ribbons. Using both hands now, he tugged out more, until the drapery was piled up around him. Most of it was cut into strips, all smelling curiously sweet and nutlike, with only the upper hem intact to indicate that it had once been whole.

Luster lifted the grass shears from the tool cupboard and clipped off a few strips of the fabric. Then he stuffed them inside his jacket pocket and put everything back the way it was. Broom in one hand, dustpan in the other, he stiffened his shoulders and stepped back inside.

"You was wise to come right on over here," Sister Gertrude Kelly declared, rocking back and forth with the same regular pace as Luster rocked in the facing chair. Between them, her old wood-burning stove sat giving off its thick, friendly heat. "It don't do no good to let on that you know what they've been up to." Her words floated across to him with a slight asthmatic wheeze. "Haunts like to get you all riled up. Makes 'em stronger." She rocked a while without saying a thing. She just closed her eyes and rubbed between her fingers and thumb the fabric pieces he'd brought, occasionally lifting a piece to sniff its scent. "Mean critters, haunts is. They laps up fear and gets fat on it. Fatter they gets, the meaner they gets." Her dark, birdlike hands rose up off the armrests, flourishing the fabric like small banners. "Takes real meanness to do this."

Luster said nothing.

"You felt it most in that plant room?" She leveled a look at him. "What you call that place?" She leaned forward, peering at him, slowing the pace.

"Ay-tree-yum." Luster nodded. "I felt it in there all right." He rubbed the back of his neck just thinking about the chill and the movement.

"Centermost in the house?"

Luster nodded.

"Then that's where it be best to do what we can do." She rocked on, eyes shut in contemplative silence, Luster rocking right along with her. After a long quiet spell, Sister Gertrude opened her eyes again. "I s'pect the reason nothin' has worked real good so far is 'cause this haunt gots a hold on somebody there. I s'pect somebody inside done left open the door. You gotta close the door on the dead."

Luster pressed his lips together, bobbing his head slightly, indicating he shared the same conviction.

"You guess it's the momma?"

Luster nodded. The charm bag under her bed was the only one missing. She was the one looking burdened. She'd put the rods back in place the last time. He figured that whatever happened this time, she had to be the one who packed up the ruined drapes and took down the rods and set them all out like they were trash. But she hadn't followed through and thrown them out.

"If she be opening the door all the time, or if she'd jus' not shuttin' it tight, haunts is goin' to keep comin' in an' out. She gotta' close the door here"—she tapped a finger on her temple—"and she gotta' close the door here"—She tapped her chest, just above her heart. " 'Specially dif'cult here." She tapped her chest again. "It ain't easy to harden your heart wif'out becoming hard yourself."

Luster lifted his brows, rocking all the while. "She sure ain't a hard lady. Soft. Real soft and nice. S'pose I better talk to her and find out jus' what's going on?" It was as much a statement as a question.

Sister Gertrude clucked her tongue. "No, no. Lordy, no. Fu'st off she'll think you as crazy as she must thinks she be. Second, you cain't say anything to her direct," she cautioned him. " 'Specially not 'round there. Only makes them stronger and more spiteful if they knows you talkin' 'bout them. Just opens the door more wide. Makes 'em come closer, makes 'em hang on tighter."

Luster didn't need to ask the conjur woman what could be done. She'd closed her eyes and was rocking faster, so he knew she was already thinking hard on that part. He clasped the armrests tightly, trying not to rush her.

"If you is gon'na say anything to her, you haf'ta get her to come away from there," Sister Gertrude spoke at last. "Somewhere where that partic'lar haunt won't go. So if it be her husband, or just a troublesome one pretending to be, you can't go anywhere it knows. And you sho' can't tell her why you want her to meet you, 'cause then you'll have opened the door yo'self and it will come along."

"Don't know what to do," Luster sighed. "Never had no dealin's with anything like this."

"Me neither. Not 'xactly. My momma taught me what I know. And I know we has to be real careful," the old conjur woman warned him. "You sho' cain't tell her that you know she's got a haunt there. Have to talk like it's just a story 'bout someplace else, so you won't make it more real. And you can't talk like it's a partic'lar somebody," Sister Gertrude stressed, "cause if you do, then it helps the haunt r'member who it was, and it helps it r'member all its old secrets, so's it can turn 'em back on her."

Luster shook his head glumly. "All we got is don't's and can't's. The missus and the chil'ren are gone off to Florida for two more days. Got the house open and a fella' workin' there now, 'spectin me to come back and help mulch some plants. Ain't there something we can do?"

"We'll do what we can do," Sister Gertrude assured him, wheezing between every few words. "But this one is nasty. Downright nasty. Won't make no never mind what we do if she come back and open the door again. You have to handle it jus' right and get her away from there and make her un'nerstand. She got's to harden her heart so's to keep from makin' it think she's invitin' it back. Rememberin' one that's died ain't the same as invitin' it back." Even in her own house far downcreek south from the Ashcrofts, Sister Gertrude was being very careful now to refer to whatever Luster had encountered only as a sexless, nameless "it" to avoid contributing to its power.

Luster clasped his hands together, tensing and untensing his long fingers anxiously. "What you want me to do in the meantime?"

The wispy old conjur woman stood and shuffled across the hardwood floor and disappeared behind her kitchen door. Luster waited. In a few moments she was back, wiping the dust off a squat glass jar with its grape jelly label still attached, only the contents now were a light-bluish, viscous substance. She handed him the jar and a small, short-bristled brush not much larger than a pencil. "I want you to paint a line around the inside of that garden room. All the way around," she told him, bent over, wrenlike, peering down at him.

Luster rotated the jar, watching the substance cling like glue to the sides. "What is this?"

"Special brew to make 'em waste away from crossing the line. Bird lime and berries, mostly, 'long with some other things. You has to go by the cemet'ry and scoop up some earth from the grave. Just a handful. Mix it in real good." She returned to her chair and resumed rocking. "You paint a little stripe 'round the inside of the garden room, cross ev'ry threshold, and up and 'round the door, and let it be. If it keeps sneaking back and hidin' in that room, this will make it weaker and weaker. Ev'ry time it crosses over, the line saps away its strength. 'Ventually it's too weak to cross. It gets stuck on one side or the other. Or it gives up and goes back where it belong." She waved her hand as if she were shooing away a pesky insect. "Then we can do somethin'. If it gets caught inside, we'll spell it till it's gone. If it get stuck outside the line, you move the line till it's all 'round the house outside, 'round the windows and the doors too. Then onc't it leave, if no one asks it back, it gets real weak and can't come in at all. Right now, it's too pow'ful to mess with straight on."

Luster rolled the jar again. "What if the missus sees the line and asks me what it is. What can I tell her?"

Sister Gertrude's round dark face creased into a smile framed in a web of wrinkles. "Jus' tell her it's to keep out 'dem household pests like you hear 'bout on the TV.

Ain't fa' from the truth. Ain't good to go fa' from de truth."

Luster returned to the house on Harborview, his truck tires skittering up the gravel drive. Kent Nelson was out by the palmetto bushes, shaking out the root-bound mums from the pots, then sinking them into holes, just as Luster had told him to do when he'd made his hasty exit almost an hour earlier. "Got everything cleaned up inside," Kent reported, coming to help unload the two extra bags of mulch that had been the old fellow's excuse for leaving abruptly. "I put the gardenia bushes and ferns inside, but I figured you would want to set them up where you want them so I haven't taken off the sheeting."

Luster nodded, trying not to show how tired he felt or how much he'd pressed to get the mulch and swing by the cemetery so he could get back as soon as he had. "You jus' keep on setting these in," he said, inclining his head toward the remaining mums, "and I'll go fuss around inside."

Bottle and brush in hand, the lanky nurseryman strolled off into the house. With the soil from the gravesite stirred in, the blue paint felt gritty with each stroke. Luster dipped and spread with the stubby-bristled brush, trying to control the tremble in his unsteady hand. All the while he half-expected the cool breeze to taunt him and show him he was not alone.

But nothing happened. Quickly he finished drawing the line along the lower edge of the room. Then he took it up and around the opening of the glass sliders. Standing back, he peered down, relieved to see that the first part, almost dry already, was barely noticeable. Once he'd slid the gardenia bushes into each corner, banked them in with a few potted ferns, then unwapped the sheeting from the branches, he figured no one would notice his rough artwork at all.

There was still over an inch of Sister Gertrude Kelly's paint left in the jelly jar. For the moment, he left the sliders open. Whistling determinedly, Luster headed for Miranda's room. He replaced her juju bag with the new one Sister Gertrude had given him, then he outlined her doorway with a thin blue streak. Still whistling, he moved on to do Eliot's room.

"Mr. Johns?" Kent called out just as he finished the second doorway. "I'm ready for the next step." Sweat-stained and flushed, the young man came around the corner of the atrium looking for him. "Mr. Johns?" He peered inside the atrium.

"Down here," Luster spoke out. "Just putting down some pest strip." The explanation came with surprising ease. "Almos' through."

Kent wiped his hands on the seat of his bluejeans and shifted feet. "You want me to do anything else outside while you finish up?"

"How 'bout you take the grass shears and cut off the tops of all the mums. Take 'em down to maybe two inches. Then go ahead and lay the mulch. Pack it good and thick. Keeps 'em snug all winter. I'll be right out."

Kent bobbed his head, then was gone again.

This time Luster tied the new juju to the frame of Barbara's bed so it couldn't fall away. He used the last of the paint and gave her a blue strip around her door. It wasn't precisely what Sister Gertrude had instructed, but he remembered feeling the cold draft in this room, not as strong as in the atrium, but present nevertheless. "Stay out of here, you no good pests. Find your own place to be." He said it aloud, hoping his voice held strong despite the tremor deep in his chest. Without looking left or right, whistling again, he strode down the hall and out into the bright November sunlight.

CHAPTER 5

> Love is like life . . . merely longer
> Love is like Death, during the Grave
> Love is the Fellow of the Resurrection
> Scooping up the Dust and chanting "Live"!
> *Emily Dickinson*

As soon as Barbara emerged from the disembarkation tunnel in Charleston, she spotted McMillan's gold hair above the group of people mingling at Gate 4. In his cream-colored cable-knit pullover and slacks, he stood out in the crowd of drab, tense winter travelers. Tanned and smiling, he looked typically at ease as he waited for her to work her way toward him. Eliot and Miranda strolled right past him, heading for the baggage pickup area.

"I thought I was supposed to get the suntan," she greeted him. "You look like the one who went to Florida."

"I was with you in spirit." He kissed her cheek as he relieved her of the canvas carry-on bag. "Actually I ran into an old buddy and we went deep-sea fishing. Froze my buns, but I got a lot of sun. I didn't want you to come back to find me pale and forlorn. You might think I was pining away in your absence." He stepped back and scrutinized her from head to toe. "You certainly look great." He softened the last word as Miranda and Eliot glanced back impatiently, waiting for the grownups to catch up.

"Basically, I loafed." Barbara waved the kids on and quickened her own step. "I ate, walked on the beach, sat in a lounge chair in the shade and read. I slept a lot. It was wonderful."

"Well, loafing sure produced some remarkable results. You look spectacular." His gaze had been riveted on her face, now it dropped and moved over her body.

By now Miranda and Eliot were stopped ahead, crowding around the horseshoe-shaped conveyor track that would bring the luggage out to them, jockeying for position closest to the ledge.

"Did you guys just loaf around, too?" McMillan asked as he and Barbara drew to a halt behind them.

"I fished with Grampa," Miranda glanced back over her shoulder at him. "I caught fish every day." Like her mother, her smooth skin was golden from the sun and wind.

"How about you, Eliot?" McMillan patted the young boy on the shoulder.

"I rode Gramma's bike," Eliot answered.

"Sounds like fun." McMillan nodded politely.

"Gramma's bike is an adult three-wheeler with five gears and hand brakes," Barbara explained. "Eliot put fifteen miles on the odometer the first day we were there."

"Then you *really* rode Gramma's bike." McMillan's tone was more impressed.

"That's what I said, sir." Eliot caught himself before his impatient reply eased into rudeness.

"Well, let's get the luggage and take you guys home." Barbara quickly intervened as the whirr and hum of machinery signaled that the belt was starting to move. Several duffle bags and some golf clubs came gliding out the opening. "That's us." Barbara pointed to the first of their suitcases, wedged with several others farther back on the conveyor track. "Grab it and step back," she urged the kids along. "School tomorrow, for all of us," she added pointedly, for McMillan's benefit as well as theirs.

McMillan chuckled and moved along beside her, grasping the handle of the suitcase she was reaching for, close enough that his upperarm brushed her shoulder. "Don't worry, I'm just here as the chauffeur tonight," he whispered. "I'm not going to put any moves on you, lady."

Miranda fell asleep on the way home from the airport. McMillan carried her straight down to her room, then helped Barbara deposit the baggage in the foyer. While she flicked on the lights in the remaining bedrooms and started Eliot working on getting ready for bed, McMillan waited just inside the kitchen entry.

"Thanks for everything," Barbara said when she came back from the bedroom wing.

"My pleasure. I'll call you tomorrow. Nice to have you back." He clasped her hands, kissed the back of her fingers, and left. Relieved and somewhat surprised by his accommodating attitude, she wandered back down the hall, hurried Eliot on to bed, unpacked her suitcase, and avoided the den and study wings completely until the house was quiet and the two youngsters were sleeping.

"Well, I'm back," she said softly as she finally backtracked down the hall into the apricot study. She didn't bother to turn on the lights. There was illumination enough from the moonlight, pouring in unobstructed on all sides. "If you're still here, I just want you to know that I'm back for good. You've frightened me. I may even be a little crazy, but I'm no quitter." In the darkened room, she passed from one piece of furniture to the next, trailing her fingertips over each object as if she were making contact with an old friend.

"I don't know what you want with me or why you've been doing the things you've done, but I'm stronger now." Her voice wavered only slightly as she delivered the speech she had thought through while she was gone. "This is my home and my children's home. If you are still here, T.J., then I'll try to let you off the hook for what went on before." She took a deep breath. "But even if it isn't you, let's make our peace now. You have to stop. I'm not going to cave in. I'll get through this. Whatever happens, you have no right to invade my life. You have no right to manipulate me." Barbara stood in the center of the dim room, speaking solemnly into the dark corners. Her slim form, small and erect, was encircled by the computer paraphernalia and T.J.'s drafting table, her heavy desk, the loveseat and glass worktable, all lifeless occupants of the house she loved. "You have no right," she spoke in clear, clipped words. "So don't try anything." Without any further comment, just as she'd rehearsed it in her mind, calmly she turned and walked away.

* * *

"They've started work on the new theater." Barbara was doodling on the notepad as she spoke to Rob Johnstone on their first December Sunday call.

The Sunday calls had become a necessary interlude in her usual routine. Rob didn't tiptoe around difficult issues. He didn't expect her to be clever or amusing. He just talked about whatever interested him, and she did the same. Their conversations were often erratic and disjointed, but the exchanges supplied something for both of them. And it was easier than talking with Karen and Louis. They were here. They would watch her with wide, kind eyes and listen carefully as she spoke.

With Rob, it was easier. It was comfortable. He didn't back down—and he didn't crowd her. And when she was finished, she could simply say goodbye. There were no eyes examining her expression, no questioning of her motives or feelings. Her privacy was intact.

"They're dismantling the interior and getting ready to do some reroofing," she reported, "so I can't really say it's actually under construction, just that something is going on down there."

"That's great. From what you said about the location, it should add a new twist to the downtown cultural life." Rob's enthusiasm lifted her spirits. It had drizzled the entire week since she'd returned from her Florida retreat, and she missed the sunshine.

"How long will the renovation process take?" Rob asked. The theater had been one project that had captured the interest of both T.J. and Rob—for varied but complementary reasons. On one of Rob's earlier visits, after T.J. had led them all on a waterlogged tour of the building site of the Ashcrofts' new house-in-progress, they returned to their present home to dry off. While Barbara oversaw the towel drying and reclothing of Eliot and Miranda, Rob and T.J. moved into the dining room. Fortified with cups of hot coffee by the fireplace, they spread out the blue-lined sketches for one of T.J.'s proposals—the one that would replace the dilapidated interior of a once-beautiful old Charleston single house with an experimental theater. Charleston and the College needed another performing facility. Starting from the ground up would be unfeasible financially. But when this house went on the market, several alumnae put together the funds to buy it. It was T.J.'s job to try to make it functional.

"McMillan has charge of the project now," Barbara noted. "He thinks it may take four or five months . . . March, maybe April," she estimated.

"That long?" Rob quizzed her. "I'd have thought interior work would go fast in this cold weather."

"Normally it would. But the agreement with the College was that student labor would be used. All the stagecraft majors are involved. T.J. took to heart what you said about giving the students in the theater department solid, physical experience in construction." T.J. had talked to Rob at length that night, listening to his suggestions and picking up details from a performance perspective. Then he had backed off and let everything jell. The revisions would be expensive, T.J. had noted at the time.

"So it's my fault," Rob joked.

"Maybe so, but I think you deserve some credit as well." Barbara scratched a few more lines on her asymetrical drawing. "Student labor was the edge they needed to get the project accepted costwise. McMillan and the contractor will have to meet with the student workers to see what kind of actual skills they have. If they're talented, things will move along quicker than that."

"What about restoring the exterior?" Rob continued. "How much student labor goes into that?"

"That depends on the students." Barbara shaded in part of her drawing. "McMillan said that within a couple of days on the site everything will fall into place. The students with talent will emerge. The ones who make good gofers will be familiar enough with the routine to do the backup work. And the contractor will know who to trust for what part of the job. They'll have to fill the gaps with regular construction workers throughout the entire process. But McMillan will try to keep a lid on the high-paid manpower required."

"Sounds like they're giving the students some incredible experience in destruction, construction, and innumerable other things," Rob said. Barbara smiled at the intensity of his interest as he spoke. "I'd love to get some of my students in on a project like this." He suddenly shifted focus. "Do you think it will be finished by Spoletime? When is the festival this year? Late May?"

"No one is promising anything yet," Barbara replied. "The College is being cautious about committing it to use until they're sure how the work is proceeding. The word is maybe it will be ready by Spoletime," she said quietly. "They aren't saying much around me." She didn't have to explain her last statement. Everyone involved with the theater had been discreet about discussing the renovation in Barbara's presence, since the project originally had been T.J.'s. But more than that, they all knew he'd been drawn into it through Barbara's commitment to the festival. She had been active as a volunteer worker for the children's activities connected with the Spoleto U.S.A. Festival for several years, partly because of her interest in the arts, but also because the Spoleto Festival was when she and T.J. met. She was the one who got him interested enough in the theater to help out.

Barbara loved Spoletime. She loved what it brought to her children, to herself, and to her community. So she volunteered, along with hundreds of others, mailing out flyers, phoning friends and businesses for financial support, proofreading playbills, even arranging accommodations for the multitude of student and professional performers who would come in each May. The three-week festival of arts filled historic Charleston's theaters, churches, parks, and streets with art and entertainment. The event brought singers, actors, musicians, dancers, and artists and craftmen of skill and distinction from all across America and from abroad. Locals and tourists flooded the streets seeking inspiration and enrichment. Drawing on its own facilities and people, Charleston let time stand still for this artistic celebration.

When she started back to teaching, Barbara enlisted the aid of students in the festival, recruiting them to man exhibits, hand out information sheets at street activities, and serve as guides. Even her "throwbacks" got involved. When she turned to them expectantly with jobs that needed doing, they didn't let her down. T.J. hadn't let her down either. He went along with her and the children to parks and outdoor shows. Evenings he attended other performances with her and their grownup friends. Finally caught up in her enthusiasm, he contributed his time and money, just to keep that light in her eyes.

Now everyone was cautious, waiting to see if this year that glow that Spoletime inspired would return to her.

"I suppose you have all your students lined up on committees this year," Rob commented deliberately.

"Nothing specific yet," Barbara replied vaguely. "There's still plenty of time."

"Maybe it is a bit early for that," Rob conceded. "You've got your hands full just getting ready for Christmas."

"Yes, Christmas," Barbara said softly. "We're getting the decorations down this week." Her sentence fell flat, mere fact without elaboration.

"That might be a pretty emotional time for all of you," Rob sympathized, guessing how she may be dreading all the preparations this year. "Lots of memories there. I'm sure this first one without T.J. will be pretty shaky for all of you." He listened to the long silence.

"I have to send off Christmas cards," Barbara's tone was reserved and preoccupied. Solemnly she placed her pencil atop the completed doodle and pushed them both aside. Again there was a long silence.

"If it starts to close in on you, Bobbie, I could come up for a weekend," Rob spoke at last. If Barbara wanted him there, he would have shifted plans accordingly. "Or maybe you should spend this Christmas with your folks. You could even fly over to Lauderdale and spend a couple of days with me. Perhaps the impact of all the change would be less awesome from a distance."

"I can't keep running away from home. I'm a big girl now. I just spent Thanksgiving with my folks," Barbara reminded him.

"But these are not normal circumstances. A few days with your folks and your kids may not have been enough of a break for you, Bobbie. You could do with some real time off—all to yourself, without an audience," Rob stressed. "If you left the kids with your folks, both parties would be content, and you could come here alone. From Sarasota we're talking thirty minutes by plane. I've got plenty of room, during the daytime I'll be working on a play with my students, so I won't be underfoot."

Barbara said nothing.

"You think it over." His usually gentle voice was firm. "Spend Christmas with them and come here by yourself for New Year's."

"Let me think about it," Barbara replied. "I have friends here. There will be lots of get-togethers. It may not be so bad."

"Not so bad isn't good enough," Rob said flatly. "The offer is open. Come if you choose."

"Thanks. I'll let you know." Suddenly she was anxious to get off the telephone. It was almost as if she had intended only to replenish something but had taken on more than she'd planned.

"Call you next week," Rob concluded. "Give my love to the kids."

"Talk to you then," Barbara agreed and placed the telephone back in its cradle. She stood there a moment staring at the drawing she had made, of a slender, slightly unbalanced version of a tree much like Keats, who stood beyond the kitchen window, gray and damp in the winter drizzle. She had drawn in extra branches and flourishes and floated circles among the leaves. Like Christmas ornaments, she observed.

"No sense putting this off," Barbara said with a sigh. With her mouth set in a firm line she proceeded to the hallway near the den, where a pull-down stairway led upwards to the attic.

"Christmas cards," she breathed aloud as she pulled the cord and drew the stairway down. Somewhere upstairs, amid boxes of Christmas tree lights and tissue-wrapped balls, there would be a box of cards diligently selected and purchased in the post-Christmas sales the year before. "From Barbara, Miranda, and Eliot." She rehearsed the revised notation each card must bear. "This really is tough, T.J." She steeled herself as she grabbed the railings on the wooden ladder and began her climb into the dim attic.

Below, the slam of the kitchen door echoed through the house as Eliot and Miranda returned from their afternoon expedition in the woods. "We found a friend for Henry!" Miranda squealed.

"Hey Mom, where are you?" Eliot called.

"In the attic," Barbara called down. "How about bringing me the flashlight?"

"I found a cricket," Miranda yelled up at Barbara

"Wonderful. Where is it?"

"In the kitchen," Miranda replied proudly. "In a jar on the counter."

"Not any more," Eliot announced as he returned with the flashlight in his gloved hand. "You forgot to put a lid on it, dummy. It's hopping around on the floor." Miranda disappeared with a shrill wail. Eliot proceeded up the ladder and delivered the flashlight.

"Dummy." He shook his head as Miranda's distant wail turned to sobs.

"Now, Eliot," Barbara cautioned him. "She was too excited to think about a lid. Go calm her down and tell her I'm getting down the Christmas stuff. Maybe she'll cheer up."

"What about the cricket?" Eliot demanded as he poked his hand into a box of electric lights.

"Forget the cricket," Barbara groaned. "It will show up sooner or later. Right now, get the little kid with the big tears calmed down and then bring her back and help me with these boxes."

Eliot shrugged and climbed down the ladder. Beneath his breath, he muttered something that sounded much like dummy.

"Eliot," Barbara growled.

"I'm going," he answered, "Mother."

On hands and knees, Miranda was creeping about the kitchen, making the same clicking sound that usually got Henry to trill. "He's probably not as smart as Henry. He doesn't know enough to answer," Eliot informed her. Then he looked at her reddened nose and tear-stained face. "He's probably scared and hiding. Just give him some time to get settled and he'll start making noise. When he does, we'll jump him."

Sniffing to herself, Miranda kept up her dogged inspection, peering under counter ledges.

"Come on. Give him a break. He's scared. Mom is getting down the Christmas stuff. She wants us to help." He stood watching her.

"I just want to find him." Miranda crept around, with her chin barely missing the floor.

"Mom will be mad if you don't come and help. Just let the cricket go for now. He'll show up. Maybe he'll hear Henry and go down and find him all by himself."

"You think he'd do that?" Miranda sat back on her heels, looking up at him hopefully. "Maybe I should bring Henry down here."

"Maybe you'd better," Eliot glanced cautiously toward the center of the house. "Remember that stuff Mr. Johns put around the atrium? You know, that sticky line of bug killer? You wouldn't want the stupid cricket to get into that."

"What should I do?"

"You get Henry. I'll scrape off the goo," Eliot suggested. "Just don't tell Mom." He rummaged through the utensil drawer for a blunt-end spatula. "Go on, get Henry and put him in here. And maybe you should sprinkle a little sugar on the floor like we put nuts out for the squirrels," he added as he hurried out the kitchen door.

"Eliot? Miranda?" Barbara's voice came from the opening in the ceiling.

"Be right with you, Mom," Eliot answered, shooing Miranda on to her room. For the moment, he put the tool down by the atrium door. He'd shuttle boxes until Miranda finished her part. Once she got Henry in place, he'd get rid of that line.

"I've put this off as long as I can," Barbara muttered as she spread stamps, two pens, several snapshots of the kids taken in Florida, her address book, and the closed box of Christmas cards across the tabletop. Outside, Miranda had lined up several of her dolls against Byron's convoluted roots and was busily setting out small dishes for a tea party. Clad in sweatshirts, Eliot and his buddy Billie Hobach were swinging on knotted ropes, performing serial stunts for the audience of dolls.

Ashcroft, Ben. Barbara began with T.J.'s brother and his family in Oregon. This year's cards had a little cedar in the snow, its branches hung with pinecones and berries, its base surrounded by squirrels and birds. "Looks like our Christmas lineup," T.J. had said when he picked up the box from the sale table the year before. When they bought their first house in Charleston—years before the new house was even a blueprint, before the overgrown lot on the point had been purchased—T.J. had started a tradition of purchasing a living Christmas tree from a nursery, with roots wrapped and ready for planting. It would spend the holidays inside with the Ashcrofts. But right after Christmas, they would move it outside to be planted in the soil next to its fellow trees.

Barbara stared at the solitary little tree on the card. Seven such cedars in varying heights lined the southern front of their lot, all but the last uprooted and moved to this location under Luster Johns's careful direction. Six were there when only the oaks and shrubs and the surveyors' stakes shared the property. Last year, the first Christmas in the new house, the seventh tree sat in the atrium, then joined the others outside—like the family, relative newcomers. This year, without T.J., all the traditions would have to be carried on.

Gingerly Barbara lifted off the plastic cover of the card box and slid the first card from the stack. When she flipped it open to read its inscription, it bore the simple wish—Peace.

Ashcroft, Ben. Barbara concentrated on the address as she willed away her tears. She had dreaded this ritual, this sending of good wishes to distant friends and relatives. But one had to go on, she reminded herself, sounding more and more like her mother. She had to take charge of the rest of her life—one step at a time.

She had signed and slipped the first card into its envelope and licked it closed before she noticed the folded piece of drafting paper that lay on top of the next envelope. She lifted the folded paper, opening it slowly. The words on the paper were half written, half printed in fine-line ink, unmistakably in T.J.'s scratchy penmanship.

"Who says I'm not romantic?" it began. Then he had printed one her favorite poems, a sonnet by Elizabeth Barrett Browning that began "How do I love thee? Let me count the ways." Barbara read each line intently, with a half smile forming on her lips, until she reached the final lines.

I love thee with the breath,
Smiles, tears, of all my life!— and, if God choose,
I shall but love thee better after death.

She read and reread the last lines, seeing them differently than she ever had before. Then her eyes shifted uneasily from the paper to the open box of cards. It was her job to send the cards out each Christmas. She'd often teased T.J. about not being particularly romantic. He'd apparently wanted to surprise her, so he must have slipped the note in the cards the previous year when they put away all the Christmas paraphernalia. He knew she would be the one to open up the cards and write the messages on them. She lifted up the box, sniffing for some trace of his cologne. There was none.

The note had been left here last year, Barbara reassured herself. Nothing more. It wasn't starting again.

Gently she pressed the note against her chest and took a long breath. "Thank you, T.J.," she whispered for the message from the past. Resolutely, she put the note aside and continued with the cards. This time, her eyes lingered on the single word within. *Peace.* "Just what I need." She smiled ruefully, then flipped through to the next address on her list.

From time to time as she wrote brief notes and signed the cards, her hand would rest on the creased paper that had been hidden away from her. Then the message would filter through her mind, intermingling with other thoughts. *I shall but love thee better after death.* The words pushed their way into her consciousness. Then would come the reassuring chorus. *Peace. Peace.*

* * *

"Is this really where you want it, Mrs. A.?" Kent Nelson asked as he held the central shaft of the little cedar tree in one hand. His other hand, clad in T.J.'s weathered leather gardening glove, supported the burlap-wrapped roots. Under Miranda's direction, Kent had carried the tree into the den, to the far end of the room, well away from the heat of the fireplace. They'd bypassed the atrium, where T.J. had placed it the year before, knowing it could be seen from every room, so Kent questioned its current destination.

"The kids want it in here this year," Barbara explained, guessing what Kent was thinking. "This is where they spend the most time. This will be fine." Barbara tugged off her kid gloves and stuffed them into her jacket pocket. Then she spread out some newspapers so Kent could rest the tree on the edge of the pool table for the time being. "Eliot," she called toward the hallway. "Bring the box in here quickly, please!" She flinched as erratic thumping sounds preceded her son.

"Sorry, Mom." Eliot apologized in advance for whatever scratches and dents he was making along the way. Finally he turned into the den doorway, dragging the Christmas tree box into view. The two-foot-square green box with rather tarnished brass fittings was a find T.J. had resurrected from an old townhouse garden. He had stripped and repainted it, lined it with heavy polyurethane so it wouldn't leak, and had the fittings dipped in brass so it looked appropriately festive for holding their cedar tree each year.

"Families need traditions. This is something with a bit of history behind it," T.J. had declared, pleased with his results. However, this year they were departing slightly from several traditions T.J. had begun. This year, their cedar tree would not stand in the heart of the house— the glass-walled garden room. Instead, Barbara had asked Luster Johns to bank the atrium with pots of red poinsettias and put a garland of holly around the outside. There was no use pretending anything was like it had been the previous December, their first Christmas season in the new house. Then the paint had not been completely dry in the bedrooms and some carpet still had to be installed. The garden room had glowed with Christmas lights, great wreaths hung over the fireplaces, and the house had smelled of cedar, pine, and bayberry when the warm air circulated throughout the wings of the structure. This year, the memories were too close, too painful, so a few changes had to be made. Moving the tree was a quiet but significant one.

"Put the box here," Barbara directed her son. "Hurry, before Kent's arm wears out."

"I'm all right," Kent insisted, refusing to acknowledge the strain from holding the balled cedar upright. He shifted his grip. In his blue and white jacket with the varsity basketball letter neatly stitched on the right chest, Kent looked taller and more muscular than Barbara had noticed before. Newly turned seventeen, he was losing his adolescent gangliness. In deference to Kent's steadfastness, she overlooked the tremble in his arms as he steadied the lacy tree.

"Let me give you a hand." Barbara grabbed one side of the box and helped move it into place.

"I'm doing the best I can," her son defended himself.

"I wasn't criticizing. You're doing just fine. That's it." She stood back and sighed. "Now for the landing." She helped Kent aim the cloth-bound root ball into the box. The pretty cedar slowly listed to one side.

"It's crooked." Miranda's voice came from behind them. She'd been helping Luster move seventeen pots of poinsettias into the space vacated by the gardenias.

"Don't worry. Kent and I will pack wood chips around it." Barbara refused to sound discouraged. "It will be perfect. You guys bring in the box of lights. Kent can get the cedar chips from Mr. Johns," she directed them, eyeing the tree. "Go." Kent, Miranda, and Eliot wandered off in single file towards the hallway, leaving her momentarily alone.

"This is more than a little grim, Bozo," Barbara muttered. She bit her lower lip as she struggled to correct the angle of the pretty little tree. Getting it home and set up each year had been T.J.'s job. He'd take the kids to the nursery, pick out the tree, bring it in, and stand it up in place, ready for decorating. Barbara's duties in the procedure were the indoor ones. She tested the lights to see which ones needed replacing. She unwrapped the ornaments, located hooks, and set out the boxes in the order they would be used. Once the tree was in place, T.J. orchestrated each progressive level of decorating—lights, ornaments, holly garlands, candy canes, bows, tinsel—so nothing was out of sequence. But Barbara was the artistic director who kept stepping back to make sure everything balanced and no angle was overlooked. This year there was no division of labor. Everything was her responsibility.

"Mother, Miranda is crying again," Eliot reported. His pale face was barely visible behind the boxes of green-wired lights he was carrying.

Barbara glanced over her son toward Kent, who followed with a sack of cedar chips from Luster's truck. "Can you guys work on lining up the tree for now and let me have a little time with Miranda?" she asked softly. The previous night, Miranda had wept at the sight of the closed boxes labeled "Christmas" all lined up at the den door. Tonight, the boxes were open. All the memories, like ornaments packed away in tissue and foam, would be unwrapped and brought into the present.

"We'll take care of the tree," Kent sounded confident. "Maybe we can even get the lights strung on it. Once we get them set up and turned on, Miranda will feel better." He gave a hopeful shrug.

"Maybe." Barbara eased past him. "Thanks, you two." Outside in the hall by the boxes, Miranda was indeed crying again. Clasping the tiny wooden Snoopy and Charlie Brown, two of her special ornaments, she crouched beside the box with cardboard dividers that housed the small, handpainted decorations they'd collected over the years. Beyond her, barely visible within the steamy glass walls of the atrium, Luster Johns moved back and forth arranging the new plants in tiers.

"Daddy left a lot of reminders," Barbara murmured, kneeling beside the little girl. "He left us lots of things to let us know how much he loved us and how much fun he was." Carefully, Barbara unwrapped the Raggedy Ann and Andy ornaments.

"Look at these." She lay them in Miranda's lap. "You were only two when we got these."

Miranda looked at them and sniffed.

"And Winnie the Pooh," Barbara continued, fumbling amid the paper, "and Tigger too." She raised a second creature triumphantly. "And here's Garfield." Miranda slowly nodded.

"It's okay to cry, Miranda." Barbara hugged the youngster. "You miss Daddy. You will always miss Daddy. But when you see things that remind you of him, if you look carefully, under all that sadness, you'll find a little smile, a tiny happy memory that will always be there, too. Like the time Daddy dropped Snoopy in his hot chocolate. Or when Eliot had bronchitis and Daddy wrapped him in blankets and rolled him in on his wagon so he could help decorate. Remember that?"

Miranda nodded her head.

"How about the time we popped all that popcorn and made strings with cranberries to put on the trees outside. And all the birds came." Barbara rocked Miranda back and forth, patting the sobbing child until her slender body no longer trembled with grief.

"Kent and Eliot are doing the lights," Barbara finally spoke. "Maybe we could whip up a little spiced tea and cookies and take a break. Then we'll do a little work on the tree." The suggestion was received with a slow nod. Hand in hand, the twosome proceeded toward the kitchen.

When Barbara came in the den to get the boys, the tree was standing straight, already strung with several strings of tiny lights. Kent had just plugged them in to take a look. All the red ones seemed to occupy one side of the tree. It wasn't quite the sight to cheer up Miranda.

"Time out. You guys come on into the kitchen," she summoned them away. "Let's just switch off the lights and leave it like that for now. We can finish it later."

Eliot turned to launch an indignant protest but halted when Barbara raised a threatening finger to hush him. "Miranda's having a rough time with this. I think we'd better switch to something else for now. How about helping Mr. Johns with the wreaths?"

"I wanted to do the tree tonight."

"So did I," Barbara said simply. "But putting together the wreaths is important, too. Mr. Johns needs someone to operate the glue gun."

Eliot narrowed one eye suspiciously.

"I don't want Miranda left out of decorating the tree. Maybe by tomorrow she'll feel more like helping."

Eliot wrinkled up his nose.

"I have cookies waiting. But how about me throwing in a grilled cheese sandwich for both of you?" Barbara embellished the peace offering.

At last Eliot grinned. "Come on, Kent." He grabbed his tall companion by the hand. "Food."

Luster Johns declined the cheese sandwich, but he sat munching cookies with Miranda out under Byron while the boys ate theirs indoors. Then he took out his thermos and filled his cup.

"You should come out to my place. See my angels. Got four of 'em done now," Luster told the little girl. He'd been looking for a chance to talk to her momma, but there was always someone about, and he couldn't say what he wished to say. Today, delivering the cedar tree and the poinsettias, he'd been inside and had seen that the strip of pale blue was gone from under the atrium door and across the base of the children's doorways. He'd been worried ever since. Even when Eliot told him there was a "wild cricket" loose in the house and admitted that he and Miranda had peeled off the strips, Luster still wasn't sure what he should do. Last time, he'd used up every drop of the paint Sister Gertrude Kelly had given him. That meant another trip to her house and then to the cemetery for a scoop of earth from the grave. And with the small cricket still wandering about somewhere, he'd have to convince the children it would only stick to the line, it wouldn't die, so they'd leave the strip in place.

Meanwhile, along with the cedar tree and the poinsettias, Luster had brought a number of special twigs and vines from the woods and backcreek to weave into the sweetgrass wreaths that his daughter had made for each of the outside doors. He had mountain ash and mistletoe for good luck and protection. Cattails for peace, and white heather from the nursery to ward off danger. At first the Missus wasn't sure when he showed her the drab-colored wreaths, but then he'd shown her how to wrap the vine and add the cornhusk flowers that Sister Gertrude dried and dyed the same peach colors as the carpets inside. He brought clusters of holly berries, a deep orange instead of the usual red, and beautiful dried and waxed oak leaves. He told her to look up the plants in the book from the nursery that T.J. had kept with his *Farmer's Almanacs*, and she'd see what each one meant.

Sister Gertrude said the magic would be strongest if the family put the wreaths together with their own hands. So Luster had apologized for not assembling them, saying his arthritis had been acting up.

It wasn't far from the truth. Sister Gertrude warned him not to stray far from the truth, not with haunts listening in. But with the damp cold closing in lately on winter afternoons, Luster truly had aches and pains enough to slow him down plenty. Working out by the woodshed on the fourth angel one night the past week, he'd felt a stillness creep over his body, slowing him so that he thought it was his final call. He'd been singing along while he worked, "Looked over Ju'salem and wa' did I see, comin' fo' to carry me home . . . Ban' of angels, comin' after me . . ."

Then the stillness set in. The spirit was near. Not one of the petty, mean spirits that pestered folks. Not a haunt. This was the peaceful one, the great one, the one he recognized when it chose to reach out to him. He'd stood still, listening, and scared in a way, but ready to go if it was his time. But instead, while he listened, he knew four was not enough.

"Mor' angels," he acknowledged, sighing and smiling to himself. The old year was coming to a close. He'd been avoiding Everett Pierce's back shed at the nursery, half expecting if he'd touch one of the uncut trunks of wood Everett was saving for him, he'd see in it his own likeness, a sure sign that death was near. But it wasn't that way at all. He had more angels to do. At least two. So he stood shivering with the cold, gave his thanks for the notice, then put away his tools and went in for the night. No need to rush. There was plenty of time. Four was not enough. If the angels were comin', they weren't comin' for Luster Johns just yet.

"Hot glue gun is ready," Eliot called out now from the kitchen door, eager to bring Luster and Miranda inside again. Kent passed them in the entry as he left for home. In the kitchen, Barbara had all six wreaths set out along the counter, each with its equally alloted portion of berries, leaves, and vines ready to assemble. Luster saw she'd found T.J.'s book, *Folklore and Symbolism of Plants*. It was closed and set aside on the table, so he knew she'd been checking his choices.

"Fust and fo'most, twist the vines all 'round so all the ends connect. Careful not to prick yo' fingers." Luster talked them though each step. He moved from wreath to wreath, looking over their shoulders, as Miranda and Barbara held the pieces in place and Eliot squeezed dollops of hot glue to anchor them. But Luster was careful not to touch them.

When all six were completed, he glanced out the kitchen windows. The sky outside was dark, and he knew it wasn't good luck to hang a charm by moonlight. "Jus' put 'em inside the doors for the night. I'll drop by tomorrow with some wire and hooks and help you hang 'em when the sun's up. But for tonight, jus' in case there's spirits about, these will keep 'em from poking their nose in here." He broached the subject carefully. "Spirits get real peculiar when it's a special time, like Christmas, when everyone gets real soft, real sentimental. They get meddlesome. Tha's what the holly berries are best for, keeping off the mean spirits." He watched Barbara's face for some reaction, but saw none, not one opening that would suggest she was picking up the significance in what he said. But she sent the children off in relays, carrying the wreaths to their respective locations—front entry, den, her bedroom, both sides of the study, and the garage.

"Tomorrow," he reminded her as he packed up the residue from their wreath making, "I'll be back bright and early." Miranda came trudging along after him, helping carry the plastic sacks of leftovers out to the back of the truck.

"Mr. Johns, is there anything you know that would make a cricket stop hiding? I put out some sugar but it didn't work. I even carried Henry around trying to get them to talk to each other. But Henry won't sing unless he's in my room."

"You jus' leave Henry happy where he is. And don' you worry 'bout that lost cricket. He'll get found," he told her. "Tomorrow I'll bring some of that sticky stuff and we'll put it all around. And this time, you leave it be," he scolded her good-naturedly. "If that little fella' step in it, he'll be held right still like Bre'r Rabbit and the Tar Baby. We'll find him." He patted her on the shoulder and glanced back at the house. Beyond the kitchen wildflowers set aglow by the lights inside, he could see Barbara moving about in the kitchen, apparently fixing a late supper.

"I want you to get your momma to bring you out to see the angels," he said quietly. "They so pretty and sweet. One of 'em looks quite a bit like you."

"But aren't you going to put them out at the nursery?"

"Not these. These stay at home, till I hear otherwise."

Miranda puckered her lips. "Is it far where you live?"

"Not too far for a visit. Specially not if you like visiting angels. I got some other ones you might like, too. Soon's you can get your momma to take a little drive, you come see." He tried to temper the urgency he felt with some old-fashioned bribery. "My daughter Mattie always has a batch of something sweet just waiting for tastin'."

"Maybe one day after school."

"You jus' tell me when." He reached in his pocket and handed her a hard, round seed the size of a marble. "This is to make your room smell pretty."

Miranda lifted it and sniffed. "Mmmmm. Smells like cookies."

"Nutmeg. Makes me think of Mattie's bakin'. You take it in and put it in a safe place in your room." He looked up again at the brightly lit house. "You better help your momma get the dinner, young'un. And you gotta help her get the house all pretty for Christmas.

Good things are comin' but you gotta help 'em come. Go." He hurried her on her way.

Back home, Mattie and his grandson Willie Dodd would be wondering what was keeping him so late, and it would be later still before actually he got there. He had to pass the cemetery, then pay a call on Sister Gertrude before he could eat his own dinner and go out and visit his angels.

"Least we got the wreaths all done," he said wearily as he tugged closed the truck door. He just needed to bring wire and hooks so they could hang them. "Tomorrow." He turned on the key, and drove off. He didn't see the patch of dark liquid on the ground where his pickup had been standing. He pulled out easy, hardly using the brakes at all.

The fugitive cricket chirped sometime after midnight.

"Go back to sleep," Barbara moaned. Her request was answered by another serenade from the refugee insect. Loud. Rude. Insistent.

"Oh, be quiet," Barbara breathed. The persistent creature replied with a volley of enthusiastic chirps.

"Okay, okay—you asked for it." She rolled over and sat upright in bed. From the glow in the hallway, she could tell the children's bathroom lights were on. The cricket let loose another round. Barbara shoved her arms into T.J.'s robe and padded, barefoot, toward the door. Farther down the hallway coming from the atrium, there was another glow, rosy and vaguely familiar.

Against the glass doors leading into the atrium, Miranda lay curled up in the quilt she had apparently dragged from her bed. Inside the garden room, surrounded by the poinsettias, with petals like bright tongues of flame, stood the little cedar tree, precisely where it had been the year before, its lacy branches illuminated with tiny lights.

"Oh my . . ." Barbara stared at the tree, standing erect with its lights aglow. She looked at the small child bewilderedly, knowing Miranda could not have moved the tree and the heavy box it was sitting in from the den to the atrium. Quickly she lifted the sleeping child, quilt and all, and returned her to her bed. "Please don't start again," she murmured as she spread the large quilt over Miranda's curled-up body. Then she headed back to the atrium. With a soft swoosh, she slid open the glass doors and stepped into the warm, humid enclosure to turn off the lights.

"I don't understand," she barely whispered as she stood inspecting the tree. No longer were the red lights all clustered on the one side as they had been when they'd left off decorating. Now all the colored bulbs were rearranged and distributed evenly throughout the branches. Beneath one bough, a solitary ornament caught the light—the tiny Alice in Wonderland T.J. had bought her for their first Christmas together. Afterwards, he had given her others: the White Rabbit, the Cheshire Cat, the Mad Hatter. But Alice had been the first because it reminded him of her.

Barbara bent down to inspect little Alice.

"T.J.?"

What began as a sigh became instead an inquiry. She reached out to touch the ornament. It trembled and pirouetted in the glow of the little lights.

Abruptly from one corner of the atrium came a cricket's chirp. Barbara bolted upright, unnerved by the sudden sound. Behind her the glass doors slid closed.

"You know I can't stand being closed in. I don't like this kind of weirdness, T.J.," she said flatly. "You're scaring me. You're going to drive me crazy." She turned slowly in the room, peering beyond the light of the tree into every corner. There was no sound or movement in response. "Look, if you want the tree here, you can have the tree here. If it means that much to you, have it your way. But don't drag the kids into this. And don't do things I can't explain."

Her knees trembled but she fought the urge to retreat. "Now I'm going to turn off the lights and go back to bed. I want this to be the end of it. T.J., enough is enough."

She stepped to the side and reached toward the outlet to disconnect the tree lights. When she bent low, stretching one hand toward the plug, a thin bluish arc of light leaped into the air from around the switchplate. Reflexively, she yanked back her hand. But the arcing light lengthened and followed. It circled her wrist like a fragile bracelet, spiraling up her arm, making the hairs stand on end. Then the line disappeared, leaving only an acidy, sharp electrical smell hanging in the air.

Barbara stared at the outlet. Slowly she reached again for the plug. The same odor and the sizzle of electricity warned her off.

"I want the lights off," Barbara declared, fighting to maintain control. "I want them off now." She stood with her hands on her hips looking at the tree. "Damn it, T. J., where are you when I need you?"

From nowhere came a gentle draft stirring the air within the closed space, making the little Alice dance. And with it came the scent of T.J.'s cologne. One by one, starting with the lights on the lower branches, then following in sequence up and around the entire string of little colored bulbs, the Christmas tree lights blinked out. Off they went, one at a time, their slow, regular rhythm echoed by the steady da-dum, da-dum cadence of her pulse. Breathless, Barbara watched the eerie light show in stunned silence. The final light, the one on the tip of the tree, lingered a moment longer, like an exotic dancer about to discard the last fragment of covering, then winked into darkness.

The cool air in the room shifted, then grew still. Instantly the harsh electrical odor was gone, and the little room was filled no longer with the mingling aromas of cedar and Dhatri. "Oh, my God . . . Oh, T.J. . . ." Her words were lost amid the uncontrollable hammering of her heart. "Please. Stop." She stood trembling and weeping. Without her moving at all, the door behind her slid open. Numbly, Barbara turned and stepped out. With the same soft swoosh the doors closed.

This time when she went down the hall she took two tablets from the prescription bottle Tom Palmer had given her months ago in case she needed some help getting to sleep. She chased them with a glass of sherry. Finally, she climbed into bed with Miranda. Still trembling, she closed her eyes and waited for the medication to take effect. "Lord . . . deliver us . . . ," she prayed. "From ghosties . . . and ghoulies . . ."

On Friday night, Barbara sat alone at her desk in the study. Before her, stacks of plastic folders containing journals full of daily notes and comments by her students awaited her attention. Beyond the hallway door, the little cedar, now bedecked with lights and ornaments and tinsel, glittered in the heart of the silent house. Barbara had smoothed over the move, saying the tree would stay fresher and be more centrally located in the atrium. No one objected. But it had taken the remainder of the week, punctuated by occasional sighs and tears, before Eliot and Miranda had finally decorated their Christmas tree. Barbara had cajoled them with refreshments and made suggestions, but after that solitary light show, she had not gone into the glass cubicle or touched the decorations again. Kent and the kids put fresh-cut pine garlands in the den. Almost as if a truce had been struck, there had not been another peculiar occurence anywhere in the house.

Outside, the chilly winter breeze pushed Keats's barren branches into bizarre and grotesque poses against the low white clouds. "Rain tomorrow," Barbara muttered, glancing at the thick clumps of clouds outlined by the moonlight trapped behind them. Miranda had been begging her to take them out to Luster Johns to see his carvings, but every night something got in the way. Eliot had an optometrist appointment. Barbara had an evening PTA meeting. The steering committee for the Spoleto Art-in-the-Park held a session. Looked like tomorrow they'd get rained out.

"Boring," she said out loud, stretching her arms and trying to work up some self-discipline. This was her first full evening at home. Now that the children were in bed, she stared impassively at the ungraded papers, wrinkled up her nose, and tossed her pencil onto the desk. Keats seemed to nod in return. So she stared a while at him.

Some minute movement in the shadows beside the huge oak made her glance narrow and her breath catch. She lowered her head slightly, leaning her right hand against her temple as if she were merely propping up her head. To any outside observer, she would seem to be reading, but with her eyes veiled by the shadow of her hand, she could stare instead into the darkness where the movement had been.

"Jesus," Barbara whispered, as she spotted the prowler. She could see his outline—half a man—partially obscured behind Keats, partially illuminated by the moon. "Oh, no," she moaned, her mind racing about for what to do next. Already the perspiration on her palm was making her cheek moist. "Act natural," she warned herself. She wouldn't look out the window again, dreading what she might see. Resolutely, she stretched, then picked up her coffee mug. She slid the desk chair back and slowly proceeded into the hallway, then on to the kitchen. With studied calmness she filled the mug with fresh coffee, then hesitated. She glanced at her watch, then picked up the telephone and dialed.

"Louis," she smiled deliberately. "This is Barbara. I don't know what to do. I've got a prowler."

"You're sure? You mean he's there now?" Louis Belcazzio quizzed her.

"Yes, of course," she replied. "I guess I should have called the police." Her voice was shaking but she tossed back her head and pretended to laugh so any distant observer would not sense there was any urgency. She didn't want him to know she was aware of his presence.

"Can the creep see you right this minute?" Louis asked.

"I'm not sure. I'm in the kitchen. I saw him out the study window. He was by Keats. He may have come around."

"You stay there and stay on the phone. I'll stick Karen on in a second, then I'll go next door and call the cops on another line. Then I'll be up there quick, I'll get some help."

"Okay." Barbara nodded and sipped her coffee while the mumbling on the other end became more frantic and the telephone changed hands.

"Louis wants to know if the doors are all locked."

"Yes." She was trying to remember if she had also turned on the Sonitrol.

"Good." More mumbling. "What were you doing when you spotted the guy?" Karen asked anxiously.

"Sitting at my desk in the study."

Karen relayed the message. "He says to talk to me for about two more minutes—long enough for him to get the car out of the driveway, then you go back to the desk and sit there. They'll try to sneak up on him."

"Okay," Barbara agreed. Suddenly she could think of nothing more to say.

"I'll talk," Karen insisted. Then there was a long silence. "I'm too scared to talk," she whined. "Are the kids in bed?"

"Yes," Barbara responded.

"Oh, God, I wonder if you should wake them," Karen moaned. "Louis?" Her voice trailed off. "He's already on the way," she reported. "Do you think it's been two minutes?"

"More like two hours."

"I really don't want you to get off the phone. Maybe if you stay on, he won't do anything."

"Maybe if I move back in there like Louis said, it will keep his attention. I'll call you back." Without waiting for a reply, Barbara placed the receiver on the cradle. Deliberately, she picked up the coffee mug and walked back to the study. With forced ease, she pulled out the desk chair and lowered the coffee mug onto the desk. As she touched it to the desk surface, from the corner of her eye she saw the dark shape coming closer, sweeping forward next to the long window panel, swinging an arm upwards.

Instinctively, Barbara recoiled, knocking the mug over as she scrambled out of the chair trying to get away. "Don't touch me," a child's voice inside her begged.

"Mrs. A. Mrs. A," the voice beyond the plate glass called above the clatter of the scattered books and cup.

Barbara staggered to a stop, turning to see the hulking figure reassemble itself into familiar human form—with a Charleston High letter on its chest. "Mrs. A. It's me—Kent."

Barbara stood immobile, gasping, with soft, broken attempts at words erupting unintelligibly as she stared open-mouthed toward the familiar voice. Kent was standing now with his hands and face pressed close to the glass.

"I'm sorry, Mrs. A.," he called to her. "I thought I saw the lights on. I was all wound up after the game. I just figured I'd swing by. I scored seventeen points." He flopped his hands against the window as he spoke. "I didn't mean to scare you. I just thought I'd come by and tell you. I was pretty excited," he rambled on desperately, his breath making a hazy cloud on the glass. "I was just checking that you were up and didn't have company or anything. I didn't want to interrupt."

Further out in the yard another figure charged into view. Louis Belcazzio stepped out of the shadows with a golf club leveled at the midsection of the intruder.

"Hold it," commanded another voice she knew. Behind Louis, the bespectacled Mark Ward brandished a baseball bat. Jeff McMillan came around from the back of the house holding a silver handgun. Kent froze.

Barbara couldn't hear much of what came next. By the time she turned on the outdoor lights and unlocked the sliding glass doors, Louis was quietly cursing. Mark Ward was patting the pale-faced young Kent on the shoulder.

Jeff McMillan stepped toward her and wrapped an arm about her shoulders. "A simple invitation would have been sufficient," he joked. "I would have been more than happy to drop by for a quiet drink and a little friendly conversation."

"Come on. Knock off the cute crap," Louis snapped, cutting McMillan off brusquely. "She's had one hell of a scare. We all have."

"Just trying to let off a little tension," McMillan apologized.

"What say we all go inside and open the front door for the rest of the gang," Louis suggested. Two Charleston police cars were swiftly winding their way up the driveway with their headlights turned on high beam.

"Aw, gees," Kent groaned. "Cops."

"It's okay," Mark Ward deposited his bat and headed

around to intercept them near the front door. "You all go in, I'll talk to them."

"How about a drink?" Louis asked Barbara. He put his golf club by the loveseat and strode toward the liquor cabinet. "Six, maybe eight ounces of scotch?" He forced a tight smile while he studied her face warily.

"Just some sherry," Barbara replied. She finally felt like she could breathe. Louis nodded and poured a wineglass full.

"Here. Down it quick."

She took one deep swallow, then another. "How did all of you get here so fast?"

A bit self-consciously, Louis looked at McMillan. "We were having a little get-together." He avoided meeting her eyes as he refilled her drink, then poured one for himself. She could see his hands were shaking. "I'd better call home and tell everyone that things are under control up here. Karen will be worried stiff." He almost bolted from the room. Barbara glanced at McMillan and Kent then followed Louis into the kitchen.

"I told your young friend he could go home," McMillan announced when he came after her. "Poor kid is scared shitless. You'll probably get free lawn service for the rest of your life," he declared. "I've seen sorry, but that kid is really sorry."

"He was only coming by to talk about the game," Barbara started explaining. "He made seventeen points," she concluded feebly.

Mark Ward returned from talking with the patrolmen. "The police are leaving. Everything is okay."

"So where do we go from here?" Louis asked. "You want us to hang around?"

"How about you two go on back and let me stay here for awhile," McMillan offered. "I'll drive over once Barbara's teeth stop rattling."

"I'll be glad to stay," Louis said stubbornly.

"I'll be all right," Barbara insisted. She crossed the room and hugged the stocky man. "Go back to your party. I'm just relieved the kids didn't wake up in the middle of this. I'm so sorry I dragged you all away," she apologized to the trio, "but I sure am glad you came."

"If you're sure you are okay now, I think we should all get back to the house. We've all got people waiting." Louis aimed the comment at McMillan.

"Thank you again for the rescue." Barbara walked the three men to the door. Once Louis and Mark stepped out, McMillan hesitated, then backtracked. "You should have been with me tonight. I was holding off, trying to give you some time and see if you'd take the initiative. That was my mistake. I don't plan to make any more. I'll call you," he said earnestly. "Tomorrow."

Barbara smiled weakly and waved him out the door. Her face felt stiff from trying to put on the show of composure.

Moments later, after she'd locked all the doors again and set the Sonitrol, she lingered in the hallway staring at the lighted Christmas tree, feeling disconnected. Here it was holiday time. Parties were going on without her. There were get-togethers and plays and good friends celebrating, and she wasn't part of it. She hadn't wanted to be. She'd asked not to be fixed up or set up, and she'd got precisely what she'd requested—left alone.

"Couples," Barbara sighed. "And I'm uncoupled." The word sounded like something e.e. cummings would have written in a poem, with *un* and *coupled* on different lines, to intensify the fragmentation implied. "Damn it, I could use a hug," Barbara confessed aloud. Instead, she settled for another drink.

Wearily she strolled from room to room extinguishing the lights. Already the sherry was sending an easy warmth through her, so she looped back and poured another. Sipping it, she wandered into Miranda's room, then into Eliot's, putting the covers over one, loosening the wrappings on the other. She recalled McMillan's comment about the children not being enough to fill her life. And about being discreet. And willing.

Restlessly, she moved onto her own room, pulled closed the phoenix draperies, and stared at her reflection in the mirror. "I'm still in here somewhere," she whispered, studying the pale, drawn image looking back at her. "I need more than a hug." She peeled off her clothes then contemplated the faded tee-shirt and the robe of T.J.'s that she'd been sleeping in. "Neutered," she muttered. She was partly to blame. She sifted through her lingerie drawer and lifted out a gown, a lacy lavender sexy one that T.J. had bought her in one of his playful moods. Every Valentine's Day and on occasional special occasions in between, he'd give her wispy, elegant undies and urge her to put on a private showing in their room. She remembered feeling embarrassed in some of them, but T.J. would keep talking, teasing, and telling her how beautiful she was. They would laugh and murmur and finally make love. And she would fall asleep smiling.

Barbara pulled on the lavender gown, dabbed perfume on her breasts and throat, and then strolled back in front of the mirror. "Much better," she decided. She propped up her pillows and sprawled out on the bed. She closed her eyes and pressed her warm hands on her breasts and touched herself as T.J. often had. Then she rolled on her side and tucked her covers between her thighs, pressing and releasing, summoning a response from deep inside. "Please," she coaxed herself, rocking her hips as she focused on the slight tingly tremor that came stronger with each thrust. "This was mine," she whispered, feeling an urgency that bordered on anger. She barely breathed, straining to reach deeper and deeper to reclaim that part of herself.

"Mine." She was damp with perspiration, her face pushed against the pillow, then she felt it build and begin to peak. Finally, it swept her over the edge. She was lost in her own sensations, the pleasure pure and explosive, the release exhausting.

She lay there gasping, without moving, reassured. Gradually her breathing settled into an easy, regular rhythm and she finally tugged the covers up over her and surrendered to the numbed sleep of a satisfied lover.

"The kids should be in bed by eight-thirty," Barbara told Kent. "We'll be back about ten."

The tall teenager nodded and shifted his feet uneasily, avoiding looking directly at either Barbara or McMillan, who leaned against the doorjamb.

"I'll see to it, Mrs. A.," Kent asserted. "You have a nice dinner," he said politely.

"We'll be at The Trawler." Barbara left the number of the restaurant by the kitchen phone. "If you have an emergency, call the Belcazzios." She added Karen and Louis's number to the list.

"We'll be all right," Kent insisted.

"Of course you will. I'm just being—"

"A mother . . ." McMillan supplied the word.

"Cautious." She settled for that. "See you later, Kent."

McMillan held open her coat while she slid her arms into it. With a final wave, Barbara stepped out the doorway toward McMillan's car.

"Gee, we're alone," he teased as they passed the brick Country Club Estates entrance and pulled onto the highway.

"Surely you aren't nervous," Barbara kidded him.

"Nervous, no. I'm delighted." He glanced over and grinned. "I've actually got you to myself."

"Well don't get carried away, and don't get any false expectations," she warned him. "This is my first adventure into the unknown. I'm not sure if I'm going to like it."

"We'll just take it nice and easy." He reached out and closed his hand over hers. "A little dinner, a few drinks, some pleasant conversation." He paused. "Then we'll check to see if your knees are still shaking."

"My knees aren't shaking."

"Maybe with a little encouragement they will be." He grinned once more.

Barbara slid her hand out from under his. "What happened to the taking it nice and easy bit?"

"I'm really better at the easy part," McMillan replied, chuckling.

Barbara closed her eyes and sighed. "This sounds like a conversation I had at fifteen."

"Relax, I'm only kidding." He laughed good-naturedly at her obvious discomfort. "I know how to behave like a gentleman, I'm just a little out of practice. I'll do better." He gave her a sidelong look. Boyish. Disarming. Familiar.

As they drove over the Ashley Bridge and across the Charleston peninsula, the soft music from the FM station punctuated by occasional announcements served as a tranquil break between bits of conversation.

"I gather Kent is still a bit uncomfortable about scaring you the other night."

"Just a bit. I keep telling him that it was an innocent mistake, but he still feels bad about it. When he told Eliot and Miranda what happened, they were angry that they missed the whole thing. To them it sounded like fun."

Between songs, the deep-voiced announcer smoothly inserted the time and weather conditions. "WXTC . . . Ecstacy . . . Clear, cool, perfect for cuddling up by a cozy fire. Have a romantic good evening, friends."

"It's a conspiracy," McMillan noted. "Sort of subliminal suggestion to wear away your resistance."

"You're in cahoots with the radio station?" Barbara shook her head in amusement.

"Every little bit helps," he countered.

She smiled thoughtfully and looked out the window. Another soft, romantic song began. "It's surprising how much pressure there is, subtle and otherwise, to push people at each other," she said quietly. "Ten years of marriage puts one out of step with the times," she added.

"Especially if you had as good a marriage as you did," McMillan replied. Barbara suspected he'd heard tales of the harmonious Ashcrofts and their model family from Louis and Karen.

"And did you?" she asked pointedly.

"Yes and no. When it was good it was very, very good," he mimicked the nursery rhyme. "And when it was bad . . . et cetera, et cetera. I was only married five years. I've been divorced three."

"Does that mean you have adjusted well to single life?"

"I suppose so," McMillan answered frankly. "I have more sense and more money than the last time I was single. I think I'm more at ease with myself now. At times I feel as if I've been granted a reprieve."

Barbara watched the second set of bridges loom ahead. This time they were crossing the Cooper River on the opposite side of Charleston, heading toward Mount Pleasant.

"Don't get me wrong, I like being married," he said. "It was the combination of individuals—not the institution itself—that didn't work out. I'd take another chance, if that's what you're wondering."

"I wasn't wondering," Barbara said a little too quickly.

"How about you?" McMillan looked over at her. "Would you try it again?"

"I don't know." Barbara glanced across the river at the low aircraft carrier *Yorktown*, moored at Patriot's Point. T.J. liked to take the kids there from time to time. "Logically, it's possible. I liked being married. It was something I was very good at. But I'm not ready to deal with the idea of remarriage emotionally. Too many loose ends."

"Loose ends like what?"

"Unfinished business, leftover loyalties. I'm still in the process of sorting through it all." Barbara stared out over the water, watching a tugboat pulling a trail of barges along after it. It vaguely reminded her of herself, still pulling the weight of T.J.'s expectations along with her own. "In some ways I don't like what marriage did for me—or to me." Barbara turned away from the boat and looked toward the end of the bridge up ahead. "Since I've been on my own, I've had to learn to handle a lot of details that I should have been taking care of myself all along. I let myself depend too much on T.J., then I ended up feeling inept. I'm reeducating myself. I guess I'm making myself a whole person again. So, before I speculate too much about the future, I'll have to survive this part."

"I hope you aren't referring to this evening," McMillan joked. "I guarantee you'll do better than survive."

Barbara smiled. "I didn't mean to sound so negative."

"Good. Because I have some very positive feelings

about you. And I like it when you smile," he said warmly.

"You're making me edgy again," Barbara cautioned him.

"I'll take that as a sign of progress."

At five after ten, McMillan pulled into the Ashcroft driveway. The full moon flooded the yard with an ivory light and reflected off the house windows, turning them into sheets of sliced marble. The only burst of color was from the kitchen's row of wildflowers, shining like homing beacons. The rest of the interior was dark. "Of course, I'd love a brandy." He turned off the headlights and answered a question Barbara had not even asked. There was a trace of laughter in his voice. He turned and gave her a sudden, arresting smile.

"Okay. Come on in. But my liquor supply is very limited. You might have to settle for decaf coffee."

"I'll take it." He got out and came around to open her door. He had been like that the whole evening, a gentleman. They had dined in a low, wooden building with rows of shrimp boats tied up just beyond their window. While they waited to be seated, they'd talked and strolled, drinks in hand, through the gift shop. Despite her protests, McMillan had emerged with a stars-and-rainbow mobile for Miranda and a model ship for Eliot. Inside, the rustic restaurant, with its cozy tables and walls hung with seafaring gear, had been perfumed by the heavenly aroma of its she-crab soup. They'd sipped wine and feasted on Carolina flounder and shrimp fresh from the Atlantic, and they'd talked for hours. Now, packages in hand, McMillan followed her to the door. Their breath made pale clouds in the cool night air.

Kent was in the kitchen picking up when Barbara came in and started a pot of coffee. "Everything went really well," he volunteered. "We made popcorn and built a fire. They went down with only a couple of trips apiece."

While Barbara went to look in on the kids, McMillan waited for her, whistling softly, circling the atrium, looking in at the poinsettias and the Christmas tree. "Very pretty," he noted when he saw her coming.

She gave him a polite, noncommital smile and continued on with him into the kitchen. Kent loaded the three empty glasses on the counter into the dishwasher, then hesitated when Barbara pulled out her checkbook to pay him.

"Oh no, Mrs. A.," he protested, "not for tonight." He shoved his hands into his pockets. "I owe you."

McMillan stepped forward and slid a ten dollar bill into Kent's shirt pocket. "No, we owe you. There would have been no tonight without you here. Thanks." He patted Kent on the shoulder. "Goodnight, son," he said, without moving from Barbara's side.

To her it sounded a bit brusque, almost like a dismissal. "Thanks for helping out." She stepped forward, trying to make the transition easier. "Especially on a school night. I'll see you tomorrow."

Kent shifted his feet and glanced behind her at McMillan, who was leaning against the counter, obviously in no hurry to leave. "Sure. Thanks. Goodnight." Reluctantly he headed toward the kitchen door, grabbing his letter jacket and shoving his arms into the sleeves.

"I think the kid has a crush on you," McMillan said as soon as Kent was gone.

"That may be," Barbara acknowledged, still a bit perturbed at the way McMillan had taken over. "We've been through a lot together. He's like one of the family. It's all right if he has a bit of a crush on me. He'll outgrow it."

"I don't think he was too thrilled that I'm hanging around here," McMillan added. "A little jealousy there?"

"Maybe that, too," Barbara admitted. "He's being protective. It's a bad habit that a lot of folks I know suffer from. It seems to be contagious," she noted with an amused, but distinct edge to her voice.

"So you say," McMillan muttered. Then he gave her a sheepish look that for a fragment of a second made him look remarkably like T.J.

"What do you take in your coffee?" Barbara asked, turning away and taking two cups down from the cabinet.

"Black is fine."

"I saw they made a fire in the den. Would you like to sit in there?" She handed him his cup. He followed her.

"I haven't spent much time in this room lately," she remarked as she eased onto the striped sofa, slipped off her shoes, and tucked her feet beneath her full jersey skirt.

"Too many memories?" McMillan guessed.

"My head is filled with the memories," Barbara replied. "Which room I'm in doesn't seem to matter." She didn't feel the need to elaborate.

McMillan sat next to her, then shifted closer so his leg pressed against her knees. "Well?" He rested his arm behind her shoulders. "How do you feel now that you've ventured out into the world of dating again?"

"It was nice. Very nice." She sat sipping her coffee, staring into the low fire that sizzled in the fireplace, beginning to feel tense for the first time since the evening began.

"I really like you." McMillan spoke without moving. He eyed the shades of crimson beneath the logs. "Am I sounding too much like the scenario on the radio?"

"I like you too, pal," she said quietly, trying to keep things from becoming too intense.

He eased forward, put down his glass, and turned to face her. "There's more to this than being pals," he said simply. "We had a great time tonight. I think there's a real attraction going on here."

Barbara looked at him. "I'm not sure what's going on. I enjoyed being with you. But I'm feeling pretty confused."

"Then that must mean there's something to be confused about." He reached over and stroked her cheek with his fingertips. "Remember what I said about friends being able to be lovers? I meant it. Sometimes a little physical closeness can get you through the rough spot. I can hold you and make love with you without messing up your life."

"I don't know if I can," she whispered. "I had a feeling this was coming. I can't even breathe right now."

McMillan took her glass and put it next to his. Then he grasped her shoulders and eased her toward him.

"I don't think this is a good—"

"Relax." His voice was low and smooth and sure.

"I can't."

"I'll help." He brushed her lips lightly with his, then he held her against his chest, gently massaging her back. "Come on. Ease up on yourself," he coaxed her. "Nothing heavy duty. Just a little body contact so you'll remember what it's like." He held her closer.

"I just don't feel right."

"It's bound to be a bit awkward," he said calmly, still keeping up the gentle rubbing motion over her shoulders. "Starting over shakes loose a lot of mixed feelings. I'm not asking you to sort it all out. I just want you to let yourself feel some pleasure. You're a very sexy lady, soft and sweet," he whispered against her hair. "I won't let you get in deeper than you're ready to, but I won't pretend that I don't want you. Come on. Easy now. Let me hold you."

She stopped resisting and settled against him, feeling in the warmth of the contact something familiar, masculine, and strong. "I've missed being held," she said, almost wearily. This time, when he stroked her hair and then eased back and lightly kissed her, she felt a faintly comforting surge of excitement.

"See, it's not so bad."

"It's not so good either," she answered, still in a whisper. "I'm nervous."

"Nervous is good," McMillan declared with a chuckle. "Fortunately I have a healthy ego. I don't accept nervousness as rejection." He kissed her again, lingering a little longer this time, gently tantalizing her. For an instant she responded, softening her lips against his. Then she backed away.

"Some part of you is interested. Somewhere locked up inside you is a lot of woman," he observed. His gaze dropped from her eyes to her shoulders to her breasts beneath the smooth fabric of her dress. "Whenever you decide to stop holding back . . ." He left the thought unfinished and instead pulled her against him, this time with a show of passion that took her by surprise. His soft lips moved against hers, easing her mouth half open so his tongue could trace the warmth inside. Barbara didn't resist this time. Instead she felt removed from it all, as if she were an outside observer waiting to see what happened next.

With one arm, McMillan slid her legs out from under her, then moved forward with her so the length of their bodies pressed against each other on the sofa. "With a little cooperation," he said hoarsely, "we could move this relationship on to a new plateau." His hand dropped to her silken hose.

"I'm not ready for that," Barbara gasped for air. "Let's quit, please. I don't feel right about this. The kids. . . ."

"Easy," he soothed her, backing off. "I wasn't going to let anything happen." He was breathing deeply, as he shifted to an upright position. "You have to admit, I was getting to you."

"Biology was getting to me," Barbara rephrased his comment. "I'm giving myself some very mixed messages."

"At least one of those messages was real encouraging," McMillan noted. "Maybe if we tried it once more." He started to lean toward her while he brought his hand slowly up her thigh.

"No new plateaus tonight, pal," Barbara warned him, stopping the upward motion of his hand.

"I just want you to know I find you very appealing. I'm more than interested. I'm eager," he said good-naturedly, retreating dutifully. "Whenever you're ready to come out of solitary."

Upright herself now, Barbara was smoothing her skirt. "I suppose then you'll make me beg."

"Hell, no, I won't. I'll be on you like a bee on clover."

"How graphic." Barbara licked her lips, and concentrated on smoothing wrinkles that no longer existed. Her face felt warm.

"You're embarrassed." McMillan looked at her, chuckling. "I like that. Classy woman like you, and you're embarrassed." He grinned as the color deepened in her cheeks. "You are definitely a prize, pal." He reached out and stilled the motion of her hand. "And I am a man who likes to win."

"This isn't a contest," she said quietly. "And it's late. I think you'd better go. School tomorrow." She stood, still clasping his hand, and pulled him up beside her. "I had a lovely evening. At least most of it was lovely," she said, walking him toward the door.

"It will all be lovely, eventually," he insisted, trying to sound deliberately sensual. "Let's try this again. Friday. Only the two of us. This time at my place, where there aren't so many memories, and there aren't kids just down the hall. I think you have too much going on here to unwind." He looked at her with a softness in his expression that set off all the old signals. "I'll cook for you and play soft music."

"Sounds dangerous," Barbara said without looking up at him.

"Precisely." He rested his arm around her shoulder. "At least you won't have to keep one ear cocked for the patter of no-so-little feet."

"I was doing that, wasn't I," she acknowledged.

"You were. I'm not sure that having them available as an excuse isn't a way of protecting yourself from making some moves that you really want to make," he commented. "They make a relatively simple issue seem terribly complicated. Just come to my place. See what a lot of privacy can do."

"It sounds very calculated and cold-blooded."

"I think we're talking hot-blooded," he corrected her. "And as far as the calculated part goes, we aren't children. We can't pretend romance just happens. I'm not into grappling in a car. I'm into pleasant surroundings with no interruptions. Then what happens, happens, without excuses or apologies."

"And if nothing happens?"

"We'll still have a nice, peaceful evening. In fact, it would be nice if you could let the kids spend the night somewhere. Then you could have the whole night if you wanted to stay."

"I'm not that progressive," Barbara shook her head. "I think I'd like to ease off this whole issue for a while."

"You have three whole days to think about it. You can change plans at the last minute if you want. But it sure would be nice." He turned and swept her into his arms, holding her and spinning as if they were dancing. "Just think about how good it feels right now, just being this close." He slowed to a gentle, more seductive, side-to-side sway. "No, easy now." He braced his arm to keep her from moving back. "Just imagine you and me, smooth skin, smooth sheets, and no interruptions." He looked down at her. "I want to make love with you. On any terms you want." He lowered his mouth to hers.

Slowly he backed her into the darkened entry, holding one hand steady in the curve of her back but gliding the other one down to cup her buttocks and draw her against him. His warm kisses, firm and persuasive, were disturbingly tender. Burying his face near her throat, he breathed slow kisses there, making her whole body tingle with a familiar flush of anticipation. Barbara lifted her arms around his neck, drawn to him by a longing that was more powerful than she cared to admit.

"You are so delicious," he murmured.

Barbara's pulse pounded in her ears, the sound slowly accelerating, rising in pitch until it became a shrill, harsh, broken whine.

"What the hell is that?" McMillan broke away, trying to listen over the sound of his own breathing. "It's your damn smoke alarm. Where the hell is it?"

Barbara stepped back into the lighted area near the atrium as the sound became comprehensible. The noise was coming from the alarm in the bedroom wing. "It can't be the fireplace . . ." She glanced bewilderedly toward the den. "There's an alarm down there." McMillan was already halfway down the hall.

"It's okay, honey." Barbara spotted Miranda stumbling sleepily out her door, trailing her blanket along behind her.

"Momma, what's wrong?" Miranda blinked at the light, trying to wake up. She had her two favorite dolls clutched under her arms.

McMillan reached up and pushed the reset button.

"It's okay. False alarm," Barbara said, taking the child and gently turning her around and leading her back to bed.

"Mom?" Eliot called from his room "Mom?" He sounded near panic. Barbara hurried across to his room with Miranda on her heels. Eliot was sitting up in the dark, kicking at his covers, trying desperately to unwrap himself. He'd managed to grab his glasses from the shelf in the headboard, but he couldn't get loose.

"It's okay. Take it easy," she calmed him.

"The alarm went off," Miranda reported. "But there isn't a fire."

"You go back to your room. I'll be in in a minute," Barbara told her. "And you just snuggle back in and go to sleep." She helped straighten out Eliot's covers and tucked him in.

She was on her way across to Miranda's room when McMillan came back from his room-to-room search for some hint of smoke. "The damn thing just went off on its own. I can't figure out what triggered it."

Barbara sniffed the air. No smoke. "Maybe it needs new batteries."

Then McMillan paused and sniffed again, glancing toward the open bedroom doors. "Do you smell something peculiar?" he asked quietly, moving once again from Miranda's doorway to Barbara's.

Barbara drew in a long uneasy breath, dreading she would pick up a trace of Dhatri. Only the Christmasy scent of cedar filtered down though the hot air vents surrounding the atrium.

"Can I have a glass of milk?" Miranda came out of her room, wide awake now. She was still clutching her dolls.

"Okay. Milk."

"I'd really like hot chocolate."

"Can I have hot chocolate, too?" Eliot called out.

"I guess so." Barbara shrugged at McMillan.

"Doesn't it seem like it never ends?" he muttered as the children paraded out of their rooms. He was sure Miranda was stifling a smug smile. "I guess this means the spell is broken." He looked back at the two backsides ahead.

"Mom, I said to leave the door open a bit," Miranda complained. "Mr. Johns said the little cricket will try to get in with the plants." She slid open the atrium door and turned on the switch Kent had installed on an extension cord just inside the door.

"I guess the spell is broken all right." She nodded, more relieved than she cared to show.

"I think I'll go on home before the damn john starts running again."

Barbara walked him to the door. "See you later." She kissed him lightly on the cheek.

"Friday," he reminded her. "One way or another. My place, or yours if you can get the house to yourself."

"I'll see what I can work out." She closed the door quietly and turned the lock.

Once the children were back in bed, she made one last trip through the house. Miranda had left the tree lights on. Barbara paused by the atrium and looked in at the little cedar tree all decked out with ornaments and lights.

"Is this alarm business your idea of a joke?" she asked of no one visible. "I told you to stop the weird stuff," she said quietly as she eased her hand between the open doors and reached for the light switch. This time, there was no blue arcing light to threaten her. She didn't even have to get near the outlet. With a quick click, the lights were extinguished.

She smiled and let out a small sigh. "Now that's better."

Before she could move her hand back, the cold closed in around it, viselike, holding her there. Then slowly the glass doors opened a bit wider, and she was enveloped in the cold and propelled inside. Silently, the doors slid shut. With a low hissing noise and a full click, her exit was blocked. Too stunned to utter a sound, she grabbed the latch and tried to dislodge the lock. The door remained cold and rigid, confining her with the tree and the chilly, moist air, pungent with cedar and increasingly laden with bay.

She turned, facing the tree, with her back pressed against the glass door. The lights went on again all at once, with a brighter, more fierce glow than ever before. "Let me out of here," Barbara tugged against the lock, struggling to retain her composure. "What do you want from me? What are you trying to prove?" She spoke softly within the small room, fighting to keep back a scream. "I don't understand why you're doing this." Her voice became very small and strained. "Please. Let me go."

Slowly the dense air stirred around her, fluttering her skirt against her legs, then holding it there, clinging to her. The oppressive heavy aroma coated her throat and lungs, making her limbs feel weighted as if she were suspended in fluid, buoyed up by the spice-laden air. Her vision blurred, her other senses became heightened, as if each breath were drugged. Dhatri. It was everywhere. Gradually the encounter took on a sensual quality as the pressure moved in on her, touching her, caressing her, urging her to respond. It glided over her thighs and stroked her breasts like a skillful lover without form or substance. Teasing. Tantalizing. Then gradually becoming insistent.

"No," she groaned, twisting and trying to fend off the assault. But the force enclosed her hands and made them move, so she was touching herself as she had alone in her bed.

"No. I don't want this." She writhed, helplessly entrapped. "This is sick." She spat out the words. "It's evil." All motion stopped. Suspended, she stood there, off balance, but supported by the heavy air around her.

The sensation of pressure slowly subsided. The mass shifted and became increasingly warm. Damp with perspiration, she grasped for the door latch once again. This time the lock clicked; the door slowly opened with the same full hissing sound as before.

She was free to leave. Behind her, the harsh glow of lights went off abruptly, all at once.

Without looking back, she leapt out and raced along the hall into the bathroom, shoving the door closed. Swallowing hard, she collapsed on her knees before the commode. Even her saliva tasted like Dhatri. Gasping and shuddering, she clung to the cool porcelain for support, vomiting. At last, empty and weak, she leaned against the wall and wept.

"Leave me alone," she begged. "Just leave me alone."

Chilled and shaking, she stepped, clothes and all, into the shower, and stood there with her face pressed into her hands, sobbing, while the water beat down on her. Later, wrapped in a towel, she gulped down two sleeping pills. Still trembling, with a hot water bottle clutched to her chest to help drive out the icy feeling, she crawled into bed, pulled the blankets over her and fell back against her pillow, exhausted. She pressed her eyes closed and gritted her teeth and tried to control the shuddering.

How do I love thee . . . I shall but love thee better after death. The words T.J. had left in his note with the Christmas cards no longer brought comfort.

"Not like this. This isn't loving. There isn't any loving in this," she protested. "Please, go away and leave me, leave us," she pleaded. "I can manage. The kids and I can manage alone. We'll be all right. You have to leave us alone. I can't go on like this," she insisted through her tears.

Somewhere far off in the house, the small wild cricket chirped.

Henry answered.

The cricket chirped again.

Then everything was silent.

CHAPTER 6

> Remorse is memory awake,
> Her companies all astir,
> A Presence of departed acts
> At window and at door.
> *Emily Dickinson*

"I'M GOING TO take the kids home for Christmas after all," Barbara said as she poured a cup of coffee for Karen Belcazzio.

"I figured you might end up deciding to do that. I had a feeling there would be too many memories here," Karen said sympathetically, looking intently at the pale, solemn profile of her friend as Barbara poured a second cup for herself. The sunny glow that she'd had when she came back from her Thanksgiving trip was already gone. Instead, she looked tired and drawn, and she'd been acting preoccupied ever since Karen dropped in. "It's especially hard at Christmas."

Barbara gave her a distracted nod and started rifling through the cabinet for cookies.

"Have you been having trouble sleeping again?" Karen guessed.

"A few nights," Barbara admitted. "It comes and goes."

"Come on. Sit. Forget the cookies."

Barbara slid onto the seat across the corner nook from her and stirred cream into her mug of coffee. "I called my folks last night. They were relieved. I don't think they really wanted to drive all the way up here for the holidays. They'd miss being with their own friends. There are a lot of retired military in Sarasota, and at Christmas there's usually a round of parties," Barbara explained. Her voice wavered. Her shoulders sagged.

Karen reached across and patted Barbara's arm. "I guess that's another thing you'd have to deal with if you stayed here, all the usual parties going on." She hesitated a moment. She'd already R.S.V.P.'d several invitations for the upcoming weeks and knew that Barbara had been invited but hadn't answered yet. "It's probably not a thrilling prospect celebrating with a gang of people without T.J."

"Or with someone else." Barbara filled in another possibility that Karen had left unspoken.

They both let several seconds of silence pass. "Speaking of Someone Else," Karen broached the subject she'd been curious about for days. "How are you and McMillan getting along? Louis says he's very closed-mouthed about you. I keep seeing his car pass the house, and since you're the only one on this end of the road . . ."

"I know, I know." Barbara nodded. She started rubbing her shoulders wearily. "He's managed to drop in several times this week. He was giving me a hand with a few things. I guess you heard about Mr. Johns." She glanced out in the hallway toward the atrium.

"Louis said he'd bumped a tree in his pickup a few days ago. Broke a kneecap?"

"Shattered it. He had to have surgery. That's what his grandson said. He came by and said Luster wouldn't be able to drive for a while. He brought me some wire and some of that blue liquid to keep the pests out. He said Luster was doing very well except for the kneecap." She licked her lips nervously. "His brakes gave out on the way home the other night. His grandson said the brake fluid was empty."

"That's a shame. But he's an old fellow, he probably forgot to check it," Karen said, shrugging.

"Mr. Johns took care of that truck very well. He remembered to take care of everything, all his equipment. Even his watering can was scrubbed clean." She gave a quick look toward the atrium again.

"Well, I'm just glad he wasn't on the highway. Louis said they found him in his truck in the cemetery."

"I guess he made a detour on the way home. His grandson said he'd been stuck there all night. He'd been too hurt to move, so he just tugged a blanket over himself and went to sleep. He just wanted the grandson to come by and tell me that he wouldn't be in to hang the wreaths."

"I meant to tell you how nice they look. Did Kent do them for you?"

"McMillan helped. The grandson said Mr. Johns wanted me to put them up myself. But McMillan came by. He insisted on helping, and he's tall enough to do it without a ladder. Besides, he likes heights. I'm definitely a ground person."

"Well, they look great. By the time Mr. Johns is up and around again, Christmas will be over and he'll never know the difference."

"Miranda keeps asking to go and see him. They don't have a listed number phone. I'm not sure if he or his daughter would want us dropping in without calling first."

"Speaking of dropping in, let's get back to the subject of McMillan. Do all his little trips here have some significance?"

"I guess they do. We're trying to establish some kind of relationship." Barbara tried to avoid going into too much detail. "He's decided he'd like to be more than pals. I think he's trying to rush things a bit."

"Five months . . . nearly half a year," Karen noted. "I don't know what official etiquette dictates, but I'd say that's not rushing. It's past time to get back into the mainstream, my dear. I don't think T.J. would mind."

Barbara gave her a sudden look, then hurriedly glanced away and concentrated on the coffee mug in front of her. "I'm not sure that T.J. really would approve," she said softly. "Lately I'm not even sure I approve." She chewed her lower lip. Part of her wanted to open up and tell Karen what had been going on in the house, but she was afraid that her friend would think she was having some kind of a breakdown. Besides, a peculiar peace had descended again and she was desperately hoping it would last. Getting away for Christmas seemed like a good way to diffuse the tension that the approaching holidays were starting to build.

"I think you're being too hard on yourself. You need to get out and let off some steam. Or work some up, romantically, I mean."

"I'm trying, but I get swamped with so many contradictory feelings. I get lonely, then I feel guilty, then I get depressed, then something happens to cheer me up, and for a while, everything is all right. Then something goes wrong and the cycle starts all over."

"Well, I hate to add to the confusion, but I have to tell you something that may stop you from spinning your wheels." Karen leaned forward. "Life does go on. I don't think good old McMillan will just sit around and wait for you if you take off for two weeks. There are plenty of women who are eager to keep him entertained, if you get my drift." Her slender black eyebrows arched emphatically. "I could name two or three who have made it very clear they are available."

"That might be the best thing that could happen," Barbara said, shrugging. "If he meets someone else and gets interested in her, then I won't have anything to be concerned about."

"Coward." Karen crossed her arms over her chest and sighed. She kept watching Barbara's face, certain there was more going on than her friend was telling her. "I'm not saying that McMillan is Mr. Right, but he's definitely one of the better ones on the loose. He's good company. He's good-looking, successful, and he has a great body. You two seem to enjoy each other. If you don't get something straight with him before you leave, someone else will move in on him."

"Or with him?" Barbara added wryly.

"That's always a possibility," Karen answered. "Smart women go after what they want. Two weeks could give another woman enough momentum to take over."

"So maybe I'm not being smart," Barbara admitted. "But I don't really know what I want. McMillan has a lot of good qualities. And I am attracted to him. But the kind of intimacy I need with a man is not just physical. I miss the closeness I had with T.J. I don't want to jump into anything just because I'm lonely. I need some time to think things through."

"How much time did it take before you decided to make the jump into whatever with T.J.?"

Barbara shrugged. "It isn't the same thing. T.J. was very sure and I was very lucky."

"T.J. was sure about everything," Karen reminded her. "And you and I both know it takes more than luck to make a marriage work. Regardless, T.J.'s going to be a hard act to follow. But he and McMillan are a lot alike. Maybe you could be that lucky again."

"Maybe. But I can't deal with a new relationship until I've cleared up some things about the old one."

"What kind of things?" Karen inquired, staring at her curiously, frowning.

"I've been doing a lot of thinking about T.J. and me." Barbara lowered her eyes as she spoke. "About how people change over the years."

Karen sat very still, sensing there was something very important that Barbara was trying to sort through, something that had kept her awake nights and drained the energy from her.

"T.J. and I had a very easygoing relationship most of the time. The big decisions around here were T.J.'s. I was always pretty content to go along with them. But the dynamics were changing once the kids got into school and I started back to work. Now that I've had to assume all the responsibilities, I've changed even more. I'm not as accommodating as I used to be." She shook her head and expelled a loud breath. "Maybe it is the similarities between McMillan and T.J. that disturb me. They're both pushy. They both think they know what's best for me. Or at least T.J. did and McMillan is starting to." She caught herself and carefully took T.J. out of the present tense. "I'm not sure I want to pick up with someone else where T.J. and I left off. This rush from McMillan is flattering to an old married lady, or whatever I am now. I'm tempted. But I'm just not on solid ground here." She sat twisting her rings, the wedding band and the diamond that she'd been wearing on her right hand instead of her left as a concession to widowhood.

"Well, for one thing, thirty-four isn't old and you aren't a married lady anymore. And for another, I don't envy you a bit," Karen said honestly. "I can still remember dating. It was the pits then and I'm sure it hasn't improved over the years. But face the facts, Barbara. There are not a whole lot of worthwhile unattached men around. You're a young woman with a family to raise. You could use someone to help. McMillan happens to be nice-looking, financially secure, reasonably intelligent, and interested in you." She tapped her fingertip on the tabletop between them. "He likes theater, architecture, sports, and he likes your kids."

"A match made in heaven," Barbara muttered.

"You said it," Karen countered. "It isn't a bad idea at all. I just want you to think twice before you leave a hot prospect unclaimed. If you must go home for the holidays, make sure he knows whether you're interested in him. Or sleep with him. He'll need something to keep him from temptation."

Barbara glanced up thoughtfully. "Okay. I think I've finally gotten the point. Now, tell me who's after McMillan?"

Karen wrinkled her nose. "No comment."

"Come on," Barbara insisted. "You have tapdanced all around the subject. You aren't supposed to keep secrets from me. If you're telling me to sleep with this guy to save him from temptation, someone has to be breathing heavy in the wings."

Karen took a big gulp of coffee, then landed her mug with a clunk. "Well, I'm not the only one playing matchmaker. McMillan's been invited to a number of parties where the main object was introducing him to available daughters or sisters or friends. There are a couple of front-runners," she reported. "He brought one to our house the night of Kent-the-Prowler."

Barbara sipped her coffee and waited.

"Janice Benson, the realtor. The one who made the Quarter-Million Club for sales. The other is Suzie Silversmith, one of the developers in on the shopping center deal. Louis says she's found a number of details that need McMillan's personal attention. She seems to be popping in and out of the office all the time."

"Only two?" Barbara forced a smile.

"Maybe more," Karen watched her friend intently. "Louis thinks one of the gals in the office is pretty chummy with him. I tell you, Barbara, he may wait around for you to make up your mind, but he won't be waiting alone."

"I'll have to take that chance," Barbara said with determination.

"You aren't taking a chance," Karen shot back. "You're playing ostrich. Hiding your head in the sand. And you're going all the way to Florida to find the sand. I suppose it's safer not to do anything. You can't lose in a game you refuse to play."

Barbara held Karen's gaze. "It's not a game. I just need a little more time."

"We all need a little more time," Karen responded. "But when a good thing comes along, you'd better grab it whether it's convenient or not. I've seen you two together. You can joke and you can talk business, comfortably—or so it seems. You've seen him with the kids. He's pretty good for a beginner. I'm not telling you that if you jump into the sack with him you have to marry the guy. But don't just leave him to fend for himself, honey, because he will."

"Okay. Enough." Barbara felt her cheeks turn hot. "I am simply not used to jockeying for position. You can't imagine how awful this makes me feel. Slightly used, thirty-four-year-old mother of two, Bachelor of Arts degree, comes with house, car, and offspring."

"I can guess how you feel," Karen said softly. "Ever since T.J. died, I find myself spending a lot of time with Louis, being more grateful than I was. Just thinking of what it must be like to start over fills me with dread. I feel for you. You and the kids." Tears welled up in her eyes and inched their way down her cheeks. "I just want you to be happy again."

"Yes." Barbara whispered. "I know."

"Louis of course thinks I'm reaching my middle-thirties peak," Karen said, brushing away the tears and forcing a grin. "He is getting screwed into oblivion nearly every night, and all he's done to deserve it is to be himself, to stay with me, and stay alive."

Barbara shifted her gaze to the gray marsh beyond Keats. A lone sea gull swooped down into the grass then rose again with a thrashing sliver of silver in its beak.

"I'll talk to McMillan," Barbara promised.

"Maybe you could come to our New Year's party with him. You'll be back for that, won't you?" Karen brightened at the thought.

"I don't think so," Barbara replied. "I think I'm going over to Lauderdale for a few days to visit Rob."

"With the kids?" Karen regarded her suspiciously.

"No, by myself."

"Oh?" Karen sat waiting for an explanation.

"He asked me to come over for a visit, see a play, look at some videotapes, spend some time alone."

"Sounds positively thrilling," Karen observed solemnly. "Are you sure this isn't some diversionary action?"

"I don't know." Barbara sighed wearily, leaning back against the seat cushions. "I just want to go somewhere and be with someone who knows me," she said quietly. "I know you know me," Barbara said, halting Karen before she could protest, "but Rob knew me long ago, when I was just me, not T.J.'s wife, not a mother, not a teacher, just me. My mother knows me as her little girl. To my stepfather, I'm just an occasional visitor. That's all right. But there is something comforting about being with Rob. Maybe it's because I am starting over, and I haven't been just me for years, and I'm a little scared," Barbara admitted. "He's the only friend I've had all through my grownup years. He's got a lot of memories to share with me, and many don't have to do with T.J. at all." She struggled to explain her feelings. "Maybe I've lost my sense of continuity, and that's what he might help me find."

"You may find more than that," Karen added rapidly. "Nothing like a few days away from the kids to fan the ashes of an old romance."

"I doubt if there will be much fanning of ashes. What we've had over the years is a friendship. I'm sure you realize that Rob, like our McMillan, has normal healthy drives and has not pined away for me in chaste seclusion. He's had a life of his own."

"Right," Karen sounded unconvinced. "I suppose you

plan to tell McMillan about your stay with a male who has normal healthy drives?"

"He already knows Rob is a good friend," Barbara replied calmly. "But I will mention my itinerary to him, just in case you or he should suspect my motives. I'm sure he'll understand."

"Like hell, he will." Karen laughed. "The one time he met Rob was at our coming-our party when he joined the firm. I doubt if he'll be terribly sympathetic if you go to spend a few days with a tall, elegant, charming former boyfriend who has happened to remain a bachelor all his life. After all, what would give him cause for alarm?" she concluded with feigned innocence.

"I'm not amused."

"McMillan won't be, either," Karen stressed, "unless you two reach some kind of understanding before you leave."

"Maybe I won't tell him," Barbara groaned. "I don't want to cause a commotion over something that really doesn't have anything to do with him."

"Now you're giving mixed signals." Karen shook her head. "You're becoming devious, avoiding a confrontation by omitting the details. That's not like you."

Barbara's expression grew strangely stiff. "I'm not trying to be devious. I'm just tired. I hate dumping things on people, especially things that really don't concern them." She stared at the half-empty cup on the table in front of her. "But I won't make the situation worse. I'll just have a nice long reasonable talk with him and let it go at that."

"When are you seeing him again?"

"Friday. He's invited me to dinner."

"Where?"

"His house."

"Perfect." Karen smiled and rubbed her hands together. "I'll keep the kids Friday night. They can sleep over. You and McMillan can have a nice dinner and some leisurely conversation, then come home. Or not."

"I think he'll get the signal on that one," Barbara countered.

"So? You two need some privacy to discuss your situation—and you won't have to watch the clock or worry about one of the kids trooping in. Not that you two would be doing anything . . ."

"You don't have to go on," Barbara stopped her friend. "Okay. I'll take you up on it. Friday."

"You don't need to pick the kids up too early Saturday. They can eat breakfast and watch cartoons at my house." She stood and crossed the room to refill her coffee mug. "Being at his house, if one thing leads to another, you won't have to feel that T.J. is lurking about watching over you. It won't be your room and your bed. There won't be so many memories bombarding you." She did not see the color vanish from Barbara's lips or catch the tremor in her friend's hands as she clasped her cup.

"More coffee?" Karen offered without looking up.

"No . . . no thanks." Barbara barely breathed the words.

"You know, while we're on the subject of sleeping over," Karen said, suddenly pursuing a divergent train of thought, "I was just thinking about your visit with Rob. It's kind of romantic to think that years later, when both of you are older and wiser, you could meet again and find out you really love each other."

"I told you, it isn't like that."

Karen went on undeterred. "Of course, it doesn't hurt that you both are free, financially and maritally. No debts, no husband, no wife, no kids in diapers. Down there all alone, it might be possible that things will take off in a way you don't expect." She turned and eyed Barbara speculatively. "A minute ago I was pulling for McMillan, but Rob would be a good catch, too. He could surprise you. Everyone has an old love that got away somehow. He may look at this as his second chance."

Barbara was still sitting silently at the table.

"Well, how's it sound so far?" Karen joked.

"Like fiction," Barbara answered.

"I had a boyfriend in high school whose family moved to Germany when his father was transferred. I used to wonder what became of him. If I ever ran into him . . ."

"I'm sure Louis would be very understanding," Barbara teased, trying to recover the earlier, more lighthearted mood of their conversation.

"Up to a point," Karen acknowledged. "But given the choice, I'll stick with Louis."

"Given a choice," Barbara echoed the words, "I'd have stuck with T.J."

Karen crossed the room and stood next to her, resting her hand on Barbara's shoulder. "Sorry," she said softly. "We don't realize how few choices we really have."

"I'm beginning to," Barbara reflected aloud. "The little ones are left to us so we'll feel important. But the truth is, we aren't given much input on the big ones."

"You have some really intriguing ones to consider now," Karen insisted, refusing to let the conversation become somber again. "Not to be crude, but it comes down to a relatively simple issue. To bed or not to bed? And when, and with whom? Friday night, just let loose and give yourself a chance to explore all the options. When you're with Rob, do the same thing. Loosen up. Try them both. Do some comparative shopping," she added with a wicked gleam in her eye. "You're a big girl, and they're both consenting adults. Live a little. You don't want to spend the rest of your life wondering what it would have been like."

"I can't believe you're telling me this." Barbara felt the first trace of an authentic smile.

Karen gave Barbara's shoulders a hug. "I'm your friend. Who else would tell you it's time to—"

"Exercise my options?"

"At least."

"I apologize if I keep grinning like an idiot." McMillan poured two cut-crystal glasses full of wine as he spoke. "I'm a little unsettled at actually having you here."

"I'm a little unsettled myself. I was half dreading I'd be surrounded by red velvet and leopard skins," Barbara said sardonically. He watched her as she strolled around the room taking it all in. "It's been a while since I've been in a man's apartment. This is very impressive." McMillan's home was a narrow, two-story brick townhouse with ornate gables on the front. Located amid a cluster of old, elegant houses on South Battery, it was convenient to the office and unmistakably upscale. Eggshell upholstered sofas, mirrored walls, graceful Regency chairs, a geometrically patterned carpet, and minimal color heightened the illusion of space. Brass lamps and baskets of broad-leaved plants gave the room added tranquility. Several issues of *Architectural Digest* and *The Connoisseur* were stacked on the lower shelf of one end table.

"Not a room one would call lived-in," McMillan acknowledged good-naturedly, guessing what she was thinking. "I had a designer do it. The downstairs is mostly for show." He passed Barbara her wine. "It has the public pieces." The room seemed uncharacteristically formal for a man's home. "The velvet and leopard skins are upstairs," he noted, smiling as she glanced toward the stairs. "So is my workroom. You want to see it now?"

Barbara hesitated.

From the kitchen came the soft whirr of an electric timer. "Dinner is ready. I guess you see it later." McMillan stepped in and turned off the buzzer, then came right back and led her to a smaller room toward the back. This one snugly accommodated a small round dining table with elegant cream leather chairs, large pots of papyrus, a trio of glass sculptures set in lighted niches in the wall, french doors that overlooked a hedged-in patch of lawn. He'd set two places, facing each other, with a cluster of low crystal oil candles and an arrangement of pastel roses between them. "Sit here and I'll bring everything we need." He pulled out her chair, then eased her in toward the table.

"You might enjoy the view of the garden." He opened the sheer curtains and turned on the outdoor light. "Not as rustic as your marsh," he conceded, "but it has a certain charm. Unfortunately, nothing is blooming so it looks a little forlorn right now."

"It has possibilities," Barbara reassured him. "When Mr. Johns recovers, you should have him come over and landscape the place. It is so neat and—"

"And small?" he guessed what she was thinking.

"Maybe compact is a better word," Barbara suggested.

"Such a diplomat," he chuckled. "Here you live in the secluded wilds of Country Club Estates, and you can find something nice to say about my postage-stamp yard."

"To each his own. This is a very nice place."

"It's a lot nicer tonight," he responded as he ducked out of sight. Within minutes he returned with several serving dishes. "Just pretend the butler's bringing these in one at a time," he joked as he scooped salad into two bowls. In rapid succession, he arranged the entire meal before them, refilled her glass, sat across from her and offered a succinct toast. "Enjoy."

"This is lovely." Barbara speared a marinated mushroom from the spinach salad. "Should I send my compliments to your imaginary chef?"

"Hell, no," McMillan chuckled. "Save all your gratitude for me. I've pulled out some of my best stuff for this event." He lifted the cover from one platter of chicken Kiev. "I have no intentions of being humble about anything this evening," he declared.

Barbara leveled an uncertain look at him.

"I was referring to dinner," McMillan winked. "I like someone with good responses. Quick. You're very quick."

"I'm also very nervous."

"Don't be. I promise, there'll be no fooling around until after dinner." He slid the chicken onto her plate. "I'm kidding. Relax. We'll enjoy a pleasant meal together. No more sneaky remarks. After dinner, we'll have a little glass of liqueur, I'll give you the grand tour, and we'll discuss more serious matters."

Barbara smiled in relief. "You don't think it will look suspicious if I eat very slowly?"

"I won't touch that line," McMillan shook his head. "So," he continued, switching abruptly to a less suggestive tone, "tell me about your teaching. What's going on in Remedial English these days?"

Barbara stared at him curiously. "You really want to know?" she asked. "I hate to be patronized. There are other things we could talk about."

"I'm not patronizing you." McMillan continued serving them chilled asparagus, sliced tomatoes, and crusty ovals of roasted potatoes. "I'd like to know more about you. So let's start with your teaching. If I get bored, I guarantee you, I'll change the subject."

"Fair enough," Barbara conceded.

"So why are you doing what you do?"

"Why?" She paused a few seconds. "Because I like the kids and I'm good at teaching them. They're easily discouraged. I'm not. I'm patient, and I'll hang in there with them."

McMillan nodded, glancing up at her and asking questions from time to time as she continued. "These kids are verbal, but not in ways that get them decent jobs. They're tough and streetwise, but nearly illiterate." McMillan sat back sipping his wine, taking in the way her eyes sparkled with enthusiasm. "They aren't dumb, they're just unskilled. I help them talk and write more acceptably so they can present themselves better to the world."

"You don't feel like you're wasting your talents somewhat?" he asked seriously. "That night we went to the theater, I heard you talking about your classes this summer. How you liked Pirandello and Ionesco and Durang. You seem to love theater and literature. All that is way out of the realm of these kids you teach now. Maybe you'd enjoy a more sophisticated audience. Have you thought of working in one of the private schools around here?"

"So I could reach a classier clientele?" Barbara offered. "T.J. had the same idea," she added flatly.

"Classier, perhaps. The working conditions would be more pleasant. Students would be more receptive."

"That's what they kept telling me in college," Barbara said, smiling ruefully. "I was supposed to get out and spread tidbits about Keats, Shakespeare, and all those highbrow guys, but only to the good students, the ones who could already read. That smacks a bit of the elite few teaching the elite few. There are a lot of teachers willing to work with good students. Those are the ones already motivated," she stated matter of factly. "The first year I got a remedial class by default. I was a beginning teacher and jobs were scarce. Low man on the totem pole. Motivating that crew was a real challenge, but I managed. The next year, I asked to keep them. I liked the kind of difference I made."

"I wasn't being critical." McMillan's voice was soothing. "I'm just curious about what do you do with all your insights and information on those highbrow authors."

"I passed on some of that highbrow stuff to T.J. and got him interested enough in theater to work on the reconstruction that you and Mark are completing. Nothing is wasted," she insisted. "It's used in some way; it just isn't always conspicuous. Sometimes I manage to slip in bits and pieces in my classes. I read them parts of Shaw, scenes from Shakespeare so they'll at least recognize the names." She reflected a moment. "But my classes operate on a more practical level. I teach my students to survive today. To read a newspaper, understand ads, handle a bank account, write a check, use a phone book, put together a resume, and to stand their ground without resorting to four-letter words."

"And you like that?" He looked bewildered.

"I like that," Barbara laughed. "That's why I keep at it. It's like being a parent," she philosophized. "You know you can't teach them everything, but you keep trying. Besides, my students know I'm not there because I need the money. They know I could switch jobs or quit. So they figure if I think they are worth my time, they shouldn't let me down."

"And they don't?"

"Oh, they do from time to time. But so do Eliot and Miranda. But they also try very hard. I don't give up on any of my kids," she asserted.

"So you intend to keep teaching Remedial?" McMillan asked, refilling her wine and his own.

"I think so." Barbara speared one last bite. "Teaching sure helped pull me through the last few months," she admitted. "I knew I had to get up and out and keep on my toes every day. I felt anchored to something outside myself. I felt productive. Something was still going on like it used to."

"I see," McMillan said quietly. "You have everything

in some semblance of order. You've put all the pieces together. Now what? Would getting involved with me upset your equilibrium?" He reached across and covered her hand with his.

"You do have a way of getting right to the point."

"You have a way of getting to me." His voice turned soft. "So what happens with you and me? Where do we go from here?"

"I'm not sure. I'm still sorting that one out." She looked intently at him. Blonder than T.J., with dark eyes instead of the blue ones that were so familiar, McMillan emanated a confidence and sensuality that was undeniably appealing. "I've decided to go to visit my folks again. I'm taking the kids to spend Christmas with their grandparents, then I'm going to visit an old friend for New Year's, then I'll be back."

"That doesn't answer my question. What about you and me?"

Barbara licked her lips, determined to tell him what she'd been rehearsing since morning. "I want to be with you when I get back. I think I would like to move to a new plateau." She felt her cheeks flush. "But not tonight. I'm hoping that once the holidays are over and the new year begins, I'll be ready to step off this emotional roller coaster I've been on."

"You want to get a little head start tonight?" he asked, grinning. "We could pick up where we left off the other night."

"Before the smoke alarm," Barbara recalled. "That was grim."

"Part of it was very pleasant," he reminded her. "It may have been a false alarm, but I could sure feel the fire in you. I've been thinking about that ever since." He was trailing his fingertips up and down the back of her hand. Already she could feel her body responding to his touch.

"I've thought about it, too," Barbara acknowledged. "And I thought about tonight. I knew we had to talk before I leave for Florida, but I simply can't do anything intimate tonight. I'm not ready, mentally or physically."

"I hate to be blunt, but does that mean you're uninspired, indisposed, or that you aren't on the pill?"

"I'm just a bit intimidated and I'm not on the pill," Barbara responded. "I never needed to be, before."

"Are you going to start—"

"I'm going to start taking them."

"Good." McMillan lifted her hand and pressed his lips to her palm. "I realize you are taking a big step," he said gently. "Getting involved with another person is intimidating. I know you're not really used to having to talk about all this. But we can't pretend that what's going to happen is going to happen merely by chance. We are going to make love, my dear one, whenever you are ready, mentally and physically," he said, echoing her words. "In the meantime," he continued, his mood suddenly becoming playful, "let's get some liqueur, stroll upstairs, look around, then come back down here and neck." He stood and came around next to her.

"I know you've been with women who handled all this with a lot more sophistication than I do. You must find me frustrating." Barbara stood next to him, feeling increasingly foolish for putting him off again.

"In some ways, being around you is frustrating as hell," he muttered in a husky whisper. "But there's something remarkably flattering in the way you've given this so much thought. Nothing is casual with you, and I like that. I like it very much." He lowered his mouth to hers in a soft, brief kiss. "I'm gonna miss you," he whispered. "But I'm going to be smiling while I do. You are going to give real meaning to the new year."

"As long as you're being so understanding," Barbara said, sidestepping. "I'd better tell you the rest. The friend I'm visiting for New Year's is Rob Johnstone. You met him at Louis's party."

"The tall dark-haired guy who ran interference for you all night," McMillan remembered. "Old family friend, so I heard."

"An old boyfriend." She refused to keep that detail from him.

"Does that mean I shouldn't be smiling after all?"

McMillan looked at her closely. "Is there more to your visiting this guy than I'm hearing?"

"No. But I just want to keep things straight. I need to be alone for a few days. No kids, no parents, no nothing. He invited me there."

"So how can you be alone with him around?"

"He'll be busy rehearsing a play with his students. He'll be away a lot."

"And when he's not away?"

"He's a good friend. He knows enough to steer clear when I don't feel like talking. He gives me whatever space I need."

"An old unmarried friend," McMillan added.

"Who has managed his life without me for many, many years," Barbara responded.

"I hope he continues doing just that." McMillan led her toward his liquor cabinet in the hallway, old and polished like the elegant console. "It's tough enough competing with T.J., without the added intrusion of your Mr. Johnstone."

"I wish you hadn't put it quite like that." Barbara stopped one step behind him and stared at him. "I'm having enough trouble as it is. This isn't a competition. Either things work out or they don't. All I'm trying to do is give myself another chance. I'm not holding a contest."

"All I want is a fair chance, too." He reached out and gently stroked her hair. "I'd just like to have some idea of the odds. You still have some loose ends dangling with this Johnstone?" McMillan asked uneasily.

"Not if you mean romantic ones. Rob was part of my life before T.J., before you, and we've been able to remain friends through it all. There's no romance." She felt the tension in her neck and shoulders tightening. Deliberately she took a deep breath and let it out slowly, trying to ease the discomfort. "I need for this year to end. I need to put it to rest. I think I can do that better away from here."

"Okay, let's go look at my velvet and leopard skins," he kidded her as he poured the drinks and handed her one. "They'll give you something to fantasize about while you're away."

"I'll have plenty to fantasize about," she insisted.

"Sorry. I didn't mean to hassle you. Just remember that people can get mushy at Christmas. Watch yourself, Barbara." McMillan put his arm around her and kissed her again lightly. "The old boyfriend part makes me nervous. Sometimes it seems easy to fall back on an old habit. It's even crossed my mind once or twice when I ran into my ex, in rare and lonely lapses of sanity," he assured her laughingly. "Sometimes familiar and safe gets in the way of whatever else is happening. It's a lot scarier beginning with someone new, someone who has already had half a life without you."

"So I've been told," Barbara said, nodding. "I'm not going to let anything foolish happen, not in Florida, and not here."

"You mean not here until you get back." McMillan hugged her. "You'll have all that pent-up sexual energy to unleash. I get steamed up just thinking about it," he said chuckling. "So I plan to do everything I can to make you feel familiar and safe here with me, love."

Barbara's hand hesitated before resting on the bannister. Only T.J. had called her "love." The term evoked a confusing mix of pleasure and guilt.

Like McMillan said, the upper landing looked more lived in. The ivory and teak bedroom opened onto a huge open office-workroom furnished in chrome and leather, its walls hung with framed photographs and renderings of work he'd done. One unfinished room full of boxes overlooked the stairway on the opposite side. "I think this is going to be my library," he said, nudging several cartons out of their way. This room, lined with half-filled bookshelves, had a computer setup, a television–CD system, and an oriental carpet in shades of cream and burgundy and toast.

"Now this is beginning to look like a real person lives here," Barbara commented, impressed with the quiet energy in the room.

"A real person who obviously hasn't finished unpacking," McMillan noted.

"But you're getting there." She walked from shelf to shelf, browsing through the book titles.

"While you're being so diplomatic, let me pose you a hypothetical question." He leaned against the doorjamb, watching her. "What if one day you should marry again. What would you do about your house? Would you keep it?"

"Of course," Barbara answered instantly. "It's my home—my children's home."

"But would you want to keep on living in it?" he quizzed her. He put aside his drink and looked in the box nearest to him.

Barbara opened her mouth to answer, then abruptly fell silent. "I'm not sure," she finally said. "I can't imagine giving it up. It seems like a part of us. Even the trees," she said softly. "I wouldn't like to leave them."

"The trees?" McMillan had started unpacking a few books. He turned to stare at her.

"You've seen the huge oaks around the house," Barbara said, fluttering one hand in the air. "I think of them as old friends. So did T.J. Each of us had our particular favorite. He made a big deal about Byron being his alterego, flamboyant and flawed. Mine is Keats, Miranda loves Wordsworth. Eliot's tree is Poe."

"Trees," McMillan said quietly, then shook his head.

Barbara smiled and continued. "I know it sounds silly. The kids grew up playing on the lot long before the house was built. We all talked about the trees almost like they were people."

"The trees," he repeated. He'd seen the children playing under the towering oaks but he hadn't given the individual trees any particular notice.

"Maybe it would be more accurate to say we made them part of our family and we became part of theirs." She shrugged, noting his arched eyebrow and his dubious but amused expression. "We're all quite attached to them."

"Trees with names. Part of the family." McMillan leaned against the door again and grinned at her. "Your Mr. Johnstone would have one hell of a time moving them all down to Florida."

"Is that why you were asking about the house?" Barbara frowned at him.

"That's part of it," he admitted. "This will be your second trip to Florida in a month. I wanted to know where you felt your real roots were, here or there."

"I never really felt I had a home. My folks were military and we were always moving from post to post. Then they divorced. My mom remarried and moved again. But I've put down roots in Charleston. This is my first real home. This is my children's home. This is where my life is. I'm not planning to leave."

"Good," McMillan expelled a long breath. "Let's go downstairs." He led her toward the stairway. "Or we can go in my room and fool around." He reached for her, easing her back in a melodramatic dipping motion. "I'd love to give you a taste of what you'll be missing." He pressed a loud moist kiss at the base of her throat. Then he stood her back upright. "Now it's your turn." He unbuttoned the neck of his shirt and bared the top of his chest. "I want a little teaser. Right there," he pointed to the hollow above his golden chest hairs.

"Seriously?" Barbara contemplated the spot. With a good-natured shrug, she bent forward and gently kissed the designated area.

"Very nice. Let's make sure we've got the picture." He reached for the neckline of Barbara's pale green shirt. "Don't panic. Easy now," he held her with one arm, stopping her from backing away. "This is simply a two-button experiment," he promised. He slid the button free. Again he kissed her, slower this time, letting his lips linger while his warm breath rippled above her breasts.

"Your turn," he said hoarsely when he pulled away and stood up. Her hands slid over his chest and unbuttoned one more button on his shirt. She could feel his pulse beating as she pressed her lips against his warm skin. He slid his hands up her arms as the scent of his body and the warmth of their contact made her heartrate acclerate.

"You want to try for three? Please." He drew her into his arms.

Barbara didn't resist. She leaned against him while he

gently stroked her back. Just being held this way felt so familiar, so good, so safe.

"Do you really want to go downstairs?"

Barbara nodded, somewhat unnerved by the realization that part of her wanted to go on.

"Then let's do it soon or I won't be able to wait until after New Year's." He eased her away and gazed down into her eyes. "You feel so good next to me. Are you sure you want to go home tonight?" he asked softly. He brushed her temple with his lips but made no move to release her.

Again she nodded.

"Give me a minute till my blood pressure gets back to normal," he said, his breathing ragged. They stood there still embracing for a moment, breathing softly.

"If you ever doubted that I'm a gentleman . . ." McMillan left the comment unfinished.

On the way home in the car, they held hands. "I'll just stay long enough to let you check all the doors." He broke the silence as they drove across the Ashley River bridge and turned past the country club toward Harborview. "If I held you that close again, I don't think I could let you go," he stated honestly. "This agreeable, understanding side of me is just about worn out."

"I was considering nominating you for sainthood."

"Not interested," he declared. "But just to keep me from straying tonight, I'll leave my overcoat on and just walk through the house with you," he insisted. "And you try your damnedest to look frumpy and undesirable."

"Right," she agreed.

"And when you check the locks, no counting out loud," he teased her. "If I hear numbers, I may lose control. I keep seeing that top button, then the second . . ."

"No counting," Barbara promised.

Just as he said, McMillan left his coat on and walked from room to room with her, flipping on the overhead lights, then turning them off, satisfied that the house was intact. "All clear," he announced. He grinned triumphantly as they completed the rounds. "No prowlers, no leaky johns, no noisy smoke alarms."

"Then I must be safe." Barbara thanked him.

"Only temporarily, love." He caught her by the shoulders and kissed her lightly on the lips. "By the way, what time is it?"

Barbara glanced at the clock. It read two o'clock. Before she answered she caught the glimmer in his eye and realized he was thinking about counting buttons, not time.

"Read it yourself, wise guy." She shook her head in dismay.

"Just wanted to tempt you."

"You already have."

"And you still want me to leave?"

"Please."

" 'Night. It was promising," McMillan waved and ducked out the door. She locked it after him, then clicked off the outside light.

Slowly she moved toward the bedroom, pausing by the atrium to contemplate the little Christmas tree, with lights turned off and decorations barely visible in the darkness. "Well, here we are, Bozo, all alone. What have you got to say about it?" She stared at the tree. Nothing stirred in the garden room.

Finally she sighed and continued to her bedroom. Eliot's door stood open, his bed, like Miranda's, unoccupied for the night.

"I don't like being alone," Barbara announced to the large-tailed phoenixes poised on the draperies. She slid into her long flannel gown, then climbed under the sheets, shivering at their coolness. She clicked off the bedside lamp and waited in the darkness. "I'm not going to live like a nun. If you want to discuss anything, you know where I am," she spoke in the still room. She rolled onto her side, listening in the dark to the soft whirr of the heat pump as the thermostat triggered it into action. Other than the rush of cedar-tinged air and the hum of the heater, the house was silent.

"Goodnight, T.J.," she murmured. She tugged the blankets up to her chin and listened. When the heater cut off several minutes later, she did not notice the complete stillness. Barbara Ashcroft was asleep.

* * *

"How you doin' out here, Old Pa?" Mattie asked as she came around to the sunny clearing where Luster Johns was chiseling away on his latest wood sculpture. Bundled in a plaid wool jacket, leather cap with sheepskin-lined earflaps, and wearing long johns under his overalls to keep out the December chill, he'd been out there since midmorning, putting the last touches on the sixth angel, detailing the feathering in the wings. He sat propped on a tall stool with his right leg, still encased in a fiberglass cast from mid-thigh to calf, poking out to one side.

"I'm fine as sunshine," Luster answered cheerfully, without slowing the tap-and-scrape movement of hammer and chisel. When he'd awakened that morning, the last day of the year, the cool air smelled clean and crisp, there wasn't a cloud in the sky. After he got into his clothes and carried his cup of coffee out onto the porch to rock a while, the spirit came looking for him.

"I got some hot soup and sourdough biscuits cookin'. How 'bout coming in for the day and warming up?" Mattie suggested. "No sense startin' the New Year with a cold."

"Just give me a little while longer," Luster said. "Almos' finished with this one. Don't want to leave it over if I can help it."

"How many of these do you think you'll end up with?" Mattie moved around to take a good look at the face on this one. It reminded her of one of the little neighbor boys, Eugene Oliver, with his rounded cheeks and pouty expression.

"Don't quite know," Luster answered honestly. "Mo' than this, that's for sure. Quite a number mo'." Off and on for weeks, he'd had the same familiar thread of music running through his head no matter where he was. He'd catch himself singing about that band of angels while he worked on his carving. He'd start humming it when he rocked and stared out over the river. He'd been humming it when the spirit came that morning and made him listen more closely to himself. "How many angels do you reckon is in a band?" he asked her.

"What you mean by band?" Mattie gave him a sudden quizzical look.

"You know, the song 'bout the band of angels comin' for to carry me home? That kind of band."

Mattie hugged her sweater tighter about herself and turned so her back blocked the wind. "Is that what this is all about? The angels are comin'?" She lowered her voice, dreading now that Luster's call from the spirit had finally come. He'd been acting peculiar, a bit secretive, since summer turned to fall. Since his injury, he'd had her son, Willie Dodd, driving him about. They'd gone up to visit Sister Gertrude twice over the holidays and they'd stayed gone a longer while than she'd expected. She'd been wondering what was so pressing that he'd had to see the conjur woman. Doctors said his shattered kneecap was healing nicely. Now Mattie feared her father had some kind of trouble that doctors and Sister Gertrude's herbs and berries couldn't cure.

"Don't you go worrying now, sugah'," Luster said, looking up from his carving. "Other than this cussed' knee and the old rumatiz', I ain't ailing. I just knows I have to make a band of 'em. A band of angels, however many that be. And I don't get the feeling they's for me. But if they is, they is. I'm at peace with the spirit. So don't you go getting all bothered. Something's afoot. I jus' don' know yet what it is. When I know, you'll know."

Mattie studied the bright look in Luster's eyes and the gentle curve of his smile. Despite the cold weather and the knee cast, he looked more rested and spry now than he had over the past months. "Okay. But you come in soon for your soup. I got greens and hog jowls and black-eyed peas simmering for tomorrow. House smells mighty good."

"I can sniff it all the way out here." Luster looked at her again, grinning. "I'll be in right soon. You just get out some syrup for those biscuits. Jus' a little lick mo' to do," he assured her.

He started chipping away at the little angel and was whistling by the time she reached the porch. She turned and looked back a moment, drawing in a breath. "How many's in a band?" she murmured, trying to brace herself for the possibility that Luster was putting together his own escort to the other side. "If it has to be, it has to be," she sighed. Her daddy would be eighty on his next birthday. She was hoping he'd make it at least a couple more years, enough to see Willie Dodd graduate from college. "Lord willin' it don't have to be," she said hopefully, opening the door and letting the aromas from the kitchen surround her.

Luster stayed out in the cold only ten minutes longer before he called it quits for the day and for the year. Then he sprayed his tools with WD-40, slipped the chisels in leather apron pockets, and rolled them all into a neat bundle to take inside. "Happy New Year, folks. See you next year," he told the circle of carved figures before he left. He gave Inez a light kiss on the cheek.

Whistling again, he hobbled toward the house on the single crutch he'd agreed under pressure to use. Doctors had given him two, but he found them too cumbersome. They also told him to stay off his feet for a few weeks. But he had errands to do and Willie Dodd was off school and there to help out. So he went about his business on one crutch, just to keep Mattie somewhat appeased.

"Happy New Year," he said now, patting the bannister of the porch on the house before he went inside. He and Mattie had made their own good luck wreaths for their doors, not as many wreaths as he'd taken to the Ashcrofts, and not as laden with special plants. But just as he'd told Willie Dodd to tell the missus when he was too laid up to help her, the wreaths had to be hung by the folks who lived there. And when he had his grandson drive him up to check on the house the past week while the family was gone, he added new-picked cattails to their wreaths to bring peace and prosperity for the New Year. The house had felt still and tranquil when he touched it. He had Willie Dodd replenish the juniper ash circle, just in case.

"You folks have a Happy New Year." He turned and sent his wish upon the wind. "New year, new life," he said wistfully as he paused there. "Bring 'em home, safe and sound." That was as close to a prayer as Luster Johns ever came.

Barbara zipped her quilted jacket up to her neck and shoved her hands deep into her pockets. She'd followed the strip of white sandy beach for over a mile with no one except a few sandpipers and seagulls for company before turning back toward the south. Far ahead, coming to meet her, she could make out the familiar form, tall and long-legged, walking towards her barefoot in the sand. Rob still wore the same leather windbreaker that he'd owned since college. Its scars and scuffmarks, like the grayish streaks in his hair, gave a curious distinction to his appearance.

"Out enjoying the sun?" he greeted her in his casual, quiet way. There was none. It was fifty-eight degrees in Fort Lauderdale and thick dark clouds hung low over the gray Atlantic. The weather report predicted rain.

"Under my three layers of clothing, I'm wearing my bathing suit." Barbara moved close enough to use him as a shield from the chilly wind. "I guess that makes me an optimist," she laughed.

"I'll say," Rob agreed. He wrapped his arm around her. "Could I interest you in a little lunch."

"Is it hot?" Barbara asked. The cold wet sand beneath her feet made her shiver.

"It was when I picked it up. If you'd move your slightly blue feet, I'll fire it up in the microwave and try to thaw you out." Arm in arm they walked rapidly over the narrow path toward the roadway. On either side, massive condominiums spread along the shoreline, but across the asphalt beach road, behind a low screen of palmettos and palms, sat several two-story beach houses with their fronts to the street and their backs opening onto a man-made canal. Rob owned a weathered grayish house with white shutters and windows full of thick ferns in hanging baskets, a staunch holdout against the incursion of multiple-family dwellings.

"You get some plates," he told her, directing her toward the cabinet next to the window. "I'll heat the food." They moved about the large kitchen, both of them still barefoot. Rob put five unmarked white cardboard containers into the microwave oven and touched the controls. When the timer chimed, Barbara had plates, mugs, silverware, and napkins waiting. Rob arrived at the table with the boxes on a tray and a pair of his socks and a hot water bottle for her feet tucked under his arm. "This is as close to formal as we're getting."

"This is great." She pulled on the oversized socks and lined up the water bottle as a footrest.

"Moo goo gai pan." Rob opened and presented the first container with a great flourish. "And sweet and sour pork." He identified the second. "Egg rolls . . . rice . . . and something in lobster sauce," he concluded.

"I'm starving, and it all smells wonderful," Barbara leaned forward eagerly. The two of them ladled rice and dollops from each container onto their plates.

"I wonder if we should feel decadent, indulging ourselves like this?" he kidded her.

Barbara drizzled hot mustard onto her plate and dipped her egg roll into it. "I can't speak for you, but I feel great. All I've had to do is eat and sleep and stuff myself. It's wonderful."

"You're not worried about the kids?" he persisted, teasing her affectionately.

"Eliot is probably clocking his first hundred miles on Gramma's bike, and Miranda can only stay on the phone long enough to tell me how many fish and crabs she and her Gramps are catching."

"I gather that means you called them this morning," Rob smiled smugly.

"Not because I'm feeling guilty," Barbara insisted. "I just like to touch base every once in a while."

"Like once a day," Rob said, grinning.

"Okay, you got me. So pass the whatever-in-lobster sauce. Tell me how the play is coming along."

"The play is coming along fine. Everyone is speaking and moving at the same time," he said with an indulgent smile. "Now we're in the refining stage. From the way it went today, I'd say we need about six weeks."

"But I thought the play started in two? Didn't you say mid-January?" Barbara interrupted him.

"It does," Rob admitted with a shrug. "Which is precisely why I spent the morning being a surly bastard."

"Will they make it in time? And do it right?" Barbara stared at him anxiously.

"Of course they will. I do an excellent surly bastard," Rob assured her. "Tomorrow they get to spend one rehearsal being indignant, then things will begin to click. I've got some great students. Really sharp kids." His voice trailed off as he concentrated on his food. "Would you like a beer?"

"With Chinese food?"

"If you want tea, I'd have to make it," he countered. "It will take a while."

"I'd love a beer. And some tea."

"Fine. I'll get us the beers. You start the kettle," he bargained. "After we eat, I'll stick on some videotapes, and we'll have the tea with dessert."

"Dessert and movies. You'll spoil me." Barbara shook her head.

"This is a holiday. We've got nothing until the party tonight. This is a great way to spend a rainy afternoon."

"Right. Get the beer. Where's the kettle?"

"That's what I like," Rob said, chuckling. "A little flexibility." He strode out to the refrigerator with her following. "Do you want it straight out of the bottle, or would you prefer a glass?" He held the dark beer up for her to see.

"How about a straw?" Barbara suggested.

"Keep that up and I'll give you a private showing of my surly bastard routine," he warned her, picking out two tall glasses.

"I've missed most of your legitimate performances. I'll settle for whatever you've got," she shot back with a satisfied grin.

"Wiseass." He poured the two beers and handed her glass to her.

"Beer in crystal. The gentleman has class," Barbara rejoiced.

"Class, and good looks, and intelligence. Now that's settled, let's eat." They sat passing the hot water bottle back and forth between them below the table and the cartons of food above. When the rain swept in, they watched it out the long glass windows as it set the surface of the canal dancing.

"You still want to go with me tonight?" Rob asked as he cleared away the dishes.

"If you still want me to," Barbara answered amiably. "It may start some peculiar rumors. What if word gets out that you have an old flame—" She caught herself. She'd intended to say friend.

"Whatever you are," Rob said, stepping in, "all the rumors can do is help my image. Surly bastard and seducer of women. Not bad for an aging thespian," he professed. "Besides, I've got a few friends who already know who you are and that you're here. Let the rest of the folks wonder," he declared.

"What have you told your good friends?" Barbara questioned him.

"That you're one of them," he answered easily.

"Oh," she nodded. There was something vaguely inadequate about his reply, but Barbara simply smiled and concentrated on the last traces of dark beer in her goblet.

"How about some movies?" Rob suggested. "I'll set them up and you get the tea and cookies."

"Cookies?"

Rob pointed to an unopened sack on the counter. "Dessert. Fortune cookies," he explained. "I bought a dozen. If you don't like what one tells you, just keep on going till you hit one you do like."

"Good thinking," Barbara sighed and cleaned away her dish.

"So, you are Rob's Bobbie." A massive woman in a fuschia gown extended her hand. Long, pinkish-purple fingernails closed across the back of Barbara's smaller hand. "You undernourished little things have all the luck." Her deep melodious laugh accompanied the comment. "Lucie Laveau," the woman introduced herself. "I know, it sounds like a hooker." Again her laughter rippled through the room.

"It's nice to meet you," Barbara finally managed to

squeeze in a few words. "When Rob told me about you, I didn't know what to expect. Somehow I expected—"

"Less of me?" Lucie cackled.

"Perhaps." Barbara smiled. "But I was thinking of someone spinsterish," she said apologetically. "Rob said you were—"

"The old maid who runs the English Department. I am," Lucie guffawed. "And, honey, he told me you were an old friend." The big woman grinned. "I sure didn't expect such a cutie. I thought you'd be wrinkled and hobbling in on crutches. Maybe I was just hoping." She gave Barbara a wink.

"Then this is a pleasant surprise for both of us," Barbara responded.

"The heck it is," Lucie said, chuckling. "All these years I've been trying to wear down Johnstone's resistance, and I find out he's had you stashed away somewhere. You could at least have warts or crossed eyes or something." She hooked her arm into Barbara's and started leading her toward the rear of the house, where thirty or more people were clustered about buffet tables on a huge, screened patio. Paddle-wheeled fans stirred the air. "Stick with me, honey, and I'll help you run the gauntlet," Lucie promised. "If you survive me, you can handle the rest without breaking a sweat."

"I'll introduce her," Rob stepped quickly to catch up behind them and to reclaim Barbara.

"You go get a couple of drinks," Lucie dismissed him. "Bobbie and I will make the rounds ourselves."

"I think she uses Barbara now," Rob corrected her with the name he'd heard her friends in Charleston use.

"Barbara, is it?" Lucie replied unperturbed. "You still go on now for those drinks. Barbara and Lucille will be back in ten minutes, Robert." She arched one eyebrow and flicked her well-manicured fingernails towards the bar.

"You're sure?" He looked at Barbara for confirmation.

"I'm the one in charge here, and I'm sure," Lucie answered. "Besides, we've got a few things to discuss."

"We'll be fine," Barbara assured him, curious to know what Lucie wanted to say.

"So I'll see you in ten minutes." He surrendered.

"This way." Lucie swept her toward a group of three men across the patio, pausing to pick up a few hors d'oeuvres midway. "Rob said you're involved in the Spoleto in Charleston. I work with theater here. These are the guys in the sponsor range," Lucie confided. "Our sponsors donate five hundred bucks to help our productions. How much do Spoleto festival sponsors put up?" she asked point blank.

"Something between twenty-five hundred and five thousand," Barbara replied uneasily. She wasn't quite sure why the conversation had shifted in this particular direction.

"The festival has grown. You're in the big leagues," Lucie said in response to the dubious look on her companion's face. "But I know you must appreciate how scarce sponsors are. And these are three of our regulars."

"Regular what?" the short gray-haired man asked as he turned to greet them.

"Regular high-rollers," Lucie replied, beaming at the dapper gentleman. "Barbara, this is Albert, and Bernie, and Jack. Barbara is visiting from Charleston," Lucie added smoothly. "We were just expressing our admiration for people who support the arts. That definitely led us to you three. We can always count on these gentlemen to help us to get a production afloat."

"Before you make us out to be philanthropists, Lucie," Albert Abrams cautioned her, "don't overestimate our altruism. Our contributions are tax-deductible."

"True. Barbara is a volunteer who works on fund raising for the Spoleto festival," Lucie stressed, "so if you're after bigger deductions—"

"I'll keep her in mind," Abrams promised, nodding. "But it will be difficult mailing a check to her with you already camped out on my doorstep, Lucie," he joked.

"Forget her, then," Lucie responded with her infectious chuckle. "I'll be after you in the spring, for myself," she insisted.

"Best offer I've had all night." The little man looked at her with a sly smile.

"Well, the night is young," Lucie reminded him. "I may be back sooner than you expect."

"I'll go charge up my pacemaker," Abrams declared. His two elderly companions winked at each other, then nodded politely as Lucille Laveau took Barbara by the arm and moved on. Off to one side, an instrumental group set up with a keyboard, drums, and a guitar began to play softly, a rhythmical salsa number that started people swaying.

"Some of these folks are faculty members. Three over there, English department. Two there, history and humanities," Lucie briefed her as they strolled on. "Others are friends and neighbors. The white-haired fellow by the geranium is our host," she whispered. "He owns the local newspaper, and he always seems to know someone who can help out whenever we need something at the college. He's a quiet little gentleman, but he's as good hearted as they come." Lucie maneuvered Barbara through the room toward him. "Widower this past year," she added pointedly. "I guess you understand that very well." Her large, beefy hand patted Barbara's arm.

Before Barbara could reply, Lucie had her face to face with their host. "William Weizmann, this is Johnstone's friend, Barbara Ashcroft from Charleston."

The white-haired gentleman narrowed his green eyes at her. "So you did come." He held rather than shook her hand. "I am so glad you took a few days for yourself, my dear. I remember last summer Rob mentioning a dear friend had been widowed. You have my sympathy and my good wishes for the new year." His deeply tanned face spread into a genial smile.

"Thank you. I understand you have been through a similar loss. You have my sympathy and good wishes, too," she said softly, feeling a sudden bond between them.

"It's a little different at my age." Weizmann shrugged. "Not any less traumatic," he added, qualifying his statement, "but different. Mimi and I both were at an age when death was a realistic consideration. You certainly weren't. And now you have a whole new life to face. I'm just rounding out my very comfortable old one."

"William," Lucie fussed at him. "Quit sounding like an old codger. You've still got a lot of miles left on you."

"I know you're right." Weizmann grinned. "Once it finally sunk in what a great life I've had so far, and how quickly things can change, it made me want to take a few more chances in the time I've got left." He turned again to Barbara. "After the shock eases, you'll understand what I mean," he said with great tenderness. "Mimi is always with me in spirit, always reminding me to match my socks, and not slurp my tea. And always loving me." He squeezed Barbara's hand. "My memory is full of her. It's the outside world that sometimes seems a little empty," he noted.

Lucie moved between them, wrapping a large arm around both Barbara and Weizmann. "There is a tall individual with two dripping glasses of booze waiting by the asparagus fern," she announced solemnly. "If you two don't mind breaking this off for a few minutes, I think we should restore a smile to Johnstone's face." Three sets of eyes turned toward Rob.

"It's a delight to have you here," Weizmann concluded. "I wish you a Happy New Year." He leaned forward and kissed Barbara's cheek lightly.

"William," Lucie teased him. "She's a little young."

"I told you, I'm not missing any opportunities." Weizmann chuckled. "By midnight I may have run out of steam."

"Well then, I'll stay with you now," Lucie declared, giving Barbara's hand a little squeeze. "You go back to Johnstone. He looks like he'd prefer to have some time with you." She waved Barbara off cheerfully. "I'll try to get in a few dances with this guy." She took Weizmann's arm.

Barbara moved smoothly between the few people who stood conversing along the fringe of the patio. Several couples had moved to the center of the floor and were swaying to the music that had shifted from Latin rhythms to soft rock to a slow tune. "You want to dance, big fella?"

"I thought you'd never ask. Let me land these." Rob glanced around for a place to deposit the two full glasses. He wiped his hands on his handkerchief. "Pardon the cold and clammy palms," he apologized. "It's not nerves, it just that ten minutes with those drinks made me numb." Cautiously he placed one hand on the back of Barbara's gown and held the left hand open.

"Been a long time," Rob said softly as she leaned her head against his shoulder.

"It sure has," Barbara answered, finding the sensations increasingly pleasurable as she felt his arm close about her. T.J. had not been much for dancing. He had danced well enough, but for him it was merely something one did on certain social occasions. From the time she was twelve, dancing had been one of her favorite pastimes and a safe kind of physical release. In college, the stereo would blare for hours as the girls gyrated about the downstairs recreation room, inventing and mastering steps. After any ballgame, play, or concert, she would rush with or without a date to the loud boogie joints and dance the rest of the night until curfew. Often she and Rob had held each other for hours, wordlessly touching, embracing, and moving against one another, then gone home exhausted, each to a separate bed and solitary fantasies.

"Sublimation," Rob had called it years before, with more than a trace of resignation in his voice. But he loved to dance as much as Barbara did. They would cling together, or dance apart, hot and wet with perspiration, until the last possible moment.

"You still dance great," Barbara observed.

"You still feel great," Rob replied with a long-forgotten warmth in his voice. He guided her between the other dancers and swirled around to the steady rhythm of the music. Suddenly she became acutely conscious of every brush of thigh on thigh, or breast on breast, and the steady heat of his open palm on her back.

"It's okay," he said softly, as if he'd read her thoughts. "We're only dancing." But somewhere deep within her, Barbara sensed another voice, less soothing, telling her it was all right to feel what she was feeling. *Mine*, it whispered without words, as she let herself breathe in the scent of this man who was her friend. *Mine*. She felt her eyelashes graze his cheek. And the softness in the way he cushioned each sway became both comfortable and distinctly erotic. All the rules that had intervened over the years silently slipped away.

At four minutes to midnight, the party had swelled to over fifty guests, who stood shoulder to shoulder around the patio, waiting for the New Year to arrive. Weizmann had cases of champagne brought out and white-jacketed waiters were rapidly filling and refilling glasses. The trio had started playing a slightly upbeat version of Memories, which reverberated through the room. They switched to Auld Lang Syne a few seconds before midnight.

"Good health, good friends, and love," Weizmann proposed, raising his glass. "Happy New Year, everyone." He barely got the words out when Lucie Laveau planted a moist kiss on his smiling mouth.

"Happy New Year," Rob said to Barbara. He had one arm around her. With the other he reached down and tapped his glass against hers. The band was pounding out the music, noisemakers buzzed and squawked, and the crowd sang and cheered. Amid all the celebrating, Barbara hesitated, then turned to face him. His dark eyes studied her with a curious intensity, somewhat guarded but incredibly tender.

"Happy New Year, Rob." She lifted her lips to his. The first kiss was intended to be brief and innocent and friendly, but the voice inside whispered and she let her mouth linger just a second too long. The kiss turned surprisingly tantalizing. When their lips no longer touched, neither one moved away. Rob studied the play of emotions on her face and lowered his mouth to meet hers again, slowly and more thoughtfully this time.

Barbara slid her hand around his neck, steadying herself as his mouth became irresistibly soft against hers. *Mine*. The word came pulsing through her. Rob's embrace loosened momentarily, but when she didn't make any attempt to pull back, he gradually drew her closer, so her body pressed against his. For a few seconds, they were both lost in the delicious heat between them. He was the one who recovered first and broke the embrace.

"Bobbie, what's going on here?" Rob's dark eyes reflected glimmers of light as he held her away from him and whispered.

"I'm sorry. I don't know," Barbara answered, breathing deep uneven breaths. "I'm not being cute. I'm sorry." Embarrassed now, she felt the tears spring to her eyes. Rob slid an arm around her shoulders and leaned her against his chest.

"Come on, it's time to call it a night," he said with forced calm. "Before one of us fails to find this amusing. Let's say goodnight." Obediently, Barbara moved with him from guest to guest, singling out the ones who had to be bade farewell. Lucie Laveau and William Weizmann walked with them to the front door. At last, with his jacket pulled about her shoulders, Barbara was safely belted into the passenger seat of the car while Rob strode around to the other side.

"Are you a little drunk?" he asked her quietly as he backed the car out of Weizmann's driveway.

"I don't think so," Barbara answered honestly. "It would be a lot simpler if I were."

"Or if I were," Rob noted.

"You always were a great kisser," Barbara tried to joke.

"I suppose I should take that as a compliment," Rob muttered. "Why do I suddenly feel so guilty?"

"I don't know. I feel guilty, too." Barbara began to cry softly. Rob glanced over at her then smoothly pulled the car over to the curb.

"Please, just keep driving," she insisted. "Let me sort this out all by myself." She managed a weak smile through the tears.

"I wish you'd tell me what is going on inside your head. This is a big deal, and we'd better talk about it."

"I just can't," Barbara lamented. "Everything is so messed up."

"You're telling me."

"I didn't want to get you all tangled up in my problems," Barbara sighed. "I feel like I'm falling apart inside. Please, just drive."

"If you'd give me half a chance, I'd be glad to help hold you together." His warm voice trembled.

"I think I'm supposed to do it myself."

"Says who?"

"No one," Barbara sobbed. "Maybe me. Please, just get us home."

Rob took a long look at her, then pulled the car back out into the light traffic. For a while neither of them spoke.

"I gather things at home have not been going along as well as you've been indicating," he said, pressing her. "All the times I called you, you never even hinted at how shaky you were."

"Maybe I didn't know," Barbara defended herself. "Maybe I didn't want to talk about it."

"Maybe," Rob acknowledged.

"Maybe I just didn't want to sound like some hysterical idiot."

"By telling me what?"

"I can't tell you." Of all people, she didn't want to see the expression on his face change to bewilderment or disbelief or despair if she started talking about ghosts or poltergeists or whatever spirit form had been haunting her house. She couldn't bear it if he thought she was crazy.

"Bobbie, how can I help if you don't open up?"

"I can't talk about it."

"Is it only the unimportant things we can talk about?" His mouth set into a firm line as he swung onto the highway. The next turn was onto the street that led along the beach road toward his house. Without speaking, he parked the car in the driveway and came around to get her.

They walked through the dim house in brittle silence. Barbara climbed the stairway up to the guest room. Solemnly she undressed, tugging a long tee-shirt over her head. Then she sat on the edge of the bed, staring out at the night sky.

Finally Rob knocked softly at her door. "Come on

out," he called. "Let's be friends. I've got a shoulder you can lean on." Barbara crossed the room and tugged open the door. Standing in his shirtsleeves, with his tie dangling at an angle, Rob waited for her to come out. "I don't want to start the new year like this." He held up an unopened bottle of champagne. "Let's get drunk," he suggested. "We'll sit and drink and watch the sun come up."

"I don't think I want to get drunk." Barbara shook her head.

"What do you want to do?" He examined her intently.

"I want you to hold me," she said in a whisper.

"Bobbie, I don't think I can." His voice broke. He stood there with the bottle dangling at his side, looking at her desolately. "Not knowing what to do with you is tearing me up. But I can't just hold you." She could see the naked hunger in his eyes.

She stood barefoot in the doorway looking up at him. "Do you have a few hours you can give me, with no questions asked?"

"What does that mean?"

"It means I don't want to be alone and I don't want to mess up anything between us, but I do want to make love with you. Without explanations or promises or anything."

"Do I have any other options?" he questioned her.

"Not right now. I don't want to talk or think or sort things out." Her shoulders drooped as she spoke and her eyes brimmed with tears she could not explain.

He stood in the dark hallway. "No questions."

"Then come in." She stepped aside, her hand still on the doorknob, and waited for him to enter.

"You don't have to close the door here." He reached out and stopped her. "We're all alone. Just us."

Barbara stood still a moment, savoring the impact of his comment. "Just us." She smiled at how wonderful it felt. Then she turned toward him. Without a word, she slid into his arms. His lips were warm and sweet on hers.

"I gather this isn't about dancing," he said hoarsely. Between each word, he covered her mouth and face and throat with the softest kisses, while a few unnoticed tears trailed down her cheeks. "All these years and I'm nervous as hell," he groaned as he lifted the shirt over her head. Standing naked in the pale moonlight, Barbara untied his tie and unbuttoned his shirt. With his hands, like velvet, caressing her, she stepped out of time and let the old year slip away.

CHAPTER 7

> —the best gesture of my brain is less than
> your eyelid's flutter which says
> we are for each other: then
> laugh, leaning back in my arms
> for life's not a paragraph
>
> And death i think is no parentheses
> *e. e. cummings*

"THESE ARE A few special ones for you," Rob said. Just as they announced the arrival of her flight, Rob handed Barbara a stack of boxed videotapes tied neatly, complete with a rubber carrying handle over the string. "Some we didn't get to," he explained. He and Barbara had spent hours New Year's Day sipping tea, talking theater, and watching segments of tapes of student productions he'd put on over the years. A few were ones in which he'd also acted in minor or character roles. It was a crash course in his creative work as teacher, performer, director, stagecraftsman, and occasionally choreographer, and there had been an impressive range of talent and technical effects represented. But these few, for some reason, he'd held back.

"I'll let the kids watch them with me," Barbara said as she grasped the bundle. The twelve-seat plane that would take her across Florida taxied into position ready to unload one set of passengers and pick up the next. "Thanks for everything."

Rob shook his head. "I don't want any of the usual departure conversation to spoil our last few minutes here. You're going away, but you're not leaving me," he said quietly. "You never really have."

Barbara's chin trembled. "I'm really not as nice a person as you think," she blurted out. She took a deep breath to steady herself. "There's a lot I wish I could tell you."

"I never once said I think you're nice." Rob towered

above her. "You're just you. I never expected you to be anything else. And I don't sit in judgement on you, Bobbie." He sounded typically calm. "And as for things you should be telling me, that goes both ways. But I think we're both doing what we can, under the circumstances."

"There's a lot you don't understand."

"Never have, never will." He lowered his voice so the other passengers could not overhear their conversation. "I never felt I had to understand. You're the one who always tried to make sense out of things. Even when nothing seemed to fall into place, you always managed to work out some kind of pattern. I don't worry about tidying everything up." He rested one hand on each of her shoulders. "None of this, not what happened to T.J., nor whatever is bothering you at home, nor what's happening between us, none of it fits in any logical order. Life's a grab bag. It's all just there." He caught her by the lapels of her overcoat and gently tugged her toward him. "Take what you get, and make the best of it." He brushed a soft kiss across her forehead.

Barbara blinked back more tears. She wished they'd had more time and fewer secrets. She couldn't tell him anything about the happenings in the house. She'd barely mentioned McMillan, who would be waiting for her to come home. She'd left her life in Charleston behind her for a few days, and now she was leaving this one. All kinds of second thoughts and regrets had surfaced.

"Give yourself a break, and quit trying to be so . . . responsible," Rob suggested, struggling for the right word. "Screw up occasionally like the rest of us. Act selfish, or downright mean if you want. I won't abandon you. Even if you show me all your warts and scars, I'll still be here."

"I wouldn't count on it," Barbara sniffed, more miserable than she imagined she'd be.

"Look, you." Rob tightened his grip on her coat lapels slightly. "You are messing up one of my best going-away speeches. I am being supportive and reassuring. I'm not asking for anything." He regarded her intently. "I don't know why we did what we did. Personally, I loved it. I think you loved it, too. So I don't know why the hell you are going off like you are, all guilty and unhappy and weepy. It must be something outside of you and me left to resolve. Whatever it is obviously can't be fixed here at the airport. So relax. It took us a lot of years to get where we are, separately and together. I'm not going to rush things now. You go home. Do what you have to do. Just know that I'm here. I love you. And I want you to take it easy on yourself." He glanced behind her. "It's time to go. Don't say a word. Just go."

Barbara turned and followed the dwindling line of passengers toward the departure ramp.

"Try being devious, deceitful, unreliable, and sloppy," Rob called after her. "Get drunk and throw up on the carpet," he suggested. The bewildered airport attendant stared from the tall gentleman in the well-aged leather jacket to the reddish-haired woman hugging a stack of videotapes to her chest. Barbara crossed the tarmac and climbed onto the plane.

"Take it easy on yourself," Rob said as he leaned against the glass and watched as the plane door slid closed. "Get whatever it is over with. Then please come back to me," he whispered.

"They don't show this part in the movies," Barbara muttered as she inched away from the damp spot and slid out from between the sheets. Wrapped in McMillan's beige bedspread, she crossed the room, then disappeared behind the bathroom door. Efficiently she wrapped her hair in a towel and stepped into the shower, turning it on lightly so only a chilly trickle came out. Finally the water turned warmer.

"Damn," Barbara growled as the warm spray shot above her head, soaking the toweling turban. At home, the nozzle was adjusted to her height now, and with T. J. gone, she'd gotten out of the habit of realigning it each time. Quickly she lowered the angle of the spray and let the warm water cascade down her body.

Devious, deceitful, unreliable, and sloppy. She recalled the words Rob had called after her as she left Fort Lauderdale a week before. "I'm sure working at it," she sighed as she scrubbed the scent of Jeff McMillan from her body. She had even gotten drunk. "Almost drunk," she noted more precisely. But she hadn't thrown up on the floor or anywhere else. Instead, within one week of her return to Charleston, she had made love with McMillan in the ivory and teak bedroom while a loud thunderstorm sent great sheets of rain across the Charleston peninsula. It was a perversely satisfying act of independence, exercising her option to indulge herself, to enjoy something simply because it felt good. And it had felt good. Warm, intimate, reassuring, and much like any other sexual encounter she'd had. It had been incredibly romantic and the parts all worked. It was the aftermath that was starting to feel uncomfortable.

"I wanna' go home," Barbara sighed as she stood in the steamfilled room and stared at her reflection in the mirror. She didn't want to go out to face him and make conversation. She just wanted to roll over and go to sleep and wake up in her own room.

"Barbara?" McMillan's voice came through the door.

"I'll be right out," she answered automatically. Anxiously she looked around for something to cover herself. "This is really stupid." She wrapped a damp towel around her naked body anyway. He'd already seen it all.

"Hi." McMillan smiled at her when she emerged. He had pulled on a pair of jogging shorts, but the sight of all that exposed tanned skin made the color rise in her cheeks. "Well, you're still alive and breathing," he observed, leaning forward and kissing her cheek lightly. "I wouldn't like to guess what kind of things are rushing through your mind right now. All those old spooks coming out to haunt you?" He unwrapped the turban from her head and gently ruffled her soft copper curls. "They'll go away," he assured her. "Some of them already have."

"Maybe so," Barbara nodded. She stood in the bathroom door, framed by the light, feeling awkward.

"Let me take a quick shower, then we'll get you home," McMillan suggested. "Your young friend Kent can scowl at me again and you can get us a cup of coffee." He spoke evenly, with just a trace of a smile. "We made it this far. Let's see if the lightning strikes us there."

"I doubt if we're in that kind of jeopardy." Barbara finally smiled.

"We're not." McMillan eased her aside while he stepped past her. "I just wanted to see if you still had your sense of humor."

"I imagine I'm going to need it." Barbara headed toward the heap of clothes beside the bed. She dressed rapidly in the pale strip of light coming from the bathroom while the steady surge of water in McMillan's shower again filled the bathroom with steam.

By the time they reached her house, she was having trouble staying awake. She tugged her coat close about her as McMillan helped her out of the car. He zipped his windbreaker, then fell in step beside her as they crossed the driveway. "It's pretty late." She kept her eyes on the lighted kitchen windows ahead. The wildflower windows glowed in the night. She wasn't in the mood for cheery. "Maybe we could pass on the coffee."

"No deal. The running-away routine is over. I'm not going to let all your old spooks crowd me out, not without a fight," he answered solemnly. "I'm not dropping you off, then leaving you to rehash this alone. You are going to sit and have a brief but civilized conversation with me, coffee or no coffee."

"I don't respond well to authority," Barbara replied coolly.

"I thought you responded just fine." McMillan reached past her and grasped the handle of the door. "One of the more memorable responses, which I will cherish forever." He grinned at her flustered expression.

"Hello, Mrs. A." Kent Nelson unlocked the deadbolt and stepped back. "Mr. McMillan."

"Hi, Kent." McMillan helped Barbara out of her coat then very conspicuously removed his own and hung it on the coatrack in the entry.

While she went to check the children, Kent silently gathered his schoolbooks from the counter, then pulled on his letter jacket. "Tell Mrs. A. I'll drop in tomorrow and haul in some more firewood." Kent spoke without looking directly at McMillan even when he pulled out a ten-dollar bill and handed it to the teenager. "Thanks. Goodnight, sir," Kent said. He stepped out into the cool night air. Seconds later McMillan smiled as the motor on Kent's Mustang turned over and the car slowly pulled out onto the street.

"He's already gone," McMillan said aloud. He plugged in the coffeemaker and looked over at Barbara, who had come back into the kitchen. "He was bit standoffish. Perhaps he suspects what we've been doing. He's worried that you're slipping away from him."

"We're friends. That's all. And we'll stay friends," Barbara insisted, dismissing his comment, unwilling to speculate what Kent must have been thinking.

"Friends like you and the Johnstone guy?" McMillan said, catching her by surprise. "Someone who hangs around on the fringe and doesn't make any demands on you?"

Barbara's mouth dropped open. "You sure know how to bring a perfectly pleasant evening to an abrupt halt."

"We can still have a perfectly pleasant evening, without ducking certain issues," McMillan insisted. "You haven't said much about your visit with good old Rob," he noted. "As long as we're waiting for the coffee to perk, why don't we just sit down and you can tell me all about it."

"There's not much to tell. We had a very nice time. We ate, drank, walked on the beach, visited friends." Barbara shot back a list of details. "We went to a New Year's party, then I flew back to Sarasota. We also watched videotapes of some of the plays he and his students have done. He gave me several we didn't get to." Barbara's delivery had increased in volume and intensity as her list progressed.

"How respectable," McMillan teased. "I don't see what there is to get all worked up about."

She abruptly lowered her voice. "I'm not worked up."

"My mistake." He shrugged. "How about some coffee?" He lifted two mugs from the cup rack and set them side by side on the counter.

"Fine."

"It's more than a little difficult trying to get close to you when I have to fish for information." McMillan put cream and sugar in his cup. Barbara ignored hers. "I know you're still recovering from T.J.'s death. I know you need old friends to comfort you. I just don't want them comforting you too much. I even feel a little uneasy about taking advantage of you."

"I wasn't drunk tonight," Barbara protested.

"I'm not talking about tonight," he replied impatiently. "I mean in general. I think you're more vulnerable than you realize. It's a problem of timing. I'm torn between wanting you for myself and giving you time to readjust. I don't want someone else moving in while I'm not looking."

"I appreciate your dilemma."

"I'm sure you're feeling some of the same things," McMillan asserted. "Let's face it, we both know a good thing when we see it." His familiar wide grin reappeared. "I'm so sick of angry divorcees or weary career women or wide-eyed cuties with more miles on them at twenty than I'd like to count."

Barbara gave him a sidelong look, surprised by the sharp edge to his voice. In the harsh kitchen light, the thin lines around his eyes and lips seemed more pronounced, minute erosions from hundreds of smiles and frowns. "So now you're turning to older women," she felt compelled to joke.

"Not women," McMillan said as he looked into her eyes. "I want you."

"That specific? So much for my attempt at levity."

"And so much for *True Confessions*," McMillan responded with a smile. "We've got a good thing here. I want to keep it." He glanced at his watch. "Since lightning hasn't struck us both down, I think it's safe to go back to my place. You're okay?"

"I'm fine. Just tired." Barbara stretched and covered a yawn.

"Well, I'll still respect you in the morning." McMillan bent down and kissed her on the nose. "I'll even call and whisper sweet nothings into the phone."

"I hope you don't. I'm not really comfortable with

that kind of thing. But if you ever launch into anything personal, make sure it's me and not one of the kids on the other end," she warned him. "I'm not sure they'd appreciate your comments."

"I promised I'd be discreet," McMillan reminded her. He grabbed his jacket and slid his arms into the sleeves. "I won't even honk the horn when I pass Louis's house."

"You won't have to. I have a feeling Karen will be riveted to the window."

"Nosy friends you got, lady."

"They say they're just looking out for me." She stood and walked him to the door.

"So am I." He gave her a hug then zipped the jacket emphatically. "So am I."

Soon after McMillan's car had disappeared down the driveway, Barbara turned out the lights and strolled into the study, staring out the long window. Keats stood dark and glistening after the heavy rain. The grass sparkled in the bright light of the moon. Beyond the marsh grass, the water of the Ashley River lay smooth and black and shiny. In the week that she'd been back, it had been like this. Cold. Still. Beautifully tranquil. There had been no sign of anything unusual, no disturbance of any kind in the house.

"Is it over?" Barbara asked, still feeling a lack of completion. "Is this how it ends?" She sat motionless in the loveseat, remembering McMillan's comment about knowing a good thing when he sees it. Maybe it was the rhythm of his voice she just wasn't used to yet or the edge of arrogance in his smile that sometimes made his remarks come out too glib, too self-assured. But T.J. had had that same assertive quality of deciding what he wanted and then going after it. McMillan said he wanted her. But Rob Johnstone had simply let her go again.

She leaned back against the headrest, tucking her bare feet between the seat cushion and the arm. *Life's a grab bag*, Rob had told her. *Take what you get, and make the best of it.* Barbara sighed and scrunched down lower, hugging a loose cushion to her chest for comfort. "I'm trying," she said. She only intended to rest there for a moment when she rolled onto her side and closed her eyes. But when she slowly blinked them open again the grayish dawn was already inching its way through the mist and hours had slipped away. Cold and tired, Barbara unfolded herself and trudged off to bed.

"Momma." Her daughter's warm breath on her face summoned her from a sound sleep. Barbara groaned and cracked open one eye. Miranda knelt beside the bed, her chin on the pillow inches from Barbara's nose. "Something sad has happened." Miranda blinked back her tears.

"What is it, baby?" Barbara struggled up onto her elbow.

"I found a dead bird."

"Oh, that's too bad," Barbara symphathized. "What time is it?"

"I don't know."

"It feels awfully early. Can I go back to sleep for a little while and I'll help you take care of the bird later?"

"I guess so."

"Snuggle with me a while."

"No, I'll just wait." Miranda quietly withdrew from the bedroom.

Barbara lay very still, hoping that she'd drop off to sleep again. But she knew Miranda would undoubtedly be moping around the house somewhere, anguishing over the plight of the poor dead bird. "I give up," she finally groaned. "I'm coming," she called down the hall. "At least it's Sunday," she consoled herself, figuring she could work in a nap later. She tugged an old sweatshirt over her head, grabbed her faded jeans and her tennis shoes, and aimed toward the doorway. But the room tilted. "Oh, boy," she muttered as she leaned against the doorjamb to steady herself, feeling a slight bit hungover. "The old body just ain't what it used to be."

Miranda led her mother toward the study window. "It's out here. Look." She pointed down to a clump of brownish feathers laying on the deck outside.

"It was a dove." Barbara squinted at the dead creature, then slowly shifted her line of vision upwards, reversing the path of the fallen bird. On the glass, just at eye level, was a bloody smudge with several tiny pieces of feathers still clinging to it. Barbara crinkled her nose and took a step back. Her stomach lurched. For a few seconds she was afraid she was going to throw up. She took a few quick swallows.

"The poor thing must have thought this was an open place and crashed into the window," Barbara concluded. She reached down and cradled Miranda's head against her side. "Go get the big matchbox by the fireplace. Dump out the matches and bring the box here. We'll bury the little guy in it."

"I'll get Eliot." Miranda began to get enthused. "He can help."

"I'm not sure Eliot would like being awakened for a bird's funeral." Barbara tried to discourage her.

"I'd better ask him, just to be sure," Miranda insisted. "Maybe you could find a nice piece of material and we could stuff it in the box so it would be pretty, just like Daddy's," Miranda suggested. "We could make a marker for the grave and everything." She wandered off, totally engrossed in her preparations.

"I really didn't need this." Barbara stood with her hands on her hips staring out at the tiny corpse. From the bedroom wing came the sound of two voices in unclear but earnest conversation. "At least they aren't fighting." She strode toward the kitchen and poured some cold coffee into a cup to fortify herself.

"Momma," Miranda yelled from the den. "Can you get me some material?" The question was punctuated by the electronic ping of the microwave. Barbara lifted the now-steaming coffee onto the counter, then fumbled in the refrigerator for the milk.

"Give me time to drink my coffee," she pleaded. "Try looking in the closet by my sewing machine."

"Eliot!" Miranda's piercing shriek echoed through the house. "Momma, Eliot is pushing me."

"Now they're fighting," Barbara said into her cup. "Eliot!" she yelled down the hallway.

"Yes, Mother," came the disgruntled reply. "I know. Don't push your sister."

"You got it, Ace," she sighed.

* * *

"Dearly beloved . . ." Eliot's serene voice drifted over the small gathering of mourners that Miranda had recruited from the neighborhood. Amy Petillo, the dark-haired granddaughter of the Franklins, two houses farther in, stood next to Carrie Hobach and Ricky Watford, two of Miranda's regular pals. Carrie's older brother Billie, nine like Eliot, shifted his feet uncomfortably and tried to appear bored by the entire event.

"We are gathered here today to bury our bird Brownie," Eliot proceeded with great dignity. Barbara squelched a slight smile at the revelation that the small dove had now acquired owners and a name.

"Brownie died this morning when she hit the glass window in the Ashcrofts' study," Eliot explained formally. "We are now going to put her to rest." He turned and nodded to Miranda, who gingerly placed the matchbox into the hole that Billie Hobach had dug. Billie frowned impatiently while Miranda adjusted the box so it sat flat in place, then he shoveled half a spadeful of dirt on the makeshift coffin.

"Ashes to ashes, dust to dust," Eliot said clearly. Billie scraped up a second shovelful, but Eliot signaled for him to wait. "They read this poem when my dad was buried." Eliot lifted up a piece of folded white paper and opened it up. He'd asked Barbara to help him find it. "It was written by William Wordsworth, the guy this tree is named after," he added in his matter-of-fact manner. "So I want to read it for Brownie, too," he insisted. "It's not long. It's really just part of a poem."

Very carefully he unfolded the paper then pulled himself erect and read,

Though nothing can bring back the hour
Of splendor in the grass, of glory in the flower:
We will grieve not, rather find
strength in what remains behind.

Now Eliot nodded for his friend Billie to continue, and the last two scoops of dirt filled up the opening. Each of the smaller children placed a fistful of dry leaves on the dark soil and each of them dutifully withdrew under Miranda's close scrutiny.

"Whenever you see a dove, think of Brownie. She was an okay bird. Amen," Eliot concluded with a satisfied smile.

"Now can we have the apple juice?" Carrie Hobach asked, appearing at Barbara's elbow.

"I guess so." She managed a stiff smile for the upturned face. Eliot stood a few feet off, refolding the piece of paper and then tucking it into his jacket pocket. His bright blue eyes looked up through his horn-rimmed glasses. They met Barbara's and held her glance for an instant. "Very nice," Barbara said quietly with a respectful tilt of her head.

Her son nodded back at her. "Miranda was the one who wanted to make a fuss over it." He tried to shrug off his part in the ceremony. "It was just a bird."

"You did something very nice." Barbara stepped toward him and held him against her. "Don't ever apologize or be embarrassed for doing something good and kind and loving," she said, speaking just to him. "I'm proud of you. Your dad would have been proud of you too, Eliot," she whispered. He nodded silently, then began wriggling within her embrace. Billie Hobach was still there, shovel in hand, waiting.

"You guys want some juice?" Barbara offered cheerfully. "Maybe a couple of cookies?"

"Yeah, sure, Mrs. Ashcroft." Billie nudged Eliot.

"Okay, Mom," Eliot agreed. "But not with the little kids," he pleaded.

"You and Billie can have yours in the den," Barbara said quietly. "Come on, everyone." Miranda and her congregation fell in step behind her. Eliot and Billie Hobach poked along behind, dragging the shovel between them. Behind them all, amid the gnarled roots at the base of Wordsworth, the little stack of leaves lay, slightly scattered by the cool afternoon breeze.

Barbara was propped up in bed, reading the sections of the Sunday paper she hadn't had time for during the day, when she saw the slight shift in the shadows beyond her door.

"Can I come in with you for a while?" Eliot stood silhouetted by the pale glow of the bathroom light farther down the hall.

"Did you have a bad dream?" Barbara asked. She pulled open the covers and made room. Eliot crossed the carpet soundlessly, then slid in next to his mother.

"I was just thinking about Daddy." Eliot's voice was a mere whisper. Barbara closed the sheets over him, leaving her arm resting across his chest.

"You're feeling sad," she said gently. Eliot nodded without turning his face toward her. "Sometimes I get sad too," she said evenly.

"I was thinking about that stupid bird, too," Eliot muttered. "Dumb old thing just flew into that window and konked itself."

"And it makes you angry?"

Eliot sat hunched against the pillows, rigid and silent.

"Are you sometimes angry about Daddy, too?" Barbara pressed him.

Eliot shrugged. He rolled over, keeping his back to Barbara.

"I get angry sometimes," Barbara confessed. "Not at your dad, exactly. I get angry because he's not here. I have to take over all his stuff around the house—fixing the fire, locking the doors at night, taking out the garbage, even putting gas in the car. He used to do all those things and I didn't even have to think about them." She looked at the crossed arms of her son. "I get angry when there's someplace I'd like to go and he's not here to go with me. Or something neat happens and he's not around to hear about it. I get angry because T.J. and I had a deal—we were going to stay together and love each other and raise you kids and grow old together. Now the deal is off." Barbara sighed. "I kept my part of the bargain. I'm still keeping it. But dying wasn't his fault any more than hitting that window was Brownie's."

Eliot turned to face her in the dim light. She could see the damp splotches on his cheeks. "It isn't fair," he finally sobbed.

"Nope, it isn't fair," Barbara agreed. "In fact, it really stinks. But we aren't really mad at Daddy, or at the poor dumb bird." She pulled Eliot over to her and held him against her chest. "We're just sad and frustrated because it isn't fair. It's tough having them go."

Eliot clung to her and wept quietly. Barbara simply held him, stroking his pale blond hair and slowly rocking him to and fro.

"In that poem you read today at Brownie's funeral, it said we would find strength in what remains behind," she reminded him. "Your dad left a lot of good things behind—good memories, good jokes, this house, you and your charming sister." Barbara smiled, a trembling teary smile. Eliot stopped sniffling and gave a "Harumph" after the charming sister part. "Your dad would have grumbled that this wasn't fair," she went on. "But he wouldn't have let it get him down, not for long," she added. "You're a lot like your dad." She kissed the top of his head. "You just go ahead and feel angry or sad whenever you want to. It helps to let the hurt out. Maybe next time when you think of him, it won't hurt quite so much." It was the kind of a talk she'd had with Miranda from time to time, and with herself as well.

For a while he sat next to her, looking over the comics while she read the city news. "Mom, do you really think people go somewhere when they're dead?" Eliot asked. "I don't mean to a place exactly, but do you think the spirit parts go somewhere, then come back in another body?"

"I don't know," Barbara answered softly. She'd never been particularly religious, and had more questions than answers lately. "Some people think so." She didn't like the way the conversation was heading.

"Maybe if you die, you just become invisible," Eliot continued, pursuing his own train of thought. "Mr. Johns said the spirit is the part that doesn't die."

"I think there's a little more to it than that," Barbara responded. Already her palms were damp from the uneasy feelings this talk was provoking. "Maybe instead of being separate things, like this person or that bird, our spirits or souls or energy fields all become part of something immense we can't see. Part of the universe," she philosophized.

"Like the wind?" Eliot seemed to like that idea.

"Like the wind."

"Then maybe Daddy is still somewhere around," Eliot said pensively. "He may be keeping an eye on us like Mr. Johns said. Except the wind doesn't have eyes. Maybe it just knows things." He sighed with satisfaction and went back to reading the comics.

Barbara pressed her eyes shut, not trusting herself to comment any further.

Eliot stopped and looked up at her. "Mom, I wanted to ask you to do something."

"What's that?"

"It's about that window. Can't you do the window for it before another bird hits it? I don't want another funeral."

Barbara nodded. "It takes a long time to do a window."

"I know. You said that before. But maybe you could start working on it. I'll help."

"Can we get some sleep first?" She glanced at him and smiled. "Or do you want to get up and start right away?"

"Birds don't fly at night. We can do it tomorrow. Maybe we could hang a picture or something in the space until the real thing gets finished."

"Right." Barbara put the papers on the floor and inched down under the sheets. "I'm already finished. I'm pooped. I'm turning off the lights."

"Okay. I think I'll go back to my room." Eliot flung his legs over his side of the bed. "Goodnight, Mom. And thanks about the window."

"You're welcome. Stop in the bathroom on the way."

"Stop in the bathroom," he repeated, mimicking her tone.

"Eliot."

"Goodnight, Mom." He ducked out the door rapidly. "Goodnight, Dad," he said aloud in the hallway. "Goodnight, Brownie."

"Eliot."

"Goodnight, Mom."

* * *

It was the warm space he left behind and the pushed-in dent in the pillows that started her thinking. She slid her hand out, remembering other beds, other warm spots and other rumpled pillows. The morning with Rob had been the nicest time. Not the most exciting. It hadn't even been sexual. But she'd awakened surrounded by the warmth of him and the smell of lovemaking. Then she'd closed her eyes and lay very still, holding on to that morning feeling as long as she could.

He'd moved first. He'd pulled a blanket over her, and he'd stayed there, holding her, for the longest time. But he made no attempt to initiate anything more. He just slid out of bed, put on the coffee, and showered. And she had sprawled out on the still-warm bed and wondered if she should have opened her eyes and let it start again.

Deliciously aroused now, she rolled onto her side, imagining. She pressed the blankets between her thighs, tensing and releasing, remembering how surprisingly unhurried it had been with him. While they kissed and touched with arms and legs gliding over the other, he had put her hand on his wrist and made her guide it to the places he should touch. Without a word, he let her lead him, keeping the contact or changing it as she wished. She'd never done that with anyone. With T.J. it had taken years of patience, and laughter, and trial and error. But in the dark with Rob, their faces masked by shadows, she had felt no need to rush to please him, no reason to hide what pleased her. Their contact was marvelous and tender and complete, and more haunting because she never imagined there would be a next time.

But she had him with her now, in her mind. She drew in low, deliberate breaths, locking onto the sensations inside her and the tension slowly but steadily increasing. She was almost on the edge when the cold set in. She pulled the blankets higher and shivered beneath the coverings but she didn't stop. She could block it out.

"Concentrate," she said, keeping her eyes closed and focusing on finding that release of energy on her own. Suddenly she felt the motion of the air against her cheek, and stared, alert now, around the room. The bathroom light still cast its glow in the hall, but her room grew increasingly dark and oppressive. Dense, moist scented air settled slowly over her, bearing down with tangible pressure, molding the bedcoverings against her body. The moving currents, like gentle, languid caresses, stroked and embraced her as she lay outspread beneath the cloudlike canopy of incense. *Like the wind.* Eliot's image had been disturbingly accurate.

She didn't want to continue, but the coolness clung to her, the moving air seemed to sigh with her, and the pressure around her body and between her thighs became increasingly direct. There was nothing gentle or patient in the purposefully orchestrated contact.

"I can't do this," she gasped in soft, sad breaths. "Not like this. Not because you want me to. Not with you." Summoning her strength, she twisted back, kicking away the blankets, struggling out from beneath the awesome fragrant weight. She leapt out of the bed on the far side, lunging toward the dark drapes and grasping for the pulls. With labored, desperate jerking movements, she yanked open the phoenix draperies. Then she unlocked the sliding glass doors, flinging them open for the clear, clean night air to enter. Instantly the fragrance of Dhatri inside disappeared as the river breeze swept through the room.

She leaned against the folds of the draperies, shuddering from the cold, but breathing in the fresh wind from the marsh. Outside, Wordsworth stood as he always had, wide and dignified against the cloudy sky. Black shadows cloaked the spot between the tree roots where the little bird was buried, but Barbara stared intently at the base of the grand old tree, gasping, until her eyes began to blur the shadows and distort the shapes.

"Damn it, if you're dead, stay dead," she rasped out into the night. Nothing outside moved.

"We had a deal. Past tense." She looked up into the sky where clumps of pale gray and silver wisps clustered to the southwest, ready to lead the approaching cold front out to sea. Beyond the clouds, the full moon struggled to be seen.

"I kept my part of the bargain," she declared. She

crossed her arms over her chest as she contemplated the bleak, moon-washed setting beyond the doorway. "I'm still keeping my part." She hesitated. "Well, mostly." She straightened her stance. "But the deal is off, at least that part of it that has to do with me and my body. I have a right to some privacy. I want something more than this." Her heartbeat thudded a loud, steady rhythm like a war drum. "I like making love. I like being touched and kissed and held. I like having a family and a husband. But it can't be you anymore. I want to get on with being me, and I don't want to be monitored. And I don't want to be handled like that. It was never a case of pushing buttons or running down a checklist with us, T.J. Or was it?"

Stonily, she waited for a response. None came.

With brisk, tight motions, she pulled closed the doors, relocked them, then returned to the bed. This time she didn't pull closed the drapes. She let in the moonlight. She curled up under the blankets again and shivered. From a distant corner of the darkened house came the cricket's chirp, not Henry's rich strong burst, but a less robust one from the wild cricket loose in the house.

"You don't belong here, either," she insisted. "You should be outside, roaming around free." The warm spot she was creating gradually grew. At last the trembling stopped. She lay awake, listening, but the high-pitched trill of the insect never broke the silence of the house again that night.

Luster Johns was waiting on the back of his truck when Barbara brought the kids home from school the next day. "Mr. Johns," Miranda squealed, and leaped out the moment Barbara brought them to a full stop. Eliot took off after her.

"Missed see'n yo' bright faces," he said, bending down to give them each a hug. "Santa Claus was good to you?" The youngsters were bombarding him with tales of their Christmas with the grandparents and their escapades fishing and biking in Florida when Barbara came around from the garage to join them.

"Good to see you up and about." Barbara went up and clasped his hand.

"Good to be back to work. They just kep' makin' me take mo' time away. Finally told 'em I had folks to see." Behind him, waiting to be carried inside, were the new plants for the atrium, six large hanging baskets of brightly colored fuchsia. "I know the list for the month said snowdrops," Luster started explaining, "but these came in so pretty and kinda' tropical. I figured that after all the Christmas colors were gone, you folks might like somethin' mo' cheerful than snowdrops."

"These are beautiful." Barbara reached out and touched the bushy plants covered with magenta and scarlet teardrop flowers. "You figured right."

"If you want to give me some help movin' 'em, you can have 'em now, I'm not s'posed to be carrying much," Luster said, looking closely at the tension in her pretty face. Appeared to him she hadn't been sleeping too well.

"I'll help all I can."

"Me too." Miranda and Eliot both volunteered as they crowded onto the truck bed.

"Whoa, now. You folks better change out your nice clothes, 'cause we got six of 'em to carry. They're too big and too wide to set on the hand truck this time."

"We could use the cart you put the fertilizer in," Miranda suggested. "Just sit the thing on top and pull it."

"Good idea, but change anyways," Barbara told her. "If there is any dirt around, you have a knack of getting it on you."

"I'll need to check the ceiling and make sure there's enough places for hooks. If I could use your ladder."

"You aren't going up any ladder," Barbara insisted. "Eliot will have to do that part. I don't like heights, but I'll do whatever else you need. You just get your stool and supervise. You can plot it all out while we change."

"Jus' lead the way," Luster said obligingly. "I'll get my pointin' finger ready."

The atrium was empty except for a few ferns Sonny Pierce had left behind when he took out the Christmas plants the past weekend, but the granite floor was still covered with dropped leaves and petals and spilled potting soil. Overhead, the skylight louvers were open to let in the heat. Luster moved all around the glass-walled cubicle, before he went inside, placing his hands on the surface, checking the feel of the place. Then he bent as low as he could, studying the transparent line that Willie Dodd had repainted for him. Only then did he venture in alone. Carefully he adjusted the vents to hold in a bit more heat so the fuschias would thrive.

He'd just set up his folding stool in one corner when he spotted Miranda's elusive field cricket. Its stiff little carcass was stuck fast with one leg held imprisoned in the pale bluish substance. Both wings were ripped out. Luster swept the area with his hand, but the wings were missing.

"I forgot to tell you about Brownie," Miranda announced as she came galloping down the hall.

"Let me tell him." Eliot came bursting out his doorway, trying to catch up. "I did the funeral."

Luster quickly scooped up the dead cricket and slipped the remains in his shirt pocket so no one else would see it.

While they brought the ladder in, Miranda and Eliot told him about the dove that died and the subsequent ceremony. Luster promised to find a suitable plant from the nursery and bring it by to mark the burial place. "Better sweep the floor last, after we walked and spilled and messed it up real good," he said, stopping Barbara from cleaning the floor prematurely. He and Eliot set up the stepladder and stared at the ceiling, determining whether the jaw-action hooks he'd brought would clamp around the crossbeams on the ceiling. "Now here's how they work." He squeezed open one hook and showed Eliot what to do. "We want 'em in three rows, cross from each other, and out a bit so's they don't bump against the glass. I'll point where with the broom handle."

Eliot nodded, stuffed the hooks in his pockets, then climbed up to the first position. Barbara held the lower legs steady, Luster pointed, and Miranda frowned. "I want to do some. Save some for me," she insisted, watching with narrowed eyes every move he made. "I can do it."

Eliot ignored her.

"Save her a hook or two," Barbara said after they'd moved the ladder forward and he'd placed the second and third hooks. "Come on," she coaxed him. "You don't want to have a sister who can't hang a flowerpot."

"I'll save her one," he said grudgingly, apparently acknowledging Barbara's point.

"You two are good helpers," Luster commended the youngsters when they'd slipped the last cord on the last pot over the hook. He swept up the debris while Barbara was out in the garage getting the hose for the vacuum cleaner to do the final cleanup. "Sorry I didn't get to see you help your momma put up them wreaths for Christmas. Saw 'em when I came by here once while you were gone. They were real pretty."

"I didn't get to do much that time except hand him things," Miranda grumbled.

"Hand who things?" Luster stopped sweeping.

"Mr. McMillan. He's been here a lot and he takes Mom places," Eliot answered.

"He put up them wreaths?"

"He's tall. He's an architect like my dad. Mom doesn't like ladders so she let him do it," Miranda explained. "Kent took them down."

"I suppose if we'd left them up, Brownie wouldn't have hit the glass."

"Which window?" Luster asked.

Miranda stopped and pointed toward the study. "That one."

Luster leaned on his broom and stared over her head toward the end of that wing. It was the same window that she'd tried covering with the striped draperies.

"Those are just some stupid stickers Mom put there," Eliot muttered, indicating the patches of color on the pane. "Ducks and hearts and bears and stuff. She said they'd do until she got started on the stained glass. My Dad didn't want that left blank like that. If she'd done the window—"

"The little dove may just as well have flown into the

door," Luster interrupted before Eliot said any more. "Now let's get this straight so your momma can vacuum." He took a cautious look around the atrium, suddenly anxious to be out of there. "How 'bout you two helping me put this ladder back. Then you can boost me up into my truck. This old leg don't bend like it used to." He kept calm and moved without haste, but he reached out from time to time to touch the walls with his fingertips, running them over the surface.

"How's Henry been doing?" Luster braced himself a little on Miranda's shoulder as they stepped outside together.

"I think he's mad at me for leaving him. I let Karen keep him at her house over the holidays. He hasn't been singing at all since we brought him home," she reported.

"Jus' give him time." Luster kept moving toward his truck. Eliot loped ahead and got the door open for him. "I really want to talk ser'ous to you chill'un," Luster lowered his voice to a whisper. "I want you to get your momma to come see my angels. Soon as you can. You have her carry you over."

"I asked. She said she didn't want to bother you at home." Miranda flopped her arms in a resigned shrug.

"Well, you tell her she'll be hurtin' my feelin's if she doesn't bring you chill'un to see what I been doin'." He puckered out his lips and gave them a distressed look. "I been wantin' you to see 'em for a long time. You bring her tomorro' and I'll have my daughter fix us her pound cake. Don't you forget now. We got some catchin' up to do."

"Are your feelings really hurt?" Miranda looked at him with a wide-eyed, worried expression.

"Not yet. Will be tomorro' if you forget to come." He hated to put so much pressure on the youngsters, but he kept remembering what Sister Gertrude Kelly said about haunts getting nastier the longer they stayed around. And how they connive and twist old memories and play possum, then come back meaner than ever. It bothered him that Henry hadn't been singing at all. He knew critters could sense something wrong long before a person could. He puckered his lips again, trying not to chide himself too much for what he was about to say. "Bring your momma to see me. May not be 'round fo'ever so you better visit while I'm spry 'nough to show you all 'round."

He had to look away on that one. He could see the dark fear inch into their eyes and he knew he'd hit a nerve. But he'd been pussyfooting around too long. "While I'm sitting home tonight, I'll whittle you a little marker for your bird. Have it ready for you when you come visitin'."

On the way out the drive, Luster tested the brakes twice, just to feel them grip. Palms moist, throat dry, he drove slowly home, checking before each intersection to make sure the truck would halt. He ignored the ones who passed him, beeping horns or thrusting fingers in the air because he'd backed up traffic and held them back. But he took no chances, and when he finally turned into the lane to his house, he drew the first deep breath he'd drawn in over an hour. Then carefully he took the cricket from his pocket, wrapped it in a napkin, and lay it on the seat.

He walked around his house three times before he went inside. Willie Dodd watched him from the window.

"That Ol' Paw out there?" Mattie peered over her son's shoulder.

"Sure is."

"Goin' counterclock?" she asked, quiet and serious as she stood behind him, watching like he did.

Willie Dodd nodded, wondering what had got his grampa all superstitious. But he'd grown up with all the charms and spells and magic, and he'd seen enough from time to time to know there was something to it. Nothing he'd admit to his classmates at college. But enough to make him real respectful when Luster insisted on doing something a particular way.

"Get out his whiskey and honey for a toddy. And put another log on the fire. Get Gramma's quilt." Mattie guessed he'd be sitting up for hours, rocking by the fire, mulling over whatever was troubling him enough to make him walk the rings around the house. She watched him tie it off at the end, carefully stepping in the exact shoeprints where he'd started, then stretching in a sidewards step and backing the rest of the way to the house. Made the spirits think he wasn't home, that the footprints only led out and circled and left. She knew it wouldn't do no good to ask him what was troubling him. If it was bad enough to make him ring the house, it was too serious to talk about just yet. Maybe too serious to talk about at all.

"Ham and redeye gravy and some cornbread sound good?" she called out when she heard Luster at the door. The last gleam of light from the sun still lit the sky and he stepped inside, welcomed by the familiar smells and warmth.

"Mighty good," he answered wearily, stopping to take off his shoes and put on his old soft-soled slippers. He headed straight for the rocker by the fireplace. He smiled when he saw Willie Dodd bringing in the old quilt Inez had made. Wrapped up snugly by the hearth, he rocked and sipped his toddy until supper was ready. Then afterward he washed and Willie Dodd dried the dishes while Mattie tidied up. Then Willie Dodd went upstairs to study. Luster took a piece of fruitwood from the box where he kept his whittling pieces and he sat back in the rocker, nicking and scraping and smoothing away.

"We're havin' company tomorro'," he told Mattie when she joined him, with her tray of pale sweetgrass and darker bullrush and palmetto thread at her side. She'd finished the spiral coiled bottom of a basket the night before, and now she'd work her way up the sides.

"Who's comin?"

"The chillun' and their momma."

Mattie nodded, painstakingly coiling the grass and listening for more. She'd been wondering what was going on at the Ashcroft house off and on over the past months. She'd been watching him making juniper ash and carry it off in his truck. She knew he'd gathered all kinds of vines and plants for them to add to her sweetgrass wreaths. And he'd asked for six of them. Most families in Charleston just had one, passed on from generation to generation, and hung on the front door for luck. And he'd been there again the night he had the accident in the pickup. Only over Christmas when they were gone had he seemed at peace. Now he'd been to see them again, and something troubled him enough to make him stop and ring the house to cover his trail.

"I thought maybe you could make us one of your pound cakes," he said gently. "I need to talk to the momma. Figure you could keep the chillun' plenty busy with some of that cake."

Mattie arched her eyebrows and gave him another nod.

For a while they rocked in silence, her coiling and whipstitching the basket, him whittling away on the wood. "Makin' a little angel?" Mattie asked when she saw him carving tiny lines in the feathered wing. Despite what he said, all the angels lately, now six finished and a seventh begun, had her nervous.

"Nope." Luster turned it in his palm so she could see the whole thing. It was a plump dove, wings spread only partway out. Mattie couldn't tell if it were just about to take flight or settle down to earth.

"The chillun', Miranda and Eliot, had a bird die. Hit a window. I'm just fixing something to mark the grave."

Mattie gave it another look. Now she could see that he'd made the wings look like a small canopy, held out, shielding whatever lay below. "Real pretty," she said. Then she started rocking again, humming in her rich low voice.

"Don't you worry," Luster told her, knowing full well that beneath her show of calm, she was most likely stewing, trying to put it all together and yet knowing better than to ask. She'd been raised knowing most of the time there's no sense talking about the bad; talking only makes it worse. Better to think and listen. Better to reflect and draw strength from the peace around, then do whatever can be done.

"You jus' be careful, Ol' Paw," she said without looking over at him, swallowing to ease the knot in her throat.

"Spirit's lookin' out for me. Lookin' out for all of us. But I'll be careful," he assured her. "I know what I can help and what I can't," he declared, rocking steadily. "I'll do my piece. That's all a soul can do."

"Amen."

After Barbara finished vacuuming the atrium and Miranda and Eliot were showered and in pajamas, she let them eat their supper in front of the TV so they could watch the first of Rob Johnstone's tapes on the VCR. "Float some of this in your soup." She passed the bowl of parmesan popcorn to Miranda, who was giggling because Rob was involved in a very romantic scene with "that Nellie person."

Now the blonde-haired Nellie turned to face the hero. This time she sang to him, her voice clear and young and strong. He reached out and touched her hand. A moment later, he sang to her and held her in his arms.

"He's kissing her. He really kissed her!" Miranda squealed, cupping her hands over her face and wriggling her feet.

"He had to. It's part of the play," Eliot muttered.

The gold-haired actress, an eighteen-year-old sophomore at the junior college, moved from one scene to the next, baring her midriff to dance in the sand, then shaking her cap of shiny wet hair while she sang about washing that man right outta her hair.

"I fell in love with this leading lady, too," Rob had said when he thumbed through the stack of videotapes selecting the ones he planned to send home with Barbara. "She was an honor student, ran track, and when she opened her mouth, she had this great voice. She was wonderful."

"And what happened to the romance?" Barbara had asked, trying not to sound as curious or envious as she felt.

"She was eighteen," Rob stressed, smiling as he thought about it. "There was no romance. I'm talking fantasy here. She was a self-indulgent kid, like any other sophomore. I never stopped being the ever-so-professional teacher, except occasionally in my mind, and she went off and screwed some rock band drummer every night. But on stage," he sighed, "we were great together, for precisely eight weeks from casting to ripping down the sets. That basically has been the way my luck has run. The illusion lasts for the performance, but when it ends, I go home and I recognize the face in the mirror. I know where the fantasy ends." There had been a blend of humor and melancholy in his assessment, then he had shrugged good-naturedly and looked for another tape.

"Nellie still likes him," Miranda proclaimed between bites of sandwich. "She's just pretending she doesn't."

"This must have been breathtaking," Barbara commented, amazed by the professional lighting effects that made the sunsets glow and the jungle paradise look mysterious and magical. "Look how the scene changes are done." She sat forward, with her elbows propped on her knees, watching an island rise and a rain forest sweep aside as huge circular insets in the stage revolved.

This production was far more elaborate than the few plays on the tapes they watched when she was at his house. Apparently he had held this one back for some reason. *South Pacific* had been the past year's premier production showcasing the new facilities in Rob's theater department. He had been rehearsing in the new theater and had talked about its state-of-the-art equipment, but she hadn't been prepared for anything as elaborate as this, not for a junior college.

All the earlier performances they'd watched used a traditional stage. Here the sets were incredibly multidimensional and mobile. The video camera taping this play zoomed and retracted, angles shifted from side to side, whereas the early productions had been videotaped from a stationary location. Before, the leads and most of the minor roles were all young actors Rob had directed, but now he and several other faculty teacher-performers were up there with the students, singing and dancing and making make-believe love.

"He doesn't really get killed, does he?" Miranda blurted out when the Frenchman played by Rob was reported missing. "I don't want him to get killed."

"He doesn't get killed. He comes back to Nellie at the end," Barbara assured her daughter. She hugged Miranda against her, waiting for Rob's Emile to reappear.

"Oh, Mother," Eliot groaned. "Now you've spoiled it."

"Sorry." She patted his leg. "Some of us can take the suspense, some of us can't."

"Well, don't do that again. I like to see how it works out for myself." T.J. had been like that, Barbara noted. He never read reviews of plays or books or movies until after he'd been through them cold. He'd stalk from the room if someone was about to reveal a crucial part of a film.

"Why do you think the damn climax is at the end?" he'd badger them. "So you have to wonder all through the first part and be surprised. If they didn't want you surprised, they'd tell you right off that he dies or the girlfriend's ex-husband did it or the bomb goes off and kills everyone. A little cliff hanging is what makes it fun."

"I can look under Miranda's bed or in Eliot's closet and get enough cliff hanging to do me," Barbara would insist. "And if I want a dose of violence, corruption, and unhappy endings, I can read the newspaper. When I want to be intellectually stimulated, I'll take a class or read a book. But when all I want is to relax and be entertained, I prefer something at least a little cheerful. If I know it has a good ending, I can ease back and enjoy it." She didn't totally avoid the heavier subjects. But she'd wait until a film came out in video if she knew a favorite actor died at the end. She wouldn't watch tearjerkers in public. She could understand Miranda's anxiety upon hearing that the Frenchman was missing.

"You're going to like this part," she whispered in her daughter's ear, ignoring Eliot's dark looks.

In the last scene, Nellie Forbush sat with two children on a flower-bedecked terrace overlooking the ocean. Off to one side, Emile stepped into view, unshaven, slightly bedraggled, but alive.

Some enchanted evening,
you may meet a stranger . . .

The deep melodious music filled the room. The tall familiar-looking hero crossed the terrace and paused by the table a few steps away from Nellie. The two lovers looked at each other and clasped hands across the table. In the movie, the hand holding had been under the table, Barbara remembered. But in Rob's production, he had done it up front, right where the children on stage as well as the audience could see and understand.

"He sings pretty good." Eliot was grinning, despite the fact that the ending made him a little teary.

"He's so handsome," Miranda gushed.

Barbara sat between the two of them, balancing the bowl of popcorn on her lap, seeing a side of Rob she'd only imagined, in fantasies of her own. She stared, transfixed, at the screen while this appealing Emile and radiant Nellie Forbush were framed in a magnificent sunset.

"Nice touch." She smiled to herself as the music faded. Miranda was drooping against Barbara's side, sleepy but delighted she had made it through the entire two and a half hours.

Eliot sat staring at the curtain call, nodding contentedly. "Pretty good," he conceded. "I sure didn't know Rob could sing."

Miranda plopped across her mother's lap. "Will you carry me to bed?" she moaned helplessly.

"Sure." She pretended to be taken in by Miranda's theatrics. She scooped up the semilimp form and began the procession down to the bedroom wing. "Teeth . . . hands . . . toilet," she noted for Eliot's benefit.

"Right," he replied from somewhere behind her.

Moments later both children were finally in their rooms. "Quit stalling," Barbara warned Eliot, who suddenly wanted to ask about some of the other tapes Rob had given her. "You can look through them in the morning. Now be quiet and go to sleep," she called from Miranda's room.

"It was kind of sad at the end," Miranda said softly as Barbara tucked the covers over her. "I know it was happy really, but it still made me kind of sad."

"When that happens you say that it was very moving." Barbara helped supply the words to describe Miranda's mixed emotions. "If it touches your heart, or your feelings, even if it brings out several different feelings at the same time, and you get kind of choked up, you can say that it was moving, and people will understand that it was happy and sad."

"Like Brownie's funeral was moving," Miranda said quietly.

"It certainly was." Barbara smiled in the dark and patted Miranda's chest.

"Christmas was moving," the little girl added.

"It was," Barbara agreed.

"Thinking about Daddy is moving," Miranda persisted.

"I know," Barbara agreed as she leaned down and kissed Miranda's cheek.

"If I have to shut up, why doesn't she?" Eliot's protest came loud and clear.

"Goodnight Eliot," Barbara called back. "Goodnight Miranda," she said loudly so Eliot could hear that, too.

"Goodnight." His voice came back. Even without looking in at him, she could tell he was lying there listening to make sure Miranda was silent, and probably grinning.

"Wiseass," she muttered to herself as she headed back to the den. *Just like your Dad*, came the involuntary response from within. Barbara hesitated, pleased but a little uncomfortable to feel something positive and funny and loving about T.J. She hadn't had many thoughts like that since she'd left the house for Christmas.

But it was another man whose face haunted her now. Since she'd left Rob in the airport in Lauderdale, she had tried not to think about him or dredge up the memory of her interlude there. Like him, she knew where the fantasy ended. So she had focused only on putting her life in gear in Charleston, and that had meant moving ahead with McMillan. Deliberately, she paused by the atrium, looking in at the cascades of fuschia with the tiny flowers Luster Johns had call "lady's teardrops." They reminded her of the terrace on a South Sea island and a patio filled with people welcoming in a new year.

Quietly, Barbara walked over to the tape machine and pressed the button, rewinding it a little way. Then she played the last part again, the part with Emile coming out of the forest onto the terrace and then holding hands with Nellie. The camera zoomed in and she saw the gentleness in Rob's expression. She'd seen a similar softness when he came in from the hallway and took her into his arms. Only then there was no one watching, no audience at all. And for that night, it had been wonderful.

Suddenly there were tears trickling down her cheeks, and she wasn't sure why. It had to do with endings and timing and ships passing in the night, but she couldn't sort it out. All she felt was incredibly lonely and confused.

She leaned forward and turned the volume higher so the sound of her sniffling couldn't be heard over the soundtrack. She remembered how comfortable and simple and elegant Rob's life was, with good friends and students who adored him, with a beautiful house nestled just a few steps from the ocean. How at home he was there. McMillan had nailed it when he said he felt better knowing Barbara wouldn't leave her home in Charleston. He figured there'd be no way Rob would uproot himself and leave a tenured position. Certainly not one with a theater as magnificent as this one.

When it ends, I go home and I recognize the face in the mirror, Rob had said, level-headed and honest as usual. And he had made love with her, then let her go, just as she had asked him too. "It could never work," Barbara told herself, feeling a vague anger now that she had waited until after she'd slept with McMillan before she'd allowed herself to view any of the tapes. Even after all these years, Rob still had some kind of tie with her. But it still was clear, they were miles and worlds apart. The music faded and the sadness gripped her, fiercer than ever now. "Damn you." Barbara buried her face in her hands and wept while her old friend strode into the center of the stage and took his bow.

CHAPTER 8

> To fill a gap—
> Insert the Thing that caused it.
> Block it up
> With other and 'twill yawn
> The more.
> You cannot solder any abyss
> With air.
>
> *Emily Dickinson*

"I THOUGHT YOU were going to do something larger for that one. A driftwood design?" Karen Belcazzio stood beside Barbara, studying the colored pattern taped to the top third of the long study window. She had drawn the design on translucent paper with wide black marker to indicate the lines where the caming would go. Now she was working on the color scheme, painting in with watered-down acrylics the separate colors of glass she intended to use.

"This is a quick fix. It would take me months to work on a big window." Barbara shrugged. "Eliot is after me to get something up soon. I'm not sure if it's just because of the little dove that hit the glass or because his dad had wanted the window done, but he's very anxious about it." She brushed a few strokes of pale pinkish orange in one section. "He hates these press-on things." She pointed to a stack of colored stickers she'd taken down for the time being. "I figure I'll do a framed, hanging panel for the top part. I can put it on little chains and hook it in there so we won't have to worry about this being mistaken for an air thoroughfare again. A hanging piece won't make putting up supports necessary."

"And Eliot will be satisfied?" Karen asked. She glanced outside. Eliot and his friend Billie had set up the croquet wickets all across the yard and were playing three-balls each. Miranda was wrapped up in a quilt, placidly munching saltines and watching them from the hammock.

"He's not thrilled, but he's agreed to this as a temporary measure," Barbara replied. "I only have so many waking hours, and this is all I can manage right now. This I can do here. It's small enough that I won't even have to take it to the glass shop to assemble it. I'll get Craig to help me do the full window eventually, then I'll move this one into my bedroom. I think it's pretty, don't you?" She turned to see her friend's expression.

"It's pretty," Karen agreed. "It looks sort of like overblown Victorian. Maybe like William Morris and the pre-Raphaelite decor. Definitely will go with your bedroom draperies." She cast an expert eye on the curving, open lily design with the stylized heart-shaped leaves. "What color do you have in mind for the border?"

"That's why you're here." Barbara smiled and steered Karen toward the scarred worktable at the far end of the room. "So far I've figured out the peach and ivory parts." She pointed to two twelve-inch sheets of opalescent glass, with veins in various shades of soft golden-orange. "I have two different greens for the leaves." She lifted more sheets of glass from the upright bins and propped them on the sill of the bay window so they had the sunlight behind them. "Unless you think I should mix in some clear pieces with the opalescent, then I have four good greens." Barbara added two more pieces to the lineup above the cutting table so their color could be judged in the light.

"So what does that leave for the background and the border?" Karen stooped down and gingerly touched the corners of several pieces of the remaining stock of glass.

"Not that one." Barbara stopped her. Karen had paused to examine a large piece the color of caramel. "I don't want to cut on that," she insisted. "That's for the big window. The driftwood. The one I'm not doing yet. T.J. bought it. I'm saving it."

"Okay." Karen moved on to the next piece. "How about this one?" She lifted out a darker sheet. "This is gorgeous." She held it up.

"It's called mahogany." Barbara spoke over her shoulder.

"It's beautiful," Karen stressed. "I vote for a mahogany border."

"Let's try it." Barbara looked from the glass to the half-painted cartoon she'd taped up where the finished piece would hang. "You're the artist. How about you mixing the colors so they match and we'll try them out. Do the greens, too. I'll get a pot of tea."

"Fine." Karen propped the mahogany glass in the window, then promptly picked up a paintbrush and a tube of Barbara's paint. She stirred and daubed and mixed again until the color she created matched the glass. She had the border and leaves painted in and the drawing taped back on the window when Barbara returned with the teapot and two mugs. "What do you think now?" She arched her thin black brows.

"Ornate. Decadent. Perfect." Barbara looked at it intently. "Let's sit down and contemplate awhile." She took one end of the loveseat while Karen settled onto the other. By now the kids had disappeared from view. The striped croquet balls were scattered under Keats, and the quilt lay crumpled in the hammock, swaying in the cool wind from the river.

"This contemplating part used to drive T.J. crazy." Barbara peered at the paper window panel design. "Once I had a design chosen, he always wanted me to grab the glass and start cutting. I have to leave it there and look at it a couple of days. I jumped into it once. It took me one ghastly combination and wasting a sheet of glass I'd misjudged to decide that I wouldn't cut again until I was sure. It breaks my heart to start in and then find out that it doesn't look right. You can't do much with leftover pieces."

"Well, this looks right."

"Now all I need is something for the background." Barbara narrowed one eye at the design.

"What have you got in mind?" Karen asked.

"Transparent?" Barbara asked. "I don't want it to filter out too much light."

"Maybe transparent with some kind of texture, little bubbles or cracks or something warped-looking to add to the antiquey effect. I'd try to work in a little burnt orange somewhere to add some intensity to the center."

"They have faceted pieces, circles and ovals. I could use a few in the center of the flowers. I'll have to stop by the shop and see what Craig has there. I told him I was starting in again. What color do you see for the background?" They both stared pensively at the cartoon.

"Bluish?" Karen suggested. "With a touch of gray?"

"Very light?" Barbara proposed, nodding.

"Sounds good to me," Karen said as she sipped her steaming tea.

"Now that's settled, I'll go down to the shop and snoop around," Barbara sighed with relief. "I need flux and a few other things. I'll take Eliot with me so he won't think I'm procrastinating. Besides, he likes to help me stretch the lead. We can do it with Craig's vice and save me from banging myself up here."

She sat silently for a moment. "It's amazing how many little things have changed with T.J. gone," she said quietly. "It takes two to stretch the lead caming—at least I could never do it by myself. With Eliot helping, it took three. T.J. used to line it up and squeeze it in the little vice. He'd let Eliot press down on the handle while I pulled on the other end. He'd pick me up when the lead snapped and I landed on the floor. Now he's not here to do any of that." Her voice trailed off. "But we'll manage."

"Sorry, friend," Karen said evenly.

Barbara didn't respond. She just held her mug of tea clasped between her hands and contemplated the drawing on the window. It certainly wasn't anything like his driftwood.

"Now that we've got the colors straight, is there anything else you want my advice on?" Karen broke the silence. "Anything at all." She smiled slyly. "Anyone?"

"You mean Jeff McMillan?"

Karen leaned over with a conspiratorial whisper. "How is it going with you two? And don't tell Louis I asked or he'd strangle me."

"I guess we are becoming an item, a very quiet item," Barbara conceded cautiously. "We're seeing each other and we're having some kind of a relationship, if that's what they call it these days. I don't know what else to say. I'm being very low key about this around the kids. Occasionally at his house, it's more intense." She suspected her friend had noticed the late hours they'd been keeping. "This my-place-or-yours business is a far cry from the days when we didn't have places so we necked in the car and kissed goodnight at the door."

"You mean back in the dark ages. We have progressed to horizontal romance." Karen shook a package of sweetener into her tea and stirred it. "You've got to look on the bright side. At least now it's more consumer oriented. You get to try out the merchandise before you decide to keep it." She became more animated. "Then again, that kind of openness could have its drawbacks. If I had known what Louis was going to look like at six in the morning, wearing black socks and nothing else." Karen giggled, "I'd have passed him over."

"You'd still take Louis," Barbara challenged her softly.

"Only if I knew what I know now. This time I'd choose him for all the right reasons," Karen insisted. "Last time, I just bumbled into a good thing because some sorry SOB had just dumped me for a physical therapist and my hormones were raging. Call it blind passion," she said with a chuckle. "But if I had to replace Louis, I'd have a shopping list a mile long. I'm a sucker for brains. And a sense of humor. I couldn't screw around with an idiot, even if he were tall, dark, and handsome. At least not after the first eight or nine times," she grinned devilishly.

"You mean the first eight or nine would just be test runs?"

"I've been married a long time. I think I'd shop around a bit before I settled down again. I'm just kidding, of course. I'm being so tacky." She shook her head in exaggerated dismay. "Three times maximum for a test run," she corrected herself with an evil smile.

"Whatever," Barbara shrugged. The thought of Louis being gone and Karen being without him took all the humor out of the conversation. Without children, Karen would have no one to give her a sense of family.

"Look, I know things are different now." Karen had caught the darkening shift in Barbara's expression. "In a lot of ways, that's good. When we were younger, we were such good girls that sex meant serious. These days it's just part of an evening's recreation. Enjoy being in the new age, but you take care of yourself, and I'm not just talking condoms here." Karen reached over and clasped Barbara's wrist. "I know you. And I know having sex is different from making love. Don't get caught up in one without the other, and don't get—"

"Pregnant?" Barbara breathed the word.

"I was thinking 'sidetracked' or maybe 'trapped.' I guess I just don't want you to settle for anything less than you deserve. If it's not enough, drop it. Or him."

"I'm not a kid. I'm being careful," she declared. "And I'm not going to commit to anything I'm not sure about."

"I just don't want you hurt," Karen repeated.

"That makes two of us," Barbara sighed.

"Well, I feel responsible." Karen wrinkled her nose. "After all, I did kind of shove you and McMillan at each other."

"You could say that."

"I guess I'm concerned that he might not be all that I thought he was. He's suitable and he's cute. But cute might wear thin after a while. I could have made a mistake." Karen seemed to be testing her friend.

"Maybe you did get us together. But what I did from that point on is my responsibility. I'm supposed to be a big girl now."

"Yeah. Well, if we're supposed to be big girls, then why do we keep feeling like little girls?"

Something in her voice made Barbara pause and give her a curious look.

"I was brought up to expect to have a man around. I admit it. Men come in handy. I've swallowed that construct hook, line, and sinker, and I know darn well that I won't change. And you've got a family with a vacancy. You eventually will fill it. So maybe I'm having a sympathetic reaction, and I'm getting cold feet for you," Karen muttered, suddenly looking directly into Barbara's eyes and turning serious. "If this thing with McMillan was so great, I'd see it in your face. Something isn't right here. I don't know what it is, but I feel it. If you need someone to talk to, please talk to me."

"We are talking," Barbara noted with a shrug.

"Not like we used to," Karen said softly. "You're always so busy, or there's someone around. I miss you. And I worry about you."

"I know that." Barbara patted Karen on the arm. She had missed the closeness between them, too. But there was an off-limits segment of her existence that she couldn't share with anyone, things that had nothing to do with Jeff McMillan, and that protective silence kept widening the gulf between her and everyone else. "I'm doing all right, really." She put on a bright smile, but she had to clear her throat to keep her voice from breaking slightly as she spoke, and when she did, it had a tinny sound even to her own ears. "This thing with McMillan may not be great, but it has possibilities. Like you said once, T.J. is a hard act to follow. I've had romance and a really good marriage, now I have to be realistic and look ahead. This one I have to work out on my own. Now back off, nosy lady, and pour the tea."

"Tea." Karen nodded thoughtfully then complied and reached for the pot.

Barbara stood in the center of the clearing with Luster, looking on as Miranda and Eliot walked slowly from figure to figure, running their fingers over the surface of the wood sculptures all facing in, surrounding them. "The kids have been pestering me to bring them out here so they could see your carvings. I had no idea you had done anything like this." Despite her initial uneasiness when Luster said that several of the figures were family members and pets that had died, she saw nothing funereal in his work. There was a quiet sense of joy in every expression. Standing with him in their midst gave her a feeling of having been admitted to a secret sanctuary where peace prevailed.

Miranda stopped in front of the one figure, a barefoot

angel, that looked remarkably like her. "Mom, look. This is the one." She bent over and poked the toes, then broke into an open, enchanted smile that registered how very pleased she was. Sweetly, she reached out and cupped her hand over the outturned one of the angel, holding onto it as they exchanged a silent greeting.

"It's absolutely lovely," Barbara remarked, wishing she'd brought a camera. "Is that one for sale?"

Eliot was squatting nose to nose with the carving of the bulldog Willie Dodd once owned. He seemed to feel more comfortable with the animals Luster had made than with the angels or the two children or Inez.

"I can't sell any of them just yet." Luster's voice was raspy and dry like the palmettos rustling in the crisp winter breeze around them. "But I'll remember you like that one, so's if time comes to part with it, I'll let you know." He'd brought her out there to his special place to talk, not to promote his artwork, and he felt uneasy over her offer to buy the Miranda-angel. "I can't break up the set until I'm sure it's all right. Right now, I know I'm not finished with them, and I can't do much else but keep on workin' till I get the feeling I'm done."

"Wouldn't you like it if suddenly something magic happened and they all came alive?" Miranda called out from across the circle. She'd moved farther around near Eliot and was patting the bulldog's head. She had her other arm around the weathered pelican Luster had crafted years before.

"Ain't the way of nature," Luster answered placidly. "Nature said it was time for them to go. So it be. We may miss 'em and sometimes we want 'em back. But it's real puffed-up and prideful to put ourselves above the way of nature. Besides, if they came back after crossin' over, they'd be different than we remembered. We're different too. Things change." He and Barbara strolled over and stood behind her. "A person has to be real careful what he asks for," Luster added gently. "If he gets his wish, it may not turn out like he figured after all. That old dog there was old, and grumpy, and eat up with the cancer to'ard the end. Wouldn't want to have him back, sufferin' any mo'. He's best where he is."

Miranda pouted out her bottom lip and studied the heavy-jowled dog.

"Come over here and set a bit." Luster spoke softly, deliberately leading Barbara off with him when he saw Mattie coming out to invite the children in for cake. "These old knees have been complainin' a lot lately." He and Barbara were seated on folding stools in a sunny spot near the workbench. "Just send ours out here, if you please," he called out when Mattie stepped into the circle, as if on cue. Earlier, he'd had Willie Dodd move his latest tree stump out a bit from under the overhanging branches so he would have a warm place to sit and look it over for a while. "Got another angel in there," he told his visitor, inclining his head toward the jagged edged piece that stood almost five feet tall.

Barbara looked at it respectfully. It was considerably larger than some of the others.

"Sonny Pierce had this stump of cypress forklifted out of a section that had been used as a dump for debris after a past hurricane," Luster explained. "Been scheduled for a landfill development."

Twisting as it rose from the cut off base near the roots, it had one portion of a limb thrusting higher than the other, so it leaned forward, balanced like a shapeless warrior, holding up a banner for a battle charge.

"Angels are real pleasant to have 'round. They ain't a bit like haunts," Luster started in determinedly, clasping a piece of soft, pale fruitwood, just to keep his restless hands busy. He whittled away, saying nothing for a while. Barbara said nothing either, she just sat next to him with a trace of a smile on her pretty face, apparently content to sit out in the sunshine and watch him work. Then Mattie brought a tray with slices of the still-warm pound cake and a big glass of milk for each of them. Luster put aside the little figure he'd been fussing over, thanked her, and waited until she was gone again.

"When I think of angels, I think of Inez," he stated, looking back toward the circle. "When she passed over, I figured nature had planned it that way, and it wasn't my place to question or complain. I suppose that's really what that is over there. That's Inez's angel like I remember her at her best of times, kinda sweet and fussy and gentlelike. Even that old dog is an angel in my mind. Don't need to see no wings on these, you know." He took a forkful of cake, pacing himself so he didn't rush into it and say too much too soon. "Thing that makes me comfortable with this place, is knowin' that angels is happy where they is." He could see his hand trembling, so he rested it on his lap. "Haunts, they ain't happy nowhere and they want to be somewhere." He pinched off a piece of cake and popped it in his mouth. Then he took a swallow of milk. "Lot's of stories 'bout haunts nearabouts." That was how Sister Gertrude Kelly told him to get into it. Tell her stories. So if there were haunts about, they'd not catch on to what he was doing.

"Once was a fella' lived downriver, had a haunt pesterin' him. Kep' getting in his traps at night, lettin' out the squirrels and possum so he could't get no meat for his stew. Turned out he owed a fella that died some money." He pursed his lips and gave her a quick sidelong look. She was enjoying the cake, but she was listening.

"Haunts like loose ends and unfinished business. Gives 'em a reason for checkin' in and nosin' around." He noticed the hesitation in her movement. "Now that old haunt didn't set out to be mean, but the longer he stayed 'round, the more he forgot what it's like to be human."

She was picking at the cake with her fork, but he could tell she was taking a long time to swallow the last bite. "How does the story end?" she prodded him.

"Had to put out money every night with the traps. Put money in his ol' friend's house. Nothing happened for weeks. Finally put it in the boat they use to take out fishin'. Must'a been where he was. That time the haunt took the money and went away, not that money would do a haunt any good anyhow." Luster wet his mouth with another draw of milk. He was sweating now, despite the cool air. "Just a matter of findin' out what's holdin' it back and endin' it."

Barbara nodded and managed a tight, stiff smile.

"Few years back, was an old wife who died 'fore she finished her laundry. Family kept finding the ironing board up and things out on the line. Sometimes they found clothes in their closet been taken out at night and ironed till they was scorched. Folks moved away and new folks moved in, and they kept finding same thing goin' on. Took to leaving out some old clothes in a basket, so's she'd do 'em over and over and not ruin nothin' else. Haunts get confused about what's theirs and what ain't. They keep drifting back, holding on harder and harder, but they forget what it's all about. They don't know they're not the same and we're not the same. Once you cross over, nothing is like it was before."

He let that one rest a bit.

"Folks round here know you have to be careful what you say or do 'round haunts. Talkin' 'bout them in particular, or worse yet, talkin' *to* 'em in particular brings 'em in. Gives 'em an opening, like an invitation to come near. Then they start meddlin'." He took the side of his hand and swept some crumbs off his lap. "Sometimes things happen that we jus' can't explain. Sometimes the line between what makes sense and what doesn't is real thin, so thin that we slip across it without realizin' it. We find ourselves on the wrong side and we don't know what we did to get there. Chances are that means there's a haunt afoot, movin' that line. Takes a while to figure out a way to put it back where it belongs." He bent forward, took the handle of his fork and drew a line in the dirt and wood chips by his feet. "Everyone has to keep drawin' their own line from time to time, whether anyone else can see it or not. Haunts know if it's there. If you get careless, they'll slip through an opening in a heartbeat."

Luster's own heart was hammering in his chest as he spoke. He remembered the night he'd left for home in his truck and he'd hit the brakes and hadn't stopped. He was sure he was going to wake up on the other side. He'd been trying to protect the family then, just as now. Only here, he was surrounded by his angels. Here, his line was drawn clear.

"How 'bout coming to fetch the chil'un and warm our toes by the fire. You might want to look at some of my daughter's sweetgrass baskets?" Luster offered, tired from talking and worrying and trying to give her a lead. Mattie would take over being social once they came inside. "She's workin' up a nice collection for the springtime for all those art shows she goes to." He was on his feet now, ambling off through the center of the circle toward the house, with the tray under one arm and the empty glass in the other.

"This is the peacefulest place," he said, pausing long enough for her to catch up. "Anytime you need a peaceful place, you're welcome here. Don't have to fear nothing when you got angels all around." Sister Gertrude Kelly had told him this was as far as he could go, as much as he could say. Until the next time.

If anything in Barbara Ashcroft's life connected with what he was saying, the next step was for her to come to him. It wouldn't work if he offered; it only worked if she asked. Favoring his one knee still, he walked on toward the house. Barbara stood inside the circle alone a few seconds longer, looking at the sculptures. Then she tugged closed her jacket and hurried on after him.

"We're going to ride down to the boat," Eliot announced from the front seat of the bicycle built for two that Jeff McMillan had rented. Miranda clung desperately to the second seat, bracing her feet on the crossbar instead of on the pedals. She'd pulled her strawberry blonde hair back into a single ponytail that wobbled frantically as Eliot slowly steered the bike down the dirt path. "Sit still," his voice commanded. Gradually, the bike seemed to stabilize as the two children moved through the park and out of sight.

"Alone at last." McMillan turned toward Barbara and grinned. That was hardly the truth. Even on a cool January day, Charles Towne Landing had plenty of other visitors who'd decided to get outside. Barbara had chosen a picnic table partially in the sun behind a low buffer of shrubs that blocked the wind. Several other families had followed her lead, so within a thirty-foot radius, four separate groups were spreading out their blankets and baskets of food.

"Don't get carried away," she warned him when he came toward her, "I'm not into public displays of affection."

"I'll settle for intense private displays." McMillan dutifully grasped the other end of the tablecloth and helped her spread it over the concrete table. "Let's run the legs off the little darlings," he suggested, "then maybe they'll collapse promptly at nine or nine-thirty, and you and I can fool around."

"At nine-thirty-one?"

"I'm not in that big of a rush." McMillan moved nearer. "I'm eager, but not desperate." He reached past her, retrieving the thermos of coffee from their basket.

"I must admit it, the thought of fooling around while the children are in the house makes me uneasy." Barbara abandoned her unpacking and sat down next to him.

"They are always going to be there," McMillan observed dryly. "Times have changed, and people adapt."

"I realize that," Barbara said softly. "I'm not ready to drop this on them, not in their own house."

"Like I said," McMillan reassured her, "I'm eager, not desperate." He leaned nearer. "I won't misbehave."

"Bologna?" Barbara reached for the ice chest in time to avoid his embrace. "Potato chips?" she offered smugly, holding the bag between them.

"I'll take anything you got, lady."

Barbara paused and stared at him curiously. He sounded just like T.J.—playful, suggestive, and confident she would be accommodating. Only coming from McMillan, it was beginning to sound a bit pushy. Somehow it brought back Karen's comment about cute wearing thin after awhile.

"Here, have a sandwich." She held out an open Tupperware container. "Bologna, peanut butter and jelly, ham and cheese." She pointed out the choices.

McMillan took a ham and cheese, then leaned back against the table, his long legs stretched out toward the bike path, hot coffee by his side. Much later, Eliot and Miranda came pedaling back from the old fortified area of the park, where the replica of a trading ketch was moored. Red-faced and puffing from the cold and the workout, they flung themselves onto the bench, groaning for food and drink.

"Eat slowly," Barbara warned her son, who stuffed

half a peanut butter and jelly into his mouth in one gulp. "Eject," she ordered. Eliot promptly removed most of the sandwich, then settled down to a calmer pace, methodically devouring almost everything in sight and chasing it with hot chocolate.

"You want to try a ride on this thing?" McMillan patted the two-seater bicycle. "The kids can finish their lunch, and you and I can whizz around the park. How about it?"

"Mothers can't ride bicycles," Eliot teased.

"Oh, do it, Mom," Miranda squealed. "You two ride. See if you can."

"Okay, you asked for it." Barbara accepted the challenge. "I want a guarantee that you two will stay with the table and clean up after you're through." She directed her next command at Eliot. "Don't fight with your sister," she said almost from habit. "We'll be back soon."

"You ride up front," McMillan suggested. "I'm tall enough to see over you. Besides, I like the view from here."

"If I thought that meant you'd be admiring the flora and fauna, I'd take you up on it. But I think you should ride up front so you can steer. I'll stay back here so you won't get distracted."

"I'll get the scenic view sooner or later," McMillan said quietly, glancing behind him to make sure the kids weren't close enough to hear. As they pulled away and accelerated down the path, the chilled wind caught him square in the face.

Barbara simply rode along, enjoying the sunshine and the feeling of having someone else doing the steering for awhile, someone else in charge. He wasn't T.J. and she wasn't breathlessly in love, but for now, it was as close as she could get to comfortable. She closed her eyes, propped her feet on the seat tube in front of her, and coasted.

The kids were in bed by eight-thirty that night. McMillan had poured himself a scotch and was sitting in the kitchen nook sipping it when Barbara finished overseeing the bedtime ritual. "You succeeded." She brushed aside a drooping curl as she returned from the bedroom wing. "You wore them out. They're both unconscious." She had just left Miranda, spread-eagled and open-mouthed, asleep in her bed. Eliot hadn't even wrapped his blankets about him in his customary cocoon. He'd just crawled under the covers and collapsed.

"It must have been the hour of frisbee." McMillan sighed and stretched contentedly.

"No doubt," Barbara shook her head. "You gave them a workout. Would you like some coffee?" More out of habit than desire, she began setting it up to brew.

"I'm fine with this." He got up and came toward her. "How about stoking up the fire and we'll sit and neck for awhile?" He pressed a light kiss to her temple. "Remember sitting by the fireside?" He brushed the side of her neck with his lips.

"I remember." Barbara put coffee in the filter and slid the drip basket into place. "But you remember what I said about the kids. I don't want to do anything with them in the house. Maybe we should call it a night."

"Don't worry. I'm not planning on staying over," he replied amiably. "Just sit a while. I'll behave."

"Fine. You work on the fire. I'll be there in a couple of minutes as soon as I've picked up a bit and the coffee is done." McMillan left her there while he strolled toward the den.

Standing alone in the kitchen, Barbara rinsed out the thermos and put away what remained from their picnic. She remembered going through this solitary process innumerable times when T.J. was there. She'd tidy up the leftovers of the day's activity while he worked or read or put the kids to bed. Then he'd come to find her, urging her to leave the rest until morning because he was feeling romantic and wanted her.

Now there was another man waiting, wanting, and all she really wished to do was to sink chin-deep into a hot tub and soak, alone. For a few seconds, she simply stood, staring into the sink, trying not to resent the feeling that even now, in her own house, she'd let herself get talked into something she really didn't want to do. Glumly she watched the soapy water circle and disappear down the drain.

McMillan wasn't in the den when she went to meet him there. She saw the movement by the study light through the atrium and rounded it in search of him. He was at the far end of the room, drink in hand, looking at the pieces of glass laid out on the worktable. "I just wondered how the window panel was coming." McMillan adopted a polite conversational tone as he waited for her there.

"Slowly," Barbara admitted. "I'm still cutting the center part. It's trickier than I expected."

"How so?" He sipped his scotch and looked at her. Standing like he was, outside of the harsher circle of light on the table, he reminded her of T.J.—tall, golden, boyish to a degree, and expectant.

"The opalescent stuff splinters. Some of the edges aren't as smooth as they should be."

"Is that where you got those little scratches?" He put down his mug and clasped her hand. Slowly he turned it over, inspecting several small cuts, mainly on the thumbs.

"One of the hazards in the pursuit of art."

McMillan lifted her hand to his mouth and gently kissed her palm. It was a gesture T.J. had often made. Barbara stiffened, then slowly began to withdraw the hand.

McMillan tightened his grip. "Come here, let me hold you," he said quietly. "I've been waiting all day to have you to myself." The night he died, T.J. had said the same words. Feeling strangely detached from the moment, Barbara set her cup on the end table, then let him pull her toward him. He held her across his lap, gliding his hands over her hips and buttocks and up to her breasts.

"Just remember what you said about behaving."

"This is ridiculous." He lowered his mouth to hers.

"Easy," she breathed between half-parted lips.

He moved his mouth over hers, teasing and tantalizing her with his tongue. "Come on. They're asleep." His kisses lingered, as his warm breath caressed her face. With one easy motion he drew her with him down onto the soft apricot carpet as his body pressed against hers. "Forget what I said about not being desperate." He reached under her sweater and stroked her breasts. "I can hardly breathe for wanting you. Let's make love." He rolled her on her back and stared down at her. "How about it?"

"Not here. Not now," Barbara said a bit unsteadily.

"You want to go outside?" He eased back, not willing to give up so easily. "We could take a blanket out under the stars."

She shook her head from side to side. "We'd freeze our buns."

"I'd keep your buns warm." McMillan stroked her backside. He eased one leg over hers and kissed her once more. He made it seem so right, so natural, so easy.

Mine. A vague sense of urgency whispered. It was ridiculous, having to run off to his apartment to make love instead of being free do it here and wake up in her own bed. *It isn't because of the children at all.* The accusation drifted on the periphery of her mind as she felt the exhilaration of purely physical arousal. She'd been avoiding it here because it was T.J.'s house, and she was afraid of repercussions that did not involve the children at all.

Mine. Her body moved against McMillan's invitingly, almost as an act of defiance. *Mine.* She slid her arms around his neck and drew his mouth to hers.

"I love it when you get all soft like this." His voice, gruff with excitement, rumbled between deeper, hungry kisses. Eagerly, he slid off her sweater and undid her bra, kissing and sucking as his hands moved constantly over her skin. "On fire," he murmured, covering her with warm moist kisses that set her blood pounding. "On fire," he gasped, tugging off his sweater so he could feel her naked skin against his. He was on his knees, pushing down his slacks when the first ring cut in.

The phone was on the second ring before Barbara was fully aware of what she was hearing.

"Let it go," McMillan whispered sharply, nearly undressed. "Don't answer it." It rang again, harsh and loud. He lay down next to her, cupping her face in his hand. "Don't . . ." It rang and rang again.

Barbara opened her eyes reluctantly. "If I don't get it, it might wake up one of the kids. It might be some kind of emergency." She crawled to her knees as it rang again.

"Damn." McMillan rolled over on his back like a wounded soldier. "Tell them it's a wrong number, then leave it off the hook."

Barbara gave him a quick sympathetic pat, then hurried to the desk and grabbed the study phone, clasping her sweater in front of her.

She covered the mouthpiece as she relayed the message. "You're going to love this one." He was still spread out on the carpet in front of the loveseat. "It's the police. The burglar alarm went off at the office. They've got officers there, but someone has to go over there and check the place."

"What happened to Louis?" McMillan protested. Barbara held up her hand, listening to the caller. "Ten minutes," she said and hung up. "Louis and Karen were going to the symphony tonight. I'd told her you were spending the day with us. Apparently Louis gave the security company this number. I guess he didn't want anyone to interrupt the concert."

"They sure as hell interrupted something else." McMillan scowled as yanked on his clothes. He sat on the loveseat and stuffed his feet into his shoes. "Phone, smoke alarm, kids. Next time we get a babysitter and go to my place. I always leave the phone off the hook."

"Obviously, you've had a little more experience at this than I have." Barbara straightened out her sweater and pulled it over her head.

"You can see where it has gotten me," McMillan laughed. "Here I am heading out into the cold on a Saturday night with a bad case of the 'I wants.' "

"We have a definite problem with the logistics," Barbara sympathized. "The wheres and whens and hows get a little complicated."

"As long as the with-whom part isn't in doubt." McMillan stood and hugged her. "We've got that part straight." He kept his arm around her as he strode to the kitchen to retrieve his jacket. Then he glanced at her bare legs below her oversized sweater. "You want to know how much I hate to leave you knowing you're standing here bare-assed?" He kissed her quickly and stalked out the door.

Barbara stood alone in the kitchen after he left, staring out into the dark night, remembering a hallway in Fort Lauderdale, and being bare-assed with another man who took her in his arms and held her all night long. It wasn't a comparison she found reassuring. Looking out toward the river, she watched the moonlight catch the bank of low fog and close in like a curtain of smoke.

Somewhere in her consciousness stirred the image of a tall man stepping out of the bushes into a clearing. She remembered one of her first visits to these lots right after T.J. had purchased them for this house. He had gone off into the underbrush to look for a boundary stake, then the fog came in and he stepped out of nowhere, grinning blissfully like an explorer discovering paradise.

But suddenly the man emerging in her memory stepped into a brighter light. He had dark hair and he was singing *Some Enchanted Evening*. The song echoed inside her head just as the recollection of Rob's gentle dark eyes suddenly made her shiver. "With-whom," she murmured, shaking her head in confusion. Regardless, she left on a light in the kitchen in case McMillan finished with the office inspection and decided to come back.

She had only taken a few steps inside her bedroom when her fingers connected with the circular knob and she had light. Strewn ribbonlike across the rumpled bed were her nightgowns, all the sexy, lacy ones that T.J. had given her over the years. They were scattered about, all in shreds, all slashed in thin, precise, even strips, just like the study draperies, all saturated with the dreaded aroma of T.J.'s cologne.

"No, please." Barbara walked toward the bed and picked up a few pieces very gently. "These are mine. These are mine, and I remembered wonderful things about each one of these. You've ruined them. How could you ruin them?" She found part of a pretty white one that T.J. had bought her when they spent their first night in the house. He'd opened champagne and they'd toasted every room. And they'd made love in here for the very first time.

"This is sick." She cradled the strips of the gowns and picked up handful after handful of the others, trying not to cry and determined not to scream. She didn't want Eliot and Miranda to see any of this.

"How could you? Get out of here! And don't destroy my things!" She wheeled around looking for someplace to direct her anger. "These are my memories." She scooped up the last of the ruined gowns and started stuffing them back in the drawer they'd come from.

"I'm starting over again. I have to." Her hands were shaking. She clenched her fists to subdue the vibrations. Her words were low and choked. "I don't want an audience," she insisted. "And I won't ask your permission to have a life without you." Instantly the lights in the room clicked off, caging her in total darkness.

The reply was immediate, catching her from the side, like a slap. As if she were no more substantial than a leaf in a breeze, a burst of chilled air flung her against the wall, holding her motionless there, open-mouthed and terrified, before slacking off and letting her slide like a ragdoll to the floor. The scent of bay and perspiration pressed against her face in the darkness.

On hands and knees, she lunged for the door, scrambling to escape. The icy air stopped her, knocking her back. It kept on, blocking every advance, steadily backing her into the center of the room. A current caught and spun her around. Disoriented in the dark, she tripped over the open drawer, then fell stumbling against the dresser. Slapped again by a crosscurrent, she wheeled into the closet doorjamb until the cold pressure forced her inside it. The door slammed after her. She grabbed the handle, cold like ice, then yanked back her hand. The frigid presence stayed on the other side. Dazed, she stood motionless, listening, but the only sound was her own uneven breathing.

Chilled bone-deep and shivering, Barbara rummaged in the inky interior of the closet for something to warm her. She slid on her quilted jacket and a pair of sweatpants, then found a long coat and a robe to use for blankets. Shaking and sobbing, she crawled into the farthest corner, huddling under the clothes, dreading that she'd touch something unfamiliar or some movement inside the dark space with her would bring back the terror of that dumpster and have her screaming uncontrollably. "Mustn't wake the kids. Keep them out of this." Her teeth kept chattering as she waited.

She stayed there for hours, dozing off and on until the thin gray strip of light below the door told her morning had come at last. Still bundled in the heavy coat, she tested the door again. This time it opened effortlessly. She eased it wider, bracing herself for the destruction she expected to see. But the room was immaculate. Every piece of furniture was in place. The bed was made. The draperies were open. Not even the bottles of perfume on the dresser were disturbed.

She stepped toward the center of the room, taking it all in, trying to make sense of it all. *Sometimes things happen that we jus' can't explain. Sometimes the line between what makes sense and what doesn't is real thin, so thin that we slip across it without realizin' it. We find ourselves on the wrong side and we don't know what we did to get there.* Luster Johns's comments from the day before came into sharper focus. She had tried to pass it off as mere coincidence that the ramblings of the wispy old man had touched upon a secret part of her existence. Now she realized he must have suspected she'd been caught up in something beyond logic. He was trying to warn her. *Chances are that means there's a haunt afoot, movin' that line.*

On the bedside table, the telephone was off the hook, neatly placed upside down beside the cradle, just like T.J. had occasionally left it when he didn't want them to be disturbed. She put it back. Everything looked as if nothing had happened, as if she'd imagined it all. She grabbed the lingerie drawer and pulled it open. The gowns were there, all shredded and stinking of Dhatri, and disturbingly cool to the touch. "T.J., damn it," she whispered, wishing it had all been a terrible nightmare.

Have to be careful what you say when there's haunts

about, Luster had said. *Some things may not mean to us what they do to spirits.* He'd been talking about the angels then but his conversation had drifted onto haunts and spirits, and Barbara had tried not to react to what he said. *Haunts don't set out to be mean, but the longer they stay 'round the more they forget what bein' human is like. They just get confused about what's theirs and what ain't. They keep drifting back, holding on harder and harder, but they forget what it's all about. Once you cross over nothing is like it was before.*

Barbara remembered him talking about how he missed Inez and how missing people sometimes makes you want them back. *Tha's real puffed-up and prideful*, he'd declared. *Tha's putting ourself above the way of nature.* He'd hated having Inez go, but he figured nature had it planned that way, and it wasn't his place to question or complain. *I take it as it comes, but it ain't often as I'd choose. But a person has to be real careful what he asks for. If he gets his wish, it may not turn out like he figured after all.*

"I certainly didn't want this." Barbara stopped herself before she said any more. Talking out loud had become something she did. It stopped little things from piling up inside. It let out the frustration. She just dumped it. *Have to be careful what you say or do 'round haunts*, Luster had cautioned. *Brings 'em in. Gives 'em an opening, like an invitation to come near.*

In silence, Barbara got a trash bag from the kitchen and wadded all the shredded gowns into it. Then she carried the thing all the way outside, her breath making little vapor puffs in the air. The sky was a few shades lighter now, but a front of low clouds off to the east was still holding back the first slanting rays of sunshine. To the rear of the house, beyond the dull brownish marsh grass, the fog had drifted off and she could see a low tanker inching its way out to sea. Nearer in, a pair of tugboats were moving a line of barges in toward the docks. It all seemed ridiculously normal after her nightlong ordeal.

Everyone has to keep drawin' his own line. Haunts know if it's there. If you get careless, they'll slip through a weak spot in a heartbeat. Takes a while to figure out a way to put it back where it belongs.

"Six." She glanced at her watch. Sunday. The kids would sleep late. She walked into the study and contemplated the lily panel, her work in progress on the glass table. *Just a matter of findin' out what's holdin' it back and endin' it*, Luster had said. Pressing her lips together to keep from commenting out loud, she took out the driftwood design that T.J. had wanted, and spread it out on the floor. It was big, complicated, stark, but with Craig Kerfberg's help, possible. Luster had said haunts like loose ends. *Keeps givin' 'em a reason for checkin' in and nosin' around*. Barbara rolled out the translucent paper over the original and traced the driftwood pattern onto it. Then she taped the cartoon to the blank window panel, trimming the edges to fit.

Her arms were aching now. She could feel the tender places on her legs where there would be bruises. Wearily, she lifted out the sheets of caramel and grayish brown for the wood and the opal pieces to make the patches of sand for the beach. She lined them along the ledge of the bay window. She didn't have nearly enough colors or textures to work with, but it was a beginning, one she'd been putting off until now. So she mixed the washes and spread color over the sections she was sure about and left the others blank.

The sun was breaking past the cloud cover when she finally stopped, too tired and her hands too unsteady to continue. It was still early and the children hadn't stirred. She dragged a quilt and her pillow from her bed back into the study. Wrapped up, she lay in the loveseat, watching the colors begin to glow and change as the light shone through. She chewed her bottom lip, and sighed, and smoothed her hair and stared bleakly off into space, wishing to speak to someone, anyone. But she remembered Luster's comment. *Talkin' 'bout them, or worse yet, talking to them in particular . . . brings 'em in.* She shook her head, and remained silent. She blinked slowly, her eyes burning and dry, then finally she couldn't open them again. Sleep dulled the aches and stilled the turmoil, old familiar songs came to comfort her, and there was no need for words at all.

Barbara tapped the wooden wedge with her little hammer, aligning the glass with the lines on the pattern underneath it. Then she pressed onto it the next strip of lead channeling, holding it with another flat-sided horseshoe nail until she had the next piece ready. Bracing it all at one end with the wooden box clamped to the workbench, she worked the stained glass lily design like a jigsaw puzzle from one side toward the other. Occasionally, when a piece didn't quite fit, she slipped on work gloves, pulled down the goggles, and turned on the grinding machine. The upright post whirled, smoothing away the irregularities. For each new section, she tugged out the nails, eased the section into the lead channel, then tapped the whole thing into place again. Piece by piece, she gradually filled the frame. Then she brushed the joints with liquid flux and waited for the soldering iron to heat.

She hadn't realized how intensely she'd been working until she glanced at her watch. She slept until eleven-thirty, fed the kids, and sent them off to play, then she'd started in on one loose end on her own so she could clear the space for T.J.'s driftwood. In an hour and a half, she'd got the Victorian piece assembled. The soldering would take half an hour more. Rubbing her shoulders, she started for the kitchen for a quick cup of coffee when the phone rang.

"I called earlier but you were asleep. I asked Eliot to have you call me back when you got up. I've been trying to be patient, but I finally figured that he probably got busy and forgot to give you my message." McMillan's voice on the other end of the telephone sounded distressed.

"I guess he got sidetracked. We didn't eat breakfast until noon, then he and Billie went outside to work on their tree house." She poured the coffee and stirred in creamer. "We're a bit off schedule today."

"What happened last night? I came back after I left the office and all the lights were out at your place."

"So there wasn't any break-in?" she asked, avoiding a direct answer.

"False alarm. Probably some mouse strolled past a motion detector and set it off. We'll have the company check it out tomorrow. But what happened to you?"

"I guess I fell asleep. What happened with you?" She propped the phone against her shoulder, set aside her coffee mug, picked up her soldering equipment, and started floating little puddles of liquid metal over the joints.

"I got finished with the police, so I called on the car phone. Your line was busy. I came back to check on you."

Her steady movement with solder, flux, and iron halted. She remembered how she'd suddenly been thrust into the closet, then everything got very quiet. Now she wondered if McMillan's return had somehow interrupted what had been escalating inside.

"I'd hoped we could pick up where we'd left off. I was right outside your room. I almost knocked on the sliders."

"Don't ever do that."

"I know. I remembered that night with Kent at the window. I figured it would scare the hell out of you. But maybe we should set up some kind of system, maybe a key outside, so I can get in if something like this happens again. I could just slip in and snuggle up next to you."

Barbara stiffened defensively. She didn't want him or anyone coming in and out whenever he chose. He was taking a lot for granted. The thought of waking with someone in her house, in her room, much less in her bed was terrifying. "I don't think—"

"How about I come over now and we'll work something out?" He kept right on talking. "Maybe we could grab a movie."

"Hey Mom," Eliot called from the side doors. "Mom." His voice had that high-pitched edge of urgency that set her maternal antenna on alert.

"What's wrong? In here. I'm on the phone." Barbara moved closer to the door to answer him.

Eliot just kept yelling from where he was. "Can you

come out? Right now. Billie and I need someone to load some stuff on the pulley."

"How about Miranda?"

"She went to Amy's. We need someone strong. And tall. And not dumb."

"Give me a few minutes, Eliot," Barbara replied testily. "Let me finish my conversation then I'll come out and give you a hand."

"We need you now."

"Just wait."

The only response was the thud of the heavy door closing.

She went back into the kitchen and leaned closer to the window, still holding the phone, trying to see what kind of construction crisis the boys were facing. They had two-by-fours nailed across a gap between Byron's lower branches to frame part of a floor. Several wider, flat boards were stacked in a crevice slightly above, ready to be nailed into place. Billie stood on the ground tying a stack of short boards into a bundle while Eliot climbed back up. He braced himself on the floor frame while he tried to yank the new supply aloft with the pulley they had rigged. He tugged. It rose slowly, then inched back down. Eliot just didn't have the weight or strength to keep it airborne.

"Can you hold on a minute or let me call you back? I'd better give Eliot a hand with something on his tree house," Barbara apologized. As she glanced out again, the board behind Eliot's feet drooped, and started pulling loose from the tree.

"Eliot!"

"What's the matter?" McMillan demanded. "Barbara?"

She let the phone drop and sprang for the door as the board gave way, leaving Eliot dangling by one arm fifteen feet above the ground. She grabbed for the garage door handle. Cold as ice, it didn't budge. Desperate, she turned and raced for the entry on the opposite side. Icy and unmoving, it didn't open either.

"Damn it, let me out." She slammed her hand against the door, then swung around and ran to the study. The sliders there wouldn't unlock. "Eliot!" she called. Frantically, she grabbed the stool from the workbench and beat it against the plate window again and again until the glass shattered and the opening was clear enough to step though. "Eliot," she gasped, racing around the end of that wing, expecting to see him crumpled on the ground.

But there were no shrieks of pain, no cries for help, no moans of anguish. Instead, she rounded the kitchen wing, breathless, and found Eliot and Billie Hobach standing side by side at Byron's roots, grinning and nudging each other.

"You shoulda' seen him!" Billie stood wide-eyed, arms flapping, as Barbara raced up to the tree. "Man, he just flipped over and swung out." Billie pointed to the spot where Barbara had expected Eliot to have landed on the stack of supplies. "Then it was like a see-saw. He came down, then they went up. He just passed the boards and landed on his feet!" Billie was obviously impressed. "Even his glasses stayed on."

Eliot stood beside his friend, still grasping the thick rope in his right hand. Every trace of color had faded from his face. The boards were up top on the landing as if he'd planned it that way.

"Are you all right?" Barbara gasped in disbelief. Her visions of crumpled limbs and puddles of blood suddenly dissipated into relief.

"My hand hurts. I just held on." Eliot stared from the rope burn on his hand to the platform above where the bundle he'd tried to lift sat balanced on the remaining stable two-by-four. "I turned clean over, I think," he added uncertainly.

"Just like in the movies!" Billie gushed enthusiastically. "It was really great." He shifted feet as he stuffed his hands in the back pockets of his jeans.

"We'll get you something for that hand." Barbara walked back under the branches, inspecting the position of the pulley and the angle of the two low-hanging limbs. "I don't know how you did it." She pressed her hand on Byron's trunk. When she lifted her hand from the damp bark, it brought with it the faintest scent of bay and almond that had soaked her lingerie. She wiped her palm against her jeans, trying to rub the scented residue away.

Eliot was smiling now. The color slowly began returning to his slender face. "Byron wouldn't let me get hurt," he said as he looked up at the towering tree.

"Yeah," Billie Hobach agreed. The idea had a certain appeal.

"I doubt that Byron had anything to do with it. Just don't push your luck and try anything like that again." Barbara turned on both boys. Her voice wavered, more from relief than from fright. "You need some help before you take that much stuff up the tree again."

"I asked you to come out," Eliot challenged her.

"I was busy." Barbara began to lose control. Byron had been T.J.'s special tree, now it smelled of Dhatri. Eliot had lifted a load three times his weight. She had something to say, but not here, not to these children.

"You were just talking on the telephone," Eliot came back at her.

"You're right. And I left the phone off the hook," she snapped. "I don't want to get into this now. Let me go in and calm down a bit. You get some peroxide and clean off that rope burn." She turned abruptly. "I'll have a talk with you later, young man."

Eliot just stiffened his jaw and shrugged at his friend. "Mothers," he grumbled. "Come on. Let's get back to work, down here."

Billie Hobach grinned and patted his friend on the back. "It was great, just like Indiana Jones or a ninja or something."

McMillan was no longer on the line when Barbara returned to the phone. She hung it up and slouched into the nook in the corner. "My constitution can't take this," she moaned, then flopped forward, pressing her cheek against the cool surface of the tabletop. Finally she propped her chin on her hand and stared out at Byron and the two boys poking around the base of the tree. The scent of Dhatri was still on her. "If you did this, if you kept him safe, I'm really grateful," Barbara murmured, remembering that Luster once said spirits that stay often watch out for the ones they love. Regardless of what the old man said about not inviting contact, she couldn't keep silent if somehow T.J. had helped to save her son.

Then another ominous, clammy feeling crept over her as she realized she may have been misled. She rubbed her shoulder where she'd hit the doorjamb the previous night. Uneasily she looked from the roots to the upper branches of T.J.'s tree. Eliot hadn't fallen until she was there, watching. And she'd been kept from him by the same door that had opened easily just now when she came back in. "Don't you start doing things to them. Don't you dare try to use them to get back at me, or to scare me, or to keep me in line, or whatever it is you're doing," she whispered. "He's just a baby. He's your son. My God, T.J., how could you even think of using Eliot? You scared him. You hurt his hand. I can't believe you'd ever do any of this. What's happened to you?"

Far down the gravel driveway, she could see McMillan's black BMW swing into view. "This is all I need," she breathed aloud. His car swerved around and braked by the entry. She stood and walked wearily to the door.

"What's wrong?" He hurried toward her. "Are you hurt?" His eyes scanned her hands and her face. None of her marks showed.

"I'm fine. My son fell out of the tree," Barbara announced evenly. "He landed safely on his feet. I'm just taking a few minutes out for a nervous breakdown."

"That tree?" McMillan asked, breathing easier as he watched Eliot and Billie stacking boards beside Byron.

Barbara nodded. "That tree," she barely whispered.

"Let me see if I can give them a hand. A little professional advice never hurts." He started to walk off then he turned to look at her closely. "You are all right?"

"Of course." Barbara forced a smile. "You go help the boys. I'll make something." She wandered off toward the kitchen. McMillan headed out into the yard.

"Lemonade." She spotted bright lemons in the wire basket hanging over the counter. The boys had heavy shirts on and the winter air was cool. Some lemonade sounded good and normal and back on track. She grabbed the knife and cutting board and plopped a couple of lemons in front of her. Her hands were trembling so violently that the knife kept skidding and clicking onto the board.

"Easy." She gritted her teeth and concentrated. The knife skidded again, barely missing the tip of her finger. She slammed it down on the counter. "So, we'll settle for apple juice."

When she turned toward the refrigerator she could see McMillan and Eliot and Billie standing and talking under the umbrellalike form of Byron. "Please stop," she pleaded, "before I can't even remember you the way you were. Don't leave me with nothing."

"I know it's late, but I was out at rehearsals. How are you?" Rob's voice on the telephone sounded the same as always. The only difference was that this was Tuesday and it was almost eleven. He usually waited until the weekend to check in.

"We're all pretty good," Barbara replied. "How about you?"

"I'm fine. I just got the strangest thing in the mail and figured I'd better call to see if it came from you." He hesitated as if he expected her to say something. "Do you have any connections at the College of Charleston?"

"Not really. Why?"

"Someone sent me the *Chronicle of Higher Education*," he started explaining. "It advertised a job at the College. It was circled," he added.

"It wasn't me. I don't even know anyone who gets the *Chronicle*. What about the job? Does it sound interesting?"

"It sounds like I wrote the specifications myself." Rob paused, then read the required courses over the telephone. Stagecraft, Fundamentals of Musical Productions, Masters and Styles in Fine Arts. "They want someone with production experience, and they aren't after a Ph.D.," Rob noted. "Sounds like me?"

"It certainly does," Barbara agreed. "I just never suspected you'd consider leaving your job."

"I hadn't given it any thought until this came up. It just sounds too good to be true. Now comes the delicate part." Rob spoke cautiously. "I want to write for an application and set up an interview."

"So?"

"So I don't want you to feel like I'm encroaching on you in any way. We seem to have done all right as long as we're far apart, or as long as our visits are infrequent," he said tactfully. "However, if the job comes through, I may be relocating to Charleston. That's your turf. How do you feel about that?"

"I think it's great." Seeing him again, even if only for a day or two when he came to interview offered an unexpected chance to reassess. "We've been watching the tapes you gave us. They're excellent. I'm sure any review board will be impressed with your work. Give it a shot. Write for the job. In the meantime, I'll see if Karen and Louis know anyone who might have some influence."

"Okay," Rob sounded ill at ease. "I have your go-ahead on a professional level," he continued, pressing her. "How about personally? Any reservations about that?"

She was having trouble shifting gears, imagining what it would be like if he were near enough to see him face to face anytime she wished. "It would be different, that's for sure. I'd enjoy having you in the area. The kids would love it if you moved to Charleston." She mouthed the words with more certainty than she felt. "Karen and Louis and I would help you find a place and get settled. We have lots of really interesting friends you can meet." She suddenly felt she was talking too much.

"It's pretty premature for any plans about moving," Rob said calmly. "I just wanted to let you know that there is a remote possibility."

"It would be fine," Barbara blurted out, hoping she hadn't made it sound like she intended to orchestrate his social life. She was floundering, uncertain about what he expected from her or what she actually would do if he moved nearby. "There are wonderful people here. I'm sure you'll find your niche. I'm getting out on my own more now." She wished she could shut up. "And I've been seeing someone, so you wouldn't have to concern yourself about me." She was trying to be encouraging without being intrusive, but nothing was coming out the way she intended.

"I'm glad you're getting out," Rob replied with a slightly bewildered tone. "I guess it takes some getting used to being single again."

"I've been dating McMillan."

"Ah, the new fellow. I remember him. We met at the Belcazzios' party."

"Well, we've been seeing each other," Barbara reiterated.

"So you said."

"I guess I did."

"Are you all right?" Rob asked apprehensively. "You sound a little peculiar."

"I'm fine," she declared, stiffly, not feeling fine at all. Everything they had been to each other seemed to be fragmenting as they spoke. She kept remembering how gently they'd made love, then quietly agreed to put that night aside. Denying the impact of that intimacy hadn't worked, even with them miles apart. Keeping those feelings compartmentalized would be difficult if he lived here. And burying her other secrets would get complicated with someone who could read her as well as he could nearby. "Really, I'm fine. I've had a long day. I went down to the glass studio after dinner today and I just got back in."

"I should let you go then."

"I'm doing the big window. The driftwood. Craig Kerfberg has been giving me some pointers."

"How's it going?"

"Slow. But I'm sticking with it. Maybe I'll have it done by the time you come up." She hadn't told him of the accident with Eliot or her putting the stool though the study window. In the interim, she'd had the glass plate she'd broken replaced with plywood.

"Well, I just wanted to ask you about the *Chronicle* and the job. Maybe one of my old professors or a colleague or a former student spotted it and sent me the ad. It certainly sounds like it's worth looking into. I'll call you in a week or so and let you know what I hear back."

"Good luck."

"You're sure you're just tired?" he persisted. "Nothing's wrong?"

"I'm just tired."

"Take care of yourself," Rob said earnestly. "Call me anytime if you want to talk."

"I will."

"Goodnight, Bobbie."

Barbara stood by the telephone several seconds after she had placed it back on its cradle. "Why did I do that?" she moaned. "I talked like an idiot." She sauntered across the kitchen mocking her own words. "I've been seeing Jeff McMillan." It sounded like adolescent one-upsmanship. "I've been doing a hell of a lot more than 'seeing' him." She stopped and stared at the phone, confused by the barrage of unsettling emotions Rob's call had triggered. Why had she felt compelled to give him a dating report? She knew if he were interested, he'd ask. She shook her head embarrassedly, wondering what she was trying to prove and who she was trying to prove it to. "To whom?" she corrected herself.

She set the Sonitrol, turned off the lights, and wandered down the hallway, pausing to check on each sleeping child. She undressed in the bathroom, pivoting naked before the mirror, sobered by all the bruises. So she turned off the brighter overhead lights and left on only those backlighting the iris window set into the wall. Now everything looked mauve and purple. She filled the tub with hot sudsy water and settled down neck deep, looking at the glass work she'd done. Rob had said she had a knack for fitting the pieces together. *Like your jigsaw puzzles and sewing*, he had kidded her. *Somehow you get it to work out right.*

"I'll get this damned window right, too," she groaned wearily. "Maybe tomorrow." She poked her toes out at the far end and braced them against the wall. Then she sank down up to her earlobes and soaked, barely rippling the deep steamy water.

* * *

McMillan yanked off his tie and pitched it across the kitchen counter. It caught on Barbara's metal fruit basket and dangled down over the side. He'd already helped her hang the Victorian panel she'd finished, and he'd taken her out for dinner. The rest of the evening was uncommitted. "I guess there isn't much need to be subtle."

"I guess not," Barbara agreed, since she'd planned it so they could have this night in her house by themselves. Eliot was spending the night with Billie Hobach and Miranda was at a sleep-in birthday party for Billie's sister.

"Do you want to have a drink or sit and chat?" Barbara asked, knowing already what agenda he'd planned. McMillan had his shirt unbuttoned to the waist.

"Follow me." She clicked off the kitchen light and headed for the bedroom wing. She'd had three glasses of wine with dinner, but she was far from being drunk. "No extenuating circumstances. This is wide awake, let's-do-it-tonight time," she'd declared over dinner.

"With the lights on?"

"Don't push your luck," Barbara had countered. She had no intention of letting him see her body with all the bruises.

McMillan stayed one step behind her all the way to the bedroom. She didn't turn on the lights. She didn't even open the draperies. "I need to do something in here. Just go ahead without me." She made it sound playful. But she undressed in the bathroom alone.

"This is really happening." McMillan chuckled wickedly. He pitched his clothes onto the chair and slid under the covers, waiting. She had a robe on as she crossed to the bed, then quickly dropped it and got in next to him. With a sudden intake of air, he pressed her against his naked body. "This is heavenly," he murmured, "and I don't have to get up and take you home. I'd hate going back to my place, then spending the rest of the night without you." He stroked her bare back.

Barbara wrapped her arms around his neck. In twelve days, T.J. would have been dead precisely seven months.

This would be the first night she had not slept in her bed alone.

"Damn it, Barbara, this is no time for horseplay." He thrust his hand behind his neck and grabbed her arm. "All right, where is it?" He bolted upright in the bed.

"Where is what?"

"The water. You brought a glass of water back with you?" He felt behind him on the mattress. "It's wet. How about you take that side."

"What are you talking about?" She sat up and peered at him in the dim light.

"Oh shit. There it goes again." He swiped at his shoulder. "I thought you were playing games or something." He flung the sheet off and shifted toward her. "There's water dripping from somewhere." He slid out of bed and stalked about the room staring at the ceiling. He turned on the light. "Damn fuckin' conspiracy," he muttered vehemently as he stared at the massive dark spot on the sagging ceiling. "What the shit is up there?" he demanded. The wet mark above them covered almost a third of the room. Its center bellied down directly over the bed, dropping irregular dollops of water where they'd been lying.

"Water pipes. An auxiliary tank. Part of the solar heating system." Barbara had pulled her robe back on to cover the bruises.

"Get the bed out from under there before the ceiling gives way," he ordered. "Grab the mattress." He shoved the wet coverings aside. "Hurry up. Grab on," he barked at her. Totally naked, he grappled with the king-sized mattress. With her helping, they stood it on its side against the far wall. They were heading back for the box spring when the bulge in the ceiling split open and dumped its load of trapped insulation, water, and wet sheetrock.

"Damn fuckin' tank," he muttered. He heaved the soaked box spring onto its side as the bed frame collapsed, one corner drooping awkwardly to the floor. "How do you turn off the water?"

"In the atrium." Barbara struggled to keep a straight face. It was hard to take a flush-faced, cursing, naked man seriously. "I'll show you. All the valves and meters are in the corner nearest the den." She hurried ahead of him.

"Goddamn," McMillan bellowed as his toe struck the edge of the slider. "It's not funny," he growled as Barbara clutched her mouth to stifle a smile.

"I know it's not funny. It's terrible." A faint thread of hysteria knotted her voice.

McMillan bent down to examine the plumbing. He pulled open valves, closed them, twisted and turned knobs, muttering all the while. "I hope to hell it's off." He turned to face her.

Her nervous smile abruptly collapsed as she remembered T.J. bent like this, adjusting the dials on the system he'd designed. He'd been the one who'd had the solar pipes set in the ceiling so he could add to the system whenever he chose. "This is ridiculous." She started trembling, then she burst into nervous, high-pitched laughter, unable to hold it back. McMillan wrapped his arms around her. She shuddered, then stood there, sobbing against his chest, until he guided her back down the hall.

"It will be all right." He spoke calmly now. "So it's a mess. It'll be all right."

Barbara continued sobbing uncontrollably.

"What we need is a stiff drink." He led her into the den. "And a plumber," he tried to joke. He deposited her on the sofa and grabbed a bottle from the liquor cabinet. "Here." He poured some scotch into a glass and gave it to her. "This will calm you down." He sounded more hopeful than certain.

Barbara managed to stop sniffing and take an even breath. Some part of her still struggled for control.

"Don't take it so hard," McMillan teased. "There'll be other nights." He glanced down self-consciously at his naked body. "I think I'll get dressed," he said with a shrug. "If you've got any lumber, I could shore up the rest of the ceiling."

Barbara sat sipping her drink as McMillan headed back into the hallway aiming for the bedroom. "Damn fuckin' plumbing . . ." his words were lost in the darkness.

* * *

"Whoever connected all the pipes up there simply forgot to glue that last section to the tank." The heavy-set plumber stuffed his hands in his overalls as he stood between Barbara and McMillan. "I checked around up there." He kept his eyes riveted to the wet sheetrock that McMillan had braced up with a ladder and several of Eliot's two-by-fours. "Everything else is neat as a pin. All wrapped and sealed. It's tight as a tick now," the plumber assured her. "Sure is a shame about the ceiling, though."

McMillan had already called in a contractor to start repairing the damage. It would take six new sheetrock panels and respraying the entire ceiling to repair the waterlogged spot.

"I'm exhausted," he admitted as they left the bedroom together. He and Barbara had spent most of the night shoring up the sagging places and vacuuming up debris and water to try and save the bedroom carpets. Then they were up at six, trying to reach a contractor and the plumber. "I think we should both lay down for awhile."

Eliot and Miranda arrived home at noon after their night with the Hobach family. They found three trucks parked in the driveway and several workmen in coveralls going to and fro across the lawn. Soggy grayish hunks of ceiling material lay on the grass between Wordsworth and Barbara's bedroom door. The carpet crew was dragging out the wet wall-to-wall and the padding.

"It didn't get my room, did it?" Miranda wailed when she and Eliot found Barbara dozing in the study. "All my dolls . . ." She started off down the hall.

"Whoa. It was just my ceiling. My room," Barbara calmed her. "Just the middle part. It leaked at the connection where the pipes and the tank meet. Nothing important was hurt."

"Can I go down and watch?" Eliot backed toward the hallway. "I'll stay out of the way. Promise."

"I just want to see my dolls," Miranda insisted.

"Go ahead." Barbara waved them off wearily. She followed them into the inner hall and watched as they proceeded past the atrium, down the bedroom wing. Miranda turned into her room. Eliot passed his and stopped at the end in Barbara's doorway. Quietly she crossed the hall and peered into the den. McMillan was sprawled out on the sofa, sleeping soundly. His pantlegs were still rolled up to his knees from his labors with the heavy-duty shop vacuum. They'd taken turns sucking up water from the bedroom carpet until nearly dawn.

Barbara watched him for several minutes, studying his tanned relaxed face, listening to his steady, regular breathing. She could list all the right reasons. He was considerate, good at his job, financially secure, hard-working, reasonably good with the kids, and cute. "A real Boy Scout," Barbara muttered wryly.

"Growing kids need a father," Louis had philosophized one afternoon when he drove her home after a board meeting. "But don't go looking for what they need. You're the one who has to spend your life with the guy." Unlike Karen, Louis always hesitated to speak of her relationship with McMillan. Barbara suspected he had some misgivings, too. Possibly because T.J. had been his best friend as well as his partner, and he sensed the same sense of betrayal as she often did. Possibly because he felt, like Karen did, that there was something not quite right about the situation with McMillan.

In the distance, the erratic hammering of the workmen echoed through the house. Occasionally the sounds would subside as someone stopped to measure or to talk. There had been familiar, productive noises like these when she and T.J. would come and watch the construction underway as the house and T.J.'s vision came together and took tangible form. Then, using routes that no longer existed, they would walk from room to room, stepping through the spaces between the two-by-four studs that would be covered with drywall and closed in. Now there were walls, visible and otherwise, blocking her way, keeping her confined. And someone else was trapped in there with her. No one, except perhaps Luster Johns, could comprehend how twisted things had become.

CHAPTER 9

> It sounded as if the streets were running,
> And then the streets stood still.
> Eclipse was all we could see at the window,
> And awe was all we could feel.
>
> By and by the boldest stole out of his covert,
> To see if time was there.
>
> *Emily Dickinson*

LUSTER SPOTTED Miranda coming into the nursery first. She turned left, prowling along the rows of cacti and succulents, glancing over her shoulder occasionally to see if anyone would notice when she reached out and poked the spines.

Eliot headed in the opposite direction. He liked the saltwater aquarium Everett Pierce put in near the office. Luster figured Barbara wouldn't be far behind, so instead of going over to chat with either of the children, he kept on with what he was doing, heading back toward the truck dock to check on a shipment of indoor plants that had just arrived. Most were showy greenery for businesses and restauraunts that Pierce Nursery serviced regularly, some were flowering plants and bushes special-ordered for private customers. If Barbara wanted to talk, they'd have a little privacy out on the loading dock. According to Sister Gertrude, she had to come to him.

"They mentioned you'd just got in some new plants," Barbara said as she crossed toward him, the click of her high-heeled shoes echoing through the warehouse.

"Got some real pretty primroses." Luster turned slightly toward her, trying to act casual. "I'll be bringing some out your way later in the week. Unless you'd rather have some tulips and narcissus. They look real good." He bobbed the end of his pencil toward the rows of pots with buds about to open. "We're kind'a moving spring ahead a bit."

"I'm all for that. Goodness, it's chilly back here." She tugged her coat around her and moved closer.

Luster studied her profile. She was paler than usual. There was a slight sag to her shoulders and shadows under her eyes that indicated she hadn't been getting much rest.

"Busy day at school?"

Barbara seemed to be only half listening. "I didn't go. A water tank leaked over the weekend and I had workmen in all day yesterday and today. I just picked the kids up and thought we'd come by. It's always so pretty here." She was patting her coat lapel distractedly and looking around as if checking that they were alone.

"Which tank broke? Kitchen?"

"The one over my room. The auxiliary tank. Part of the solar heat. If it isn't one thing, it's another." She shugged. "Sounds like some of the stories you were telling me the other day, about things that sometimes happen, things that don't make sense in the normal way." She wasn't looking at him directly. "Tanks leak, the smoke alarm goes off, doors slam shut and won't open. Cold drafts." She licked her lips and gave him a fleeting sidelong glance, then looked about the warehouse warily. "I get edgy with drafts. At home, there are chilly currents of air when nothing is open to let one in."

Luster remembered the shift of chilled air that had spooked him. Knowing she'd felt it too only confirmed his suspicions. "Strange things happenin' often means something is restless." He knew better than to say too much or get too specific, even out there. "Specially after someone passes over. All kinds of things can get pent up inside a house where there's been sadness."

"There's probably a perfectly logical reason for everything, including the water tank. Something about glue," she said nervously, backtracking just like Sister Gertrude told him to expect her to do. "Folks feel foolish talking 'bout spirits," the conjur woman had counseled him, " 'cept in a jokin' way or in stories. What worries 'em is that it jus' might be true. And if it is, then we have to face up to fact we ain't sure of anything we thought we knew to be. Wise man knows nothin' is sure and everythin' is possible."

"Probably there's a reason fo' those troublesome curtains doin' what they did." Luster kept his nose to his clipboard as he spoke.

Barbara stood in stunned silence, unable to reply. She hadn't realized Luster knew anything about the shredded draperies.

"Nature got a lot goin' on that we can never know 'bout, we jus' suspect. Tha's why we have stories, so's we don't have to deal with it direct."

He proceeded checking off pots of foliage while he talked, hoping she'd catch the message and realize they had to be careful what they said. "Fella downriver a piece had his wife up and die. Moaned and groaned about bein' left all alone. Couldn't go to bed at night without waking and hearing the furniture or dishes or somethin' bein' moved about. Went to the conjur woman to help him get rid of the pesky haunt that was hangin' about. Seemed to be the wife, but ain't no way to be sure. Conjur woman gave him a broom to leave out at night. Old haunt started sweepin' the floor. Left out some wax. Haunt swept and waxed the floor. Left out a mess of peas. Haunt shucked 'em. Kep' leavin' out mo' and mo' to do. Haunt finally ups and leaves, tired of doing people's work."

"So it was the wife?" Barbara's whispery voice followed him.

"Don't know, don't matter. What matters was that it went away before it started being mean," Luster stressed. "So the fella hung little mirrors in all the doors and all the windows like the conjur woman says. Once a spirit is out, won't come back past a mirror, won't come back past a blue line, won't come back past a circle of ash— 'less somebody calls it back."

"Why would someone call it back?"

"Not on purpose. Just by accident. Just because of bein' lonely."

"How would he call it back?"

"By speaking to it, by wishin' for it, by talking about missin' it and lettin' it think he wants it back there. Spirits don't understand that we say lots of things we don't mean exactly the way they hear it." Luster turned to look at her. "Saddest part, is that once they stay too long, you have to work extra hard to make them go. They get real possessive. They have to believe you don't want 'em round. Not in your house, not in your heart. Give 'em a little, and they take over."

He was trying to repeat everything Sister Gertrude Kelly had told him, just as she'd stressed it to him. "Got to harden your heart, without lettin' it turn you hard," he cautioned her. "Trouble is, you end up dealing with the worst part of them. They's tough. They don't play fair. They don't play at all."

Barbara stared at him, desolate and confused. "I can't believe we're actually talking like this. I can't believe anyone talks about things like this. It all sounds so matter of fact, but it can't be true. Nothing like this really exists. It's crazy."

"Then there's lots of crazy people in the world. Lots of folks been through mighty peculiar times." Luster turned his attention back to the clipboard to try to diffuse his own tension. He felt the cold rising off the cement floor like an incoming tide, but it was a cold that just came with the weather.

"Worst of times comes when the moon is full. Spirits come closest then. Lots of stories 'bout things happening on the full moon." He had to warn her that much. The full moon was on them.

Barbara was staring unfocused off over the plants, shaking her head.

Sister Gertrude had said it would be like this. Part of her knowing Luster spoke the truth, part of her afraid to admit it was possible at all, another part thinking that a body could get lost in the midst of it all and never find the way back. Luster could see the conflict in her expression and he ached for her.

"Scary when it comes down to your turn to move the line a little," Luster said sympathetically. "Specially since you don't know what it is that might be on your side now. Takes a while to figure out a way to put it back where it belongs. Wise man knows nothin' is sure and everything is possible," he quoted Sister Gertrude.

Barbara still hadn't moved. She had her arms crossed over her chest, hands clutching the lapels of her coat, like she was holding on, keeping everything together as best she could.

Luster could see Miranda and Eliot heading their way through the heavy plastic dividers that hung from ceiling to floor separating the colder dock area from the heated section of the warehouse. "Story is that haunts can only be somewhere they been before, someplace important to them. You come out and visit me and the angels," he added quickly. "Don't have nothin' to fear out there." He hoped the urgency in his voice got through to her.

"Mom, we're hungry," Miranda called out. "Hi, Mr. Johns."

"Did Mom tell you about me falling out of the tree?" Eliot strolled up to them, grinning at the tall elderly nurseryman.

"No, I didn't. You're not hurt and that's the main thing. Mr. Johns has work to do and we've got to get home before the workmen leave. We'll pick up some dinner on the way." She caught him by the shoulder and turned him around.

"I'll tell you about it later," Eliot promised, allowing himself to be propelled along. "It was neat."

Luster stood looking after them, shaking his head slowly. "Fallin'?" he rasped, wondering what more there was to it. "Po' little lady. Trying so hard." He pursed his lips. Cold drafts and curtains were one thing, but anything to do with the children said serious, loud and clear. Luster shook his head again, hoping it was just another childhood tumble, one he'd chuckle over when Eliot got around to telling him the details. But he couldn't shake the image of the cricket with its wings ripped off and the clean straight cuts on the drapes. "Worse an' worse," he muttered, hurrying to finish up. He had some "what if's" to run past Sister Gertrude, some "jus' in case's" that he needed to get straight.

* * *

DARK WINDOW 317

Barbara jerked her head up just as her pencil dropped from her fingers. The paper beneath her hand still lay ungraded, its lines of irregular writing blurring before her eyes. She glanced at her wristwatch.

Eleven-fourteen.

She carefully stacked the ungraded pages separate from the graded ones, lying her marking pencils side by side. They'd have to wait. Scuffing along in her thick socks, she put her empty coffee cup in the sink, turned off the front lights, and set the Sonitrol. Then she came back to shut off the desklamp.

It was there again, like it had been months before. The glass of sherry just beyond the circle of light. *"Once there was a fella' downriver,"* she whispered aloud, just as she'd heard Luster Johns do when he started a story. "He couldn't leave the room without comin' back and findin' somethin' left out for him." She bit her lower lip thoughtfully. "Frankly, I thought being crazy would be a bit more glamorous."

She rummaged in the desk drawer for the sleeping pills Tom Palmer had prescribed the past summer. She popped one into her mouth, lifted the glass, and took a sip. "Why couldn't you just make a nice clean break of it like anybody else?" she sighed, then took another long sip. "I'm working on the new window. If that's what you're hanging around for, you should be happy. It won't be long until it's done." She stared across the room where the glass lily panel still hung, in the place where the large driftwood piece would go.

"Momma?"

The voice from the hall jolted her.

Miranda stood in the doorway in her nightshirt. "I got up to pee. I thought you were talking to someone."

"I was talking." Barbara crossed to the child and hugged her. "You know how sometimes you like to talk with your dolls?"

Miranda looked at her mother solemnly. "You don't have dolls."

"I talk to windows. You've heard me grumble at things when they don't work."

"Sometimes you say bad words," Miranda noted with a smirk.

"Sometimes I do. So now that you've gotten the idea, you can go back to bed." Barbara took her hand and led Miranda back to her room. "Did you go to the bathroom?"

Miranda nodded.

"Did you get a drink?" Barbara asked patiently.

Again Miranda nodded.

"So snuggle back in your bed." Barbara lifted the covers then lowered them over the child.

"Sometimes I talk out loud when I'm on the toilet," Miranda confided.

"Sometimes you even sing." Barbara patted Miranda's backside.

"I didn't think anyone heard me," Miranda grinned.

"Well, I didn't think anyone was listening to me either." Barbara kissed the angelic face. "Goodnight." She patted Miranda once more.

She began to get that on-stage, fishbowl sensation as she headed back to the study. Uneasily she looked back over her shoulder, then checked that the atrium sliders were closed fast. "Come on, disconnect." She tried calming herself. She filled her glass again then quickly swallowed a second pill. Standing in front of the long window in the dark, she sipped her sherry, waiting for the medication to take effect.

"There was a woman downriver had her husband up and die," she breathed the words quietly, testing. Her warm breath made a foggy spot on the glass. She stared out past Keats at the grassy marsh bordering the Ashley River and thought about what Luster Johns had said that afternoon. There are times when the spirits come closer. The *Farmer's Almanac* indicated the full moon was still one day away, but the entire yard was already bathed in light.

"Strange things started happening in that woman's house and made the woman very upset and very confused and very crazy. And she couldn't sleep," Barbara continued the tale grimly. *"Friend told her that strange things happening mean something is restless."* She turned her

back to the window and studied the solitary silhouette that the moonlight sent across the dull carpet. Her dark figure stood within the elongated rectangle of white, motionless and silent. *"Restless."* The word also fit her.

For a moment, as she stared, the outline on the carpet stayed precise and intact, duplicating her slightly angular stance. Then her vision blurred. The dark form shifted and expanded like drifting clouds against the sky, reforming into two of them, one behind the other, with the larger one enveloping then separating from the first. Inside the room it felt cooler.

"T.J." Barbara whirled around. She was still alone. The silver-gray marsh grass swayed gently in the evening breeze. Keats stretched his branches across the clear star-filled sky. But there was no one else, nothing else there.

"Once upon a time . . ." She pressed her forehead to the glass dejectedly, her arms drooped at her sides. Finally she felt that pleasant fuzziness that meant the medication was ready to ease it all away. With heavy steps, she walked down the hall, staying close to the wall so she could brace herself occasionally. At her bedroom doorway she stopped and took a deep breath. The room smelled of fresh paint. The new mattress was on the springs and set back in place. She stepped inside, turned, and with her fingertip drew a line across the threshold. "You know it's there. I know it's there." The room was shifting on her now, the floor rising, cushioned with each step. The back of her throat was dry, but when she swallowed, she tasted saliva and she felt clammy and weak. Without looking back, she crawled into bed and pulled the covers up.

"I'm playing hooky again." Barbara showed up on Karen's doorstep the next morning after dropping off the children at a neighbor's who'd agreed to ride them to school. Bluish half-circles beneath her eyes made her face appear unusually thin and drawn. "Did I wake you up? Maybe I should have called."

"I wasn't sleeping. Come in. You really aren't feeling well, are you? I hear the flu bug is going around."

"I'm just tired," Barbara replied dully. "I'd been

camped out on the sofa while they were working on my room and I was having trouble sleeping there, so I took a couple of pills and went to bed in my room last night. I think I should have waited another day or two until the room aired out. I guess all the fumes and the mess with the pipes and the workmen finally took its toll. I threw up a couple of times this morning and I have got a crashing headache."

"How about some juice? Better yet, I'll put together an eggnog. You could probably use the nourishment. Go sit out back. I'll be right there."

Barbara was in the wicker armchair, staring out at a foursome of early golfers on the course, when Karen joined her. "Should I drive you down to Tom's office and have him check you over? I love you dearly, but truthfully, you look dreadful."

"I'm also a bit hung over," Barbara admitted, clasping her hands around the glass to keep them steady. "I had a few glasses of sherry with the pills. I know it wasn't smart, but I just needed to numb out."

"So now we're talking paint fumes, pills, and sherry."

"I know. Not bright."

"What was it you were numbing out?"

"A bit of everything."

Karen cleared her throat uneasily. "Honey, I think you'd better get a checkup." She propped her feet on Barbara's chair and slumped against the cushions of her own. "Didn't you say you'd started taking birth-control pills. Maybe they have something to do with this, too. It's been years since you were on them. I've heard about all kinds of weird side effects—high blood pressure, water retention, nausea, loss of appetite, insomnia." She stared at Barbara's pale face solemnly. "Add to that sleeping pills, the sherry, and the amount of stress you've been under, and maybe a little Victorian guilt."

"And you get a basket case," Barbara muttered.

"You get a tired, distraught human being whose health is suffering."

"A basket case," Barbara repeated stubbornly. "Karen, I'm really not doing too well right now. Sometimes I think either I'm having some kind of paranoid reaction or there's something strange going on in the house."

"Strange like what?" Karen asked. She remembered that Rob had mentioned a similar conversation months ago when Barbara was spooked by being at home.

"Just strange." Barbara expelled a long breath, realizing she was on precarious ground. She didn't want to scare her friend, but she was slipping farther away from everyone and she desperately wanted to reach out for some kind of understanding. "I keep having the feeling that there's something there," she barely whispered.

"What does that mean?"

"It's like I'm being watched." She chewed her lower lip, wondering how much to say, then sidestepped, trying another tack. "There's just too many coincidences. The other night when McMillan and I were just about to make love, the alarm went off at the office. He got called away. Once before that, under similar circumstances, the smoke alarm went off. This weekend when the water tank leaked, we'd just got into bed." She looked at Karen and saw her bewildered, worried expression. Instantly she regretted having said anything at all. She was trying to draw Karen over the line with her so she wouldn't feel so terribly alone. "I'm rambling. I'm tired and hung over and strung out." She forced a half-smile and waved her hand as if she were erasing what she'd been saying. "Forget what I said. I'm just a little wacked out."

"I think you're exhausted, physically and emotionally." Karen leaned forward, resting her hand on Barbara's arm. "Those things that happened involved rotten timing. Why they happened doesn't have anything to do with you and McMillan. Aside from pipes and alarms interfering with your love life, maybe the real problem is how you reacted to those interruptions. You obviously connect them with some kind of sexual betrayal."

Barbara shrugged and took a sip of her eggnog. "It's not just things involving sex. Sunday afternoon, Eliot and Billie were out working on a treehouse. They needed help and I didn't come right away. Then I saw Eliot start to fall, and I ran to get to him, but I couldn't get the door to open. All the doors stuck. When I did get out, he was all right. He'd landed on his feet."

"You don't think the doors were conspiring against you?"

"Not the doors. They opened all right later."

"Then what is it you're saying?"

"Nothing," Barbara replied. She looked away, leaving the line intact. "I'm just frustrated. I keep thinking I'm doing fine, then something happens."

"Something always happens. I think you're making more of it than you should. Maybe you need to see some kind of counselor to learn to be a little less judgmental on yourself. Maybe you simply have to let up," Karen suggested, saying all the things Barbara had already tried to tell herself. "T.J. had unusually rigid standards for himself, and that was his way. But it wasn't yours. I'm worried that some of his driven quality has rubbed off on you. And since you're my friend, then that makes it my business," she added with a harder edge to her voice. "I'm no shrink, that's for sure," Karen continued, "but whether you realize it consciously, unconsciously you obviously internalized a lot of T.J.'s rules. That's why you're always feeling guilty. T.J. was a good guy, but he wasn't perfect by a long shot. Don't let his standards squeeze the life out of you. Don't do it to yourself or the kids or even to McMillan. Bury everything about him for a while."

Barbara shifted her eyes to Karen's oval face, trying not to reveal any more than she already had. Luster had told her to harden her heart. Now Karen was telling her something strikingly similar.

"I think you need to see a doctor, a body doctor," Karen said firmly. "Have him check you completely. Maybe get some vitamins to build up your energy. How long are you taking off work?"

"A couple of days," Barbara replied, staring out the window.

"Good. What about Eliot and Miranda? Do you want me to take care of them? They could stay with us. I was going to make lasagna tonight anyhow. You know how they love my lasagna."

Barbara glanced out the window again. Luster had said that spirits came closer on the full moon, and tonight the moon would be full. If it was time for a confrontation, she'd feel better knowing the children were safe and away from it all. "Staying over might be a good idea. You and Louis can fuss over them, and they wouldn't have to keep fussing over me."

"Okay, okay, it's settled," Karen said, brightening. "You need rest. So go ahead home and rest. But be careful what medicine you take and what you take with it. I'll check in with you later. If you aren't doing better, I'll get Tom to drop by," she insisted.

"Don't worry. I'm not going to do anything foolish."

Karen stood and collected the two milk-coated glasses they had used. "I just want you healthy. And I want you out of this funk you're in."

"That makes two of us."

"More than that," Karen said quietly. "A lot of us are pulling for you," she noted, frowning as she walked away.

Barbara spilled the bag of mirrored discs from the craft shop out on the kitchen table. Carefully she threaded each one with transparent fishing line so it would dangle from the tiny hooks she'd put up over every window and door. She hadn't rested like she'd told Karen she would. She'd followed Luster's veiled suggestions instead.

"Okay, let's get this over with." She glanced out the window at the last glow of sunset over the river. She'd spent the entire day getting ready. She'd scraped all the ash from the fireplace and put it in a bucket so she could spread it around the house later and make a circle like Luster Johns had mentioned. She'd bought several packs of blue markers and outlined the top and sides of every window and every door. She would put in the fourth side, closing off the opening, when she felt it was over. At times she'd stop, warning herself that these were nothing but backriver superstitions, but she'd remember the solemn way Luster Johns had spoken to her, and she'd remember the curtains and the gowns and the closet. Doing something was better than doing nothing, so she'd kept on. The mirrors would go up when she was sure the presence was outside.

Gradually darkness closed in and she waited for the full round moon to rise higher in the night sky. A low cloud cover blocked the light. For a while she sat at her worktable in the study, tracing the pattern on milky patches of opalescent glass that would form the lower third of the driftwood piece. Still propped up, facing her in the bay window, were the larger sheets of glass for the driftwood itself, the strong, darker colors obscured in the darkness. Every so often she'd stop and walk from room to room, waiting for some shift in the air currents to confirm what Luster Johns had said, then she'd come back and work a little longer. By nine, the muscles in her back and shoulders ached. Even her jaw muscles were taut from silently rehearsing what she wanted to say, though she said nothing at all.

Finally at eleven, exhausted, she went to her room, wrapped herself in her bedspread, and stretched out on the bed, staring out into the night. When she closed her eyes, they burned from the strain. But she couldn't sleep.

A little past midnight, the heat pump clicked on for the fourth time, sending a soft whisper of warm air through the house. In resignation, she flung back the covers, changed into her pajamas, and grabbed her snug robe. She left on the pair of T.J.'s socks that she'd worn to scuff around the house. With soft, silent steps, she moved down the hall past the children's rooms, pausing by habit to glance in each door. Finally she ended up where she had for the past three nights, standing in the darkened study by the long, empty window.

"I'm not going anywhere." She spoke in a low, determined voice. "This is my house." She strolled off to the den for the large bottle of sherry, then settled obstinately in front of the window and poured a full glass.

She was on her second glass when the thick gray line of clouds broke and drifted apart, and the full moon finally emerged. She turned slowly to stare at the squares of colored glass gradually coming to life as the light from outside poured through them. Caramel, mahogany, bark gray, and opaque pearl overlapped, casting a patchwork design across the table that spilled forward onto the carpet in long, leaner stripes.

Barbara filled her glass a third time, then slowly capped the bottle and pulled herself to her feet.

"This is my farewell." She raised the glass in a solemn toast to the window, to Keats, to the river beyond. And to T.J. "It's time to call it quits, Bozo, wherever you are." A bit unsteadily, she circled the loveseat, pausing in front of the worktable to ponder the somber light show. She deposited her empty sherry glass on one corner and began rummaging in the glass bins.

"There you are." She slid out a lighter butterscotch-colored sheet she'd bought at that glass shop when she picked up the tiny mirrors. "Let's check you out in the moonlight."

Already the sweet liquor was making her movements more expansive. She propped the butterscotch sheet on the table, bracing it with one hand while she shifted the other colored pieces to the right. Then she put the butterscotch piece in line with the others, rearranging the smaller ones next to it, some with colors overlapping. She stood back to examine the effect.

"How about it, Bozo? If I do this window, am I off the hook? Will we both be off the hook?" She leaned forward, gazing into the sleek, translucent surface of the golden-brown glass. *Bury everything about him for a while*, Karen had said. *Harden your heart*, Luster phrased it. Blinking back tears, Barbara tried to keep resisting. But mellowed by the liquor, she couldn't keep out the softer, gentler thoughts. The swirling patterns had all T.J.'s colors—the gold of his hair, the creamy shade of his throat, the darker bronze of his body. The blending colors gradually merged into the hazy image of his face. Slowly the vision sharpened, abstract shapes assembled into familiar features, and from the glass T.J. was staring at her with deep, penetrating eyes. The cool air brushed her hair against her cheek. She could feel his breath, smell his skin, almost taste him. She swayed and righted herself, reaching out with her fingertips to caress the glass.

"T.J.," she whispered. "You know I loved you."

She barely had the words formed when the end sheet shifted. Like a row of playing cards, all the other sheets of colored glass touched against one another and began to teeter forward. For a few seconds they stood on edge, then in slow motion, they tipped end to end.

"Oh no," Barbara gasped. "No." In a sudden reflex action, she thrust out both hands to block the collapse. The smaller sheets simply flopped onto the table, chipping or snapping as they hit each other or some object in their path. But the larger caramel sheet descended majestically in one motion. Its top edge flipped downward, slicing across her outstretched hands almost at the wrist junctures. Her golden vision was suddenly shot through with streaks of deep liquid red.

"Oh, my God. Oh, no," Barbara whimpered as she felt the warm blood spreading onto her palms and spilling over onto the wood beneath. One at a time, she dislodged her hands from under the still-intact sheet of caramel glass. From the one handprint, twisting rivulets of her own blood trickled down the surface toward the other. Hooking her hands tightly towards her so the gashes would stay closed, she raced for the kitchen, flicking on the light with her elbow.

"Please, no," she gasped when she saw the sleeves of her robe were soaked with blood. "Please don't let me die." She took a teatowel and wrapped it tightly about one wrist, then wrapped the second with a clean apron. "Karen." She grabbed the phone and hit the memory button. It took four rings before anyone answered.

"I've had an accident, Karen. Some glass fell and I'm cut," she explained, hastily relating the details. "Could you get me to the hospital?"

Karen relayed the scant data to Louis then he started giving instructions. "Louis says to sit on the floor, wrap a towel around your wrists, and press them together. Keep them elevated, put your hands up on a chair or something, then put your forehead on them for extra pressure. We're on our way."

The Belcazzios didn't take Barbara anywhere. They rewrapped Barbara's wrists with ice packs, Louis used fresh towels for tourniquets, and each of them held one arm elevated until the pulsing red light of the ambulance illuminated the kitchen.

Louis relinquished the arm he was holding long enough to admit the first two attendants. "I'm the one who called. This way." They worked hastily, clinching straps, administering shots, and inserting a plasma I.V., then they lifted her onto the wheeled stretcher. She was pale and weak, but conscious.

"There's a perfectly reasonable explanation for all this," Barbara told the men as they slid her into the rear of the ambulance. One paramedic climbed in next to her.

"Yes, ma'am," he replied politely, his bright eyes riveted to the I.V. connection on her forearm. "You take it easy now," he said calmly. "You're gonna be okay."

"It was a dumb accident," she kept explaining as the ambulance pulled out of the driveway. "I didn't want the glass to break. Am I going to be all right?" she asked under her breath as a peculiar lightness overtook her. "We were supposed to say goodbye." She was slurring her words now. "I really loved you, T.J.," she whispered as the anesthetic took over. "I really did. But it was time to go."

The young attendant gave her a curious look, then refocused his attention on the monitor by her side. "You're fine. Just rest. You'll make it, lady," he assured her. Barbara drifted in a rolling sea of golden light that gradually darkened and grew quiet.

"There were two policemen at Karen's house this morning," Miranda began chattering the minute she finished hugging Barbara and taking a good look at her bandages. She'd been a bit white around the eyes when she first stepped through the doors of the hospital room. She'd relaxed once she saw her mother was sitting up, sipping a coke. "One of the guys was named George. He had coffee with Eliot and Karen and me. He was really nice." Her twin ponytails bobbed as she made a quick inventory of the hospital room. "George was real worried about your accident."

"Hi, Mom." Eliot had followed his sister into the room. His cautious blue-green eyes scanned the unoccupied second bed, then settled on Barbara. "How are you doing?" He contemplated her bandaged wrists.

"I'm a little embarrassed," Barbara admitted. "I guess Karen told you that the glass sheets in the window fell and I reached out to stop them. It was a dumb thing to do."

"Yeah." Eliot seemed to breathe easier hearing it from her. "The cops thought you might have done it on purpose. But then they looked at the mess in the study. I guess now they just think you're clumsy."

"They've got a point," Barbara admitted, shaking her head. "First I'm dumb, now I'm clumsy."

Eliot answered with a weak smile.

"How many stitches did you get?" Miranda settled on the side of the bed.

"I'm not sure," Barbara answered. "Maybe twelve."

"Each?" Eliot stepped nearer.

"Each. But they were small stitches," she assured him. "It really wasn't as bad as it looked. There's just these two veins on the bump where your thumb starts. See." She rolled Miranda's hand over to demonstrate. "I guess I knicked them both."

Eliot looked from Miranda's hand to his own, stretching the skin so the bluish vein was more visible. "So it really was your hands, not your wrists at all." He seemed more comfortable with that.

"Right. But I won't be moving any of this for a while or I'll mess up the repairs." She rolled her hands over so he could see the fiberglass brace that kept her wrists from flexing. "So I guess this means I can't beat you," she said with a grin, "or throw a football."

"You can't throw a football anyway." Now Eliot broke into a small grin.

"Karen said you can get out right away." Miranda bobbed up and down on the bed.

"I think so. Did you bring me some snazzier clothes? This thing's a little airy." She turned one shoulder so they could see the split back of the hospital gown.

"Karen has a suitcase thing with some slacks and a sweater."

Eliot crossed to the window and peered out. "She

stopped to talk with some doctor. She'll be here in a minute."

"I told her to bring your lipstick," Miranda declared, at her most efficient. "And some perfume," she added smugly.

"I thank you." Barbara made an exaggerated bow. "I do hope you also thought of underwear."

"We did," Miranda smiled. "Karen and I thought of everything."

"Did you bring anything to eat?" Barbara tested her. "I'm starving."

"Karen said we'd have to see when we got here," Miranda responded. "She wanted to check with your doctor."

"She would," Barbara sighed. "I guess I gave Louis and her quite a scare. It was pretty messy."

"It isn't now," Eliot announced. "It's all cleaned up. At least it will be. Karen sent in her cleaning lady. Louis and Mr. McMillan are there now finishing up."

Karen Belcazzio's cheerful voice interrupted them. "I thought you two would be here." She bounced into the room with a small overnight case in one hand and a stack of official-looking papers in the other. She plunked the case on the bed between Miranda and Barbara. "Get dressed. We're bailing you out. Just sign these." She waved the papers in the air. "Insurance, discharge papers, you name it." She leafed through them. "I need your signature where they put the check marks." She stopped abruptly as she glanced at Barbara's bandages, then looked away quickly, trying not to be caught staring at them. "Can you write?" She realized she may have hit a slight obstacle.

"I can do something that will pass for writing," Barbara insisted.

"Then let's get on with it," Karen said. "You know how I hate institutions." She handed Barbara a pen, pointed to several locations on the various papers, then stacked everything neatly. "Your watch and rings are in the little brown envelope. Be back in a minute." She waved and was on her way.

"Do you need some help?" Eliot offered as Barbara

slid out of the bed and began lifting garments out of the case. Like Karen, he would look at the bandaged wrists, then shift his eyes away nervously.

"First, let me have a little privacy." She grasped her slacks and lingerie and flounced toward the bathroom with her back-opening gown held closed. "I will call you if I need you," she said, then pulled closed the bathroom door. A few seconds later, she peeked out. "I forgot the sweater."

Miranda grabbed it and handed it to her.

"Better?" Barbara asked when she reappeared, fully dressed. The rolled cuffs of the pink sweater covered most of the bindings around her wrists.

"Better," both younsters agreed.

Only when Miranda had finished packing all the hospital lotions and cotton pads in the carrying case and snapped closed the latch did she finally show the signs of the strain. Her large blue eyes widened with concern as Barbara fumbled putting on an earring. It was a simple task she'd seen her mother perform with ease innumerable times. But now, with the wrist braces, the action became momentarily grotesque. Miranda's lower lip stiffened.

"It's okay, baby," Barbara reassured Miranda, catching the image watching her in the mirror and turning to hug the little girl. "It's a bit scary, but I'm okay." She held Miranda snugly, rocking her back and forth. Eliot hovered around, just out of arm's reach, but Barbara saw the uncertainly lurking behind his brave little smile. She'd have to comfort him when he was less guarded, in the car or maybe at home. Eventually, she'd get a chance to hug him in private and chase the fears away.

The minute she stepped inside she could see that everything had been thoroughly cleaned. The kitchen floor was now spotless. Every towel was fresh and neatly folded. The scent of lemon wax and a peachy potpourri was in the air. Nothing antiseptic like the hospital. There were several pots of tulips and narcissus at one end of the counter. "Gnomes," Karen said, inclining her head playfully. However, none of the gnomes were there to meet them.

"Take your mom's stuff to her room." Karen waited until the children were on their way down the hall to talk to Barbara. "There's a slight catch to all this." She handed Barbara a glass of cold ginger ale. "When I sprang you from the joint, I had to make a few promises, one of them to Tom Palmer."

"Okay, what did you promise?" Barbara waited for the details.

"I told him I'd get you to see somebody," she broached the subject dutifully. "Someone who can help you sort out your problems and get you cheered up again. In fact, one of the papers you signed sort of said that you'd see a shrink."

"A shrink," Barbara acknowledged.

"Right." Karen tried to sound enthusiastic. "Tom wants you to get a good physical. He and an officer assigned to help you suggested you have a little counseling."

"There's an officer assigned to help me? You do believe this was an accident?" Barbara turned to stare at her friend.

"I'm not sure what it was," Karen answered honestly. "I don't think you were trying to hurt yourself," she insisted. "But you've been under a lot of strain lately. And you've been putting some strange mixtures into your system. I think a lot of it is probably physical. But it may be that your subconscious was signaling for help of some sort. This business sort of moves things along." Her eyes fleetingly dropped to the bound wrists. "I figured if you wanted to get home, you could put up with a few sessions of therapy." She posed the last as a feasible explanation.

For a moment Barbara said nothing. She turned and walked toward the study doorway, and stood there looking in. "Actually, I'd rather settle for being dumb and clumsy." She forced herself to joke about it. "But I gather you guys are taking it a bit more seriously. Is that why the cleaning crew did such a thorough job?" She tilted her head towards the workbench where the accident had occurred.

"Louis and Jeff McMillan worked on that part," Karen told her. They had totally stripped the room of anything to do with glass work. Besides mopping up the blood, they'd removed the broken pieces and sheets of glass, the books and patterns, the grinder and soldering equipment. The only thing on the cutting table was a big basket of primroses. Even the long window was decorated. It boasted a drooping Swedish Ivy plant with shiny green leaves and a few sprays of tiny white flowers. "Mr. Johns thought the plants might help. He was fussing around off and on all day."

"But I promised I'd finish," Barbara protested. Then she saw the tiny silver-white flash as the oval caught the light. On the outside, beyond the hanging plant, one of the mirror pendants she'd bought was hanging. Stepping nearer, she noticed the blue line she'd drawn was painted over by a beading of transparent glue or caulk and it was closed off across the base where she had not finished. Luster had done more than see to the plants. He'd finished what she had started, and he'd helped in ways Karen could not imagine. Barbara took a quick look at the sliders and the bay window and saw Luster had attended to them as well.

"Doing that window can wait." Karen misread her attentiveness. "Tom Palmer and the rest of us think you should take some time out to talk about everything, including the window, with a shrink. You can't keep blocking out whatever is bothering you. You were upset before your bull-in-the-china-shop routine last night. And you were becoming a tad obsessive about doing the piece T.J. wanted," Karen stressed.

"Obsessive, huh?" Barbara studied Karen's intent expression.

"Just a bit." Karen refused to back down.

"Maybe," Barbara conceded. "Do you happen to have the name of a suitable shrink?"

"Gwen Henderson," Karen reported with her customary efficiency. "Tom Palmer says she's super. Of course, you'll have to judge that for yourself, but he likes her a lot."

"And do I have an appointment?" Barbara inquired.

"Monday and Thursday at three," Karen smiled slightly. "You have to call and confirm the time, but if you go back to school on Monday, then you could go right after. The kids could stay at my house until you get home."

"I'm supposed to go back to school like this?" Barbara held up her slightly bent and bandaged wrists. Although Karen and Eliot could barely stand to look at them, she knew the "throwbacks" would be fascinated.

"Tom suggested you go back next week. You certainly can't do much around here," Karen responded. "Mr. Engler says he'll give you a classroom assistant to handle papers and things. He said your students really miss you."

"My students will love these." Barbara contemplated the bandages.

"They'll ask questions," Karen acknowledged. "You can handle that. They'll probably all pitch in to help."

"I can hardly wait," Barbara sighed. "They have a not-so-subtle way of expressing their curiosity." She shook her head. She could already imagine their gaping looks and the first flurry of comments. 'You tryin' to waste yourself, Mrs. A?' 'You sure done a lousy job.' 'We thought you had more imagination.' It would be a no-holds-barred inquisition. "Clumsy . . ." She would make them believe her.

"How will I get to school? I can't drive," Barbara suddenly realized.

"Louis said he'd take you. He'll leave a few minutes early every day," she declared. "No problem."

"And I suppose he'll pick me up and take me to the psychiatrist and bring me home?"

"McMillan volunteered for some of that," Karen informed her. "Kent said he could help. I get whatever's left over."

Barbara shook her head. "Boy, did I cause a mess. I've turned you all into taxi drivers. I've got everyone in an uproar. I'm so sorry to put you through this."

"Maybe this is what it takes to finally reach a turning point," Karen said optimistically. "After you hit the low end, everything else is up."

Outside, car doors slammed and the sounds of male

voices grew louder. "Party time," Louis Bellcazzio called as he led the procession into the kitchen. He was carrying boxes of fish and chips and a bucket of she-crab soup. Jeff McMillan brought up the rear with rolls, crackers, the salad, and a container of ice cream. Miranda and Eliot came galloping down the hall to join in.

"How about some plates and soup bowls," Louis called out.

"You want the good ones?" Miranda asked.

"Let's just keep this informal and uncomplicated," Karen suggested, handing out paper plates and squat soup mugs.

"Sort of a welcome-home celebration." McMillan took Barbara's arm and escorted her to the corner nook. Like the others, his cheerfulness seemed a little forced. His wary, appraising look returned to her wrists again and again, then shot away. "You relax. I'll bring you some of everything. You and your bandaged appendages are the guests of honor here," he teased her.

"I'd like a lot. I'm hungry." Eliot sniffed the pale, creamy soup.

"Take what you get, just like the rest of us." Karen handed him a mug. "Then ask for seconds," she said, weakening.

Louis was the last one to squeeze into the corner nook. "I only have a couple of things to say." He waited until he had everyone's attention. "Thank God that's over. We love you. Good to have you back," he sighed.

"I'll second that," McMillan spoke up.

"This is crowded. Could I please take mine into the den?" Eliot flashed Karen his most ingratiating smile.

"I'll second that," Miranda chimed in.

"You guys are bailing out?" Karen gave them a disgruntled look.

"We'll be back for dessert," Miranda promised.

"Business as usual," Barbara said, laughing for the first time in days.

Sister Gertrude Kelly pulled the knitted afghan over her knees and rocked back and forth while Luster poked another piece of firewood in her pot-bellied stove. He stoked up the fire and took his seat across from her again.

"Don' know what to make of it." She thrust out her lips, puckering up her raisin face, as she thought awhile. "Don' know what to say. Never hear nothin' like this in all my years. Haunts do nasty things to folks. They make noises and move things and tip things and cause a mess. They can scare a body to death. But they don't draw blood. Blood is of the livin'." She tapped her fingertips on the arms of her rocker. "But one thing I do know. Blood will sanctify a place. Blood will keep the spir'ts at bay so's they won't come inside no more. Leastwise not for a long, long time."

"Hope so. Just in case, I put everythin' around like you said," Luster told her. "She already started linin' the windows, but I went over them with yo' paint. And I put conjur bags in all the plants fo' I took 'em in. Put the mirrors she bought all 'round the outside. Tol' her chill'un it would keep the li'l birds from bumping them. Which it will," he added emphatically.

"You can wait pas' the next full moon. Then you fetch them mirrors an' bring 'em here. We'll take 'em out to the cemetery and bury them, put to rest any spirits that been lookin' in. Put up new ones till the next moon passes. Then we'll do it again. Keep on as long as we mus'." Her voice was dry and crackly and weaker than usual. She'd tugged on her knitted cap to keep her head warm. Only a few white hairs poked out at the back.

Luster looked at her uneasily, wondering how this latest turn was wearing on her. "You up to this?"

"I'm old, but I ain't done yet." Sister Gertrude narrowed her eyes and peered at him. "You're no spring chick either, ol' man. Bes' we both take care. Jus' wish I knew if this blood spillin' scared 'im off for good. May not have 'tended to hurt her. May have jus' wanted to give her a fright. Maybe things jus' went too far." She blinked her birdlike eyes and puckered her lips. "Then again, maybe not. Wish I knew for sho'."

Luster leaned forward and stopped rocking. "What you mean 'maybe not'? You s'pect this was on purpose? Lady could'a died."

Two deeper lines of worry appeared between her brows amid the web of lesser wrinkles. " 'Member the story of the out-island boy who loved a pretty gal whose daddy grew the indigo? Fella' was killed accidental one day. Came back with the moon at night to court the indigo gal anyway. Left her pretty things. Whispered in her dreams. Kep' telling her to cross over and be with him." Sister Gertrude stared off into space, telling the tale in a whisper soft voice that made Luster's neck skin tighten.

He was nodding, recalling the tale his gramma had told years before. "Indigo gal loved him so much she hanged herse'f so's they could be together always. Did it on the full moon." His mouth felt dry and cottony.

He'd heard the talk in the house while the Belcazzios were there with the cleaning lady. He'd been in and out all afternoon. He'd heard them talkin' to each other and talkin' on the phone. They'd been saying things about her being depressed. He'd heard them mention suicide. The moon had been full the night it happened.

"Maybe he's been invitin' her to cross over. Maybe he's been keepin' at her, wearin' her down. Maybe this was her way of sayin' yes." Sister Gertrude looked at him.

Luster held the look for a long moment, then shook his head. "Can't be. I see her with those chill'un. I see her with her friends. She wants to do right by them." He rubbed his chin. "Maybe what she did was tell him 'no.' "

Sister Gertrude stopped rocking and rubbed her arms with her small angular hands. Luster's comment gave her the chill. "If'n she did, it sure didn't set well with 'im. I hope he listen'd good," she spoke at last. "Sometimes ain't easy for one of us to take 'no' for an answer, much less one of them. Puffed-up and prideful, haunts can get." She sat on the edge of her chair now, looking down at the flashes of flame visible through the vents in the stove door. "Up to her now."

"I warned her 'bout callin' 'em back. I'll wait a bit and tell her again. Nothin' else to do?" He looked at the old conjur woman hopefully.

DARK WINDOW 337

"Nothin' to do but hope fo' the bes' and take it as it come."

"As it comes," Luster echoed her words. With a deferential nod, he stood and took his leave. His knees ached. He drove home slow.

Later in the evening before he went in for dinner, he stood in the circle out back, looking from face to face. "Know you'd help if you could," he said softly. "Know that you'll help me to do what I can." He hugged his coat closer around his tall lean frame. Another frost tonight, he speculated, looking up at the sky and feeling the damp cold below his knees. Turn all the dew to diamonds. They'd sparkle like they had the night of the full moon, pretty and shimmery, like the mirrors he'd put up to keep her safe. Her and the children.

"Don't wan't nothing to hurt that lady," Luster muttered, thinking now of all the bloody chips of glass he'd seen them sweeping up. He'd almost got the warrior angel completely blocked out. Arm thrust up, it stood out in the clearing with shavings of wood like snowfall around its feet. Still had to find the face. Then he felt the peace settle in over him like a soft warm cloak. He smiled a long, slow smile, studying the roughed-out shape more closely. Somehow he'd left enough of a swell at the chest to still make it work. He could see her clearly now. Her brave pale face, her stiff shoulders, the curve of her body, the defiant tilt of her chin. And next time when she came out to the clearing and saw her angel, she would understand more than he could ever say in words. Survive. Fight on. Do not despair. Hold your ground. It would all be there.

"As it comes," Luster said, nodding thankfully, knowing he'd be able to get on with it and finish the angel now. "Night, ev'rybody. Night, Inez. Night, little lady." He patted the warrior. Humming to himself, he headed back to the house where Willie Dodd would have the checkers set up and waiting and Nellie would have liver and sausage and onions hot and ready. But he walked counterclock three times before going onto the porch. And he spit over his shoulder. No sense in taking any chances.

CHAPTER 10

> We grow accustomed to the Dark—
> When light is put away. . . .
> Either the Darkness Alters—
> Or something in the sight
> Adjusts itself to Midnight—
> And Life steps almost straight.
> *Emily Dickinson*

"I COULD SAY that I just happened to be passing through." Rob Johnstone leaned against the doorway when Barbara opened the front door. "However—"

"I didn't know you were coming now," Barbara broke in, bobbling her bandaged arms slightly, then hugging him as she usually did. "It's great to see you. Come on in."

"When I heard of your accident, I called and bumped my interview up a week. Figured I could be useful. Maybe do something with the kids."

"Where's your luggage?"

"In the car. I've got a reservation at the Holiday Inn."

"Nonsense. You stay with us. Get your things."

"I don't want to give you any extra trouble," he insisted. "I heard your mobility was a bit impeded. Impressive bracelets." He inspected the slightly frayed bandages. "How are you doing?" He held her hands gently as he spoke.

"I'm doing all right," Barbara answered cheerfully. "Now get your things and we'll get you settled."

"If you're sure."

"I'm sure. Come on." She hurried him along. "News travels fast. I've only been home from the hospital a couple of days."

"I know. I talked to Karen." Suitcase in hand, he followed her to the den. "She said you were coming along okay."

"So she's the one who told you. What can I say? It was a dumb accident. The stitches and bandages come off next week. I'm still working on the stupidity part." She shrugged then glanced back over her shoulder. "I suppose she told you I have to see a shrink for a while."

"She mentioned it. You're managing to get around all right, driving and chasing kids?" He looked about for the children.

"I can't drive. But the kids are at a movie with Kent," Barbara explained. "They had the day off school for a teacher planning day. I start back on Monday, so I figured I'd do my planning here. I had a sub all week and I've got all kinds of papers to grade."

"One of the joys of teaching."

"Tea? Coffee?" She motioned him toward the kitchen. He slid into the comfortable nook while she emptied out the coffeemaker. "You said you bumped the interview up. When is it?"

"Tomorrow morning. Ten.

"Tell me what they've said so far. What's the prospect at the college?"

"They said they'd like to see me. This interview is just a preliminary thing. It means I'm in the running for the job. It also means I need some of the videotapes back. They're looking for a sort of show-and-tell time," he joked easily but his eyes never left her hands as she filled the coffeepot and set in a new filter.

"Let me copy some of them first," Barbara protested. "I really love some of those tapes."

"I'll have them make a copy. You can have them back."

"Good. We've enjoyed them. Then I'll let them go for a while." Barbara plugged in the coffeemaker and crossed to join him.

"I've sent them everything else from my college transcripts to still shots to playbills and programs from my productions. Now it's time to bring in the tapes and let them see if they're interested." Rob seemed surprisingly impassive.

"Aren't you a little nervous?" Barbara slid in across from him and looked at him closely.

"Sure. But there's nothing I can do but show up and

present my stuff," he replied calmly. "Either I'm what they want, or I'm not. It's their move next, not mine."

The coffeemaker hissed and sputtered and the aroma filled the room. "How about you stay put and I get the cups?" he suggested, unfolding his long legs. "Tell me about your therapy," he said as he focused his attention on the cupboard full of assorted mugs.

"Mental or physical?"

"Which do you feel like discussing?" He gave her a sidelong look.

"I'd like to discuss what you heard about all this." She crossed her arms on the table and leaned forward, watching him closely. "I suspect Karen told you that they were worried I may have done this to myself."

Rob nodded thoughtfully. He deposited the mug of steamy coffee on the table in front of her. "She's a friend. Friends worry. I'm your friend, too," he reminded her. "She told me you had been depressed. You were mixing drugs and alcohol. And you'd been sorting through a lot on your own. I knew some of that already. It's perfectly natural to be depressed once in a while—especially in your circumstances," he stressed. "Dealing with it is another matter. You kept insisting on working it out for yourself. Now this happens." His eyes shifted to her wrists. "I can see how she might see a rather ominous progression in that."

Barbara stared at her hands, knowing he was right.

"I do buy the accident bit, incidentally," he added gently. "I know you wouldn't hurt yourself or anyone else. The cuts will heal in no time." He reached out and cupped his hand over hers. "But I'm glad you're finally getting some professional help with the rest of your concerns. Take advantage of the situation. Maybe your shrink can get you to unload. Your friends can't seem to." He blew softly over the surface of his coffee.

Barbara gave him a quick look. The criticism in his tone had startled her. "Do I catch a little testiness here, Mr. Johnstone?"

Rob met her stare and suddenly chuckled. "I guess there's a little bitchiness in all of us." He grinned, seeing he'd sparked a response. "It's an indication of sound mental health. Everyone else has probably been babying you. You don't need it from me. In fact, I'm not sure what you need from me, but I came anyway."

"What hotel did you say you were staying at?" Barbara arched her brows.

"Now who's being bitchy?" he kidded her. "Finish your coffee," Rob insisted. "I've got a car. Let's go for a drive. What time will the kids be getting back?"

"They went at one. I think the show is over at three. Kent said they may roam the mall a bit. They'll be back for dinner."

"So let's call the hotel and cancel the room. I'll take you out for ice cream or something, then when the little folks return I'll take you all to dinner." He looked at her intently. "Or did you have other plans? I don't want to get in the way."

Barbara avoided his even stare. Apparently Karen Belcazzio had been passing on information about more than Barbara's physical condition. "I have adaptable plans," she said, shrugging. "Louis and Karen and McMillan are going to a meeting. They're all working on the Historic Foundation house tours, which are next month. The firm is one of the sponsors. They said they might drop by later for a drink."

"Why weren't you going with them?" Rob studied her profile.

"I haven't been out in public with these except to visit the doctor and the shrink." She propped her hands up in the air. "Besides, this is the company image we're dealing with. I really think it's best if I keep a low profile until after everything heals." She glanced his way briefly. "You know how people can make something out of this." She flopped her hands like little wings.

"That was your idea?" Rob persisted. "The low-profile bit?"

"We came to that conclusion jointly." Barbara hedged. "We just didn't think it was a good idea."

"We?" Rob waited for clarification.

"Well, McMillan and Louis and me." She waited a moment. "Actually McMillan brought it up," she confessed. "He didn't want to put me under any more stress.

People do gawk. And talk. Besides, there's a lot they need to cover tonight. I'd rather not be added to the agenda."

"You don't have to convince me." Rob rested his hand on her arm. "I doubt if you have an outfit that matches those wrappings anyway." He linked his fingers softly with hers. "I'm just glad you're okay."

"Me, too," Barbara whispered. Silently she contemplated his large slender hand enfolding the bandages. Other than Eliot and Miranda, who conducted occasional inspections, he was the only one who had felt comfortable touching them, touching her, since the accident. "Do I still get the ice cream?" she said at last.

"Sure." Rob cleared his throat before he replied. "You even get to ride in the front seat and get out and come into the shop, bandages and all." Even his teasing made her comfortable.

Comfortable. The word crept out of nowhere and made Barbara suddenly uneasy. Comfortable, warm, and safe. Being with Rob was like that, she noted, even here. It had been difficult on his first visit after T.J. died, when all the parameters were shifting. But in the salty air of Rob's beach house, they had made love with each other and drank tea and ate Chinese, and for a time there were no parameters. She had regained a sense of intimacy and acceptance that she had thought was gone forever.

But she had come away from Rob and promptly jumped into another man's bed. And everything had worked just the same, only with McMillan it hadn't been comfortable. Afterwards, she hadn't imagined McMillan climbing a hillside and singing her a love song. Or walking barefoot on a beach. Or reaching across the table to hold her hand. Now Rob held her hand again, bandages notwithstanding. She hadn't realized how much could be communicated in a touch.

This time with Rob in her own house, in T.J.'s house, she felt a peace with him that had always eluded her. With him, there was nothing she needed to be. Nothing to hide. She'd been fragmented, living in stages, scenes, and moments, always trying to make it all fit together for someone, even herself. Rob just took the pieces as they came, at their own pace, without pattern or form or explanation. He accepted her more completely than she had been able to accept herself. But he didn't know everything.

"Let me put on some makeup and get a jacket." Barbara almost leaped from the booth. "I'll be right back." She plunged down the hall toward her room. "Oh, T.J., I'm so sorry." She leaned against her closed door. "I loved you. I really loved you. But it always had to be your way. This is something else. This is something separate and scary and all mine."

She grabbed a cool cloth and pressed it over her face, trying not to push the present into some kind of pattern for the future. "Just let it alone. Let it be what it will be," she warned herself. *Good old Rob, your bodyguard*, McMillan had called him condescendingly. Karen, eager to see Barbara coupled again, had hinted that it would be easy rekindling an old romance. Everyone had something wise and logical to say, some label to apply. But somehow the touch of an old friend had cut through all the categories, eliminated expectations, and simply made it important just to believe in each other.

"Come on. It's only me. Don't fuss," Rob called down the hall.

"I'm coming," she answered as she spread a rosy foundation over her slightly blotchy face. She fluffed up her hair and touched her lips with bright color, and practiced her bright public smile. Then she shook it off, hating the artificial feel of it. "Oh, brother," she groaned and dashed out to join him. "Where's a good shrink when I need one?" she sniffed. Then she turned into the hallway leading to the kitchen. When she saw him leaning over the sink, rinsing out their cups, she stopped and let out a slow breath. Comfortable. Without even knowing she was near, he had touched her again.

There was nothing formal about the afternoon sessions Barbara had agreed to attend each Monday and Thursday. At the first meeting, she and Gwen Henderson each sat sipping herb tea while they chatted and looked each other over. After asking quiet, carefully phrased questions, the pretty silver-gray haired psychiatrist sat attentively, listening as Barbara talked. Her dark, liquid eyes would follow each gesture with keen interest, without making Barbara feel that she was being dissected. There was no pressure to suddenly expose her private thoughts for inspection. Someone was simply listening. Someone almost motherly. Someone who didn't know her at all. She could dole out little portions of whatever that day allowed her to share.

"How are you today, Barbara?" Gwen Henderson poured them each a cup of tea and settled into the armchair in one corner of the office.

"I'm pooped." Barbara collapsed into her chair. "I had a houseguest all weekend and forty-seven compositions to grade. I put the papers off until yesterday afternoon, and it took me till midnight to get through them. I think I need a nap."

"School went all right today?"

"About as I expected. The students were curious. There were a lot of rumors flying. They got on me about what they called my hatchet job on myself. But we talked about it. I threw a tennis ball at one and he caught it. Then I asked what would have happened if it was a raw egg or something hot or sharp or sticky. That was Rob's idea. They got the point about reflex action and how it makes us do things with consequences we can't always predict." Barbara nodded and smiled to herself. "I think it was a good day all in all."

"And you had a pleasant weekend with your company? Is that the Rob you mentioned?" Gwen settled back in her armchair across from Barbara and waited.

"I guess that means it's time to cut through some of the chit-chat." Barbara met the steady dark eyes across from her.

"Let's give it a shot," Gwen suggested with a nod.

"I haven't said much about Rob," she began slowly. "I guess I was still mulling that one over. I still am." She shrugged. The single session the previous Thursday had been a cautious, getting-acquainted one. Most of the conversation had centered on T.J. and the kids. Some had involved Jeff McMillan. A considerable amount had focused on the details of the accident. Barbara had talked about her commitment to finishing the driftwood window, and the combination of stress, sherry, and guilt that had put her at the worktable that night.

"I was an accident looking for a place to happen," she'd conceded. Afterwards Gwen had ordered some blood and urine tests and a thorough physical. Then she started Barbara on vitamins with iron and calcium but restricted all other chemicals—no sleeping pills, no birth-control pills, no alcohol, no coffee. They were treating the symptoms, as both of them knew, and until they dug beneath the surface, at least they'd eliminate some possible complications. But this time, they didn't need the get-acquainted period.

"I had a difficult weekend in some ways," Barbara confessed as her bright smile faded and she became less defensive. "I've had to do some reevaluating. I always thought that things never worked out between Rob and me because we were young, broke, and going in different directions and didn't love each other enough. But part of it was simply me. I never told him then how I felt. I expected him to do the talking and make all the plans. But he was too passive, too unassertive. Now those are the things about him that I like most. Only now he just seems gentle and accepting, not weak or indecisive."

"You think he's changed?"

"Some. But I think I'm the one who's looking at this differently."

"So you've changed?"

"I think I have. My family moved a lot when I was growing up. I was terribly insecure. My father was a bit of an alcoholic, military, often inconsistent, but always very authoritarian. My mom always smoothed everything over. I always behaved. Then my folks divorced, and my mom remarried. My stepfather is a dear man, but he's quiet and reserved. I was used to being told what to do. I thought I needed someone to give me some sense of direction, something stable. I wanted a husband who was in charge. I wanted a home."

"And T.J. gave you all that?"

"He did. T.J. was a man who knew what he wanted.

He took a lot of responsibility early in our relationship. He made most of the decisions. Karen says he made them all. I was too busy and too content to disagree. My babies and T.J. were everything to me."

"Did that change?"

"A bit. When the children started off to school, I had more time to do things I wanted to do. I got involved with a lot of community projects. I took some classes. Then I started substitute teaching. I liked it so much that I decided to go back full time."

"And how did T.J. feel about that?"

"He wasn't thrilled about me going back to work. He worried about me getting tired. But he didn't complain about it as long as it didn't interfere with what he called our real lives."

"That real life sounded exceptionally idyllic."

Barbara paused. "I guess it was," she agreed. "There weren't any drastic changes or confrontations through the years. No terrible traumas to work through. We worked things out. And he was a wonderful father. He did a lot with the kids."

"So your recollection of the marriage is a pleasant one."

"I'd say so. There was something solid that we shared. Our life together had real substance. Our family and our home was our own work of art."

"You mentioned him not being really pleased about your going back to work. But you were going to do it anyway."

"I told him it was important to me."

"And did he agree?"

Barbara paused and thought a moment. "I don't know if he agreed, but he didn't make an issue of it. He just grumbled a bit now and then."

"So it wasn't actually resolved."

"T.J. always said that in the cosmic scheme of things, some issues weren't significant. They weren't worth getting upset over."

"But if he'd dug in his heels and insisted you didn't work, would you have stood your ground and insisted on doing it?"

"That wasn't his way. He didn't give ultimatums."

"That's not what I wanted to know. I just wondered if you would ever have stood up to him to get something your way?"

"I never needed to. We just worked things out." Barbara licked her lips and took a deep breath, determined to remain calm and pleasant.

"How did T.J. feel about your friendship with Rob?"

The shift in direction caught Barbara off guard. "They liked each other."

"No jealousy?"

"T.J. knew that we hadn't been physically intimate, so I think that made things easier."

"I don't doubt that both men were extremely civilized when they met," Gwen commented. "But human relationships are far more complicated then they often appear to an onlooker. Are you sure this T.J.–Rob acquaintance was that good-spirited? Did you ever ask them, apart from each other, how each one felt?"

"I never asked," Barbara answered. "They never said anything to make me think there was any kind of problem."

"Would they have behaved well because they were trying to please you?"

"Perhaps. I wanted them to get along well. They were both people I loved. If it wasn't as congenial as it seemed, I'd think someone was being childish."

"And possessive?"

"And possessive." Barbara nodded.

"Who would be most apt to be the childish one?"

Barbara gave her a startled look.

"If you had slept with Rob earlier, do you think T.J. would have had a more difficult time being friends with him?"

"I'd say so. I think any man would feel a little edgy."

"Have you made love with Rob since T.J. died?"

"Once. In Florida at New Year's."

"And do you wish you hadn't become intimate with your friend Rob?" Gwen asked quietly. "After all these years?"

"I'm not sorry about that," Barbara answered immediately. "I don't like to analyze what happened with us that night. It's almost like putting words and explanations to it will ruin it. It was very special," she whispered.

"And what does Rob say about it?" Gwen asked.

"He wouldn't say anything. I asked him not to, so he won't."

"He hasn't said anything? He never mentioned it again?"

Barbara shook her head. "I don't know if I want to hear what he has to say. It may change something. I'm just not ready to deal with anything that complex."

"So he has to keep his thoughts to himself to keep from upsetting you?"

"I guess that's right. It sounds foolish, doesn't it?" She frowned, struggling with the uncertainty that the questions had triggered.

"It sounds like he's incredibly patient."

"I told him I had some things to work out."

"And are you working them out?"

"I am now. At least I'm beginning to. That's why I'm here."

"You're also here because of those." Gwen dropped her eyes to the bandaged wrists. "They're a pretty grim reminder that when you keep everything inside and the pressure builds, it can erupt in ways we can't anticipate."

"So I'm trying to get some of it out," Barbara replied with a slight edge to her voice.

"So am I," Gwen said reassuringly. "I'm on your side. I want to help."

"I know. I'm trying to help too," Barbara insisted.

"Okay. Let's just backtrack a little," Gwen suggested. "What was your weekend like?"

"It was just a nice relaxed weekend. No fireworks or romance. He had an interview for a job at the college. Mostly we talked theater. It's like everything is back to normal."

"Is it really?"

"No." Barbara's hazel eyes turned somber as she glanced down at her wrists. "Nothing is normal anymore. It hasn't been normal for a long time. Everything is a little off-center from what it was." She furrowed her brow thoughtfully.

"What do you mean by off-center?"

"A lot of peculiar things have been happening." She felt her mouth becoming drier.

"Peculiar like what?"

Barbara paused. Her slim fingers tensed in her lap. "A couple of nights when I was up late, I found a glass of sherry set out for me, just like T.J. used to do. I've smelled his cologne, but there's none in the house anywhere. I've felt a pressure in the room, like someone is there. Once the newspaper was in and coffee was brewed and the Sonitrol was still activated. I've had doors close, and not open when I tried them." She said each one cautiously, testing. When she finished the brief, carefully edited descriptions, she looked up. Gwen's face was impassive, solemn.

"You said you missed him terribly."

Barbara nodded.

"All those things make it seem like he's still there."

Barbara nodded again.

"Perhaps you want things like they were when T.J. was here, so much so that you keep leaving little reminders for yourself."

Barbara held Gwen's gaze. She had not told the doctor about the slashed drapes and lingerie, the bedroom ceiling and smoke alarm, or Eliot's slow-motion fall from the tree. She knew she hadn't caused those things subconsciously or otherwise. But they had stopped. Everything had stopped since the accident.

"Perhaps." Barbara nodded without conviction. She stared off into space as if something in the distance was gradually becoming clearer. "I don't think he wanted me to forget how it was with us. How he was," she added wistfully. "Then again, maybe he didn't like the new me."

"Or maybe you didn't like the new you," Gwen offered.

"That subconscious stuff again?"

Gwen could tell by the look in Barbara's eyes she had lost her temporarily. She'd retreated behind that smile.

She had been edging toward something important and suddenly backed off.

"It's almost March. T.J. died in July. For half a year now, you've been working on a life without him, and you've been doing pretty well. But change is scary. Maybe you felt you were moving ahead too fast." As she spoke, Gwen kept a close watch on the movement of Barbara's eyes, hands, fingers. "It's perfectly normal to go through periods of backsliding. It's a way of making things feel less precarious, of negating change. Recovering is a two-steps-forward, one-step-back kind of thing."

"I realize that."

"Do you think you might be testing yourself with these occasional expeditions into sexuality, with Rob and with McMillan, then you run back home and study your reactions and try to hold time still while you struggle with all the feelings of betrayal or whatever?"

"Is that what you think?" Barbara sounded surprised.

"I'm just giving you possibilities to mull over," Gwen reminded her. "That happens to be one. The downswings after intimacy with others, physical or otherwise, are to be expected. They're part of the process of adjustment. They can prompt some peculiar behaviors."

"We're back to the subconscious business?" Barbara brooded.

"We're back there, but hopefully each time we'll discover a little more," Gwen noted. "There are other ways of looking at this. T.J. literally took over for you. He designed a life for you instead of letting you create your own, and you lived it. You were lucky enough to also enjoy it. But it wasn't your design. Now it has to be, and you're second-guessing yourself. It's almost as if you're waiting for his approval."

"I'd just like some peace."

"You have to find that yourself. And you won't find it if you're feeling guilty about betraying or disappointing a man who is dead."

"I know that."

"You idealized T.J. You idealized the marriage. But I keep getting the idea that everything went well because

T.J. had no real cause for complaint. You played by his rules."

"Mostly," Barbara admitted.

"Didn't you get tired of being so agreeable? Didn't you get angry at him once in a while?"

"I don't usually get angry. If something bothers me, I usually think it over and straighten it out without a lot of fuss."

"You don't like making a fuss?"

Barbara was careful to keep her tone neutral. "No. I'd rather work things out quietly."

"You said your father was a bit of an alcoholic. Were there a lot of arguments in your home when you were a youngster?"

Barbara hesitated, sensing the direction Gwen Henderson was leading her. "I guess there were. When my dad drank, he and my mother would bicker a lot."

"And then what?"

"Sometimes my dad would yell."

"Very loudly?"

"Yes."

"Did a neighbor or anyone call the police?"

"A couple of times."

"And what would your mother do when they came?"

"She'd cry." Barbara wet her lips with the tip of her tongue.

"Was she embarrassed?"

"I think so. They never arrested my father or anything. My mother always talked to them and they would go away."

"And what would you do while this went on?"

"I'd stay in my room."

"Then this business with the ambulance and the police and your neighbors rushing over when you were hurt must have been difficult for you."

"It was. I don't like making a fuss."

"And you don't like bickering."

"Right," Barbara agreed. Her smile was gentler now, but no less frustrating. She had begun the session with a show of enthusiasm, a dutiful unburdening to show that she was taking this counseling seriously. But bit by bit, the more the conversation turned to what was going on inside her mind and inside her house, the agreeable demeanor and the wall of restraint emerged.

But Gwen Henderson had made a chink in the wall. Rather than keep hammering at it, she'd let it rest a while and take a different tack. "How do you feel about Rob moving here, if he gets the job?" she added the last before Barbara could.

Barbara took a slow breath, still reeling from the last series of questions. "My first reaction is that I'm pleased." She took a moment to choose her words carefully. "But I'm also a little apprehensive. We've been long-distance friends for years. I liked being able to talk to him on the phone or drop in on him way down in Florida when it's convenient for me. It was nice to have him come here every once in a while. This will put us on a daily basis." She paused for a moment. "I'm just not sure what might happen between us now."

"Would you consider marrying him?" Gwen asked.

"He's never said anything about marriage." Barbara's chin line became more rigid.

"Are you angry that he's never brought it up?"

"I think I was angry years ago. He just let me go on my merry way. I wanted him to stop me. But that wasn't his style. Even with this job, he isn't pushing. He simply says that either he's what they want or he isn't. He says it's their move now."

"Perhaps the same applies to you. Maybe it's your move."

"I'm not sure I'm ready to make one."

"From what you tell me about him, I'd guess there's no rush," Gwen declared earnestly. "Everything takes time."

"I'll say." Barbara leaned back and sighed.

"You ready to call it a day?" Gwen reached out and rested her hand on Barbara's arm. "Home and a nap sound good?"

Barbara glanced at her watch. It was four-fifteen.

"You did it again. You crammed all this into forty minutes and ended up on time. I thought we'd been here hours."

"Don't forget the you-left-me-with-all-this-to-think-about part." Gwen took her arm and walked her to the door. "Think about the price you may have paid for being so nice and so agreeable most of your life. Try to think of a few things that make you upset. On Thursday we'll work on not bottling up strong feelings. They have a way of backfiring."

"I'll do my homework. See you Thursday." More exhausted than she liked to show, Barbara tucked her purse under her arm and strolled toward the elevator. "I'll have new wrappings and no stitches by then." She waved one bent hand in farewell. When the elevator doors slid closed, she leaned back against the cool wall. "Nice and agreeable," she muttered, shaking her head.

Jeff McMillan was waiting for her beside his car in the parking lot. "Hi," he called to her. "How'd it go?"

"It went fine." Barbara crossed toward him. "Thanks again for the taxi service."

"Not at all." McMillan opened the door for her. "I'd like to stop off at the office for a few minutes," he said as he slid behind the wheel. "Is that all right with you?"

"Sure. Louis said he had something for me to sign this week. Besides, you're the one who's doing the driving." She watched his profile as he maneuvered through the afternoon traffic.

"Have you and Dr. Henderson come up with any revelations?" McMillan inquired. "Or is it none of my business?"

"No revelations," Barbara answered. "Lots of interesting conjecture, but nothing specific."

"Have you discussed the house with her?" He tried to make the question sound casual.

"The house? You mean about the window or the ceiling caving in?"

"I mean the whole house. The fact that it means so much to you, that it's almost a part of you and it's part of T.J."

Barbara propped one arm along the back of the seat and turned to examine him curiously. "I'm not sure I get what you mean."

"It's just something curious I noticed," McMillan tried

to explain. "When you're out there teaching or at my place or at the office, you seem to be all right. Most of the problems seem to come up when you're in that house. Maybe she would see something in that." He shrugged.

"A lot of good times are in that house too," Barbara said evenly. "I love the house."

"I know." McMillan's voice had a curious edge. "That may be part of what's troubling you. I just wonder if Dr. Henderson might think you should make a clean break of it and start over in new surroundings."

"You mean move?"

"You said yourself there are a lot of memories there," McMillan commented.

"Precisely." Barbara turned to stare through the front window.

"Just a thought." McMillan hesitated. "Something you might consider." He glanced over at her inscrutable expression. "Look, pretend I never mentioned it," he apologized. "I didn't want to make you angry."

"I'm not angry." Barbara kept her voice light. "Just surprised. You and I talked about the house before. It's my home," she said simply. "I thought you understood that. I can't leave my home."

"I do understand," McMillan insisted. "I just wanted to point out that if the house has something to do with the stress, then I'd think about living somewhere else. Even on a trial basis."

"At Christmas, Rob and I talked about the aftermath of things," Barbara explained. "It was something he'd picked up in a book about acting, but it had to do with trauma related to the death of a family member. Anyhow, it said that after some terrible emotional upheaval, like a death or a divorce or a serious health problem, the people most affected should not make any change in their lives, at least no big changes, for at least a year."

"Why not?" McMillan regarded her quizzically.

"Things need to be settled on familiar territory. If you move, it wouldn't be clear if a person was reacting to the first trauma or the added ones caused by the changes in physical surroundings. The point was that one would not be in the right frame of mind for major decisions or for added adjustments." She turned and looked out the window. "I'm definitely not in the right frame of mind for a major decision. I'm struggling with the minor ones."

McMillan continued to drive in silence.

"The house has given us something to hold on to. I don't think the kids would have handled it as well as they have, not without familiar surroundings, the house, the river, the trees, and the crickets." She smiled slightly as she added the last one.

"Crickets?"

"Miranda has a thing for bugs and crawly things."

"Crickets." McMillan nodded, apparently relieved that the somber mood had lightened a bit. "I used to collect butterflies." Deftly he steered into the parking place labeled JRM in block letters. "I'll get the door," he said as he ducked out his side.

"You'll get no argument from me." Barbara dangled her bandaged hands helplessly.

She and McMillan parted company in the reception area of Ashcroft, Belcazzio, and Associates, Architects. He headed to his office while Barbara turned down toward Louis's domain. "So what do you need my scrawly signature on?" she greeted him.

"Let me close the door."

"Is it something secret?" Barbara teased.

"Private, not secret." Louis seemed to relax once they were closed off from the hallway. "It's about McMillan." He paused to phrase his comments carefully. "He's been with us almost half a year this month," Louis noted. "He is interested in buying in as a partner and becoming more conspicuous in the firm."

"Conspicuous how?"

"He'd like to add his name to the list before Associates," Louis explained. "Ashcroft, Belcazzio, McMillan, and . . ." He left the last unfinished.

"He never mentioned it to me," Barbara said, shrugging. She was more surprised than upset.

"I didn't think he'd mentioned his offer to sit in on the partners' meeting last week while you were recuperating from your screw-up with the glass," Louis shot back. In spite of the terminology, Barbara appreciated Louis's conviction that her accident was simply that—an accident.

"I didn't know there was a partners' meeting."

"I didn't tell you," Louis smiled. "It was just the usual crap," he reported. "If it was interesting or important, I would have dragged you in on it. That's how this company name business first came up," he spoke frankly. "McMillan wanted to sit in for you, temporarily, so he said. I told him that it wouldn't be necessary. We'd just have an informal session. He slid in his suggestion that we work him into a position with more visibility."

"He could have mentioned it to me."

"Last week you were laid up. No one wanted to put any more pressure on you than you already had. He asked me not to mention it to you." Louis shrugged self-consciously. "Until things settle down a bit. So I'm not mentioning it."

"Okay. What else aren't we mentioning?"

"I know the two of you have a personal thing going. And that's fine. But you and I are friends, and I don't like to see him maneuvering you personally, then working that into some kind of a business agreement without my input. McMillan is a real go-getter, and I don't want to lose him. But he's a lot like T.J. in some respects. He's a slick operator, always setting things up to his advantage. I'm glad he's on our side," Louis insisted. "Regardless, he's a bulldozer."

Barbara sat quite still, considering Louis's remarks. "So what about the partnership?" She eyed him intently.

"I say not yet. T.J. stipulated a full year, but that isn't legally binding. You could change that if you wanted. But I say wait. We're not in a rush. He shouldn't be, either."

Barbara nodded, remembering the aftermath time frame—no major changes for a year. "I agree," she said softly. "He made an agreement; he'll have to stick to it. Tell him he can bring it all up one year from the day he started," she suggested. "It will give us all a chance to evaluate the situation."

"Now you sound like you've been taking lessons from T.J." Louis winked. "He was a stickler for keeping agreements. I waited a year before we talked it over and became full partners."

"I remember," Barbara said quietly.

"Yeah. He was a pistol." Louis's voice suddenly turned hoarse. "I sure miss him. He'd come in handy on this phase of the theater we're doing."

"You mean the Moffatt?"

"Right. Everyone is waffling about the final details. McMillan let them make some changes and it's plodding along like a turtle on valium." Louis frowned. "I could use a shot of T.J.'s stubbornness. He could come on like a real freight train when he wanted to get things moving his way."

Barbara felt her throat becoming dry. She looked down at Louis's desk and hastily changed the subject. "Wasn't it supposed to be finished soon?"

"Funny you should mention it." Louis rocked forward in his chair and reached for a pile of papers. "Here, take these." He pitched them across to her. "Some guy from the College wants us to take part in a grand opening or something when the place is finished. Sometime next month," he added. "Apparently they've scheduled another production for the Festival but they want to do this one early, before all the Spoleto rehearsals begin, more for the community than for the tourists. The tourists get the second one."

Barbara scooped up the papers. "Then it will be finished?"

"I've got some ass to kick, to put it delicately. And McMillan will have to put in some extra time there. But we'll get it done."

Barbara looked at the ticket request forms and the seating charts he'd given her. "It was my idea to get the company involved with the Moffatt in the first place," she said. "I suppose if I walked out of here with these, McMillan could think this is what we were discussing in here."

"I guess he could," Louis responded with a wide smile. "Meanwhile, I'll work on reiterating the one-year policy," he promised. The two of them emerged from his office and strolled down toward McMillan's. He was still on the telephone conversing with someone. He looked up and pointed to his watch. Five minutes, he signaled.

"Come on, I'll get you a cup of coffee," Louis turned down the hallway toward the small kitchen.

"No coffee," Barbara sighed. "Gwen is drying me out, except for the odd cup of tea she allows me."

"Are you sleeping better?"

"I'm sleeping better," Barbara confirmed. "Without pills."

"How about a glass of water?" he offered.

"I'll take it," Barbara followed him.

"How'd the interview go for Rob at the College?" Louis called over his shoulder as he stepped into the tiny kitchen and reached for a glass.

"I don't know what they think yet. He liked them," Barbara responded from the doorway. "He showed them all his tapes, at least parts of them. He left some others for them to look at later." She shrugged. "He said he'd call if he got word one way or another."

"When it comes right down to it, there isn't much anyone can do in a situation like that. He's either right for the position or he isn't," Louis remarked.

"That's what he said."

"That's about what T.J. said when he hired me. Either I was right or I wasn't," Louis grinned. "Of course, I was right."

"You certainly were," Barbara agreed, patting him with her bent hand.

It was T.J.'s distinctive laugh, sliding down the hallway of the home he had built, spilling into the kitchen where Barbara stood, that made her breath catch in her throat. She was shredding lettuce for the salad and froze in midslice when T.J.'s unmistakeable cackle reached her.

After weeks of nothing, not the slightest disturbance, this was happening in broad daylight, inside the house. Just beyond her, a tiny mirrored oval dangling just outside the window caught the late afternoon light. The beaded blue line around the frame was unbroken. "It can't be." Her heartbeat accelerated, thundering louder and louder as she listened for the next sound. But all she heard was someone talking, indistinct television noise from the den. She stood rigid, holding her breath, staring in desperation at the heap of lettuce on the cutting board for some reassurance that she was wide awake.

In the week and a half since the accident, she'd begun healing more than physically. She'd started taking for granted that it was over, whether she understood what had happened or not, whether or not she believed in mirrors and ash and blue lines. The bizarre game that T.J. or some other nameless haunt or even the dark side of her own psyche had been playing had gotten out of hand, and somehow, with her injuries, it had ended. Or so she'd thought.

The television noises continued. Her shallow breathing resumed in rapid, uneven gasps. "I'm not crazy." She gritted her teeth and concentrated once more on the cold lettuce in her hand.

She stepped toward the sink. "Green peppers. Don't forget the green peppers." Then she heard it again. The pepper rolled from her hand and plopped into the dish drainer. Still clasping the paring knife, Barbara turned toward the laughter. It was coming from the den.

Miranda and Eliot were in there, watching TV. This afternoon they had been allowed to watch Tom Palmer take the bandages off and remove the few stitches that were visible. When they arrived home, they carried the packages and raced for the door ahead of her. Miranda unlocked it and held it open for her. Eliot went to the mailbox and brought in the mail. "Mostly junk," he reported as he dumped it on the counter, "except for this." He held up a carton containing videotapes addressed to "R. Johnstone, c/o B. Ashcroft," from the College of Charleston.

"It's our tapes. Let's watch Nellie and the Frenchman again. Please," Miranda begged.

Eliot groaned. "Let's watch one we haven't seen." Tonight they were celebrating the unveiling of the wrists with the Colonel's fried chicken and salad and ice cream cake for dessert.

"No fighting. How about the two of you trying to work this out while I start dinner? Surprise me." So the youngsters had taken the videotapes into the den to look over the selection and negotiate.

But this tape certainly wasn't of Nellie and the Frenchman. There was no music. No singing. The low voices were male voices. None of them were intelligible at first as Barbara moved cautiously from the kitchen into the hallway. Then she heard T.J. clearly and she stood still again, struggling for a plausible explanation.

"The children." Barbara struggled for control. "My babies are in there." It came out as a whimper. She moved toward the archway, still clutching the knife. As she reached the opening, she could peer around and see part of the room. Miranda and Eliot sat transfixed, their faces aglow in the grayish-blue light from the set. Eliot was open mouthed. Miranda almost smiling.

"Look!" Eliot exclaimed. His voice made her jump. "Mom, look. It's Dad. We've got a tape of Dad." He stared back at the image on the screen. "Come on, look," he demanded impatiently when she didn't move.

"My God." Barbara stepped, robotlike, toward them. "T.J." She stared spellbound as whatever apparition she had anticipated yielded to the sandy-haired, blue-eyed image of her husband on the television screen.

"Sometimes we have to separate interior from exterior in accomplishing what is needed," T.J. said clearly. "We have to take chances with the aesthetics."

It was T.J. all right. He was demonstrating the scale model of the downtown theater project, the Moffatt. "We've already got several fine theaters in Charleston," he was telling someone off-screen. "They vary in capacity, but they don't vary that much in form. Audience here. Performance area there." He held out his hands to illustrate the standard opposing locations. "What we could use," he said, pointing to his model," is a structure consistent with the heritage of Charleston on the outside, but innovative and flexible, again like our heritage, on the inside."

Barbara remembered seeing the model almost a year before when he was building it in the study. She vaguely remembered something about him needing it for a presentation. But she hadn't known there was a videotape of it all. "Where did you get this?"

"Mother, please." Miranda inched sideways so Barbara did not obstruct her view. "Daddy's talking." She said it without shifting her eyes from the face on the screen.

"It was with the others," Eliot explained, jerking his thumb toward the opened package of tapes from the college.

Slowly, Barbara lowered herself on the ottoman beside Miranda, sitting with knees clasped as she listened to T.J.'s explanation. She remembered telling him this part herself. A Pinter play, an American premier, had been withdrawn from the Spoleto Festival just before T.J. began work on his design for renovating a single house, essentially for technical reasons: too large a seating capacity, too distant a stage, too structured a setting.

"We have nothing intense and intimate enough to place new demands on the theatergoer. We have nothing to jar the numb television viewer—who is used to seeing things close up—and draw him into live theater. We have theaters that make few demands on the audience," he said. "This one does."

The camera zoomed in so his multilevel open-space model occupied the center of the screen. "We'll remove the second floor and be able to see the entire height of the building interior. We can create vertical as well as horizontal movement patterns," T.J.'s voice-over continued. "Stairways, ramps, and galleries circle the room. At several levels there are landings from which larger areas, performance areas, or small stages, protrude. Audience seating is not fixed. They can select their own vantage point and mix with or be surrounded by the action."

Barbara found her heartbeat becoming regular as she sat enthralled by the voice of the man she had loved. Hearing him talk, seeing him move, having that vitality so close again was oddly soft and comforting. Parts of what he said she remembered from conversations they'd had. She'd forgotten details of his expressions, how he crooked one eyebrow, how his smile was lopsided, how he seemed to always be in motion.

"This theater has another advantage that has a profound financial impact." The camera angle shifted and T.J. stepped back onto the screen. "It doesn't require a new facility. It can be created within a standing building. We're talking primarily of moving something dynamic and new into something old, dilapidated, familiar, but still sound." T.J. smiled slightly as he delivered his main point. "We are creating a vital future within the shell of a fading past."

Barbara remembered the clammy, close sensation of the presence that had tormented her as she sat here watching him speak. There was nothing threatening her now. T.J. looked straight into the camera, straight into her eyes. "Whenever we breathe new life into an existing structure and create a new beginning, we open up a window in time."

She crossed her arms over her chest, cupping her upper arms with her hands to smooth away the tight, prickly sensation that had crept over her. *A window in time.* The phrase reverberated within her as T.J. proceeded smoothly with his presentation.

"A friend of mine, Rob Johnstone, teaches at Atlantic in Fort Lauderdale," T.J. went on. "He used something like this for a college production of *Steel Magnolias*. Then his students added some scenery and costuming and did—"

"*The Taming of the Shrew*," Barbara spoke at the same time, recalling that she and Rob had watched the tape of that production when she visited him.

"Mother," Miranda shushed her.

"Any production can become more challenging in an environment like this. The play doesn't have to be experimental or modern." The camera panned from the model back to T.J. "This environment can be used creatively with any play. It lends its own vitality to the piece."

At that point another man, apparently someone from the theater department at the College, took over and began explaining how various plays could be adapted to

DARK WINDOW

this ramp-tower-open landing style of theater. Miranda and Eliot lost interest.

"Play the part with Daddy again," Miranda insisted.

Barbara nodded slowly but signaled for Miranda to wait.

"But this is boring," Eliot complained, taking Miranda's side as they watched the gray-haired drama professor drone on about the possibilities of taping television productions and recitals in such a facility.

"Let's just watch it till the end." Barbara quieted them. "If you don't want to watch, then leave. You can replay the first part later."

Miranda simply huffed, then she sprawled out on her stomach on the carpet. Eliot left.

Barbara sat through ten more minutes of what apparently was a fund-raising pitch by the College budget committee. It had worked. The project had been accepted and funded and was now almost completed. T.J. had done precisely what he had described. He had breathed new life into a familiar old landmark. He had opened a window in time.

Silently, Barbara rewound the videotape, catching the beginning for the first time. The gray-haired man was making the introductions. He joked about money. T.J.'s cackle rippled through the air. The gentleman spoke of surprise and innovation and executed a sudden pratfall that produced another off-screen cackle from T.J.

Miranda sat upright again. Cross-legged and wide-eyed, she stared at the screen. "Eliot," she called without moving. "It's Daddy again."

A second later, Eliot came loping down the hall to take his seat next to his sister. "When are we having dinner?" He directed a disgruntled question at Barbara but he never lifted his eyes from the screen.

"In just a few minutes." She stood up and smoothed her slacks as she took another look at the moving figure. He was smiling. She'd been imagining him with darker looks.

"I'm hungry," Miranda added pointedly.

"All right, already," Barbara surrendered. "I'll get dinner."

The plump green pepper still lay forlornly in the dish drainer where she had dropped it. The carton of once-warm carry-out chicken, with circles of grease soaking through its sides, awaited her. She moved briskly, first thrusting the chicken into the microwave, then putting the greenery into a wooden bowl with croutons and some dressing drizzled over the top.

In the cosmic scheme of things. Barbara had been slowly seeing all the good years of the marriage diminished and edited because of the outbursts over the past six months. In her mind, T.J. had become monstrous. But the tape brought the better times back vividly, visually.

On the screen, T.J. was assertive, dynamic, much like the freight train Louis had called him. Only someone who knew him well would suspect he'd had to research and rehearse to sound so smooth, so knowledgeable. But he knew what it took to be convincing, and he was relentless in searching for the precise details. That determination was the edge that made him so successful.

It was reassuring having that little glimpse of him in action to confirm how he was and why she had loved him. It was something timeless, something permanent, for the children and for her.

"Windows work both ways," she found herself smiling unexpectedly. This one offered a glimpse from the past, a moment that she had not witnessed, existing now for all of them in tangible form. It was a remarkable treasure. That outrageous cackle, the wonderful laughter of his, could be played and replayed through the years. It would keep breathing new life into the fading recollections that were so difficult to hold on to on their own.

The ping of the microwave sounded as Barbara finished lining up trays so everyone could carry dinner to the den. "Come wash your hands and fill your trays," she called. "Switch to one of the plays. You can run the one of your dad again later." At least now, whenever they needed him, he'd be there.

Outside, the base of Wordsworth was surrounded by clusters of bright yellow daffodils, some barely budding, some in full bloom. March had slipped in like a lamb and spring had finally touched the yard. When Louis dropped her off after the Thursday session with Gwen Henderson, Kent was down by the river with the kids, watching a few brave souls in wetsuits jetskiing out beyond the grassy marsh. Luster Johns was up by the house, moving in pots of violets and lily of the valley to replace the tulips and narcissus that had faded. She met him at the kitchen door.

"How's it been?" Luster stopped and stooped a bit, looking at the thin bracelets of gauze that she wore in public while the marks still looked a bit gruesome. The swelling in her fingers had subsided and she was wearing her rings again, on her right hand. His dark, bright eyes met and held hers.

"It's been peaceful. I saw the mirrors and the other things." She tilted her head toward the kitchen window. "I really appreciate your help."

"Sister Gertrude says that eve'ythin' helps, but the blood may be what ends it. Those on the other side can't spill the blood of them that's here. Blood sanctifies. Keeps 'em at bay. Leastwise inside the house." He looked at her wrists again. "Sorry price to pay. Glad you're okay now."

Barbara's mouth went dry at the mention of the blood. She remembered it being everywhere when it happened. All over the kitchen floor where they were standing. She remembered trying to stop it. "I'm more than okay," she assured him, swallowing.

"One day soon, when you're feeling up, you come see me again. Got a story for you, 'bout an angel. Got a new angel fo' you to see." He glanced over his shoulder, almost as if he were checking that no one was eavesdropping. "Meanwhile, you be careful to keep the door closed." His hand rested over his chest. His solemn face was a network of lines. "Harden that heart. Ain't no time to get soft. These things get started and slip out of control, even from theirselves. You keep drawin' the line. Hold it fast."

"I will." She reached out and grasped his large bony

hand. "Thank you. I don't think I'll ever understand any of this, but thank you."

"Anytime I can." Luster nodded, placing his free hand around her wristband like a second layer of protection. "Don' forget. Real soon. You come see me."

"I'll come see you," she promised. For a few seconds they stood there, the tall dark nurseryman and the slim bronze-haired woman, holding onto each other's hands.

"Bes' I better get on with that." Luster bobbed his head and took his leave. By the time Barbara changed clothes and came out and made a pot of tea, Luster's old pickup was nowhere in sight. The atrium was lined in pots of purple and white, and the sweet perfume smell of the violets and lilies of the valley was drifting through the house.

"Teatime," she called. She took a tray outside while the late afternoon sun still flooded the west side of the yard with warmth. Kent and Eliot and Miranda spread a blanket under Wordsworth and they all ate cookies and drank hot tea out beneath the newly green boughs.

"Here's a poem by Wordsworth that may remind you a little bit of the one Rob told you a while back about the grasshoppers and crickets." She read them William Wordsworth's piece, "I Wandered Lonely as a Cloud," about the golden daffodils fluttering and dancing in the breeze.

"It's about memories. Good ones. Like having that discussion by your dad on tape. It makes us feel good to see it and remember. When Wordsworth remembers the beautiful daffodils, even years later, he gets back the same good feelings." She read them the last two lines again.

And then my heart with pleasure fills,
and dances with the daffodils.

Despite what Luster Johns or anyone else said, she felt the children were entitled to keep alive whatever remembrances of their father they could. Regardless what had happened to her, T. J. was their father and she didn't want them to feel the loneliness as acutely as she had when her parents divorced and her father transferred overseas.

"I sometimes feel my heart is dancing," Miranda insisted.

"When does your heart dance?" Barbara asked.

"Usually it has to do with boys, though. Or sometimes it happens when I come in and I hear Henry chirping."

Eliot moaned and nudged Kent.

Miranda conscientiously ignored them. She picked one daffodil and trotted around to lay it on the far side where the grave of Brownie The Bird was still marked with the little carving Luster Johns had made.

"Do you want to take some flowers out this weekend to put on Daddy's grave?" Barbara broached the subject when Miranda returned.

Miranda simply shrugged and shook her head no. They had driven out there twice. The children had looked at the floral wreaths with interest the first time. The second time, they read the pale gray headstone and cleared away some dried flowers and were very solemn. From then on, they simply didn't want to go, so neither had she. But occasionally she would ask.

"I think Dad would like it better if we left them here," Eliot answered for his sister. "He isn't in that place," he spoke with quiet confidence. "If he wants to see daffodils, he knows where we have them."

"I guess you've got a point." Barbara sat listening to the update of their day, then collected the residue of their tea break and stood to leave. Kent walked back with her partway, then headed home to do his schoolwork, leaving the two youngsters still sprawled contentedly beneath the tree. "Wherever you are," Barbara said softly once she was alone, pausing to look at Byron and the treehouse she and Kent and McMillan had helped the kids finish, "I hope you know you've got some very nice kids. You'd be proud." The phone inside started ringing and her thought was left hanging as she made a quick dash for the door.

"I got some tickets for the Candlelight Tour this Friday," McMillan announced over the phone. "It takes you though four houses and ends with a chamber music performance and cocktails. Do you want to go?" Other than him bringing in dinner once, they hadn't spent an evening together since the accident.

"I'm going to the ballet Friday night."

"You are?" He sounded surprised and a little distressed.

"Yes, I am."

"Would it be impolite to ask who you're going with?" The paternalistic quality in his voice was vaguely irritating.

"I'm going with me," she informed him, "and no, I don't want you to change your plans to go with me. I'm going out into the world alone."

"What on earth for?"

"Because it's time I did. It's time I found out what it's like to rely on my own company. Besides that, I like the ballet."

"I'd be glad to go with you," McMillan insisted.

"That would defeat the purpose of the expedition," she responded. "If I'm going to stand on my own two feet, I'd better start now. This way, if anything else I want to do comes along, I won't be too intimidated to do it alone."

"Are you upset with me for something?" he asked.

"No. It doesn't have anything to do with you," she stressed. "It has to do with me. I need to rely on myself more, so I'm taking myself to the ballet."

"I hope you have a wonderful time with yourself." His words oozed insincerity.

"Come on. Now don't get uppity," Barbara reprimanded him. "This is nothing personal. I'm being a good little girl. I'm seeing my shrink regularly, I'm taking my vitamins. But I'm easing off making any complicated decisions for awhile. And I'm taking a breather from any personal entanglements."

"I gather that means me."

"I need some time to myself. In the words of some unnamed philosopher, 'Either it will work out, or it won't'."

"You're sure you aren't angry?" he pressed her. "No one's said anything about me that has upset you?"

Barbara sighed and fought the urge to say something

rude. Louis's comments about McMillan's interest in an early partnership had made her cautious. She hated questioning his motives, even to herself. And his awkwardness since the accident made her uncomfortable. "No one's said anything," she assured him. It wasn't the truth. "And I'm not angry."

"Good." He was silent a few seconds. "Would you be upset if I took someone else on the Candlelight Tour? I'm not too thrilled about going to these things alone. I'm sure you'd hear about it from someone if I took another date. I really would like to make an appearance at least," he explained, "just to show my support for the Historic Foundation."

"I think you should definitely go." She was surprised how sincerely she meant it. "Take someone along. It should be a lovely evening. I've been before and I enjoyed it. I certainly have nothing to be angry about if you take someone else," she conceded. "You gave me a fair chance."

"Fine," McMillan concluded a little uncertainly. "I'll call you later in the week. We'll get together."

"Sure." Barbara suddenly wanted to get this over with. "See you later," she said quickly. "Bye, now." The phone was back in the cradle before the last syllable of McMillan's goodbye.

"Well, you've done it now," Barbara told herself. "Nuts or not, you're on your own."

Rob called after nine that night. "Are the kids asleep?" He sounded peculiar.

"They sure are," Barbara replied. "Is something wrong?"

"That's what I'm calling to ask you," he stressed. "I got the damnedest thing in the mail. The drama department at the College sent me all the videotapes addressed to you. 'B. Ashcroft care of R. Johnstone.' They got the addresses mixed up," he explained. "That was all right, but then I got this letter saying that I might be interested in passing some interview tape along to you at a suitable time. Only there was no tape with the letter."

"There was an interview tape with the set I got," Barbara replied.

"There was?" Rob repeated apprehensively.

"They came a couple of days ago."

"My God. What did you do with them?"

"I thought they were the ones you said we could have back, so I let the kids open them," Barbara confessed. "Miranda wanted to see *South Pacific*, but it wasn't in this batch. The extra one was T.J.'s presentation to the College budget committee."

"Oh, my God," Rob said softly.

"It's all right," Barbara assured him. "It scared the daylights out of me at first when I heard his voice, but it turned out to be something really great. The kids love it, I love it," she insisted. "You'll have to see it. He even mentions you by name."

"Really." Rob was guarded in his response. "It must have been quite a surprise."

"That's putting it mildly," Barbara admitted. "Once I realized what was going on, it wasn't such a shock. I'm glad someone at the College saved it."

"I must admit I'm relieved," Rob sighed. "I had no idea what had turned up. I called because of the foulup with the addresses. I didn't want you blindsided by anything that would upset you or the kids."

"Actually, it was very informative," she told him. "I know T.J. wasn't really into theater, but he certainly didn't come over that way. He made a good case for the flexible design. He mentioned you. It sounded almost as if you'd written parts of his dialogue. It all involved the new theater."

"I remember him asking me about it. I lent him a book called *Theater, Spaces, Environments*, about some innovative projects."

"He must have read it. He certainly did a convincing job. At least the model. I haven't seen the building itself, but I've been thinking about going down there."

"I heard that it was almost finished. Lucie sent off for some brochures about the Spoleto Festival. Apparently there is a production scheduled in it."

"More than one," Barbara noted. "There's a play

there in two weeks, a grand opening thing. Then the Festival has it booked for an experimental production. Something by Sam Shepard."

"*The Tooth of the Crime*," Rob said, supplying the title. Obviously he'd read the brochures Lucie Laveau had received.

"Is Lucie coming up for the Festival?" Barbara asked eagerly. The large, outspoken woman had left a vivid impression on her. "I'd love to see her."

"A whole group of us are coming. She's planning on bringing William with her," Rob replied. "You remember William Weizmann?"

"I certainly do. I remember them well. That was a wonderful evening."

"It was, wasn't it?" Rob responded solemnly, obviously thinking of more than the friends and the party. For a few seconds they were both silent.

"Yes, it was a lovely evening. All of it," Barbara said firmly. "One of these days we'll have to talk about it."

"Really. That sounds like some kind of progress. I'm interested in talking, of course, but I'm in no hurry," he said with a faint trace of amusement in his voice.

"We've got plenty of time."

"Speaking of which, I'll be coming up with Lucie and William and the others. We've all booked reservations at the Mills House Hotel. We're planning to eat our way through the historic section while we're there, so leave as many evenings open as you can. I don't know what your schedule will be, but I would like as much time as you can spare, and Lucie and William want to see you."

"Are you sure you wouldn't like to stay with us?"

"I'd love to, but I've promised to show the others around. We'll be trying to catch a lot of performances, including matinees. You'll be teaching. The kids have their schedules. Rather than turn your place into a madhouse with all the coming and going, I'd be better staying downtown." Barbara was nodding, already imagining the chaos that would be involved and the hectic trips across the bridge to downtown Charleston in the unpredictable Spoletime traffic.

"We're close to everything at Mills House," Rob continued logically. "We can run in and collapse between shows or change or grab a bite to eat without having to think about parking or traffic or conversation or anything. You can jump in and join us when you want. You'll have peace and quiet at home, and the kids won't feel like mailsacks being dropped off and picked up at all hours."

Barbara smiled at the description. "You're right. We're not used to the pace."

"Me neither. I'm used to my own peculiar brand of serenity. But this is short-term frenzy. Things will get sane again," he stressed. "We just have to ride it through." There was a slight shift in his voice that made his statement ambiguous.

"You'll all have a great time."

"We all will." He altered her word choice. "That includes you, I hope."

"It includes me."

"Good. Give the kids a hug for me. I'm glad the tape mixup didn't upset anyone."

"It didn't. One of these days you might want to watch it. You may find it interesting."

"Frankly, it's always been the other members of your family who interest me," Rob said quietly. "I'll be seeing you soon, I hope. Take care," he added.

Afterwards, on her way to bed, Barbara stopped and checked on the children. She didn't give them the hug Rob mentioned, but she watched them a moment and smoothed their covers and tucked them in. *Mailsacks*. She smiled and shook her head as she looked down at Eliot in his blanket cocoon.

It's always been the other members of your family who interest me. Rob had spoken without a trace of rancor, but his point was clear. Gwen Henderson had asked her if she knew how either Rob or T.J. felt about each other. She'd only been able to describe what she had seen: pleasant talks, pleasant expressions, amiable dinners, then the visit would end. She'd always assumed the relationship was as friendly as it seemed. But Rob's comment indicated she had missed something.

Admittedly, she liked smooth surfaces, neat packages,

and everyone being polite. She'd been brought up that way. Gwen had suggested that in her effort to please everyone she had often bottled things up, refused to get angry or stand her ground. She'd cautioned Barbara about being habitually "nice and agreeable." Now Barbara wondered if it was a game she'd inadvertently forced the others to play, if the pleasantness between T.J. and Rob was simply an effort to please her.

In the cosmic scheme of things. There were countless times she'd backed off from an issue because it held no great consequence on the cosmic level. But she had been the one to capitulate. She'd been the one to turn off the TV show or put aside a book or her sewing because T.J. wanted her. She almost passed up the certification classes because he didn't think she needed to work again. But she signed up anyhow and felt like a deceitful child when she did. Now she was ducking McMillan to avoid having a confrontation, personally and professionally. Gwen said there was a price for being "nice and agreeable." It made some people protective, some pleasant, and others manipulative.

"Damn," Barbara muttered, pressing her hands to her temples. "What did we do to each other?" She headed to the den and slammed the interview tape into the VCR. She sat there staring and listening, trying to see beyond the surface, trying to get some sense of what was once so clear.

CHAPTER 11

> A Light exists in spring
>   Not present on the year
> At any other period.
>   When March is scarcely here
>   *Emily Dickinson*

"How's it been going this week?" Gwen Henderson asked as she settled back and let Barbara catch her breath before starting in. March had started gently, with a few days of sunshine and sea breezes, but the remainder of the month had been punctuated erratically with torrential rains that backed up traffic and made driving in downtown Charleston a precarious and tense experience. Gwen had canceled the Monday appointment because the electricity was knocked out in a heavy storm. Now after being caught in the after-school congestion, Barbara was already fifteen minutes late for this Thursday session.

"It's been okay. A little frazzling with all the rain, but otherwise not bad." She took a sip of the apple cinnamon tea and let out a small sigh.

"Anything in particular you want to get off your chest?"

"Maybe." Barbara pressed her lips together. She'd been running a few possibilities over while she drove through the latest downpour to keep this appointment. "I figure I've been ducking McMillan, and it's gone on long enough."

"You've been ducking him?"

"I've been deliberately busy lately and I've begged off doing anything with him. I suggested he see others while I put things on hold for awhile. Actually, I was looking for excuses," she admitted. "I was just afraid to tell him that it won't work between us. I've been playing ostrich, hoping he'd get involved elsewhere and lose interest in me, so I wouldn't have to make any decision one way or another."

"And has he lost interest?"

"I'm not sure. I've decided to come out of hiding and check."

"But you're sure you're not interested in him?"

"I'm sure. I've had to face the fact that I was confusing sex and convenience with something else."

"And the McMillan thing wasn't that something else?"

"No. He was a lot of other things I needed at the time. I needed reassurance. It was nice to have someone attentive. And sexually, it was very, very nice."

"But?"

"But there isn't enough there for a long-term commitment. I've been analyzing why I found him so appealing. He's a lot like T.J.—blond, good body, confident, good at his job. He fit into the picture I'm used to without too many ripples."

"But?"

"But I was fitting him into someone else's life, not his own," Barbara said aloud what she'd been ruminating over for days. "That sort of smacks of what happened to me when I got married. I fit myself into T.J.'s vision. If I kept on seeing McMillan, I'd be doing that to him. I'd be trying to recreate the old life, the one T.J. designed, not the new one that has to start with this version of me." She leaned forward, balancing the cup with both hands, staring out the window at the rain as she spoke. "The old life doesn't even fit me anymore. If I'd keep on being that agreeable, nice, accommodating person I've been, I could work out a passable relationship with McMillan. For a while it would probably be as idyllic as the last one. That's what's disturbing. I could make it fit for a while longer. But I honestly don't feel it would end up being healthy for either of us."

"You have been doing some soul searching."

"I've been trying to understand how my being nice and agreeable and accommodating has affected me and everyone around me," Barbara explained with a glimmer of annoyance in her eyes. "I've been lazy. T.J. and my friends tried to take care of me, and I let them do it. I don't like confrontations, so everyone tried to spare me. Worst of all, I learned to avoid conflicts by letting others have their way. Especially with T.J. If I gave in, things were fine."

"At least they seemed that way."

"Right. I could see it happening with McMillan."

Gwen tilted her head, listening without speaking.

"It isn't like that with Rob," Barbara said. She glanced outside again, fleetingly recalling the rain that New Year's night months ago in Fort Lauderdale. "He knows we have to talk. And we will. He doesn't push me. So until the time is right, we tiptoe around certain issues, but we know they're there."

"And that bothers you?"

"To a certain extent. He won't make my decisions easy for me; but with him, I don't need to have all the answers. I don't even need the right questions. But underneath it all, there's something comfortable between Rob and me that's going to take some time to get used to." She glanced at Gwen, catching the gleam of amusement in her eyes. "Don't get ahead of me here," Barbara insisted, barely able to keep from laughing. "We're friends. I'm trying not to set up any expectations with him. But I also don't see any point in avoiding something inevitable as far as McMillan goes."

"Like what?"

"Like letting him totally off the hook. Telling him flat out that I'll be his friend but not his lover."

"You're sure about that?"

"I'm sure the lover part is over. In fact, I'm a little iffy about the friendship."

Gwen looked up at her curiously.

"He's said a couple of things to Louis about moving things along faster in the business. His motives may be a bit suspect. My motives weren't too noble either," she admitted. "But I want someone to love me for being me, not because I'd be helpful in advancing his career. Not that we weren't compatible," she added quickly. "We were getting along very well in a lot of ways. But I'm concerned that he's more taken with surface than with substance. Probably we both were."

"That can happen," Gwen agreed.

"Once he pointed out that we're both good prospects.

That doesn't necessarily make us right for each other. I think we were going a little too fast too soon, trying to fit some image of what a couple should be. If we could be friends without forcing anything more, I think we'd both end up happier."

"Sounds like there's another 'but' coming along."

"But I need to get together with him and iron this out. I don't want him thinking we can go on from here. We can't." She shrugged. "He was there when I needed him. I'd like to salvage something with him. Something nonphysical."

"So?"

"So, I guess I'll have to see him face to face and deal with it. I was thinking about what a friend said. He told me sometimes we have to harden our hearts. In a way, he was talking about being firm and ending false hopes, not leaving loose ends dangling. He says we have to keep drawing lines that mark certain limits. I have to learn to do that better."

Gwen nodded. "Your friend gave you some very good advice. I think you're on the right track."

Barbara's smile broadened in satisfaction. At least she'd worked through some of the clutter in her mental closet.

"As long as we're talking friendship and salvaging and hopes of one kind or another, how do things stand with Rob? Any word on the teaching job at the college?" Gwen's tone was noticeably lighter. Barbara guessed that meant their session was nearing its end.

"No news yet. His students are rehearsing for a spring production of *Barnum* and he seems to be busy with that. He'll be coming in May for the Spoleto regardless."

"So where does all this put you socially?"

"I'm not sure." Barbara set aside her empty teacup. "I'm not ruling out any possibilities anymore. There are functions I attend where there are men. If I run into someone, I'd think about going out. But, I'm not looking for a quick solution or another temporary replacement. Things have leveled out. I think I'll be taking it real slow."

Gwen gave Barbara a quick grin and put her cup down

next to the other one. "You made it easy for both of us this time."

"We're through?" Barbara asked, looking at her watch.

"I think you've worked out a lot for one afternoon."

"So you're pleased?"

"You don't have to please me."

"I have to please me."

"And?"

"And I think I'm doing all right." She nodded and straightened her shoulders. "I'm working on the things that I can do something about. So I'm pleased."

"I think you should be. And so should your friend."

When Barbara dropped Eliot off at the ballfield Friday afternoon, his two coaches were already there with large bulky sacks of bats and gloves and balls. The field was spotted with puddles and dark soggy areas from the rain that had persisted through the weekend, but they'd decided to squeeze in the Monday practice anyhow. In his ragged jeans, peaked cap, and striped team shirt with "Astros" in large letters and "Ashcroft" in smaller ones, her son trudged toward center field amid a cluster of his teammates.

"One of the coaches is divorced," Karen had told her. Her golfing friend, Patti Caldwell, mentioned needing an extra player on the Little League team her brother was coaching. "Bob doesn't have custody, but he spends a lot of time with his son. I figure if Patti or you mention to him that Eliot's father died, he'll make a special effort to take him under his wing."

Barbara had agreed that Eliot could use some other male influences in his life.

"Patti says the coach's son has a good attitude. He plays on his dad's team, but he lives with his mother. I know it's Patti's own brother she was talking about, but she assures me he's an excellent coach and he isn't win-crazy. He's big on sportsmanship. He gives everyone a chance to play. She's sure he'll watch out for Eliot," Karen had insisted. "Besides, he's supposed to be real good-looking. Available. He's a plumbing contractor."

Barbara had laughed and said she wished she'd known him when the auxiliary tank above the bedroom ceiling was put in. But she'd taken Karen's fact-gathering effort seriously and signed Eliot up for the team. Now that she was driving again, Little League was a regular addition to her after-school itinerary.

She watched a few minutes until the team started warming up. She glanced at the stack of envelopes on the carseat beside her. "Okay. Let's face the music." Most of the packets contained tickets she'd picked up at the Gaillard Auditorium for performances during Spoletime, still over eight weeks away. But the shows would sell out. So she'd made advance group purchases for people at the firm—Mark Ward, the Belcazzios, McMillan, and herself. The rest were for the Fort Lauderdale contingent—Lucie Laveau and William Weizmann, Albert Abrams, and Rob. She glanced at her watch and drove toward the Ashley Bridge. She'd have time to drop the tickets at the office, have a few words with McMillan, pick up Miranda from her art class, swing by the dry cleaners, and still get back in time to pick up Eliot when practice ended.

"Toilet paper and milk," Barbara reminded herself as she pulled into the parking lot behind the office. She took out her small notepad and scribbled down the items. "And tea," she added, with a sigh of pleasure. Gwen Henderson had given her a reprieve about the caffeine. Last week she was allowed coffee; this week she could start having an occasional cup of tea other than the herbal ones they had at their sessions. "You can have a glass of wine now and then," Gwen had also suggested. "Just to make you feel civilized."

In the parking lot of the firm, Barbara propped the shopping list on the center armrest, sifted though the tickets, and removed the ones she had to deliver.

"How's it going?" She greeted the familiar figure crouched on the workroom floor. Karen Belcazzio muttered without looking up. She had several large posters laid out in front of her. "For the Homebuilders Show?" Barbara guessed, looking over Karen's shoulder.

Karen nodded and sighed impatiently after removing

a pencil from between her clenched teeth. "I'm having a problem with the lettering."

"Maybe I'd better leave you with it," Barbara proposed.

Karen brushed a trickle of perspiration from her brow and smiled gratefully. She cast a dissatisfied look at her designs. "My language is getting a little blue and my disposition is definitely purple."

"This should cheer you up. I got all the tickets. Excellent seats." Barbara stepped past her. "I'll leave them with Louis." Karen had already stuffed the pencil back in her teeth and was concentrating on her artwork. But she looked up and nodded anyway.

"I've got—" Barbara waved the tickets in the air but broke off as she turned into McMillan's office. He was bent over his desk, examining a city map. Beside him, a brown-haired woman pointed with a well-manicured fingernail while her other arm draped across McMillan's back.

"Oh, excuse me," Barbara said, halting. The twosome stared up at her. The woman in the camel-colored suit did not alter her position. McMillan straightened so the arm dropped away.

"Barbara." He greeted her with an uncertain grin. "We were just locating a building site. This is Janice Benson. She's a realtor." The brown-haired woman smiled politely. "Barbara Ashcroft as in Ashcroft and Belcazzio," he completed the introduction.

"Nice to meet you." Barbara smiled slightly. "I'm sorry if I interrupted. Here are the theater tickets. I've got a few more to drop off." She handed the envelope to McMillan and left. She could hear him say something to his companion. A few seconds later he was behind her in the hall.

"Barbara. Hold on a minute. How have you been?" He caught up with her and rested his hand on her arm.

"I'm fine. How about you?" She managed to sound noncommittal.

"Back there, that was simply business," McMillan began explaining without being asked. "I've really missed you. You're always on the run. I've been up to my ears in work, too. I wish we could get together and talk." He kept his voice low.

"We talk off and on."

"I mean really talk," he added deliberately. "Like over dinner."

"Well, you're busy now and I've got to drop the rest of these off, then pick up the kids. Maybe later this week."

"How about Thursday?" McMillan persisted.

"Eliot has a game at seven-thirty." She shrugged.

"How about if I go with you?" he suggested. "We can pick up something to eat after."

"It would be a little late for the kids on a school night."

"Saturday?" He tried again.

"I'm going to the Symphony Designer House."

"Alone?"

"Yes." She stopped and remembered what she'd said about straightening things out face to face. "Unless you'd like to go with me."

"Sure I want to go with you."

"Fine." Barbara waved and strode off toward Louis's office with the next batch of tickets.

"I'll call you about the time." McMillan waited in the hallway until she was out of sight, then finally he stepped back into his office. When she passed by on her way out, she noticed this time, alone or not, he'd closed the outer door.

The Thursday game didn't come off as scheduled. Barbara and eight other parents sat in the stands while the Astros warmed up. The black-shirted members of the other team, the Pirates, moved about their dugout area waiting for the rest of their players to show up. At starting time, the Pirates only had seven boys. The game was a forfeit.

"Sorry folks," Eliot's coach said, coming over to explain what had happened. "Practice Tuesday in the batting cage," he called to the boys. With large steps, he climbed the stands and sat next to Barbara.

"I've got Brian for a few hours. Could I interest you and your kids in some hamburgers? Burger King's just a few blocks down." There was more than a casual edge in his voice. Up close he was as handsome as Karen had reported.

Barbara considered refusing. Then she reconsidered. The children were all keyed up and bright-eyed. Eating out would be a satisfactory substitute for the canceled game, and it would give the kids time to unwind. Besides, it would let the adults get to know each other. "Sure, let's go," she agreed. "You want me to follow you?"

The dark-haired coach frowned. "How about we all go in my car, then afterwards I'll bring you back here for yours," he suggested.

Now Barbara frowned. "We're talking a lot of zigzagging. How about I take my car, you take yours, and we go home from there? You have to get Brian home and I have to get my two to bed."

"This isn't exactly what I had in mind, but it makes the most sense," he conceded.

"I want to ride with Brian and Coach Caldwell," Eliot insisted.

"Me, too," Miranda whined. "Please."

"Sure. You kids pile in."

"First, I've got to have a word with Eliot." Barbara tilted her head so Eliot would step aside with her. "What's your coach's name?" she whispered.

"Coach Caldwell," Eliot replied indignantly.

"I mean his first name."

"Bob, I think," Eliot said with a smirk.

"Bob, I think," Barbara echoed. "Well, behave yourself in Bob-I-think's car and use the seatbelts," she reminded him. "Meet you at Burger King." She let him join the others. "See you there."

"The joys of single parenthood," she murmured as she backed out of the parking spot. A quick bite at a burger joint with three kids and Bob-I-think. At least she was trying to be open to possibilities.

By the time the burgers were eaten, she'd already heard enough about hunting and camping and fishing and jetskiing to know that she wasn't interested in Bob-I-think. He liked long weekends tenting in the mountains.

"I'm the hotel-by-the-beach type," she made it clear right away. "But I appreciate you taking your free time to coach these boys." She managed to steer him into talking about his plumbing business and solar water systems. They laughed about her ceiling collapsing. The evening ended early and on pleasant terms. But Barbara left nothing unclear between them, no uncertain openings. On the way home, she found herself humming contentedly while the kids drooped and dozed, belted upright in their seats. "Nice enough but not wishy-washy," she murmured to herself, with a quick, satisfied glance in the rear-view mirror. "Luster would be proud of me," she concluded, humming again.

The year's Designer House was a three-story brick house built in the early eighteen-thirties, facing Colonial Lake in the heart of old Charleston. For the event, each room had been refurbished by a different local interior design firm, from wallpaper and drapes to floral arrangements and doorstops. Most of them had preserved the feeling for the period by relying on superb antiques and plush appointments. Some of the daring designers had been more eclectic, blending the old with startlingly modern pieces of furniture and artworks.

"I'm always dazzled." Barbara took McMillan's arm as they strolled along the lakeside walk afterwards, moving toward his parked car. "But I'm also relieved to get home and walk around in bare feet and sit in my already-paid-for furniture."

"Is that an invitation?" McMillan smiled. "I'd like some quiet time with you."

"I guess this wasn't the best place to have much of a conversation," she admitted. They had been constantly surrounded by other tourgoers. "How about coming home for a drink?"

"I'd be delighted." He stopped and unlocked the passenger door.

Barbara paused and looked back. Across the small lake drifted the sweet perfume from white-blossomed trees and thick clumps of flowering shrubs that were just showing their spring blooms. She loved the subtle changes that marked the shifts in the Charleston climate.

"Well?" McMillan touched her arm gently. "Let's get going." He urged her along. "You've got your own water to look at if you want." He closed the door behind her a bit abruptly.

"Pushy," Barbara muttered while he made his way around to the other side. When he climbed in beside her, she said nothing.

Twenty minutes later, she poured herself a glass of wine and stared out at the moonlit marsh. McMillan stood behind her, sipping the drink she'd given him.

"I thought we were going to talk," he reminded her. "Come on, sit." He sat and patted the loveseat next to him.

"Okay." She kicked off her shoes and settled down on the opposite end. "Was there anything in particular you wanted to talk about?" She was leaving an opening for him to bring up anything, from his friendly realtor to revamping the company name.

"I guess I just want to know where we stand." He leaned forward slightly and looked at her. "I was wondering if we could start again like we were before all this happened." His eyes shifted for a few seconds to her wrists. "I know I probably didn't handle this as well as I should have."

"There was a lot to handle," Barbara admitted. "You walked into a real mess here. You did a lot to make it better."

"Past tense? I'm getting an uneasy feeling about where this is going."

Barbara steeled herself and kept on. "I don't regret anything we did together. And I don't know how I would have gotten through a lot of this without you."

"Just wait," McMillan interrupted her. "Before you drop the axe. You have been through a lot, and you seemed to want some time to yourself. Then you gave me the go-ahead to see other people. At the time I figured you just weren't up to working on a relationship. My mistake was in letting you slip away and losing the momentum. I was wrong." He waved his hand in a gesture of dismissal. "Look, I don't know what you've heard or what you think I've been doing. Maybe that business at the office with the Benson woman bothered you, but there's no one I'm interested in except you. And if you'll think a minute, you'll admit that you and I have a lot going together. You may be throwing away a perfectly good relationship just because of all the other things that went haywire over the past months."

"This really hasn't anything to do with momentum or the Benson woman or things going haywire," Barbara persisted. "It has to do with knowing when things are right and when they aren't. Besides the fact that we had good sex, there wasn't enough else that was right between us."

"I thought we got along great."

"We did. Up to a point," Barbara conceded. "But I think we both had some mental checklist that we were ticking off. According to the list, we should have made a great match. But I was using an old list. I've changed. I've done that version of me before. I want to work on a new one."

"So let's work on a new one. Tell me what you want."

"I can't tell you. It's just something I feel. There is no sense trying to make the pieces fit," Barbara tried not to sound impatient. "We're talking square pegs and round holes."

"You don't have some other man?"

"It's not another man. It's me. I'm not as accommodating as I used to be."

"You don't want us to have any kind of a relationship? We were better than good together in bed," he pointed out, his tone decidedly suggestive.

"Sex with you was better than good," Barbara agreed, feeling as if she were talking to a petulant adolescent. "Occasionally it was as earth shaking as it's cracked up to be. But that still isn't enough to build a life around. And that's what we're talking about here. Building lives. Very complicated lives. When I find out what I need besides good sex, I'm sure I'll still remember how everything works. But I can't be casual about it."

"You can't just shut down your sexual desires."

"We're not talking desires. We're talking behavior. There's an important difference between having an orgasm and having one with a partner."

McMillan's drink nearly spilled as he looked at her, wide-eyed.

"I'm giving up the partner part temporarily," she said, keeping her gaze level. "I think I'll survive."

"A man just can't live like that."

"I'm not suggesting you have to. I'm just telling you that you won't be doing it with me," Barbara countered sweetly, drawing the line and underscoring it.

"If you are worried about becoming pregnant, and you can't take pills," McMillan seemed to miss the point, "I can take precautions. There are other things to use."

"I'm not stupid," Barbara said gently. "That's not what bothers me, it's everything else. But while we're setting things straight, you are right that I do not want to have another child."

"Ever?" McMillan asked, surprised.

"No more kids," Barbara said calmly. "I'm thirty-four. I have two children already. We're all healthy. In a couple of years they'll be moving into the puberty stage and out of the bodily function period." She looked at him intently. "Don't get me wrong. I loved having my kids. I loved my babies when they were babies. But I don't care to see another budding tooth, urine-soaked diaper, or runny nose until I'm a grandparent, if then."

"You mean if you married again, you wouldn't want one more child?"

"Why one more?" Barbara shot back. "To check off something else on a list?"

"Maybe so your husband would have one of his own."

She flopped back against the cushion. "Raising the two I have is a big enough challenge. They are both finally big enough and mature enough to go places with me. We got out to dinner and they eat off their own plate. At the theater they sit in their own seat. We can actually play badminton together. We can all ride bikes." She made each detail sound like a significant sign of progress. "They have so much to see and do and learn," Barbara declared. "A baby is a new person who needs love and care and time. It's a different kind of time than I want to give. So, no," she stated uncompromisingly, "no babies."

"You wouldn't negotiate that with a husband?" McMillan persisted, making one last effort.

"No," Barbara answered softly. "Before I'd marry again, I'd make sure the man feels as I do, for his sake as well as my own. A marriage and two kids is more than enough these days, especially if people want time for each other." She paused a second, then took a slow breath. "If you have the remotest thought that you could change my mind about this or about reviving anything between us, you're wrong. But if you think you can change the fact that you want a child of your own," she stressed, "you are probably wrong about that, too. Listen to your heart and stick to what you want. It's a no-compromise situation," Barbara declared. "If you compromise, or if you tried to get me to, someone would end up resenting someone else. Both sides lose something."

"Maybe so," McMillan admitted, surrendering.

Barbara sat forward and studied his handsome, solemn face. "I like you. I like a lot about you," she asserted. "We had something really nice for awhile. Neither one of us is battle scarred," she reminded him. "We can be friends."

"You think so?" McMillan asked, finally managing a weak smile.

"Let's make the best of an impasse. Don't clutter it up. This is it. You get a friend." She reached out and offered him her hand.

"Actually, now that you mention it, I don't have a lot of those." He held her hand. He didn't shake it.

Once McMillan was gone and she closed the door behind him, Barbara turned and let out a relieved sigh. "You did okay," she announced. "You're getting better."

She made her customary check of the sliding glass doors and clicked the deadbolt in the kitchen door. Then she walked in the moonlight through the study to collect the empty glasses.

"If you're still nosing around . . ." she began with an amused smile. Then she suddenly stopped, realizing that she was yielding ground. She glanced at the wood worktable with the fern where the glass grinder once sat. "No more weird stuff," she said. She lifted the glass and held it up toward Keats. The last bit of wine sparkled greenish-gold in the night. "We're doing all right on our own. Finally."

She carried the two empty glasses into the kitchen, slid the rings off her right hand, squirted out some detergent, and thrust the first one under the running water, scrubbing it clean. The second one skidded in her soapy hands and hit against the faucet, snapping off at the stem. She caught the pieces then stared at them apprehensively. Same reflex, this time no cuts.

"I didn't want to hurt myself that night. I didn't cause it," she said aloud, remembering the blood that had trickled down the sheet of stained glass. There had been a lot of blood all the way to the kitchen. Something had been there that night; something made the glass fall. Something evil.

Shaking her head, she remembered the lines from the Pirandello play she'd been reading the night T.J. died. *When a character is born, he instantly acquires his own independence, even from his own author.* Independence was a given.

She leaned against the counter, recalling what Luster had said about haunts getting worse as time passed. "I don't know whose creation this thing is," she whispered, "and I don't know who was supposed to be in control that night. But I could have been crippled, or I might have bled to death." She felt her voice waver as she stated her case. "Don't ever hurt me again. Don't ever scare me again." She rested her fingertips on the whitish scar at the base of one hand and glanced out at the beaded blue line and the tiny dangling mirrors outside. She picked up the rings, but this time, she didn't put them on.

With one finger trailing along the window ledge, she walked the length of the room, drawing an invisible line. Then she put the broken pieces of the glass in the trash, dried her hands, and walked away. T.J.'s wedding band was in her jewelry box, where she'd put it after the funeral. She put her two rings with it in the little drawer. Then she pushed it closed.

"Have you been locking your garage door at night?" Louis Belcazzio asked as he stood on Barbara's doorstep in cut-off jeans and a ragged sweatshirt on Saturday morning.

"I guess so." Barbara stood back and invited him in. "Why? Is something wrong?"

"Some kids have been spooking around after gasoline," Louis muttered. "The gas tank on my bass boat was drained and someone has been tampering with the lawn mower. It was in my garage," he said indignantly. "Came right up on my boat dock and in my garage," he grumbled.

"I don't have a boat or a dock, Louis," Barbara reminded him. "And the lawn mower is in the garage, empty. Kent cleaned it out and put it under a tarpaulin last November. I guess it's still there." She hadn't been out in the garage except to get in or out of the car in months.

"Maybe I'd better take a look," Louis suggested. "My guess is that some young kids are coming in the back in a canoe or a runabout and are swiping fuel. I don't think they're coming by land. I found two cigarette butts on the dock. Face it, anyone stupid enough to use a siphon and smoke, apparently in the dark of night, is also stupid enough to blow up themselves and my damn boat."

"That's pretty ominous," Barbara admitted.

"Yeah," Louis, now on a roll declared. "And if the fools drag a siphon and some cigarettes into my garage . . . kapoweeee," he concluded impressively, making elaborate explosion gestures with his hands. "They have no business endangering all of us like this. I'd like to tell the jerks to fuck off."

Barbara thrust a mug filled with coffee at him. "Let's look around." She preceded him out the side door of the kitchen. She pushed the button that opened the overhead door so there was more light and room to move around. The door slowly raised and a gust of clean air swept in.

The inside wall against the study was lined with tools

and half-empty sacks of fertilizer and peat. There were shelves full of magazines, old issues of *House and Garden*, *Architectural Digest*, and *Smithsonian*, intermingled with cardboard cartons of papers, lesson plans, tests, and answer keys from her classes.

Louis spotted the metal gas can by the door, crossed to the far wall, yanked back the tarpaulin, and inspected her lawn mower. "It looks all right," he affirmed. "A hell of a lot cleaner than mine," he admitted. "Anything look like it's been disturbed?" He waited while Barbara squeezed past him and inspected the rest of the garage. She paused by the closed cartons on the southernmost corner.

"That's your glass stuff." Louis stopped her before she opened them. "McMillan and I put them there. One has the broken stuff." He nudged the middle one with his toe. "This one has the bigger pieces." He pointed to the next one. "Just leave 'em here for a while until you know what you want to do with them. Keep that gas can out of sight." He backed toward the driveway and stood with one hand on his hip. "No sign of any tampering. I guess they left you alone." He took a long gulp of coffee.

"I guess so."

"Well, keep it locked at night," Louis reminded her. "And you might keep putting your car in, too," he suggested, knowing that if the weather was good, she often didn't bother.

"My car has a locking gas cap."

"They'd have to be right up in your driveway to tell that," Louis cautioned her. "You don't want stupid kids with gas cans and cigarettes up here in your yard."

"Okay, so I'll put the car inside," Barbara promised.

"I've called the cops," Louis informed her. "I told them about my place and Tom Palmer's. Even the Hobachs had a window jimmied. Everyone backing the creek. Some officers came out and prowled around. They said they'd keep an eye out and run an extra patrol through here for the next few weeks. The country club has had some of the lawn equipment drained. They're taking on an additional night watchman," Louis added. "Partly that's because there are a lot more night parties at the club now that the weather is getting nicer," he noted. "Parking lot full of cars, all full of gasoline. Easy target."

Barbara nodded.

"Just give me a call if you hear anything." Louis handed the empty coffee cup back to her. "Or call the cops. This gas-stealing crap is too damn dangerous to fool with," he declared. "Rainy season is over. Woods are getting dry."

"I get the picture." Barbara walked him halfway across the lawn. "Thanks for keeping me updated."

"No problem," Louis said with a grin. "Just being neighborly. But I still wish the little shits would fuck off. Pardon the language." He waved and drove back up the street. Barbara pushed the button once more on the way back in. With a soft whirring sound the garage door lowered and clicked closed.

Eliot turned ten on the fourth of May. Barbara carried a sheetcake and a gallon of ice cream to the practice field.

"Oh, Mother," he mumbled when his coach called the boys aside and marched them to the picnic bench where Barbara and Miranda had everything set out. He shrugged and shuffled his feet in embarassment as the kids and coaches sang *Happy Birthday*—loud, off key, but enthusiastically. Despite his grumbling, deep down inside, where ten-year-old boys don't have to act like big guys, he was tickled that his mom had thrown him a surprise party.

The presents came later, after they had driven home. There was a fishing pole from Grampa and Gramma, an easel and paints from the Belcazzios, a telescope from Rob, two videogames, and an assortment of clothes. Out back had been the real topper. Kent had pitched a bright blue umbrella tent in the yard. "Happy Tenth," was painted on a white banner and hung across the front of the zippered porch area.

"Can I sleep in it tonight?" Eliot asked after he had finished whooping and galloping around and through it with his friend Billie right behind him.

"You'll have to wait till the weekend. It's a school night," she reminded him. "But on Friday night, you and Billie can camp out."

Eliot groaned and retreated once more to the dark yard to peer at his new acquisition. Barbara divided up what was left of the cake and gave Kent and Billie extra-large shares. "Come on," she yelled to Eliot. "It will be all right out there without you. Now get in here and join the celebration!"

It was after ten when all the excitement died down and Eliot and Miranda finally went to bed to stay. Barbara stuffed the paper plates into the garbage sack, tied it with a wire twister, and let out a satisfied sigh. She poured herself the dregs of a lukewarm pot of tea without bothering to heat it in the microwave. Cup in hand, she switched off the kitchen lights and turned into the hall.

"Doors," she reminded herself as she strolled into the study. The heavy traffic had been coming and going through the east sliders all evening. Eliot had made two trips, in his pajamas, to check the tent "one more time."

"I trust you can watch over the campsite." She addressed her comment to the droopy form of Poe, hunched like a long-armed old goblin behind the blue tent. She poked her head out the doors for a moment, glancing from the tent to the marsh. Heavy cloud cover cut off the sliver of moon and engulfed the yard in heavy, still darkness. Then she remembered what Louis had said about kids, gas cans, and cigarettes.

"They wouldn't dare," she muttered, realizing that someone skulking through the marsh might be able to see the tent from the river. It had been a week since Louis and the neighbors had had the nocturnal visitors. So far, no one else on the street had noticed gas or anything else missing. A tent would be tempting. "They wouldn't dare," she argued. But of course they would, and she knew it.

"Okay," Barbara muttered, flicking on the floodlight that illuminated one section of the yard. "I really don't want to go out there. However," she focused on the blue dome, "I am going to take down that tent. And if anything moves, I will scream like a banshee and wet my pants." She stood there stuffing her feet into her tennis shoes while she mustered her courage.

Maybe they had been doing it all along. But after moving out a few steps, Barbara stopped and listened to the steady chorus, the rapid, high-pitched chirping of frogs. Occasionally a lower note—the rumbling of a courting bullfrog—would punctuate the marsh sounds.

"Okay, guys," Barbara addressed them all. "You watch the flank, and I'll break camp." She raced across the yard, pausing to yank out a tent stake, then hurry to the next one. The thin nylon tent listed, then the walls fluttered, and finally the whole thing collapsed inward while the riverside singers sang on. She rolled the tent into a bundle, flung her arms around the poles, and dangling ropes, and made a dash back to the house.

Almost out of breath, she dropped it all inside with a clatter, yanked the doors shut, and leaned against them, panting. "We did it," she congratulated the froggy chorus. "I did it." She plopped her hand on her heaving chest. She turned and switched off the light. "A small step for man." She grinned as she stared out at the pitch-black yard. "A giant step for me." She could still hear her heartbeat loud in her ears. Breathing heavily, she strode off toward her room, filled the bathtub in the iris bathroom and squeezed in an extra shot of bubble bath. She ignored the slight tremble in her hands.

"Not bad," she beamed at her reflection in the steamy mirror. "Not bad at all."

"Don't forget the opening Thursday," Karen's message on the answering machine reminded her. "We'll pick you up at seven." Barbara had glanced at the calendar where "Moffatt Theater" was already printed in for the next night. She ran the tape back, set the machine again, then grabbed her car keys and headed out. She was almost to the Ashley Bridge when she remembered that Miranda had a double session in art class that afternoon. She had an hour on her own before Eliot would be finished with ball practice.

She arched her eyebrows and kept on driving toward the Charleston peninsula. She'd driven past the theater project twice, once in the rain, and once when McMillan's car was parked out front. Today, a paving crew was finishing the parking area next to the Moffatt building, so she found a spot farther down the street and walked back. The black- and gold-lettered marquee above the door still had empty drill holes where the wiring would go for the lights. She stepped up onto the colonnade that ran the length of the renovated two-story house and tested the double front doors. They opened into a lobby area with a box office and waiting area freshly painted and carpeted in Wedgwood blue. A curving wall with offset entrances separated the lobby from the theater beyond.

Inside, she could hear voices, but none sounded familiar. She'd barely made it into the main seating and performing area when the students and a few professional actors who'd been finishing an afternoon rehearsal came streaming off the ramps and platforms, gathered their belongings, and left. For a while she watched from the shadowy periphery, remembering how T.J. had talked about this place on the tape. Then suddenly it seemed she had the theater all to herself—silent except for the occasional growl and roar of the paving equipment outside.

Finally, she ventured into the lighted area to get a better look. She walked halfway around the first elevation of seating to get closer to the actual stage areas T.J. had designed. The inner walls and most of the second floor had all been removed, opening up the entire area. The lower floor of the old house had been removed and two adjacent revolving bases were set into the central portion so entire structures could be rotated and realigned without requiring the intrusion of stagehands. Telescoping landings, attached to open staircases on three sides, could be raised or lowered, reduced or extended to accommodate the action. Seasoned, scarred hardwood had been saved and reused for cosmetic touches to balance the high-tech theater machinery with the warmth of handcrafted materials.

"Very nice," she breathed the words as she trailed her fingers over the smooth, heavy timbers of a moveable up-ramp and walked onto one stagelike platform. "You gave this place a whole new life all right. You opened up a window in time, T.J., like you said." She bent down and sniffed the rich, polished wood. "It even smells good."

"Are you looking for someone?" A disembodied voice stopped her in midstep. "Can I help you?" Barbara turned full circle trying to locate the source. In the control booth above and behind her toward the back, someone was still up there working, obscured by the tinted glass.

"I was just sneaking an early peek." She shielded her eyes and tried to make out the person who went with the voice. "I'm Barbara Ashcroft. My husband is the architect who designed this."

"I thought that was the big blond guy. McMillan?"

Barbara's expression stiffened. "Same company. McMillan implemented the design. Is it all right if I look around?"

"Sure. We're breaking for dinner. I'll just leave the lights on. Watch your step." She could see the outline of a balding fellow with a headset, standing in the control booth looking down at her. "We've got some kinks we've got to work out. Lots of last-minute fine tuning."

"I'll be careful." She could see him open a door at the back of the booth and step out of sight. When she walked across to the next landing, she could hear nothing. Even the outside sounds had ceased.

As if it were a gigantic free-form playground, she made one entire circuit of the staging areas and climbed up to a tier of balcony seating. She was leaning forward, checking the view, when she felt the coolness glide by her legs. It touched her again when she'd descended to one of the mid-level performing areas that jutted out like a diving platform over the center. Slowly her smile faded. She sniffed the air and smelled paint and fabric fixatives and sawdust, then she sniffed again and she knew he was there.

Immediately she lowered herself to the next stage and sat down leaning back against a stairway support, trying to appear more relaxed then she felt. "So this is where you've been," she said, nodding in understanding. "You've been here keeping track of another one of your projects."

The soft movement of the scented air fluttered a few typed pages of script that lay abandoned on a performing area across the open space.

She thought about climbing down to the lower level, then reconsidered. She cupped one hand over her wrist to steady herself, then went on and crossed her arms, covering the scars. She waited. Nothing moved.

"When will we all be finished, T.J.?" she asked as she stared out into the surrounding space. "When will you be finally satisfied that you can leave us? It can't just be me that's keeping you. Not here." The cool air moved in, heavier and more scented with Dhatri than before.

She reached down and drew a circle on the platform, enclosing herself. "Stay back." She sat there a while longer while perspiration beaded on her face, her eyes locked on the minute hand on her watch. Three minutes passed. Then three more. Eventually she would have to move and go to pick up Eliot and Miranda.

"I've got to go." She unlocked her arms and put her hands down to boost herself forward, planning to jump the few feet down rather than trust her unsteady legs to the open stairs.

One of the heavy crossbeams on the metal catwalk above her creaked.

Barbara leaned to the side, glancing upward toward the sound and the rows of mounted lights. One metal-shrouded spotlight pivoted its silvery face directly toward her, like the head of a curious bird.

She pressed her lips together and swallowed. "I have to pick up the kids." Soundlessly, a second large spotlight turned to gawk at her.

She inched forward, bracing herself for the jump. Then the first light broke free. With a swift, ominous swoosh, it slammed, glass-down, on the platform she had just left. Thousands of minute shards of glistening glass sprayed out in all directions, showering her with silvery fragments. Slowly, the dismembered metal head rolled off the upper ledge and ended its plunge with a dull, deadly crash on the platform she was on, inches from her fingers. But not inside the circle she'd drawn.

At first, she was too stunned to move. She stared at the heavy piece of lighting equipment, knowing it could have crushed her skull or her hand. Then she waited, expecting to feel pain somewhere. Carefully she lifted one hand, then the other, shaking the glass dust off her arms. She touched her face, then looked at her hands again, assuming they'd be bloody. But she wasn't cut. She leaned forward and shook the debris from her hair. It fell like silver stardust onto the stage a few feet below.

When she spoke, her voice was low and fierce. "You've forgotten everything. You've forgotten about trust, and caring, and honor. You hang around. You play your rotten games. You made a beautiful thing here, T.J. but it isn't yours. It doesn't need you anymore. You gave it life. But you can't give any of us that any more." She glared out into the shadows. "You've become nothing but a bully. A mean, nasty, arrogant bully. Why don't you just fuck off," she muttered with a biting sound that even startled her. "You hear me? Fuck off." This time she said it loud and clear.

With her fingertips, she pinched the front of her jacket and held it away from her, shaking it so the flakes would fall. When she stepped down onto the hardwood floor, the glass beneath her shoes grated and shifted like sand with each step. But nothing moved. Nothing stopped her. She walked straight out one aisle to the lobby and from there, out the front door. She had seven minutes to reach the ballfield.

Both the children were thrilled when she swung through the drive-through at McDonald's and told them they were going straight out to Luster's for a quick visit before they went home.

"Last time he came by he said he had some new angels. He's on number ten." Miranda had her sandwich bun open on her napkin and was neatly lining up her french fries on the tartar sauce of the fish fillet. Then she squeezed a packet of catsup over them, put the lid of the bun back on, and bit through all the layers. "He said he still had more to do," she added.

"He had a stump in his truck when he came by last week," Eliot chimed in. "Big twisted thing."

Barbara said nothing. She simply drove, trying not to let her nervousness show. All she knew was that she wanted to step inside the circle of angels and feel the panic subside.

Luster was out by his workbench. All she had to do was follow the sound of his hammer as he chipped away on the piece. He straightened and watched her as she came toward him, immediately reading the message in her eyes.

"Whatever it is, it's still around," Barbara declared.

" 'Round where?"

"Not at the house. It was downtown. In the theater T.J. designed. It made a spotlight fall. It almost hit me. Look at me. I'm covered with glass. At least, I was." She had shaken most of it off before she got in the car. "I went in to see how the work was going and I felt it there. Then the light fell."

"Didn't hurt you?"

"Just scared me."

"They'll do that, haunts will," he said sympathetically, looking her up and down. Then he narrowed one eye and leaned forward. "So what'd you tell it? Seems to me you must'a told it something. Seems to be a little touch of fire in your eyes."

"I said something rude," Barbara admitted.

"Must'a been real rude." His tight expression relaxed into a half-smile.

"It was."

"Then it lef' you be?"

She nodded.

"Good." Luster glanced back at the angel carving he'd been working on. He ran his hands over the deep cuts he'd already made, then he blew them clean. "Mustn't give an inch and mustn't back down." He stared at it a little while, then lined up the chisel and started in chipping away again. Fragments of wood leaped into the air.

"That's all you're going to say?"

"All I can say. What's done is done. Mus' not been too strong there," he noted. "Haunts are strongest where they mos' belong. Story is that a haunt who can't go home will hole up somewhere and 'ventually pine away. Can only be strong where it had good reason to be when it was alive, where it has a connection."

"T.J. spent time at the Moffatt when he was redesigning the interior. Does that mean this kind of thing can happen in any building he worked on?"

"Don't know. I s'pect so. There's part of him in everythin' he did. But I'd say it has to do with you, too. Seems like the point was to stay near you. Least, it was." He stopped carving and looked up at her. "Can't say if it still remembers."

"I'm supposed to go to an opening there this week. Do you think I should go?"

"Like I said, mustn't give an inch and mustn't back down." His dark hands were back on the wood again, carefully searching out the features hidden in the grain. The face he was discovering was strong and broad nosed and savage, but the body emerging from the twisted cypress stump was balanced and coiled like a dancer about to leap into the air.

"Won't it ever stop?"

"Hope so." Luster rubbed the angel's cheek with his thumb and concentrated on the deep-set eyes. "Fact that this thing's still around means it won't let go. Must be something left to do. Something undone." He peered toward the house, where Miranda and Eliot were sitting on the porch swing eating fresh-baked cookies and helping Mattie strip and sort grass for her baskets. " 'Nother month or so and it'll be a year, won't it?"

"July seventeenth."

"Any other special time?"

"Our anniverary. June twelfth."

"Four weeks." Luster nodded. "Lots of memories tied in with an anniversary. Real sentimental time," he cautioned her.

"I understand." Barbara patted her hand over her chest. She'd harden her heart.

"Sister Gertrude says it can't last past a year. These things sort of burn 'emselves out." He gave her a long, pensive look. "Meanwhile, it wears heavy on all of us. Wish it could all been settled nice and tidy long before."

Barbara walked back toward the circle where there was another angel she hadn't looked at up close. This one was striding forward, chin erect, curling hair pushed back as if it were caught by the wind. Looking at the determined set to the shoulders and the slightly parted lips, she could almost see the fire in her eyes and imagine what she would be saying. Something brief, and rude, and not angelic at all.

"I guess we'll go home now." She came back and stood beside him, watching the sure movement of his hands and tools for a while longer. The dancing savage was fully formed now, with roughed-out wings that he'd eventually detail in with feathers, like the others.

"I'll be 'round to check on you," Luster promised. "Got some periwinkles to help bring in the summer. Maybe I should spread some ash." His eyes met and held hers. "You come by anytime. You got all of us pullin' for you."

Standing with him in the clearing, with Inez and the children and the angels all around, Barbara couldn't help smiling. "I guess we do have whatever it is outnumbered."

"I think we got more than numbers on our side," Luster professed, looking up at the darkening sky. "Don't quite know what it is, but I feel it when I'm out here, and I think I sometimes hear it in my dreams." Like a statue himself, he remained still a long time, listening to the wind.

He was back working on the dancing angel when Barbara slipped away and loaded the children in the car. Mattie had wrapped up the rest of the cookies in foil and insisted they take them along. By the time they reached the paved road and turned toward home, the horizon was a bright orange line of flame that finally flickered and glowed, then died away. "Hurry up, burn yourself out," Barbara murmured, hoping that Sister Gertrude Kelly was right.

"Can you believe they let me off work for this? With pay. Professional enhancement, they call it." Lucie Laveau stared up at the dark wood interior of the old Dock Street

Theater. The upper boxes were filling with patrons as Lucie clutched Barbara's arm and reveled in her good fortune. "We have plenty of cultural stuff at home." She leaned close and whispered. "But this is real class. It even smells like history."

"There is something special about productions here," Barbara said, keeping her voice low as she located the row with their seats.

"I'll just be glad to be sitting awhile. I figure I've run off at least ten pounds today as it is," Lucie sighed, easing herself down into one of the cushioned seats. "Not that I can't spare the weight." She grinned, noting the close fit with the armrests. "But my ankles are rebelling. I need about twelve more hours in the day to keep up with all this. William took a nap this afternoon and missed the chamber music concert at the Methodist church."

"There's always another one." Barbara settled next to her. "That's the great thing about Spoleto. There's always something else coming up."

"So you say." Lucie fell silent a moment, watching the incoming crowd, then she nudged Barbara. "I've figured it out," she said, fanning herself with the program. "The reason there is so much scheduled for each day is so nobody can get to it all. You get so frustrated you just have to come back next year. It's a plot." She nodded. "A very effective plot."

"Does this mean I should start booking tickets ahead?"

"You might as well. We'll all be back." Lucie flapped her hands. "Look at those two." She tilted her head toward Rob and William Weizmann, who were standing down front at one side of the theater orchestra section, staring up at the boxes one moment, then occasionally glancing down at the black-clad musicians setting up in the orchestra pit. "William just eats this up—oldest theater in America, great music, marvelous performances. And the food is wonderful. And we haven't seen inside that new place, the Moffatt House, yet, the one your husband designed."

"That's tomorrow night," Barbara answered a bit uneasily. She had sent Rob some photos Louis took at the opening a few weeks earlier, but she wasn't really looking forward to going back there.

"From what I could tell, it's very avant. Rob would love to get his hands on that place. With a little luck, he just may do that."

"We'll see." Barbara rolled her program into a tight cylinder and tapped it against her palm, still watching the two men. Monday would be the last step in the selection process. During the Spoleto festivities, the College had invited three teacher-artists, Rob included, to come to the campus for a final evaluation. This time, each one would instruct an upper-level class in the theater department while the senior staff observed from the back of the lecture hall.

"I'd faint," Barbara had gasped when Rob phoned and told her the final screening procedure.

He had simply chuckled. "I've done the same kind of lecture for thirty. I can do it for three hundred. They know it's not a normal class atmosphere," he said, sounding unflappable. "The search committee wants to get a feel for how we hold up with real students, which is a valid point. Anyhow, now they'll be paying my fare to Charleston. I get to see you and the kids. I'll have Lucie and Williams and Abrams to show around town. How can I lose? We may even get a few minutes to ourselves."

So far, those few minutes hadn't happened. They'd been ricocheting from one event to the other, squeezing in dinners and sightseeing in between. When the house lights dimmed, Barbara glanced over the rapidly filling seats. Rob and William barely reached their places as the overture began.

"I just love this," Lucie whispered. "Something about the sudden surge of music and the tension before the curtain opens always thrills me."

"I know what you mean." Barbara sat slightly forward on the seat, anxious for the production to carry her away with its magic. When the house lights went off, Rob reached over and rested his hand on her shoulder. But he didn't draw her back, like T.J. would have. He simply made contact.

For forty minutes, the comic opera proceeded rapid-fire from scene to scene and song to song, without a break. Then came intermission, and the final act went on. The actors in period costumes danced and strolled across the stage, sometimes romantic, occasionally outrageous. Barbara tried to keep her mind totally occupied with the show before her, but she couldn't. The recollection of the shattered light at Moffatt House Theater kept nagging at her. She dreaded having to sit through another production there. Worrying her way through the preview at the opening had been tense enough. But as Luster said, she mustn't give an inch and she mustn't back down. She kept remembering how his hands moved while they talked and how the wood chips flew as that angel stepped out of the twisted cypress stump before her eyes.

"Barbara?" Rob touched her hand when the production ended.

Suddenly she snapped back to the present.

"It was wonderful, wasn't it?" Lucie gushed.

"Absolutely," Barbara offered, confident that it had been whether she'd been paying attention or not.

"Terrific," Rob agreed, glancing at her curiously while the last of the enthusiastic applause was dying away. They remained in their seats while the rest of the audience, smiling and exuberant, rapidly filed into the aisles and left.

"Let me just take another quick look." Rob took a final stroll down toward the orchestra and stared into the pit.

"He wants to come here so bad even I can taste it," Lucie confided, wrapping one thick arm around Barbara's waist. "But in case you haven't noticed, he's a mighty laid-back contender, and I don't mean just for the job," she stressed. "He's a gem. But anybody who wants him will have to spell it out pretty clearly. You do know how to spell?" she added coyly.

"Lucie," William Weizmann cautioned her. "Leave the two of them to work this out on their own. Butt out, my dear," he commented with the faintest glimmer of a smile.

"I do love a man I can't intimidate," Lucie cackled good-naturedly.

The elegant old theater was almost empty. Some of the musicians who were still packing their instruments chatted with Rob while Barbara, Lucie, and William moved toward the back and watched from the rear. The curtains reopened with a soft swooshing sound and a whole new kind of magic took over. The stage crew began striking the set, rapidly transporting each prop and piece of scenery into the oblivion of stage left. Rob watched them a moment, then came strolling back up the aisle.

"That was great," he declared. "Really well done." He took Barbara's hand as they followed Lucie and William through the open lobby doors. "Thanks for tonight," he said simply.

"Well, the night is not over," Lucie insisted. "Now I've caught my second wind, there's a jazz performance at the Gourmetisserie just over on Market Street." She held aloft her tourist map of Charleston.

"Not for me there isn't," William replied.

"How about you young folks?" Lucie stood with her hands on her formidable hips. "Are you game?"

"I'm not very big on jazz," Barbara confessed.

Rob shook his head. He wasn't interested either.

"What duds," Lucie muttered. "You've got no sense of adventure."

"All right," William surrendered. "I can't let you go alone. Some young fellow might just sweep you off your feet."

"Not unless he's in damn good shape," Lucie replied with her deadpan delivery.

"You two just go on your way," William insisted. "Lucie and I will boogie till dawn and come home in a taxi." He hesitated and then winked. "That is, if I can still remember how to boogie."

"Just pretend you're lining up a putt," Lucie instructed him. "Only do it to the music and forget the golf club. See you folks later."

Arm in arm, Rob and Barbara strolled along Church Street past the tall-columned arcade of St. Philip's Church. Behind it, in the parking lot, her car sat off to one side.

DARK WINDOW

"Do you want to drive somewhere?" Barbara offered him her keys.

"Let's just sit," he declined. "I just want to watch you."

"Oh," Barbara said softly.

"Yeah, oh. I've been caught up watching everything else all day." Rob took the keys long enough to open the driver's door and let her slide in.

"Do you want to stop off somewhere for coffee or a drink?"

"No." Rob tugged his tie loose and stretched his legs. "In a minute you can drop me at the hotel. I need to turn in and think for awhile."

"You mean about the lecture?" Barbara guessed.

Rob shook his head. "Nope," he said impassively.

"Is something bothering you?"

He stared out the window for a few seconds. "You want to talk seriously?" Rob broke the silence in the car.

Barbara glanced at him uncertainly. "Sure."

"Maybe sitting here wasn't such a good idea. But it would be worse up in my hotel room. Being alone with you gets to me. On the phone, we can talk without a lot else going on. But I can't stay close to you too long without losing my perspective." His voice became soft. "I keep wanting to touch you. Even when I look away, I keep seeing your face . . ." He didn't have to finish.

"It's not easy trying to know what to say to you right now," she said. "So much is up in the air." She'd been trying to think of a way to tell him that she didn't want to go to the Moffatt Theater without going into the light-crashing story. But she didn't want to do anything that might be misunderstood.

"You've had something on your mind all night," he said cautiously. "If you're building up to the let's-be-friends speech, I don't need it. I'm already your friend. If I've done anything to make you uncomfortable, just say so. I'll stop."

"It's not like that at all," she spoke up, realizing he had misread her preoccupation and her uneasiness. "I feel very comfortable with you. And I don't want whatever is going on between us to stop."

"You better think that one through, and you'd better be damned sure you know what you want." His voice was edged with control.

Barbara turned in the seat and looked at him. "I know I don't just want to be friends."

"Then the question is, what do you want to be? I may have been easy on New Year's." Rob forced a smile, "But that was for all the times I loved you and didn't dare to touch you, much less hold onto you. You wanted me then with no strings attached, and that somehow ended something," he spoke evenly. "But it also shook loose a lot. After you left, I dusted off the old memories and shoved a lot of new feelings on the same shelf. Side by side, they made me feel like I've been operating with part of me in neutral," he confessed.

"I let you go after New Year's because I wanted you to get through this recovery period without my interference," he continued. "I wanted you to look around and figure out you want me. I also wanted to hold you and protect you and become indispensable to you, but that was T.J.'s style, not mine. At night I'd close my eyes and I'd see your face," he spoke in a low voice. "Your grownup face, not the one I'd kept in my head for years. It's a whole new story now. Strings exist," he said, shrugging, "and time is precious. Trying to put this in words is scary as hell."

"I know." Barbara forced herself to speak.

"We'll be buddies if you want. But if you reach for me once more as a lover, it had better be for keeps," Rob stressed. "And it had better be this me that you want. I'm not a struggling student anymore. I think I'd be good for you now. I've done some good work. I've got good friends. I've fallen in love once or twice along the way. I'm making money doing what I love to do. I can live with what I've got," he admitted. "And I can be content. At least, I think I can. But I have this feeling that whatever we are or we were to each other is nothing compared to what we can be. I don't dabble in peoples' lives. I don't take making love lightly. If there's a next time with us, I won't let you go again."

Barbara sat very still, staring down at her clasped

hands. Apparently Rob had been doing some soul searching, too. Now she began to understand why he had opted not to stay in the house with the kids and her this visit. He was drawing some lines of his own, keeping his distance until they knew where they stood.

"We can play it safe," he spoke gently, "and leave things as they are. But if you want more," he insisted as he reached out and brushed away a curl that had fallen forward across her cheek, "it's all or nothing. It's the rest of our lives—you, me, and the two short people."

Barbara smiled and blinked back the beginning tears. In the cosmic scheme of things, her concerns about going to the Moffatt Theater no longer seemed crucial. "I didn't think I had to make that kind of a decision now."

"You don't have to make it tonight. But you'll have to make it sooner or later. How about when this college job is all settled, whether I get it or not, we'll take a breather? I'll take you and the kids off for a quiet, uninterrupted vacation somewhere," Rob stated. "You can look things over, question me at great length, and see what you want to do about the next forty or fifty years of your life. Then we'll negotiate," he suggested.

"That sound's fair," Barbara agreed, recalling what Lucie had said. If she wanted him, she'd have to spell it out.

"Until then, make it easy on me and don't look at me when you laugh at my jokes." He slid his hand softly against her cheek. "And don't smell good." He pulled her toward him. "And don't taste salty when I kiss you." He brushed his lips over hers. "Don't reach for me." He caught her hand before it touched his chest. She could feel him tremble. "Don't touch unless you're ready to hang onto me forever. Right now, there's too much festival around. We're all dressed up with lots of places to go. Things look rosy. Lots of excitement. Wait until things settle back to normal."

Barbara slowly pulled her hand back toward her.

"I've got to go. I think I'll walk from here." Rob reached for the passenger door handle. "My mind has been thrashing away all night." Suddenly he grew still and serious and he stared at her intently. "I can settle for phone calls and visits and even teaching in the same town. But I want it all," he said earnestly. "You, Eliot, Miranda, even T.J. The whole grab bag," he stressed. "We won't be leaving anything behind. It all goes," he emphasized. "Including whatever loose ends you may have trailing along after you."

"There are a few of them," Barbara admitted as he slid out and closed the door behind him. He waved and pointed to the seatbelt. Then he stood in the light from the street lights, watching her as she drove off. He was letting her go, but this time, they knew it wasn't for long.

CHAPTER 12

What we call the beginning is often the end
And to make an end is to make a beginning.
The end is where we start from.
                                    T. S. Eliot

"How does *Sweeney Todd* sound for a season opener? Do you think Charleston is ready for a bit of semimorbid musical comedy?" Rob asked, beginning his phone call abruptly. "Then to show we have a little diversity, I could opt for something intense and cerebral, like *The Shadow Box*."

"You got the job." Barbara dropped her purse and schoolbooks on the kitchen counter and slipped off her shoes.

"I sure did. Not bad for a country boy."

"You're no country boy. Congratulations. I'm so thrilled they came through. You must be relieved."

"It's nice to have it settled. I think I'll hurry out to buy an ascot," Rob joked. "Maybe a cigarette holder."

"You're probably the only man I know who could wear an ascot and not look like a fool," Barbara commented. "But you'd be a little overdressed for this campus."

"I could fly up and split a bottle of champagne with you," he suggested. "We should do something to celebrate. They called me at two-thirty today. I've been pacing around waiting for you to get home from school so you could answer your damn phone."

"It was a teachers' workday at school," Barbara explained. "You know—the usual faculty meeting and nearing-the-end-of-the-year departmental conferences. The kids had the day off. They spent it in the Belcazzios' pool."

"Are they around?"

"I told them to be here for dinner. That's not for half an hour. Sorry," she apologized. "I'll tell them the good news," she promised. "They'll be so excited." There was a brief silence on Rob's end of the phone. "Would you rather tell them yourself?" Only ten days before, Miranda had spent the evening after Rob's teaching demonstration sitting on his knee possessively while he gave a blow-by-blow report on the session.

Eliot had been equally inquisitive about the lecture at the College. "Did you get to sing for them?" he'd asked during Rob's account.

"I didn't get to sing this time," Rob replied, shrugging. "It would be a little difficult to work a song into a class on the difference between realism and believability. I think I'd be stretching the believability part."

"Did they applaud when you finished?" Eliot persisted.

"No. Do you applaud when your teacher finishes talking?" Rob patiently reversed the question.

"Sometimes I'd like to," Eliot replied with a grin. "Only because it means I can do something besides listen to her talk."

"I've felt that way myself occasionally," Rob admitted. "These guys didn't applaud, but they smiled a lot. And they hung around and asked questions."

"If they smiled, that's good, isn't it?" Miranda offered. "I don't smile unless the teacher is funny."

"I suppose that's something," Eliot conceded. "But you really sing good."

"The screening committee knows all about my singing. They've also seen the sets I've done and a lot else. This is just another part of what I do. If it all adds up, they'll call me. They're making their decision sometime next week."

"Why does it take so long?" Miranda asked, obviously impatient.

"They've got a lot to consider."

"It wouldn't take me that long." Eliot pushed his glasses up and strolled off to watch TV.

When it was time to drive Rob to the airport, Miranda had squeezed between him and her mother in the front seat, holding his hand as Barbara drove. When they called his flight, she teared up and hugged Rob's neck. Eliot stood back a pace and shook Rob's hand. Now that he was ten, he didn't like to hug in public. But he did shake Rob's hand a little slower and a little longer than usual. And he did say, "Break a leg," like Rob told him theater people did for luck.

"If you want to tell the kids yourself, I'll have them call you tonight," Barbara suggested. "As soon as they get in."

"You can tell them," Rob finally replied. "If I were there and could see their faces, I'd like to do it myself," he admitted. "But I'm not, so you go ahead and tell them. Then take them out for ice cream or something to celebrate on your end." The touch of melancholy in his voice distressed her.

"Have you told Lucie or William?"

"I told Lucie, all right," he replied. "I'd have thought you could hear her hooting all the way up there. I called her in between my pacing and phoning you. She offered to take me out for a victory dinner." He was sounding considerably more cheerful. "Speaking of celebrating, have you decided where we're going?"

"Is that a philosophical question about the future," Barbara asked, kidding him, "or are you talking about our mutual vacation?"

"Let's pick the destination first," he suggested. "Once we're there, we can discuss philosophy without this long-distance business getting in the way. What's it going to be?" He'd suggested Bermuda. Eliot liked the idea of going to the Keys. Miranda wanted to go to the Bahamas. Her dad had promised to take her there, or so she'd said at first.

"Actually, he didn't quite promise," Miranda later admitted. "He said he'd like to take me and Eliot. He said maybe one day." Miranda puffed out her lips in her typical pout. "He said I could see his pavilion." She still had the snapshot of the white gingerbread gazebo that T.J. designed for the resort in Eleuthera.

"We're still undecided," Barbara told Rob. "I'm sort of abstaining," she ackowledged. The Bahamas, specifically Eleuthera, had been their special place, hers and T.J.'s. Going to Eleuthera would mean entering into another world, one filled with beautiful memories of babies and romance and life beginning.

"I'll give you till the weekend to decide." Rob tried to speed things up. "I've got to tie up all my loose ends here. Then I need to start looking for a place to live up your way. I also have to find somewhere to ship my semiprecious belongings. Would you mind storing a few paintings and prints of mine in your house for a while? They're the only things I really need to be concerned about."

"Sure. Send them up." She remembered the bright, dramatic artwork she'd seen in Rob's home, most of it having to do with the theatrical scenes or performers. "I could put a few hooks up and hang them. They'd be safest that way."

"You're sure you wouldn't mind?"

"It would be fun," Barbara insisted. Hanging anything on the walls, even temporarily, would change the character of the place. T.J. had never wanted the walls cluttered with anything extraneous. The setting and the design of the house was to be artistry enough. He selected beautiful paneling and exquisite shelving for books. He allowed for wide expanses of windows. The stained glass windows were for color and light. But no paintings. "I kind of like the idea of seeing your art collection again," Barbara told Rob now. She looked around and smiled at the prospect of walls full of color. "They're welcome whenever you can get them up here."

"It will take a few days to get them crated. In the meantime, work on this vacation business. We all can celebrate the new job and school ending, among other things. Let's get together on this."

"I'll hold a conference with the short people," Barbara promised, using his terminology. "We'll work out a compromise of some sort."

"Compromises don't do too well," Rob said pointedly. "Pick out a place that someone really wants," he insisted. "No compromise. We'll all simply agree to that place. The next time, we'll pick a place that someone else really wants to go to. That way, someone is deliriously thrilled each time, and the rest of us are sure that our time is coming. A compromise doesn't leave anyone thrilled."

"So we're going for a one-thrill minimum." Barbara nodded. "I'll work on it."

"I'll call you Sunday."

"Congratulations again," Barbara said hurriedly before she hung up.

"Thanks. And tell the kids they can still call. Just in case they want to talk." There was that undercurrent of wistfulness again.

"I'm sure they'll want to talk."

"Good. I miss them."

"I must have left it open." Barbara turned the car around and backed it toward the open garage. Saturday morning was clean-up time. She'd planned on reorganizing the shelves to make room for whatever Rob was sending. It seemed sensible to sort through and repack a number of things of her own at the same time. "Go ahead and unload the boxes," she told the kids. She'd driven them down to the shopping center to find sturdy empty cartons and packing tape and had forgotten to hit the remote button to drop the garage door.

"We weren't gone that long," Eliot sounded unconcerned.

"Just don't tell Louis I forgot to close it. He'd get all flustered. And help me with the groceries." She handed him a bag before he got away. The box-hunting expedition had evolved into a two-bag supermarket excursion as well.

"Here comes Mr. Johns." Miranda leaped out her door and stood waving at the old pickup heading in the driveway.

"Groceries," Barbara reminded her, giving her the milk and eggs. "Let's get all this in the refrigerator before we get sidetracked. Call Kent and remind him that we need him."

"He's already here." Miranda spotted Kent's car coming in behind Luster's truck.

"Good. We'll get everything done at once."

When she came out again, Kent and Eliot had all the

empty cartons stacked up on the driveway. Kent was bent over, struggling in the trunk of his car, unloading a crate of school materials that she'd asked him to bring home for her to store over the summer. For the students, school was over for the year. For the teachers, there were two more days after the weekend.

Barbara didn't notice that the boxes of glass were missing until she started in on that end of the garage.

"Did you move those boxes of stained glass?" she asked Kent when he came in with one box of books. "Three of them. They were pretty heavy." She tilted her head toward the empty spot. "One had a lot of little pieces?" She looked around to see if they were nearby.

"Beats me." He shrugged. "I think they were here when I ran the mower in last week." He stacked the books he was carrying on the shelf next to some *Farmer's Almanacs*. Then he helped Eliot slide the box he'd hauled in onto a shelf closer to the floor.

"Maybe Mr. Belcazzio did something with them," Eliot suggested.

"Other than him and Mr. McMillan, I don't think anyone else knew about them." Kent shook his head in bewilderment.

"I'll ask Louis about them later. I sure hope he didn't decide to throw them out altogether." She remembered he had steered her away from them when he came to warn her about the gas thefts. "I thought he knew they were too valuable to trash." She started sliding some other boxes into the center of the garage floor.

"But they were broken pieces, weren't they?" Kent picked up a split sack of fertilizer and ran some packing tape over the rip in its side.

"You don't throw out pieces." Barbara took another quick inventory of the room. "They're always good for making something, petals for hanging ornaments or berries or leaves. I was thinking of teaching the kids how to make some sun-catchers over the summer. If they like doing it, I could turn them loose on little panels with lollypops or bubbles or balloons or something." She glanced across the yard where Luster and Miranda were unloading a few flats of daisies.

"Mrs. A.?"

Something in Kent's tone made her turn suddenly.

"Did you move the gas can?" He was holding up one edge of the tarp they used to cover the mower. "It was over by the door."

"Is it gone?" Barbara grimaced.

"Unless someone moved it."

"Louis told me kids were stealing gas."

"Maybe someone ripped it off."

"Along with three boxes of broken glass?"

"Looks that way." Kent pulled out the mower and checked behind it. "You want me to call the police?"

Barbara stood a moment with her hands on her hips. "I don't think there's anything they can do about it now, other than tell me I should close the garage door. Louis already told me that." She flung up her arms in resignation. "So I blew it. Maybe it's just as well. Let's just get on with this. I'll get a new gas can on my next run." She refused to let anything get them off track. Working steadily, they shifted and repacked, until there was an entire wall clear to stack whatever crates or boxes Rob was sending ahead.

"Mr. Johns said to tell you we've got all the plants in." Miranda came to give her report. "He wants you to come and look."

"Maybe I should see if he wants me to start the sprinklers." Kent followed them out. "The whole place could use watering." He poked his toe into the dry grass.

"We wet the holes we put the flowers in, but Mr. Johns says we have to wait until after dark to soak them good." Miranda turned and skipped on ahead of them.

"We're under water restrictions," Barbara reminded Kent. Charleston was suffering a temporary drought and the city officials had asked residents to water only on alternate days to conserve the water supply.

"But that's only for city water. The sprinklers are on your well."

Barbara shrugged. "Luster says it's nature's water and it isn't ours to waste. He doesn't want the sprinklers running unnecessarily, especially in full sunlight when some of the water just burns off in the heat."

"Okay, wait." Kent surrendered. "But it sure is dry." He cast a concerned eye over the wide, rolling yard. "I hope they had the lid tight on the gas can, and I hope they kept going once they got it."

"Maybe we should take a look around," Barbara suggested, her gaze following his. "Louis said the ones who took his gas left cigarette butts on his dock."

"Maybe you'd better mention that to Mr. Johns," Kent suggested. "It might be smart to get everything washed down."

"I just wonder what they'd want with my glass." She stared off toward the marsh, remembering Louis had thought they'd come into his house by boat. "I hope they didn't decide it was too heavy and pitch it in the river."

"Jerks," Kent mumbled.

Luster had rubbed his chin and pursed his lips when Barbara told him what had happened. "Gasoline. Best look around," he suggested. They'd all split up and scouted the area looking for anything the thieves may have left behind. Luster walked the edge of the marsh grass and found a place that looked like someone had pulled a jetski ashore.

"Probably nothin' to worry about. They sure couldn't carry much. They probably filled it up, ditched the can, and took off." But he agreed that putting the sprinklers on for half an hour in daylight was a reasonable precaution. While the set-in heads sprayed their circle and wedges of mist over the inner yard, Luster and Kent ran hoses and moveable sprinklers to douse the outer areas.

"After dark, you soak it good," Luster told Barbara when he loaded up to go. Then he took the back route, the old construction trail, driving between the buffer ridges, checking to see if the boxes of glass had been abandoned somewhere along the way. When he didn't come back, Barbara knew he hadn't found them.

Barbara called Karen when the kids were in the treefort midway up Byron, eating lunch. "Karen, do you know if Louis moved the boxes of glass out of my garage? You know—all the broken stuff? I don't want him to know what a dumb thing I did, but I left the garage door open. All three boxes are gone." She told her friend about the gas can as well.

"I think he would have told me if he'd done something with them. Do you want me to ask him? He's out working on the boat."

"Don't ask. Just drop a few casual hints," Barbara suggested. "Maybe he'll say something about it. I really don't want him worrying about what I did. If he hears I forgot the door once, he'll run himself ragged coming by to check all the time."

"He would do that," Karen admitted.

"Just see what you can find out. And I won't leave the door open again, I promise."

"If you do . . ."

"I won't. I'm going to be storing some of Rob's things there. I wouldn't dare let anything happen."

"Good point. I'll snoop. I'll let you know."

Barbara stood in the kitchen after the phone call, sipping her coffee and watching the kids finishing their sandwiches in the tree-fort. They had stripped off the breadcrusts and were pitching them to the squirrels and birds.

"I could use a little help with the laundry," she called to them. "Come on down." Eliot put all the cups and plates in the pulley-bucket and lowered it to the ground. Then he and Miranda came down the nailed-on steps.

"Will one of you pick up the mail? I forgot to check the box today." Both of the youngsters wheeled around and raced off toward the wood-framed mailbox at the entrance to the driveway. Eliot got there first, grabbing the handful of envelopes, holding them high above his head, and leaping back toward the house, accompanied by the high-pitched protests of his sister.

"Let's see what we got." Barbara concentrated on the mail and refused to get into the dispute about who was supposed to carry what. She spread out the items on the kitchen counter, putting aside the ones that looked like bills.

Seacoast Travel. The return address on the large business envelope caught her attention instantly. She'd booked all her travel through Seacoast for years, and so lately had Rob. "I think Rob is trying to give us a little prodding," Barbara said, ripping open the packet. Inside were travel brochures for the Out Islands—the Abacos, Bimini, San Salvador, Andros . . . and Eleuthera. The Bahamas. The enclosed computer letter requested prompt confirmation of reservations made for the second week of June. Stunned, Barbara turned the envelope over. Her lips tensed into a thin line. The name on the address portion was Mr. T.J. Ashcroft.

"See," Miranda squealed. "I told you that we were going to the Bahamas. I told you Daddy said we were going." She clutched a color pamphlet in her hand, riffling through the pages, scanning the bright pictures of the golf courses and sailboats and beachside resorts.

"Accommodations for four." Barbara read that flight and hotel arrangements had been made for two adults, two children. In three weeks it would be June twelfth, their eleventh anniversary, precisely the date reserved. T.J. had asked her if she wanted to spend their next anniversary in Eleuthera. They'd agreed on it the night that he died. But it would have been just like him—methodical, efficient, and sure of himself—to set it up even before he mentioned it to her, knowing how much she loved the island.

A cottage. Three bedrooms. The kids would have had separate rooms. So would they. He'd seen to it that they'd have some privacy. Part of the venture would be romantic and exclusive, like it had been before. "So we really were going," she said softly, "all of us."

"You mean we aren't going now?" Eliot demanded indignantly. He clutched one open brochure in his hand.

"I thought you wanted to go to the Keys?" Barbara avoided a direct answer.

"I did." Eliot shrugged. "But this is okay." He looked back at the picture of a pinkish beach with the surf fisherman standing knee-deep in the water.

"Daddy said we could go one day," Miranda pleaded. "Mother." She duplicated Eliot's distressed tone. "Pulleeese . . . can we go?"

Barbara felt the color draining from her cheeks as the aftershock set in. Dark and disquieting thoughts started tugging at her. Harden your heart. Luster had cautioned her about special times and special places. "Let me do some checking first." Her voice faded to little more than a whisper. "You two go and get your laundry together." She waved them out of the room. "Give me a little time to think about this."

For once, Eliot and Miranda cooperated without comment, both of them wheeling around and heading off toward the bedrooms. The brochures with the perfect smiling faces and scenic locales lay open across the counter. Barbara picked them up one by one, still clutching the travel agency memorandum in one hand. Then she poured herself a cup of coffee and walked stonily to the corner nook. She looked out at Keats. "What do you make of this?"

For a long time she pored over the pictures, noting the new developments that had been constructed since the last time she had been there. One large multistoried hotel loomed above the tropical vegetation, like a concrete wedge with balconies that had landed there accidentally. "T.J. would have hated that one," Barbara thought. He preferred buildings that settled into their surroundings, ones that looked like they belonged. Then she slid out the next brochure, the one for the Wellesley that he'd thought to book a year ahead. Nestled on the hillside, stair-stepped amid the lush green surroundings, were the whitewashed cottages where she and T.J. had stayed, each with its own porch and water view. In another shot, on the rise overlooking the harbor, the white gingerbread pavilion T.J. had restored sat timeless and elegant, with the island spreading out on all sides and the bright blue sky above.

"We have to go." Barbara brushed aside a tear that had dropped silently onto the slick paper. "I don't want to give this up. It was mine, too." A deep ache within her was the only confirmation she needed. "We have to go there," she repeated as the images blurred before her eyes. "I have to see it all again and say goodbye. And I have to make it mine." While more slow tears inched down her cheek, she reread the letter. She could hear the whispering in the hallway as the children tiptoed close.

"Are you okay, Mom?" Eliot called without coming in.

"I'm okay." Her voice sounded shakier than she would have liked.

More whispering. "We've almost got all our laundry together." He hesitated.

"Call us when you want us," Miranda said, peeking in at her. Then discreetly the two youngsters went away. They figured Momma was crying. It was all right. They couldn't quite understand her sorrow, but they would give her a few more minutes to think.

"Okay." Barbara slid all the brochures into a neat stack. She checked the number she was supposed to call to confirm. "Two thrilled minimums, coming up. Potentially more," she declared as she headed for the phone. Tomorrow, when Rob called to get their destination set, it would be easier to talk about. By then, she'd have it all thought through.

The label on the largest of the crates said "DO NOT OPEN UNTIL AUTHORIZED." Barbara was on her third load of laundry when it arrived. It was marked "FRAGILE" addressed to her, with Rob as sender, but unlike the two other crates of his prized objets d'art, this one had been shipped locally. Stenciled on the edge was HANDLE WITH CARE.

"I'll waste away from curiosity," Barbara groaned, but she didn't open it. She just showed the fellow with the hand truck where to put it. She still had her bags to pack and a list of last-minute chores to do before morning. The flight to the Bahamas left at dawn.

"Do you really think two bathing suits will be enough?" Miranda asked, bursting in to plead her case another time. "Can't I get just one more?"

"You can wear one while the other is drying," Barbara answered in a matter-of-fact tone. "Besides, there are stores in the Bahamas. If we get really desperate, we can pick up another one there. Maybe something totally different."

Miranda wandered off down the hallway contentedly, while Barbara concentrated on shifting a load of wet clothes into the dryer.

"I can only find one sandal," Eliot said as he came meandering into the laundry room.

"Then you'll have to hop," Barbara replied without cracking a smile.

"I'll look under my bed."

"Do people in the Bahamas play with dolls?" Miranda came back with one doll in each arm.

"All children play with dolls. Children on Eleuthera included. But only take one."

"Can I take the fishing pole Grampa and Gramma gave me for my birthday?" Eliot asked.

"It might be a little awkward on the plane."

"How about my telescope?"

"No. The pavilion has telescopes." Barbara shoved a load of clothes into the washer.

"Will I need a coloring book on the plane?" Miranda had apparently moved on to packing her in-flight entertainment.

"It would be nice to have one, just in case you get bored." Barbara leaned against the doorway. Miranda had withdrawn to the den to inventory her coloring book collection. Eliot was nowhere to be seen.

"I found it," Eliot spoke from behind the refrigerator. "My sandal." He held it up. "I found it."

"By the refrigerator?"

"I was thirsty. Hey, Miranda, you want some juice?" he yelled.

"Yes, please," came the reply.

Barbara gave her son a sidelong glance. "You said to be charming," Eliot said stiffly. "So I'm being charming."

"I'm thrilled." The beep of the dryer called her away.

"We'll look after all your plants," Karen Belcazzio promised, strolling toward the airport check-in desk with Barbara the next morning.

"Kent will cut the grass if it needs it. Mr. Johns said he'd come by and look over the place." Barbara had checked off every detail on every list she'd made the past week.

"Louis will pick up the mail every day. Everything will be fine," Karen insisted.

Louis had the two kids and a couple of suitcases and was already at the Delta luggage check-in desk. "I'll have my new boat dock finished by the time you get back," he told the kids. "You can come down and fish off it."

"What about your boat?" Miranda reminded him. "Will we get to try your new boat?" Louis had finally yielded to a lifelong urge and purchased a high powered skiboat. He'd amused them by saying his bass boat was getting a large roommate.

"All he needs is a driver," Karen joked. "It finally occurred to him that he can't drive and ski at the same time, and he certainly doesn't trust me at the wheel."

"At the helm," he said gently. "I just don't want to be out behind on a rope while she's up front sightseeing. I was thinking of recruiting Tom Palmer. You know, hands of a surgeon. Respect for pain," Louis explained with a grin. "We may have something worked out by the time you guys get back."

"Momma knows how to sail," Eliot announced. "You could teach her to steer." Barbara was already shaking her head no.

"It's been a long time," she stated. "And we're talking windpower, not twin engines. I'd probably drown us all. Besides, I don't like the noise. I like the sound of the wind."

"There should be lots of wind in the Bahamas." Karen nudged her friend. "You and Rob should go out sailing. It would put you off shore, out of range of big ears and big eyes," she stressed, "if you two should want a little time alone."

"I'll keep it in mind," Barbara replied without conviction. Besides the overall plan for all of them to play tourist together, Eliot had already asked her to surf fish with him. Miranda wanted to snorkel. Rob wanted to be with her just to relax. Somewhere in the five days they'd be gone, she had to make some time for herself. She had a few things she wanted to do on her own.

When the airplane took off, Barbara felt a slow but unmistakable wave of relief. Eliot and Miranda were across the aisle with juice and peanuts, both by a window, belted in their seats. Whatever hadn't made it into the luggage and onto the plane wasn't her concern anymore. They'd get along with whatever they had. They'd switch planes in a brief stopover in Atlanta, then they'd continue on to Lauderdale, where Rob would join them for the flight to the Bahamas. Until they touched down, she was off duty.

By the time she'd finished her first cup of airline coffee and they'd risen above the clouds, all she could see was an unreal landscape of puffy white drenched in the bright morning sun. Somewhere ahead was Atlanta. Farther east was Eleuthera. In the brochures it said the word itself meant freedom. Barbara peered toward the horizon. A new sense of excitement began to build. Everything was beginning to come together.

When she told Gwen Henderson what she planned to do, Gwen had seen a certain wisdom in the act. They had talked about the function of ritual. "Sometimes an outward procedure helps us act out and resolve some very complicated issues," she said. "Like letting go. And beginning something new. Funerals often aren't enough. They're too quick, too soon. We're in shock."

Barbara had nodded, recalling that she'd made it through T.J.'s funeral feeling numb. But she brought along his wedding band and hers. She'd left the diamond in the jewelry box, perhaps to be reset one day.

"You said there were changes in Eleuthera, new resorts going up, old ones being redone. You've made changes too," Gwen had noted, her gray eyes gentle and sympathetic. "You'll feel some tugs at the old heartstrings. But you'll feel that difference. Besides, it's a beautiful place to unwind. You've had a heck of a year. This may be an excellent time to bring it full circle and gain a sense of closure."

Gwen also said that sometimes a pilgrimage like hers would make the transition between the loss and the healing more tangible. The past simply wouldn't be there. Since Rob would be going with them, he would also help her make that separation more real, without totally losing a sense of continuity.

But now it occurred to her that maybe this journey

was not her mission alone. Spending their anniversary in Eleuthera had been T.J.'s idea all along. Even before his death. Maybe it still was. Maybe this was the unfinished business Luster had mentioned. Gradually the sense of anticipation that had been building all week was supplanted by a growing uneasiness she could not explain. Details that had not connected before began realigning themselves in new patterns. Sentimental times. Special places. Loose ends. "Now don't start getting yourself crazy," Barbara insisted, calming herself.

Throughout the past year, she'd come to accept this presence, this lingering aspect of T.J., as a given, a quirk of nature that didn't just happen in folklore or mysticism or poetry. There were people who knew, ones who suspended disbelief, and simply accepted. Luster Johns had quietly acknowledged that there were forces beyond understanding, realities that ran over into one another. And he helped protect her with some simple rituals that had been passed on from conjur woman to conjur woman for years. But because there were others who did not know and wouldn't understand, she had to learn to keep up the balancing act between two worlds. She dealt with Gwen Henderson on the issues they could talk about, and turned to Luster Johns and Sister Gertrude on the darker side that extended into the surreal.

She had tried appeasing and making bargains with this presence, as she had accommodated and pleased others all her life. Then Luster taught her to stand her ground, to harden her heart. Gwen helped her see the trap she'd built herself, and she had changed. But some part of her still needed to hang on to a past that may never have been quite as wonderful as she recalled it, just as the children needed to see Eleuthera and feel the beauty there. The island would make some things tangible. They'd have the beaches and surf and beautiful views and a lookout post that T.J. had resurrected. And they would have a sense of him again.

As the plane banked, the sunlight glinted off the wing tip of the aircraft, sending a too-bright shaft of light ricocheting in. Barbara reached up and pulled down the shade. Almost instantly the gesture brought back the image of the caramel glass, poised motionless before it crashed forward and slashed her hands. She had seen T.J.'s face that night. She had smelled the Dhatri. He had been there. A warning. She'd tried to believe that was all it was. A prank that went too far and became an accident. She rubbed her thumb over the slight ridge beneath her hand.

There had been that moment in the new theater, when she'd sat frozen, staring at the heavy spotlight that had plummeted to her side. She thought then how easily he could have moved it a fraction and taken her life away. A touch to the left and he could have made her cross over. Unless that act was beyond his power. Perhaps, like the glass incident, it hadn't been a warning or an accident, but an invitation, like the tickets and the reservations.

"An invitation to do what?" Barbara closed her eyes tightly, determined to stay calm. Eleuthera. Free. The word had always brought her a feeling of peace. Freedom was something all of them needed. Freedom and closure. A line between yesterday and tomorrow. If T.J. could be at the house and the theater, it was possible he would be there, waiting. He had created another window in time. "He wouldn't want anything to happen to me." She dismissed the ominous thoughts that had crept out from the recesses of her brain. "He only wants us to be happy."

There was the promise of liberation for all of them on the island. "We're coming." She raised her chin confidently. Even there, she wouldn't give an inch, she wouldn't back down. Without formulating any more questions, she knew that Eleuthera held the answers that would set her free.

CHAPTER 13

> The one remains, the many change and pass
> Heaven's light forever shines, Earth's shadows fly:
> Life, like a dome of many-colored glass
> Stains the white radiance of Eternity.
> *Shelley "Adonais"*

THE BRIGHT MIDDAY sun sparkled upon the surface of the horseshoe-shaped opening of Harbor Island at Eleuthera's northernmost end. Barbara stood at the window, looking down over the marina toward the point. Just beyond it was the three-mile strip of pinkish sand where she and T.J. had once sprawled out, selecting names for their unborn children. "Well?" she said expectantly. "I'm here and I'm still waiting."

She had taken the children to all the special places and sat with them on the warm sand, telling them of their beginnings on this island filled with sunshine. Miranda had ridden on Rob's shoulders as they had climbed the hilltop to the Victorian-style gazebo, now an observation pavilion with glass panels in its roof so land and sea and sky could be contemplated from the same vantage point. She had gone back there alone in the moonlight, hoping that somehow she would feel a shift. She'd even spoken his name aloud and said goodbye. Still, she felt as if whatever was to happen there, whatever release she was expecting, had not come.

The sudden rap at the door didn't startle her. She crossed the room and opened the door.

"What do you think?" Rob stood back while Miranda paraded in, modeling the new swimsuit they'd just bought.

"I think it's definitely native. Very nice."

"Good. How about this? Will I make it as a deckhand?" Rob opened the bag he was carrying and tried on his purchases. He'd managed to acquire a nautical-looking peaked cap and wide-lensed sunglasses.

"I picked out the hat," Miranda informed her mother.

Barbara looked at him and shook her head. "You'll do just fine. I'm ready if you are."

The sailing venture had been Rob's idea. After two days of "family" outings and poolside relaxing, he had coaxed Barbara into tackling something a little precarious. "I remember years ago that you used to sail," he said, prodding her. "Let's take out a boat and try it. I've heard you never lose the hang of it. If you're game, you can even teach me."

Barbara had tried to think of some excuse for avoiding it. T.J. had been the one who really knew how to handle a boat. She'd been a reasonably competent crew as long as he gave directions. But Rob had persisted. "Take a chance," he had teased. "I don't care if you're good at it or not. Even if we just piddle around out there, we'll get come sun. Quit being so cautious."

The resort youth program had made the difference. A tall tanned young man named Blake, a Bahamian with one earring and a ponytail, had rounded up the kids at ten o'clock that morning and rattled off in a jeep with them for an outing. He brought them back for lunch to pick up swimsuits. They were having a pool party by the clubhouse for the preteen set. Both of Miranda's suits had conveniently disappeared, so Rob rushed her down to the hotel shop to find one suitable. Eliot had already changed and gone on ahead to help Blake set up.

"We've got the entire afternoon to do something ourselves." Rob's dark eyes sparkled mischievously. "So let's get physical. I've talked to the guy at the boat rental. He's got a whole line of sailboats rigged and ready."

"I'm not really sure about this," she confided while they walked out the marina ramp toward the sailboats. "T.J. was the one who knew what he was doing. I hope you can swim."

"Swim?" Rob acted mystified. "I thought my part in this had more to do with tightening ropes and calling out 'Land ho' or whatever." He kept a straight face.

"You can swim, can't you?" Barbara asked, realizing that she didn't know for sure. "Be honest."

"I'm an excellent floater." He finally relented and smiled. "Once in a while, I move my arms."

"Can you swim?" Barbara asked with a frown. She had stopped in the middle of the walkway and wouldn't budge until he assured her that he could.

"Yes, I can swim," he asserted. "However, in this case I'd prefer to stay aboard. You know, dry, non-salty, intact," he said with a grin.

"I'll do my best. But wear a life vest." Barbara continued on toward the boats. "You'd better listen very carefully to whatever this guy tells us before he sends us out on our own. It's been a long time." She emphasized her inexperience.

"It certainly has," Rob chuckled.

The old Bahamian on the dock issued them two vests and a sixteen-foot sailboat and briefly explained the rudiments of sailing. "Winds 'round here can be flukey. If you tip over a couple of times, you'll be doing 'bout average," he said calmly. "Everyone flounders around when they start out. Just stay with the boat, and try to keep inside the harbor until you've got a feeling for it," he advised. "If it capsizes, release the mainsail and stand on the centerboard to get it righted, or we'll send someone out to help you."

Rob dutifully concentrated while the fellow pointed out the lines and named the parts that should concern them—the mainsail and the working jib—then demonstrated their function.

"Did you get that?" Barbara asked, nudging her companion.

"Sure." Rob smiled noncommittally and pulled his peaked cap down a bit more in front, like the boat master's.

"The best way to learn is to get in and try it." The Bahamian seemed confident. "Should be fun. If you get wet, you can always dry off."

"Then let's give it a shot," Rob suggested. "I've got an up-to-date will."

"So have I." Barbara tried to match his good-humored tone.

"Does that have any particular significance?" Rob pointed up at the whirling wind gauge atop the boat master's shed.

"It means the wind is blowing," Barbara replied dryly. "Rather briskly at the moment," she noted. Abruptly both the wind and the movement of the wind gauge subsided. "I spoke too soon."

"It's been like that all morning," the fellow called out to them. Then he glanced out across the water. "Gusty. Then nothing. If it gets dangerous, we'll blow the horn and call everyone back to shore. If it falls off altogether, we'll come and get you."

"Not at all reassuring," Barbara said, keeping her voice low. She climbed aboard and moved to the back of the craft so she could operate the tiller and the large jib. "Sit near the mast, so I know where you are." She directed him to a safe location below the mainsail boom. "And don't laugh if I mess up," she warned him. "It takes a bit more coordination than I'm used to orchestrating."

"I would never laugh at you." Rob looked at her steadily. "Smile, perhaps, but not laugh."

"Put your vest on."

He did. "By the way, shouldn't we have brought a bottle of champagne and a couple of glasses?" Rob settled in. "They do it on television."

"They do a lot of things on television that I wouldn't try in a boat."

"They're probably on a sound stage." Rob was trying to bend his legs so they'd fit without getting in the way. "And they probably don't even like each other." He ended with a preoccupied note.

"What happened to the bright-eyed romantic from days of yore?" Barbara teased him.

"He's still here," Rob insisted. "He's just had a few bouts with the real world." There was no bitterness in his voice, only a slightly exasperated quality that had to do more with his seating arrangements than his philosophy. "We'll have champagne when we get back," he promised.

Barbara adjusted the sail and tiller. "Okay. Keep your head down." The small sailboat inched off from the dock. Barbara slackened up on the rope. Instantly the boat skimmed out past the other rentals moored in the marina, then veered left, straight for the clear water in the middle of the harbor, precisely where she had intended for it to go. "Some of this is luck," she admitted, letting the wind out of the sail so they could drift a bit.

"Just tell me what you want me to do," Rob offered, clutching the sides of the craft but keeping his head down like she'd asked.

"Putting aside the jargon, you simply try to turn the sail so it catches the wind."

"What if the wind gusts like the guy back there said?" he asked diligently.

"Either you let the sail loose so the air spills out, or you steer and go like crazy, or you tip. I'd prefer one of the first two."

"So how do we go that way?" Rob pointed farther out. "And what do you want me to do?"

"For now, let me do it. You watch. I'll just sheet it in." She pulled the mainsail line. "And steer." She pushed the tiller away. "Not too much wind, not too little." Then she showed him how to release the mainsail so it flapped, and they drifted to a near-halt again. At last she was beginning to get the feel of it.

"Okay, we're turning. Heads down." The bright yellow sail snapped as she ducked, swung the boom across, and tacked out toward deeper water. "It will be easier coming in. The wind will be behind us."

"Right. But then there'll be things in the way like boats and docks and buoys. Take us out a little more, and I'll try doing the rope bit while you steer."

"Okay, duck." She tacked again. The only sounds were the rush of the breeze and the splash of the waves against the hull as they skimmed through the bright blue-green water.

They had just cleared the mouth of the harbor, past the long peninsulas on either side that sheltered the marina like two outstretched arms, when the wind dropped off. A couple of gusts came up, faded again, and finally died down completely.

"What do we do now?" Rob asked.

Barbara secured the lines, letting the boat drift, and leaned back. "We'll wait for the next breeze."

"That's it? Should I hang overboard and kick?" For the first time she looked at how he was wedged in. She'd not realized that the few inches of height he had on T.J. would make that much difference.

"I'm going to undo this darn thing a while," he said, unsnapping the belts holding closed the vest.

"You can't be comfortable. Let's switch places and find out if you've been paying attention." She offered him her job at the tiller.

"Certainly. I don't mind making a fool out of myself." He uncrossed his long legs. "Just how do we choreograph this crossover?" The boat bobbled slightly as he shifted his weight.

"I'll slide up the middle," Barbara directed. "You ease back this way."

"Is this what is known as keel-hauling? I picked that up from some play." He was sliding along on his rear end, trying to time each shift with the rocking of the boat.

Barbara tried not to laugh. "Keel-hauling is something you do to people. It has to do with dragging them under the boat on a rope. It's a punishment."

"And this isn't?" Rob winced as the boom drifted his way and he scooted down. "Believe me, I feel like my keel is being hauled."

"Just move on back here and quit worrying about the terminology, wise guy," Barbara coaxed him. She was crouched low, on hands and knees creeping in the opposite direction.

"There is something remarkably poetic about all this," he kept on in his casual, teasing way. "You have to admit, our ships have finally stopped passing in the night."

Seeing the amusement in his eyes, she laughed.

"We're finally in the same boat," he persisted, grinning at her.

"Literally," she agreed.

"Just remind me next time to get a larger boat," he moaned. "One with a motor. And a crew."

"This was your idea."

"No one said I was always right."

Midway in the exchange, the boat rocked again. Barbara's hand slipped and she rolled into him. "Sorry." She was feeling inept and awkward, and strangely vulnerable.

"Don't be sorry. This is the most physical we've been in ages." Rob wrapped one arm around her, but the bulky vests kept them apart. "I'd put some romantic moves on you, but I'd probably knock both of us overboard." He looked at her intently. "How about it, Bobbie," he whispered. "You want to start something?" The humor shifted suddenly to something more sensual.

"Not out here. But yes. I think I'm ready," she said softly. Since they'd reached Eleuthera, she'd been expecting something, some sign, some farewell, some feeling of ending. Face to face with Rob, she knew she didn't need any more signs than she already had. "I've been waiting for something to let me know that it's all right. But I really don't need permission."

"If you did, you've certainly got mine." He strained forward so their lips would meet. His new sunglasses slid down his nose.

"Let's try this on land," Barbara suggested when the boat wobbled again.

"You're the captain. You give the orders."

"It might help if we rearrange ourselves and get started in the right direction." She inched past him.

"We're going in the right direction. Finally."

Just as she reached the mast and rolled to a sitting position, Rob took his place at the stern. Even there, he had trouble fitting his legs into the limited space.

"Not yet." Barbara sat forward abruptly, trying to unsnag one portion of the line that had looped about his foot. Trying to help her out, Rob unleashed the mainsail sheet so he could maneuver the sails as she had done. Suddenly a gust of wind snatched the sail and flung it aside just as she rocked up on her knees. The heavy boom swung out, catching her on the side of the head with a loud crack. The taste of blood was the last thing she remembered.

"Bobbie . . . . . !" Rob cried, lunging toward her. The boom swung back again, this time catching him with the ropes and flinging him backward, off the side of the small boat. Before he could struggle to the surface, the current had carried the boat and his bobbing vest farther along the coastline. The riptide across the mouth of the harbor began dragging him out into the blue, cool waters beyond.

"You all right, lady?"

"Don't move her," Barbara heard the distant voice say as she struggled to open her eyes.

"I feel sick," she groaned. The steady to-and-fro rocking of the boat accentuated her queasiness.

"You be all right, lady?" The Bahamian accent finally connected with a face. "You got some nice lump on your head." His bright white teeth flashed against near-black skin.

"Beginner's luck," Barbara moaned.

Her two rescuers grinned and helped her sit up.

"We betta' get you into shore and let someone look at dat head," the darker of the two men said. "It's not a good idea to be out here in dis little boat all by yourself," he scolded her.

"I'm not by myself." Barbara steadied herself on one elbow then pushed herself up. Her head pounded. Except for the two rescuers who sat holding the lines to their larger craft, she was alone.

"Rob," Barbara gasped. "There was a man with me." She pointed to the unoccupied stern of the boat where the mainsail rope had been tied down again. Rob's sunglasses were skittering back and forth on the deck with the rolling movement of the boat. "Rob?" She crawled forward, staring out across the water.

"Ain't no one here nowhere, lady," the young Bahamian replied. "The line was loose and the sail was flappin' when we spotted you. It was mighty clear that no one was doin' the driving."

"He's out there somewhere." Barbara raised her voice. "We've got to find him." Her arms gave way beneath her as a new wave of dizziness closed in, pulling the world into a bright circle of light surrounded by black. She collapsed on her stomach against the warm deck.

"Easy now. Don' think you're going nowhere, lady," the younger man insisted. "There are plenty of boats around. If one of 'em ain't picked him up already, we'll go lookin' for your friend after we get you in. Come on, lady." He grasped her upper arm, guiding her toward his motor boat moored alongside.

"We've got to look," Barbara protested as the two men moved her into their boat. A sudden surge of nausea made her thrust her head over the side. The raging pain in her head throbbed mercilessly as she gagged and gripped the side of the boat.

"You jus' settle down. We'll look for him," the darker fellow said, pacifying her. He climbed back aboard the sailboat, lowering, then tying down the sails, securing the little sailboat behind the motor boat. The engine began with a dull roar and they headed back around the peninsula toward the resort bay.

"We got a man missing," the Bahamian yelled to the boat master who came out to watch the small procession. "He must'a gone over by Gull Point." He jerked his thumb to the northwest. "We found her drifting just south of here."

Barbara leaned forward, bracing her head on her arms. She hadn't recalled any point, Gull or otherwise. "We went out of the bay and went that way," she said, pointing to the south while she closed one eye, hoping to alleviate the hammering headache.

"There's a lot of boats out today." The boat master reached inside the shed for his radio transmitter. "I'll send out an alert and round up a couple of our crew." He took the entire episode calmly. "He had his vest on?"

"I think so." She remembered he'd unhitched it at one point.

"Good. Either he's out there waitin' for a ride, or he swam ashore, or someone already picked him up." He bent forward to inspect Barbara's bump. "Get her to the hotel and have the nurse check that," he directed the two men. "We'll take care of the search and rescue," he assured them.

DARK WINDOW 435

Barbara stared out toward the mouth of the bay. Except for a few bright sails, there was no sign of action. "You must hurry," she urged the man.

"I'll hurry." He moved back toward the shed. "You get your head looked at." He waved to a uniformed woman coming out of the main building. Apparently his initial radio message was to get medical help for Barbara.

"He'll be around. We'll get him." The man turned his attention to the radio transmitter. He was sending out information when the two men led Barbara down the dock toward the white-uniformed woman.

Eliot tiptoed into the room and picked up Miranda's sandals. He paused at the foot of Barbara's bed and looked at her closely. "Hi, Mom," he whispered when he saw that she was awake.

"Eliot." She reached up and he came closer and took her hand.

"Are you okay now?"

"I'm sore." Barbara rolled her head from side to side, "and stiff." She glanced toward the window, trying to gauge the time by the light outside, but the shutters were closed. "How long have I been like this? Where is Rob?" She peered at him. "Have they found him?"

The nurse who had met her on her dock stepped into the room. "Don't worry, ma'am. They're still calling along the coast. The boats are still out looking." The steady blue eyes did not waver as the white-haired woman replied.

"Oh, no," Barbara groaned. "What time is it? How long has it been?" The bright midday sun had gone and the room was dull and dim. "What time is it?"

"It's about five." The nurse adopted a motherly tone. "It's become a bit overcast. A little squall blew in. It's drizzling right now." She spoke gently. "It hasn't been all that long. Your mister is probably holed up in some beach hut farther down waiting for the rain to pass. Either that or he's aboard a boat on his way in," she said, sounding confident.

"I want to help look for him," Barbara started up from

the bed. Once again the rapid movement blurred her vision and made the room swim.

"Stay in that bed," the woman said, placing a firm hand on Barbara's shoulder. "There is nothing we can do other than wait."

"Where's Miranda?"

Eliot disappeared for a moment and returned with his sister.

Seeing the worried look on Miranda's face brought all the memories of that hospital stay after the glass accident surging back. Not only was she hurt again, but Rob this time was missing. The child was desolate.

"Come here, sweetie." Barbara made herself sit up. "How about a hug?" Miranda came forward slowly and hung on very tight while Barbara stroked her hair. "I got careless again. I didn't duck."

Miranda didn't say anything. She just hugged. Barbara hugged back, trying to keep the room from swimming.

"I've got to get up," Barbara insisted.

"No you don't," the woman said. "Blake is coming to pick up the chil'ren. He's going to take them to dinner in the hotel with some other chil'ren. They can watch the rain and keep a close eye on any boats that pull into the marina. The mister will be back," the nurse declared. "And when he gets here, he will be more worried about you than anything else, for sure. So you stay put. You chil'ren get yourselves ready, okay?"

They both looked at their mother.

"Go. I'll be fine. Shoes." She pointed at Miranda's bare feet. The youngsters hesitated a moment, then went back to the next room.

Barbara finally settled back against the pillow.

"Call us if Rob gets here." Miranda clasped her sandals against her chest. Her soft reddish-gold hair framed her face like a halo.

"If you hear first, you call me," Barbara asked. Miranda nodded.

"You can check in on your mum later." The nurse ushered them out. "Blake is here with the big umbrellas." Then very quietly, they withdrew, closing the door behind them. Barbara was alone again.

"Is this what you wanted?" she addressed the empty room. She pulled herself out of the bed and crossed to the long window, then stood looking out over the marina below. The moored ships bobbed up and down in the pale gray rain. "You brought me here for this?" She wept. Then she turned and looked around the bedroom she and Miranda shared. Hastily she grabbed a jacket from the closet, tugged it on over her shirt, and yanked on a pair of shorts. She'd been talking to T.J., but he had no reason to be in the cottage. But atop the hill, in the observation pavilion, she could wait and watch, in T.J.'s creation. Without making a sound, she opened the door to the patio and slipped out.

There was no one else on the hilltop leading to the pavilion. The light rain spread a luminous glow over the marina below as Barbara paused occasionally on her climb to steady herself and look back. Her wet hair hung in damp spirals against her cheeks as the tears and raindrops intermingled. Inside the pavilion, she leaned against the columns, her arms crossed over her chest, shivering.

"You wanted me here, T.J.?" Her soft voice was lost in the sound of rainfall on the rooftop. "I thought you might be here so we could end this. I thought you would let me be free. I want my own life." She turned and gazed up through the glass-paneled ceiling. Once again the memories shifted and realigned as she looked through the glass at the dull sky and sparkling drops of water on the other side, like thousands of fragments of glass.

She remembered T.J.'s voice on the theater tape as he stood there, confident and alive, telling the men of his intent. *A window in time.* Barbara tried to remember precisely what T.J. had said. He'd spoken about breathing new life into an existing structure. *You open up a window in time.* It was an idea charged with energy, rich with possibility, full of promise. "New life," Barbara whispered. "Please, don't let Rob be dead." She hugged herself. "Please, T.J.," she pleaded.

Three levels below, on the zig-zagging walkways like stairsteps down the hillside, she could see white-shirted hotel employees with umbrellas carrying trays of drinks to guests who were waiting on their small porches for the rain to end. Gradually the rain was transformed into a light mist as the wind picked up and the low sun began to burn off the few remaining clouds.

"Come back to me," she begged. The sunlight through the glass-paneled roof sent a bright starburst of light onto the floor where Barbara stood.

Her attention had been riveted on the incoming cruiser that sped up to the dock. Her two rescuers were returning, without a passenger. At first she didn't notice yet another island jeep. The roadways were always crisscrossed by jeeps taking visitors on tours or transporting luggage and supplies about. This one drove right past the hotel entrance, then swerved out toward the boat rental shed, right onto the "Guests Only" dock. The driver walked rapidly toward the boat master and the two empty-handed rescuers, who stood talking with him by the shed. The bare-chested passenger from the jeep headed toward the hotel.

In the fine haze, with the bright sun streaming through the mist, everything seemed far away and out of focus, subdued and eerie. Barbara raised her hand to shade her eyes. She didn't recognize the clothes. Something familiar in the set of the shoulders, something distinctive in the walk, brought out memories and snatches of dreams gliding layer upon layer, aligning, shifting, and separating like fragments in a kaleidoscope.

Then the first small form raced toward him with her hair streaming in the air. Miranda leaped into his arms. Eliot was right behind her. Out in public, Eliot hugged the sunburned man.

Then with a peculiar precision, the three faces turned toward the cottage on the hill.

"I'm here. Up here," Barbara called, tugging off her jacket and flapping it above her head. Eliot spotted her first, pointing her out as the others looked up to the hilltop and waved.

Like something out of an old pirate movie, Rob climbed over the low wall that separated the first porch below from the street and shoved his way through the bushes. Then he vaulted over the next wall, nodding apologetically to the bewildered occupants. He proceeded on to the next wall in the most direct path to Barbara. It was something T.J. would have done, and he'd have laughed as he did it. The thought formed before she realized how ominous it was. She stared apprehensively at the approaching man. She'd asked him to come back. She knew T.J. could breathe new life into something. But into someone? Someone else? She felt her heart begin to pound.

If he'd been orchestrating this, if T.J. had not only planned for her to come here but had intended for Rob to come as well, whose life was beginning again?

"Was it me you wanted?" Barbara wondered. "Or was it him? Did you bring us both here for this?" She stepped forward, steadying herself on the gingerbread railing as she studied the man who drew near.

"You really didn't think you were rid of me?" The words he called out seemed to come from two worlds at once. "I'm sorry if you were frightened." He was on the walkway now. He leaped up the stairs two at a time, then reached out, stopping and looking at her. "Are you all right? You're as white as a sheet."

She stood, immobile, examining the familiar form of someone older, someone new again. Stills from another tape flashed in her memory.

Some enchanted evening. She had a curious sense of déjà vu.

"I'm alive. Pinch me," Rob said with a grin. "I'm no ghost." He regarded her intently. He held her steady just as her knees started to give way. "Easy now." He walked her across to one of the benches of the pavilion, holding her against his chest. "I think you need to sit."

"You're really here," she said cautiously.

"I'm really here." He sat next to her and pulled her closer. "You don't think I'd blow my big chance by doing something dumb like drowning?" He slipped one arm around her, bracing her with the other. "Talk about a big reception. You swooned, no less," he kidded her.

"What happened out there?" Barbara steadied herself enough to ask.

"To start off, I lost my darn life jacket. Then I got

caught in a riptide," he began to explain, hoping to erase that guarded look on her face. "I was pulling against the tide, trying to reach you, then I remembered what you said about going in the right direction." He watched the curious light in her eyes. "I heard once that if you swim parallel to the shore, instead of fighting it, you'll get out of a riptide. So I headed along the shoreline, a long way along," he said solemnly. "I started swimming until I could hardly move my arms. I simply lay back and floated and let the waves take over. By the time I got out of it, I was to hell and gone."

"How long were you out there?"

"Maybe hours. Hard to tell. Especially with the rain. It got real peculiar after awhile. I started getting wacked out. Mental fatigue, or something like that rapture-of-the-deep business that divers get. All I know was that it would have been so easy just to drift down under the water. Real easy."

Barbara nodded slowly. She remembered that moment in the bedroom when the scented air settled upon her seductively, or in the study when she first felt the warm blood. After awhile, resisting the invitation was the hard part.

"I swear something was right there with me," Rob lowered his voice. "I was hallucinating, I guess. But I could feel something urging me to give up, to let go. Then the weirdest thing happened. I started having flashbacks. I could hear T.J.'s voice, over and over, telling me 'So long.' I kept seeing you and T.J. standing in the driveway of your old house, waving goodbye to me, then walking back inside together. It played again and again, like a loop of film." He shook his head and looked out over the marina. "I swear, I could hear him saying goodbye. It was the damnedest experience," he muttered.

Barbara leaned her head against his shoulder, saying nothing. Someone else had felt T.J.'s presence, someone who had nearly drowned. Someone she loved.

"So," Rob breathed. "I got angry. Really pissed. I don't get pissed often," he said abruptly. "Here I was, finally you and I were in the right place at the right time, and I was getting sent off, dismissed, so he could go home with you. Not this time," Rob said with conviction. "This time I'm going home with you. No one is going to tell me goodbye, not even a damned hallucination," he declared.

Barbara felt the first trace of a smile. She remembered the power of being pissed herself. She'd stood her ground at the theater, telling T.J. in rude terms to back off. He had. Luster had said this thing could only push so far. "Don't give an inch and don't back down," she said quietly.

"Exactly," Rob agreed. "I hung in there. I made it to an inlet, flopped on the shore. All I did was think about you and hope you weren't hurt. Then I got to some back road and walked along until someone came along with a car. I didn't know where the hell I was or I'd have started back on foot. But I'm here now. And I'm staying with you. On land. Enough of this taking our time crap." He kissed her lightly at first. She could feel his arm shaking. "I love you. And I know you love me. I've never been so scared, or so frustrated, or so determined in my whole life. Marry me. Here. Now."

"Now?"

"How about it, sailor?" He held her back and stared into her eyes. "Take it or leave it."

"I'll take it." Barbara hugged him.

"You realize that someone is going to have to break the news to the rest of the family."

"I'll do it. I'll tell them."

Rob bent down and kissed her. "Let's both do it. You got to tell them about my job. I've missed enough. I don't want to miss anything else." He stood and pulled her to her feet, closing one arm around her to keep her steady. He was sunburned and sore. She was still dizzy.

"I'm not hedging, but maybe we should put off a wedding just a little while," Barbara said as they started down the hillside. "Maybe we should wait until we get back home. We'll tell the kids now. Let things settle down a bit. A shipwreck and a near drowning are a bit much for one holiday."

"Just as long as they know what's going on."

"I think they'll be very pleased. Just don't be surprised

if Miranda starts lining up bridesmaids," she warned him. "Little girls are like that."

"Big girls are like that, too." There was amusement and affection in the eyes that met hers.

"I just want to do it right," Barbara said with a laugh.

Late that night after everyone else was asleep, Barbara climbed back up to the hilltop pavilion and sat once more in the pale moonlight. "This is it, Bozo," she said softly. "This is my goodbye to you." She took out the two wedding bands she'd brought. "I'm going home to a new life." She took a deep breath. He was there. She could feel the wind stir within the graceful gazebo and smell the tantalizing scent of bay and almond on the salty ocean air.

"I don't like being manipulated," she stated. "I don't know if that boom swung because you wanted me dead. I don't know if you wanted to destroy Rob or to claim him. I don't know if you were trying to come back to me. But none of it worked. You can't take over another person's life."

She felt the cool air close around her like a soft caress. It felt different than before, as if it were making peace with her.

"I'm not sure if I was afraid to let you go completely or if you were trying all this time for another chance. But I'm setting both of us free. If you love me, you'll let me go." She stood beneath the glass ceiling, her arms limp at her sides, her chin slightly raised. "Let me keep the past that I love and remember. Leave my present and my future for me and the ones I love here and now. Please, T.J., go in peace. This world isn't yours anymore."

She waited a moment, while the pale moonlight cast her shadowy image on the floor. Then she threw the rings as far as she could out over the hillside. The soft breeze rippled her hair and fluttered the fabric of her dress. "Peace," she whispered as the night air regained its salty scent.

"Barbara?" Rob called up from below. "Is that you?" He peered up at the pale figure in the moonlight.

"It's me."

"What are you doing here alone?" He came ahead and stepped up into the wooden pavilion. "Put this on." He unfolded the extra jacket he'd brought.

"I was practicing making the big announcement." She slid her arms into the sleeves. "And I was saying goodbye to T.J."

"Are you finished?" he asked. "Are you ready to go back? Or do you want me to leave you a little longer?"

"I'm finished here." Barbara smiled up at him. "You can take me home."

"Almost home." Rob corrected her. "But I'll settle for that." Arm in arm they walked back down toward the hotel. The ornate lookout pavilion, stark white in the moonlight, stood serene and aloof on the hilltop.

The envelope Louis handed Barbara at the airport was addressed to her. The return address read "Say's Who?" and the handwriting was Rob's.

"You're supposed to wait until you're home in the study before you read this," Louis said, delivering the message when he came to meet the evening flight back.

"In the study?" Barbara tucked the note in her pocket.

"That's what the man said," Louis declared. "While I'm remembering things, run your sprinklers tonight. It's dry as a bone. Fire warnings are out. And so were the damn kids. I found a couple of empty gallon jugs on the edge of the marsh. Looks like the little bastards who've been swiping gas have been stashing it out along the river. Sort of floating pit stops. Just remember to water," he cautioned her.

"How was the trip?" Karen tried unsuccessfully to keep from overwhelming the arrivals with questions.

"Karen," Louis reprimanded her, "it's late. The kids are tired. Let's drop them at home and let them get a good night's rest." He was grinning like the cat who had swallowed the canary. "We've got lots of time for a run-down of the trip. She's not going anywhere. She's coming home."

"Except for the boat part, the trip was great," Barbara said with a smile, "and so was the company." Eliot and

Miranda were already recounting the story of the sailing accident.

"Boy, I thought a shark had eaten him," Miranda sighed.

Eliot had covered the details. His mom got hit on the head with the boom and Rob was caught in a riptide. "He was really sunburned," Eliot noted. "And he threw away his shirt and lost his hat and sunglasses and life vest." Rob hadn't told the children quite as much as he told Barbara. "I knew that I had to get back to you, all of you," he had said simply as he cuddled Miranda on his lap.

Barbara wasn't ready to say much about the rest of the time she and Rob had spent together, not yet. The kids were already planning what they would do when Rob moved to Charleston. In the hotel room, they had smiled knowingly when Barbara had started to explain that sometimes people fall in love again. They had liked the idea that she and Rob were getting married. They were going to be a family. But they settled on engaged for now.

All four of them had walked hand in hand, even Eliot, right out in public, for the last few days. Eliot and Rob had gone surf fishing together while Barbara and Miranda snorkled and searched for shells. And in the afternoons while the children were off with Blake and the preteens, there had been opportunity enough for the grownups to spend some time alone. There was no sense of urgency. No need to hurry.

Once the decision was made, everything else followed in an easy sequence. Rob would go back and rent out the house in Lauderdale. "We'll keep it as a retirement home in our old age," he decided. He'd get his business affairs in order and move up and stay with Louis and Karen for a few weeks. Meanwhile, Barbara had his artwork and anything else she wanted to unpack. By mid July, when he got there, she'd have a small ceremony planned and the kids would have adjusted to the idea of him becoming a permanent part of their surroundings. By then too, the anniversary of T.J.'s death would also have passed. The cycle would be complete.

DARK WINDOW

Telling Karen and Louis would have to wait, Barbara decided on the flight back home. At least until they had all recovered from the plane trip and settled in. Tomorrow, or maybe the next day, she and her friends would have time to talk. Something in Louis's twinkling eyes when he handed her Rob's letter warned her that her announcement would not come as a particular surprise.

"No, we can't come in. Not even for a few minutes," Louis insisted as he pulled into the driveway and began unloading suitcases and straw bags full of souvenirs. He plunked everything in a row along the corridor by the kitchen, clasped Karen's arm, and led her off toward the car.

"Call me tomorrow," Karen pleaded. "I'm dying to hear."

Louis grinned and kept moving her along.

"Go into the study," Louis called to remind her. "Read the note."

Eliot and Miranda promptly disappeared down the hallway into their rooms. "Doing inventory," T.J. had called it. After every trip, the kids would spend some quiet time with their possessions, sitting in their rooms, getting reacquainted with familiar books and toys. Then they'd move things about so the new items had a place with the old standards, side by side on a shelf, or tucked into a drawer.

Barbara made her own inventory. She strolled around the inner garden room looking at the thick green ferns Luster had moved in with a few bird-of-paradise plants. The tiny mirrors outside the windows were new. He'd taken care of everything. Then she cleared a path, dragging the suitcases down the hall, dropping one off at each room. The unpacking could wait until tomorrow. For now, she would take Rob's note into the study and read it, as Louis had instructed her.

The note was fairly simple. "From all the pieces of our lives, the old and new, the perfect and the imperfect, we can make something beautiful and timeless."

Now she knew what had come in that crate she hadn't been supposed to open. While the four of them were off on Eleuthera, Louis and, no doubt, Kent had taken the hanging plant from the study window that she had promised T.J. she would finish. In the open space, they had mounted the long stained-glass panel. Ornate, intricate, and opulent. She recognized all the colors. The boxes of broken glass from the garage hadn't been lost at all.

The artisan who signed it was her teacher, Craig Kerfberg. He'd salvaged everything and created a beautiful tree, with branches of caramel and mahogany with leaves of orange, yellow, rust, and green.

"All the broken pieces." Barbara traced the thin lead channels with her fingertips. Rob had taken them all, like he'd take her, and he'd had this made for her. The small brass plate at the bottom was inscribed "Tree of Life." With its roots in the earth and its multicolored branches stretching up into the heavens, it held twelve golden spheres aloft. Each circle had been etched with a symbol from the zodiac, showing the unending cycle of time.

"Wow!" Eliot stepped in beside her and stared. "Miranda," he yelled. "Come and look at this."

"I remember that one," Miranda said as she stood with her nose inches from the window and poked at the pieces she recognized. "That's the one Daddy bought you." She ran her little fingers along the strips of caramel that made the branches.

"It sorta' looks like Keats," Eliot noted. "Except for the little moons."

"Boy, I thought they threw all this stuff in the garbage," Miranda marveled. "But they used it all."

"The blue is new," Eliot observed authoritatively. The surrounding glass that formed the sky above and the rivers of earth below were a bright, vivid blue. "Looks like the water off the islands. Wait till the sun hits this in the morning." His voice was pitched high with excitement. "It should be great. We've never had blue in here before." Even now, the lights from inside the study sent the myriad of colors from the window in bright patches across the outside patio onto the dark grass.

Eliot picked up the note that Rob had sent. He studied the message, then he grinned—wide, smug, and knowing. "I like that," he commented. "Something beautiful." He slipped his hand into hers.

"I like it, too," Barbara agreed.

Luster Johns woke just after midnight. There was a stillness in the room that made him unsettled.

"Somethin' botherin' you, Ol' Paw?" Mattie asked, coming out onto the porch after him when she heard the front door squeak. Luster was in his rocking chair by then, sitting with Inez's quilt over his knees, looking out over the river. "Just a bit edgy," he answered her. "Been too long since we had a good rain. Even the sweetgrass and rushes sound dry."

Mattie crossed her arms and leaned against the porch railing. She'd had trouble sleeping, too. She'd been keeping an eye on Luster lately. He'd finished his eleventh angel early in June, then he'd started right in on the twelfth, working at it every night, like a driven man.

"You got something worrisome on your mind? You finished that angel mighty fast," she pressed him.

"Just had the feeling it's coming soon. Had to be ready."

"What's comin', Paw?"

"Something. Been countin'. Twelve angels. Spirit seems to let it set at that. No more. Reached the end."

"End of what?"

"Don't right know. Sister Gertrude and me, we talked about it, patterns of twelve been 'round long time. Twelve months. Twelve hours on the clock. Constellations. Disciples in the Bible. Sons of Jacob. Steps to heaven. Stations of the wind." He rocked slowly to and fro. "And angels."

Mattie stood there, waiting for him to say more. But he just kept looking out, and she knew that meant he wanted to be alone. "You want me to get you something? Lemonade?"

Luster raised one finger. A gentle dismissal. He continued rocking until he heard her bed creak far off and he knew they were alone. Him and his spirit.

"You just let me know," he spoke out loud. "You just

show me the way. I'm ready." He clasped the arm rests snugly. "We all ready."

He started whisting softly then, hoping to hear the wind pick up in the palmettos nearby. "Could use a little rain, if it suits you," he commented as if he were chatting with a friend. Then he leaned back, rocking again, humming softly. "Looked over J'rus'lem, and whaddid I see, comin' for to carry me home. Ban' of angels, comin' after me, comin' for to carry me home." He closed his eyes and rocked a while longer, smiling as he did. He was ready, and he wasn't alone.

CHAPTER 14

> Wear me as a seal upon your heart,
>   as a seal upon your arm;
> For love is strong as death,
>   passion cruel as the grave;
> It blazes up like a raging fire,
>   fiercer than any flame.
> *Song of Solomon*

IN THE MORNING, the window was better than great, it was spectacular. Barbara stepped out into the study apprehensively, hoping that it had passed the night undisturbed. Nothing had been moved, neither the artwork Rob had sent to her for safekeeping, nor the window he'd had created for her. Now the sun shone through it, flooding the room with streams of color. Around it all, the clear blue gave the room an aura of serenity. "Peace at last," Barbara sighed.

When Eliot joined her, all he could do was mutter "Wow!" again and again. He said it five times in succession as he moved from side to side, gaping at the window and the colors it cast into the room.

"Ooooh, the window is beautiful." Miranda walked over and stood directly in the shimmering shower of light. "Look at me." She grinned. "I'm in technicolor."

"Your face is blue," Eliot pointed out.

"Speaking of blue," Barbara interrupted his teasing. "If you want to pitch your tent today, you can invite Billie over and the two of you can camp out tonight."

"Okaaayyy," Eliot cried, snapping his fingers and making a dash for the telephone to call his friend.

"Can I spend the night with Carrie? If Eliot gets to camp out, can I sleep over at Carrie's?"

"I'll call her mom and check," Barbara agreed, nodding. "But after breakfast. We have to unpack the suitcases."

* * *

By midday, the unpacking was finished and the washing machine chugged away on a load of soiled clothing. Miranda was on her way to spend the night with Carrie, and Eliot and Billie Hobach were spreading out the tent in the back yard.

"Just when do you think this wedding will take place?" Karen babbled delightedly. "Summer weddings are gorgeous," she said, beginning to make plans. "Lots of people."

"Think small and intimate," Barbara cautioned her. "And late July. A simple family event, with a few good friends. Maybe even here," she suddenly added. "We could have a quiet ceremony out under the trees." The idea appealed to her.

"How about my house," Karen offered. "We have lots of room."

"Thanks, but I think I'd like it here," Barbara said, glancing out at the yard.

"I'm delighted. Louis is delighted," Karen insisted. "I know the kids are."

"I think so." Barbara checked the progress the boys were making with the tent. "Let's give them a hand," she suggested when the tent poles tilted in different directions for the third time.

"Did you water last night?" Karen asked as they trudged out across the yard.

Barbara stopped and grimaced. "I forgot. We started looking at the window." She shook her head. "Everyone took baths. I didn't think about it. But I did lock everything."

"I won't tell." Karen brushed it off. "I guess you can't do it now or you'll drown your happy campers."

"I'll leave a note. I'll do it when they break camp tomorrow," she promised.

"Make sure you do," Karen stressed. "It's so bad now that they're talking about not having any Fourth of July fireworks."

"Not even at Patriot's Point?"

"They're talking no displays, public or private. Fire officials say unless we have a real deluge this week, it'll be too dangerous. There's nothing promising in the forecasts."

"The Fourth sure wouldn't be the same without the fireworks out over the Point." Barbara shook her head. She'd taken it for granted that they'd get together for a picnic and a fireworks show out over the harbor. T.J. and the kids had loved the noise and the flash and the color. That had been their last family outing before he died.

"This year Louis could have taken us all out in the boat to watch." Karen echoed her disappointment. "But they're saying everything is too dry and on top of that, the water supply is low. All it would take is a few sparks," she sighed. "Unless it rains."

"I'll water," Barbara reassured her. "And I'll get the boys to do a rain dance."

"I'd dance with them if it would help," Karen offered.

The boys were in their pajamas out by the tent when Barbara heard the first blast. It was a low, dull boom in the northwest, further around the bend in Wappoo Creek from where they were. She came out of the house and walked up behind the two boys. She stood staring like them out over treetops beyond the dry marsh grass, resting her hand on Eliot's shoulder. Then came the second explosion, this one nearer and louder. This time, she could see the flash of fire where Wappoo Creek curved toward the larger Ashley.

"I hope that's not near Mr. Belcazzio's boat." Billie walked closer to the river.

"Go call the fire department," Barbara told Eliot, turning him toward the house as she started for the hose. "The number is by the phone." Eliot took off at a trot. She could feel the thud of the third explosion as the air pressure shifted. "Wait, never mind." She raced after him. "I'll do it. They may not take a kid seriously." Eliot stopped abruptly.

"Don't take your eyes off the area even for a minute," she called to them. "And start getting the tent down. Then get the hoses out."

She could already hear the siren on the first fire engine

as she stepped back outside after making the call. The dispatcher said St. Andrews Number 2 was on its way. The shrill noise swept across Harborview in the direction of the golf course. Then a fourth and fifth blast echoed through the still evening air. This time she was frightened.

"I said get the tent down," Barbara yelled when the glow of fire above the treeline toward the Wappoo did not disappear as it had before. "I'm going to get the sprinklers started. Hurry with the tent." She urged them into action.

Now the scream of a second fire unit joined the first. "I can see them," Billie yelled from a land ridge near the driveway as he spotted one vehicle after another with police and fire officials aboard, cutting down the crossroad farther inland and veering off toward the country club. When a red car pulled up the roadway and turned into her driveway, Barbara knew they were in trouble.

"It's the marsh, Ma'am," the uniformed man explained. "Some kids have been swiping gas, then storing it in plastic containers. Looks like they strung 'em together and anchored them all along the creek. I don't know what started them popping. Maybe they leaked. But the wind could shift, and if it does," he said, glancing from the Wappoo area out toward the Ashley River, "you'll be cut off out here. Maybe someone dropped a cigarette. But it's running through the marsh. If the wind picks up and brings it this way," he warned her, "you'll have to evacuate."

"Evacuate?" Barbara gasped. "Leave the house?"

"Leave everything," the officer said. "If there are any more jugs out there, this thing could get out of hand. We've called in the Coast Guard on the water side," he added. "They'll be bringing in fireboats to start spraying it down from the river. I was told to alert the neighborhood just in case an evacuation is necessary. It might be smart to pack your car just in case."

"You two get your clothes together," Barbara told the kids. "Billie, you call your Dad and tell him to come get you guys right away. You can all spend the night at your house until things calm down here."

"Awww," Eliot groaned. "I can help here. I don't want to miss all the action."

"I don't like the looks of this." Barbara sniffed the gas fumes in the air. "I want you two out of here. Call your father," she told Billie once more. "And stay inside until he gets here," she added. "I don't want you breathing this stuff."

She glanced westward at the dark cloud hanging over the country club area along the Wappoo. The sky was almost slate gray. As the night closed in, the firefighters would have more trouble negotiating in overgrown swampy areas between the creek and the residential area.

"Stay away from my home," Barbara muttered between clenched teeth as she turned the sprinklers on full blast. "Don't you come this way." Now a series of explosions in the opposite direction, to the east on the Ashley, sent a flare of orange fire high into the dark sky. It was beginning to look like the Fourth of July had come early.

By the time Billie Hobach's father pulled into the driveway, the wind was increasing and was gradually inching the creek fire toward her bend where it curved and widened into the river. A patch of marshy land where they met was still untouched. The dry grass farther down the river had already started blazing as the erratic breeze pushed bright red tongues of flame from one clump of dry grass and rushes to the next.

"I've got the water on," Barbara assured Billie's father. He had loaded the boys in the car and come back for her. Eliot had a pillowcase full of special belongings, including his telescope and the fishing pole he loved. "It will probably stop before it gets this far." Barbara refused to go with them. "I'm going to hose down the house. If any sparks get close, everything here will be too wet to burn."

"Do you want me to pack up anything of yours?" Bud Hobach offered. "I've got the station wagon. I could stuff it full."

Barbara turned and stared at the house that she treasured. "I wouldn't know where to begin," she sighed. "No, wait a minute. Help me get some artwork out."

They ran into the house to strip Rob's prints and paintings from her walls. When she returned from her third trip, she handed the boys Henry in his terrarium and a pack of videotapes. "It's T.J. and Rob," she said simply. "Keep them with you for now."

"But what about you?" Hobach asked, reluctant to leave. "They've already evacuated the area west of here. They probably figure you've been told."

"I'll stick it out." Several fireboats cruised past, heading toward the creek. They started spraying beyond her place, arcing plumes of water along the dry areas. Out over the golf course, the local news station had its helicopter circling, filming the fire. "Look, I've got lots of help," she assured him, pointing toward the heavy equipment offshore. "Sooner or later, it will die down. I'll give you a call." She hurried him toward the station wagon where the boys were waiting. "You be good now." Barbara steadied her voice. Hobach slammed the door closed and backed out toward the street. Barbara straightened her shoulders and stood waving as they pulled away. Two small faces stared back at her until they finally swerved out of sight.

"Let's get at it," she told herself, trudging around to the rear wall of the garage and beginning to unwind the long hose. Then she hauled out the aluminum ladder. Half dragging, half carrying it, she moved the ladder to the side of the house and propped it up. Against the sky, she could see the bright searchlights of the Coast Guard vessels. Huge sprays of white water belched into the air as the guardsmen headed off the Wappoo blaze.

Barbara made one last tour of the interior of the house, pulling the furniture away from the windows and shutting every door. From the entry closet, she grabbed a flashlight, an old construction helmet of T.J.'s, and a yellow rain slicker. When she stepped outside, the air was thick with smoke. She went back in for a kitchen towel to cover her nose and mouth.

After turning the faucet wide open, with her battle uniform under one arm and the hose clasped in the other, she climbed the ladder onto the house roof, determined not to look down. Between the distant sounds of shouting and the wail of the incoming fire units, she could hear the crackle and whoosh of the fire. The fire on the Wappoo side seemed to be under control, and she couldn't see any flames on the opposite end, offshore from the undeveloped area farther east along the Ashley.

"You stay the hell away from here," she muttered defiantly. "Stay away." She pulled on her garb, letting the hose run all the while. Then she walked from wing to wing, soaking everything.

"Look at this," Willie Dodd said, getting up from the TV and going to get Luster. "Grampa, there's a big fire in by the country club. Come look."

Luster was already on the porch, standing still, looking at the sky to the north. The color was wrong. And the smell.

Luster hurried in and leaned forward, listening to the live reports. When they mentioned gasoline and evacuation and showed the fireboats, he picked up his keys. "We got to get out there."

Willie Dodd still was watching the news.

"I said we got to get out there," Luster repeated, his raspy voice was louder this time, just a bit, but enough to get his grandson's attention. In the kitchen, Mattie heard him and switched off the gas stove.

"I'll get the truck. You come along now," Luster insisted, heading out the door.

"Where are you goin'?" Mattie came out after them. From her father's stride, she knew he was set on something.

"Come on, gal. Help us load up," he said without looking back. Mattie peeled off her apron and hustled out toward the truck.

"Load what?"

Luster was already behind the wheel. "Angels."

He drove them straight to the circle, then he dropped open the back, hurrying them along as they ferried the statues to the truck bed.

"Are you sure about this?" Mattie panted, struggling to help him with one of the taller ones.

"Sure as any man can be," Luster answered without

breaking his pace. He slid the angel Willie Dodd had brought farther in.

"You just want the angels?" Willie Dodd paused.

"They's all angels. Bring 'em all. Bring Inez. She'd want to help." He climbed up in the truck to help move the dancer. "We just got to get them there. Gotta' hurry."

Barbara was watching the helicopter when a cache of gas-filled jugs exploded just off the northeast tip of her property, nowhere close to either of the previous fires. There was a tremendous column of flame, then another thunderous roar as a billowing puff of fumes and fire shot into the sky. The wind caught it and flung it toward her place.

Then the woods on the west end erupted, streaming in a line across the end of her property and jumping the access road in. The power lines shot off sparks as a transformer blew. All the lights went out. Suddenly she was cut off.

The news helicopter turned and started toward her, circling the area and coming back. She could see the fire trucks coming in the end of her street, then stop when they neared the downed wires.

Barbara leveled the hose at the roof again, but the stream of water drooped and fell off to a mere trickle. "What the heck is going on?" she gasped. She inched toward the edge of the roof to peer down at the faucet. Her own well and pump system supplied the water, but because of the hurricane of '89, T.J. had put in an auxiliary kerosene unit that would kick in and run off the storage unit for several days. There was no reason for it to cut off.

Barbara snapped her head toward the lawn sprinklers. They were still going strong. "Thank goodness," she muttered. She sat down on the edge of the roof wearily. Then, one after the other, the sprinklers shot an unnatural spray almost the height of the roof. The misty columns pirouetted like dancing spectres all around, then dropped down, narrowed their circles of spray, and finally cut off completely in a bizarre sequence. She felt the same creeping chill that she'd felt watching the Christmas lights blink out.

"T.J.!" She was on her feet now, yelling. "It's you. I know it's you! You can't do this. You can't let it get the house. Make it run again." She shook the hose that hung useless in her hand.

"Do something—dammit!" Barbara shouted out into the flame-streaked sky. "I'm not leaving here. This is my home. This is my children's home. You can't take it away."

The wall of flame had crept to the top of the berm along the far end of the yard and inched along the entire waterfront edge, like long fingers stretching across the ridge, poised, but not yet ready to close in.

"Can't get through there, buddy. Turn back." The uniformed officer waved his flashlight, pointing Luster in the opposite direction, while the red and blue pulsing lights flooded the area.

Luster stopped near the patrol cars that were pulled end to end, blocking the crossroad to Harborview.

"I have to get up there. Lady there needs some help," Luster insisted.

"Grampa," Willie Dodd said, trying to calm the old man.

"Power lines down. Fires popping up everywhere. Can't let anyone through there. Turn around and head back, sir," the officer said more insistently.

Luster puckered his lips and said nothing. He put the truck in reverse and executed a U-turn, glancing in the rear-view mirror. The savage dancer just beyond his shoulder stared him in the eye.

"Let the firefighters take care of this," Willie Dodd said, trying to console his grandfather as the truck wobbled a bit on the shoulder, then straighted out on the road. Luster drove away slowly, looking off to the side. "They got all kinds of equipment."

"But I got what she needs," Luster said quietly. Then he shut off his lights, cut across the oncoming lane, and took a sharp left into the underbrush.

"Grampa!" Willie Dodd yelled, bracing himself on the dashboard.

"Just stay quiet," Luster told him, hitting the lights again. "Old logging road. Used it when they was doin' all the constructing. Bumpy, but it gets us there." His high beams strafed the wall of palmettos as low branches scraped and clawed at the truck. Rocking like a boat in a sea storm, they ground their way through from one clearing to another. Smoke was hanging low. Luster tried easing around a bush and connected with a stump that smashed the right headlight and shook them all.

"If you don't get us killed, you darn sure will get us arrested," Willie Dodd complained.

"Hush." Luster hunched forward, eyes narrowed, picking out the route. He rounded the point, coming in the back way. Ahead, he could see the ridges of the berms all aflame. The house was totally encircled. "Hang on," he told his passengers. Then he shoved the gas pedal down and drove right over the earthwork and through the fiery strip.

"Just get 'em out. I'll drive, you pull 'em out. They go all 'round. One on every point. Like a compass. Then put Inez and the chil'ren out back where it's the worst."

Barbara saw the solitary vehicle with its one light come lurching out of the woods. "I'm up here," she lowered the cloth covering her nose and mouth and yelled to Luster when he pulled close to the house.

"I was afraid you'd be 'round. Where are the chil'run?"

"They're safe. They're in with friends."

"Best you come on down," Luster called back. Willie Dodd was already out the back of the truck, putting the Miranda-angel down, facing Poe, her back to the children's rooms. While Luster rolled from one spot to the next and Willie Dodd jumped in and out of the truck, unloading angels, Barbara followed above on the roof ledge.

"I'm staying. I'm not giving an inch," Barbara insisted. Luster leaned out the window of the truck, looking up at her.

"This may not be the bes' time for that," he warned

her. "Don't know what's goin' on when a wildfire gets goin'. What you doin' up there anyhow?"

"I was soaking everything."

He looked out and saw that the sprinklers weren't on. "What happened with the water?"

"T.J. did it. It was running on the auxiliary generator. Then it did some strange things and quit."

"Then you sure better come down," Luster told her before he moved the truck on. This time Willie Dodd had the female warrior that looked like Barbara.

"Not a chance."

By now there was another helicopter, this one with police markings, circling overhead, shining its lights over the yard. "You folks need to be out of there," an officer with a bullhorn called out, giving directions. "Have anyone on the premises come up on the roof," he told Luster and Willie Dodd. "We'll drop you a line."

"I'm not getting up on any roof. And sure not dangling by any rope. Keep movin'," Luster told Willie Dodd. "Just you worry 'bout the lady." He pointed up, his words drowned out by the beating of the propeller.

When the helicopter circled back, Barbara tried waving them off. "You have to evacuate," the officer insisted. He started lowering a harness.

"Go away," she yelled. She walked to the other side of the house, watching while Willie Dodd finished emptying the truck.

"How's it look out that way?" Luster asked her, pointing out toward the end of the driveway. He wasn't particularly set on retracing his last trip in.

"Stay to the right after you go out the gate. You'll miss most of it." She could see the police and fire squad just beyond the cross street. "There's a pumper on the other side." The helicopter was overhead again. "I'll tell these guys to have them cover you."

"He's going out," she called, cupping her hands and shouting to the officers in the helicopter. "Tell them to spray." She gestured with her hands. The officers inside said something to each other then the copter raised up.

"We don't suggest you try that," they said again on the bullhorn.

Luster was turning the truck into the driveway with Willie Dodd holding on next to him.

"Don't try it."

On the far side of the flames, Barbara could see the men on the pumper pulling the hose into position. They were ready to soak him down when he broke through.

She gave Luster the thumbs up sign.

He shifted gears, waved, cranked up his window, and set off in a shower of gravel with the helicopter moving along over him. It went higher when he crossed the flames, then it circled around while the firefighters and police closed in.

Almost instantly, the wall of flame leaped higher and filled in the space he'd made. Barbara stood there watching in silence as the flames spread out, closing in steadily toward Wordsworth on the North end and Poe along the back.

"You son of a bitch! These are our trees! They've been here a hundred years," Barbara bellowed. "Don't you hurt them! Can't you see how stupid and cruel this is?"

The hungry flames encircled the broad trunk of Wordsworth, then began slowly swirling up toward the branches.

"Nothing I do, nothing that happens in the rest of my life will take anything away from you. You can't take any more away from me." Tears and flying ash streaked her face as she stood helplessly on the roof watching Wordsworth's lower branches turn red and orange with flame.

"You're screwing it all up. You're fucking around with my memories and you're twisting everything. You may not have started this damn fire, but you darn sure can help me end it."

Wordsworth's lower half was totally engulfed, its life flying skyward with the ash and flame.

"T.J., don't take it all away, damn it. Wasn't it enough that we had to lose you?" She pulled herself up to her full height. "Stop the damn games. Help me!"

A sudden burst of wind, strangely cold amid the spill-over from the fire, caused a loud awesome cracking noise deep within the flame-shrouded old tree. With a sickening splitting sound, a large upper branch separated from Wordsworth and crashed to the ground.

Barbara wiped at the soot and tears with the back of her hand. She could feel the fury boiling up within her. There would be no more pleading. She walked over and shoved the ladder with her foot. It shifted and slid to the side, hitting down with a metallic clatter.

"Give me back the damn water," she yelled. "If it comes this far, if it gets the house and it gets me, it will be your fault, T.J." She stood firm. "You won't let me fight. You won't give me a fair chance!"

Behind her, on the south end, Keats had now caught fire and was sizzling and snapping. The fallen branch from Wordsworth had dropped the fire within a few feet of the house. Already the flowers and shrubs were curling into blackened, grotesque shapes.

When the police helicopter came in this time, a fireball leaped into the air directly in their path as bushes along the berms went off like roman candles. The copter banked and swung out over the river.

"Damn it, T.J.!" Barbara screamed above the roar of the fire. "If I die like this, if you let it get the house and me, I'll never forgive you. I may die." Her voice cracked and turned hoarse. "But I'll die cursing you forever!"

The creeping fire was within a few yards of the house now. It halted just inches from the feet of the wooden angels stationed all around. Then it stayed there, leaping and dancing in front of them, but it didn't move in.

One by one, the sprinklers nearest the house rose and sent a white spray out full circle. Throughout the yard, the other sprinklers burst into action like fountains in the wind, each one pouring a protective ring around itself, until all their perimeters touched and overlapped. Just as abruptly, the hose that Barbara had dropped on the roof began gushing water.

"All I asked was a fair chance," she said with conviction.

She doused the roof, pulled the towelling face mask back in place, and soaked herself down. The wall of flame coming in behind the low fingers hesitated, halted, then seemed to keep its distance from the house. Barbara maintained her stance atop her home, soaking and resoaking the shingled roof, then scooping water over her eyes and wetting down her face mask to cool her cheeks. Still the air was filled with smoldering bits of debris and clouds of cascading ash.

"It got my tree," Barbara said as she fought back the tears. The sprinklers had doused the lower part of Wordsworth, but the upper limbs were still spotted with bits of flame. Behind her, Keats had taken the worst punishment. "You hurt my trees." Keats had become a gnarled blackened skeleton, sizzling in the darkness. Barbara tried tightening the nozzle but the spray wouldn't reach. The wind died down and there was an eerie stillness all around.

"Show me you understand. Show me you and I are free. You give me some sign that it's over," Barbara demanded. She stood turning slowly in a circle, scanning the ring of retreating fire. She made a complete turn, ending up facing poor Keats.

"Show me. It must end," she repeated softly.

Like an arrow, a line of flame separated from the distant ring and made a straight path toward Byron. T.J.'s tree.

The force of the next blast sent her sprawling across the rooftop. Billowing like a flare in the night, Byron exploded, shooting tall spires of white heat into the sky. Barbara rolled down behind the peak of the roof, covering her face from the invisible wave of heat. The stench of her own hair, singed and smokey from the blaze, hung all around her. She choked on it and gagged, pulled off the face covering, and finally caught a breath of air that tasted clean.

"Okay, okay." She gasped. "You've made your point." She wiped broad streaks of sooty grit across her face. "I just wanted a little sign."

The collar of flames around the once-glorious oak flickered, then subsided with a dull sizzling sound, leaving Byron blackened and scarred and nearly leafless, but not destroyed. Tall, twisting spires of smoke stretched up into the night air, gathering above her in a pale canopy of gray.

Far off she could hear the sirens as the fire trucks down by the cross road made it past the fireline and started up her driveway. Behind them, parked and waiting, she could see Luster Johns and his grandson in their truck.

After the smoky dome had drifted away with the incoming breeze, Barbara sat on the roof, cross-legged and exhausted, staring out at the blackened fringe that had once been her lovely marsh. The noises all around below were no longer so loud or threatening. The steady churning of the pumps on the Coast Guard vessels gradually subsided as they squelched the last of the fire. All across her rutted yard, there were fire trucks, sodden hoses, and weary men. No more sirens wailed. A dull, silence settled over the neighborhood.

"Lady." She heard the ladder clank against the house. A paramedic climbed the ladder and looked at her. "Are you all right?"

"I'm okay. I'm coming down."

When she touched ground, she walked over to the bedraggled Keats. Silently she hugged the tree and patted the wet bark, soaked down by hoses far more powerful than hers. "I'm so sorry." She untied the towel face mask and used it to wipe her hands.

"You'd be surprised how trees come back," one fireman told her. "They'll fool you. Tough old fellas. They'll leaf out again in no time."

She kept walking all the way around the house until she stood beside Wordsworth. "You hang in there." She pressed her palms against the grayish bark and patted the old tree, brushing away the loose bits of debris. Then she tugged off the hardhat and coat, dropping them in a heap beside the rubble that had been Brownie's marker.

When she came back around to the front of the house, she could see the uniformed fire officers waiting with the paramedic. "You want us to ride you in to the hospital, just to check you over?" She could imagine what a picture she must be.

"Just get me to a phone." There were a few folks out there who would be anxious to hear her voice.

SIGNET BOOKS (0451)

CHILLING FICTION

- [ ] **MAMA'S BOY—A Novel of Horror by Linda Crockett Gray.** He was his mother's dream . . . until she died and still would not let go of him. Then he was every other woman's nightmare! (401514—$4.50)

- [ ] **CULT A Novel of Modern Terror by Edward J. Frail.** There is something awful in Eden. A madness that spans generations, a secret as old as time. For the curse has been cast . . . and the unthinkable begins. (401891—$3.95)

- [ ] **PRIME EVIL edited by Douglas E. Winter.** 13 new stories "on the cutting edge of horror!"—*Montreal Daily News*. From the masters of modern horror! Stephen King, Clive Barker, Peter Straub, Whitley Strieber, and many more! Here is writing that is at once eerie and haunting, chilling and nightmarishly brilliant . . . Don't miss it! (159098—$4.95)

- [ ] **THE IDEAL, GENUINE MAN by Don Robertson.** "Dark, horrifying, brilliant"—Stephen King. Herman Marshall was a good ol' boy. But now something has gotten into Herman. Something is eating away at him. Something dark. Something ravenous. And no one is safe. No one. (158016—$4.50)

- [ ] **HEAR THE CHILDREN CALLING—A Novel by Clare McNally.** Parents around the country are miraculously being contacted by children once presumed dead. An amazing blessing turns to be part of a medical nightmare where evil wears the mask of a child. (402006—$4.95)

- [ ] **DEAD RINGERS by Bari Wood and Jack Geasland.** Doctors Michael and David Ross were identical twins. But while one was good, his brother was evil. And when they switched identities for pleasure and profit, the woman who loved one and feared the other discovered a mystery she had to solve—and a force she had to escape. . . ! "Positively frightening."—*UPI* (159896—$4.50)

Prices slightly higher in Canada

Buy them at your local bookstore or use this convenient coupon for ordering.

NEW AMERICAN LIBRARY
P.O. Box 999, Bergenfield, New Jersey 07621

Please send me the books I have checked above. I am enclosing $_____
(please add $1.00 to this order to cover postage and handling). Send check or money order—no cash or C.O.D.'s. Prices and numbers are subject to change without notice.

Name_____

Address_____

City _____ State _____ Zip Code _____

Allow 4-6 weeks for delivery.
This offer, prices and numbers are subject to change without notice.